DECEPTION

DECEPTION

Dwayne Morrow Mystery #7

DARIN MILLER

ISBN: 978-1-963325-07-2 (Paperback)

Library of Congress Control Number: 2024925343

Any references to historical events, real people, or real places are used fictitiously. Names, characters, and places are products of the author's imagination. No portion of this book was created through use of artificial intelligence (AI), nor may any portion be used to train AI.

Front cover photography by James Wheeler, courtesy of Pexels (www.pexels.com).

Printed by Kindle Direct Publishing, in Columbus, OH, USA.

First printing edition 2025.

www.darin-miller.com

DARIN MILLER
Dwayne Morrow Mysteries

To Traci and Nicki
for your unwavering belief in me.

Here's to
Lucky Number Seven…

TABLE OF CONTENTS

CHAPTER ONE

We sat on opposite ends of an unyielding maroon leather sofa, the objects of Dr. Jillian Whittier's discomfiting focus as she perched cater-corner in a matching armchair, one slender leg crossed over the other. A steno pad lay untouched in her lap, a fancy rose-gold ballpoint ticking against it in sync with the obnoxious second hand of her wall clock. I tried to keep my eyes from frequenting the clock, but its persistent cry for attention made it difficult, if not impossible.

We had only spent seven minutes of our allotted hour.

Fuck.

Hi.

My name is Dwayne Morrow, and I am in the midst of my first adult relationship crisis. It would seem it's my fault, and I'm really trying to figure it out, but every single thing I do is wrong, and I'm out of ideas. It's beginning to feel like we've passed the point of no return, and couple's counseling is our last resort.

I honestly don't know what else to do.

The past few months have been awkward and awful.

Melanie McGregor is the widow of my childhood best friend, Ryan. We had only first met when Ryan's mother, Sarah, asked me to look into Ryan's unsolved murder the previous year. Despite the fact that I was no investigator, Sarah had turned to me because the police were doing absolutely nothing, and Ryan and I had run in the same circles all those years ago. She thought I might be able to shake a few trees.

Boy, did I ever.

My entire life changed with that one decision. The unexpected satisfaction of solving Ryan's murder made my already tedious computer consulting business almost unbearably boring, and I decided to pursue private investigation as a career. My attraction to Melanie was undeniable from the start, and the fact she felt the same had me pinching myself into visible bruises. She and her daughter, Jasmine, have been a constant presence in my life ever since, and we had only just recently moved in together into my big old farmhouse on a desolate stretch of Orin Way in Grove City.

And then we went home for Thanksgiving.

More specifically, we went to *her* home for Thanksgiving. Oh sure, we checked in with my folks when we were there, but they had already met Melanie a while back. I had only been tangentially exposed to a couple of Melanie's sisters—oh, *wow*, what a bad, yet sadly accurate choice of words— but this would be the whole enchilada, all gathered around to say grace and give thanks for the people and things that we hold dear.

It wasn't that they didn't like me. Well—*most* of them liked me. The trouble started when I got involved trying to help a friend of Melanie's sister, Molly, locate her missing niece.

No, wait.

That's not entirely accurate. It began just a smidge before that, when— "Mr. Morrow?"

"Unh?" I jumped at the sound of my name.

At some point, Dr. Whittier had leaned forward, peering at me through her owl-like glasses, her pen *tick, tick, ticking* against her steno pad. Had she asked me something? Where had I gone?

"He wasn't listening," grumbled Melanie, somehow shifting even further away from me and propping her chin in her palm as she rested an elbow against the arm of the sofa.

"I was *listening*," I said, if a tad too defensively. "I was just thinking about what the doctor said before."

Melanie looked at me with one eyebrow raised. "Which was?"

"Oh, you know," I fumbled. "She was talking about expectations. And setting boundaries."

Melanie sighed. "Oh, for fuck's sake. That was ten minutes ago."

"Now, now, now, Ms. McGregor," interrupted Dr. Whittier. Her tone must have been something she learned in college. It was like a smooth, sonic tranquilizer, soothing Melanie's flare-up before she could really get going. "There is no time limit on processing. The fact that Mr. Morrow is mulling an earlier concept indicates he understands its importance. This is a *good* thing."

I stole another glance at the clock and was surprised to find another ten minutes had passed. How about that?

Melanie rolled her eyes, sighing impatiently. "Whatever."

Dr. Whittier returned her focus to me. "We were talking about trust, Mr. Morrow, and its importance in any relationship, be it romantic or otherwise. It would seem this is the very crux of the problems you and Ms. McGregor are experiencing."

So *that's* how you pronounce crux—just like it looks. *Huh.*

Dr. Whittier cleared her throat and sat back in her chair, switching up which leg crossed over the other and jotting something on her steno pad. "Let's begin with you, Ms. McGregor. I want you to tell me in your own words how this lack of trust is affecting you. Nothing is off the table. We are here to listen." She looked at me over the top of her glasses. "This is especially true for you, Mr. Morrow."

I blinked. "Me? Why would it be especially true for me? I'm here, aren't I?"

Dr. Whittier's eye ticced, and I sensed her mounting exasperation. "Of course, you are, Mr. Morrow, but that isn't what I meant. This is a time for you to listen. There may be times when Ms. McGregor touches on something, and you'll feel compelled to comment, but this is her time and not yours. This is your time to listen. You'll have your turn next week."

I sat up straight. *"Next week?* That hardly seems fair."

The good doctor shrugged. "It's my process. I like my couples to have the time between appointments to reflect on what's been said by each partner. It's human nature to become defensive in the moment. A cooling off period enhances understanding."

I frowned and sat back. "A week is an awfully long time."

"I offered to schedule you and Ms. McGregor more frequently."

Melanie and I exchanged a resigned glance. We were both fully aware of Dr. Whittier's going rate, and we couldn't afford to be seen more frequently. I waved my hand for Melanie to begin but immediately shot her a warning look.

"What was that?" Melanie asked, scowling.

"Nothing," I said. "Just—keep it to what we know and not what we *think* we know."

"What's that supposed to mean?"

"You know what I mean."

What I meant was I wanted her to stay off the topic of my sister, Gina. For all appearances, Gina perished in a fiery car crash the previous summer. I have reason to believe she's still alive, but for my family's personal safety, I promised not to investigate any further. It's the big, horrible, crushing secret I've kept from my parents and brother, and when I eventually confided in Melanie, it was the final straw that blew our relationship out of the water. It wasn't what I said, but when I chose to say it. She was already upset with me for not divulging my plan of action in my last big case—a case I wasn't even technically working anymore. The whole thing was triggering for Melanie, reminding her of the multitude of secrets her late husband, Ryan, had kept from her, and she wasn't willing to go down that road again with me. In fact, it felt like a small miracle she was even open to counseling. I just wished *I* could be more on board with the concept. I didn't see why we couldn't work things out privately. Sharing our innermost thoughts with a complete stranger seemed invasive and illogical.

"—would you say that's a fair assessment, Mr. Morrow?" Dr. Whittier had launched into yet another explanation of her rules, and her eyes were once again burning holes through me. I glanced at the clock and was surprised to see another ten minutes had elapsed. I was nearly home free.

"Um, yeah, maybe." I tried noncommittal on for size, but Melanie wasn't having it.

"He's not *listening!*" Melanie objected, adding her dark and stormy glare to the doctor's microscopic probe.

"I am, I am," I said, trying to keep things from spiraling into the ugly. "It just seems to me that we should have some sort of safe word or something, you know? Something that automatically puts the brakes on."

Dr. Whittier was nonplussed. "This isn't an examination of sadomasochistic sexual practices, Mr. Morrow. We're talking about everyday communication and trust here, nothing more. We are all invested in helping to steer your relationship in a positive direction."

"I understand that," I said, leaning forward and avoiding Melanie's piercing gaze. "But before Melanie begins—and if I may?"

Dr. Whittier glanced at Melanie, who finally broke her death glare by rolling her eyes to the heavens, her exhalation a long, angry whoosh as she turned away from me, shutting me out with her body language. "Whatever."

I knew I was in dangerous territory, but I plodded along, dumbass that I am, albeit slowly. "I just believe that everybody is entitled to a modicum of privacy. Sharing absolutely everything could be needlessly hurtful—maybe even cruel. Do you understand what I mean?"

Dr. Whittier's expression was utterly blank.

"Okay," I said, sitting back on the couch and steepling my forefingers beneath my nose. "Let me see if I can give you an example. Let's say Melanie goes shopping and picks up a bunch of new clothes."

"When do I *ever* pick up a bunch of new clothes for myself?" Melanie interrupted. "I can't *afford* to pick up a bunch of new clothes. Especially now." She winced at the doctor, shrugging apologetically.

"Please, please, *please*, Ms. McGregor," implored Dr. Whittier, kneading a migraine that was practically visible in the lines of her forehead. "Let's let Mr. Morrow make his point, whatever that might be."

Encouraged, I continued. "So, she's trying on these new skinny jeans and asks me if they make her look fat. Now, me? I'm no fan of skinny jeans, but I'm a huge fan of Melanie." I snuck a peek at Melanie to see if I might have scored any points, but I only detected the ice cracking underneath my feet, and still, I stayed the course. "I would never say something I knew to be hurtful, even if I thought it was true. Not that I think it's true. In fact, I don't really get hung up on weight, although I know some guys do. I think it's really—"

"*Mr. Morrow!*" snapped Dr. Whittier, recovering her composure almost immediately when she saw my mouth hanging open, frozen in mid-sentence. Apparently, her voice was sharper than she intended.

Or maybe not.

"Prosocial lies as you describe are entirely different from the sort of prevarication Ms. McGregor believes is at fault here, and I think you already know this," she said, and I wondered if this woman ever blinked. It was unsettling. "If this were a ball game, I would suspect you were trying to run out the clock."

My eyes drifted to the wall clock to see if my strategy was working and could barely disguise my delight in discovering our session was almost over. I opened my mouth to refute her assertion, but no words came out. Lying was just never gonna come naturally to me. Out of the corner of my eye, I could see the corners of Melanie's mouth dip into a tight frown.

A soft, single chime sounded from Dr. Whittier's desk, and she sighed. "Well, it would appear you've succeeded, Mr. Morrow. That's our five-minute warning. We don't have adequate time to give Ms. McGregor the floor, and I really have to tell you, I'm just a little bit frustrated. This is only our second appointment, and it doesn't feel like we made good use of our time together. I thought I had outlined our approach clearly during our first appointment. I sent you home with a new patient packet that quite literally spells out what you should expect over the course of our sessions. Did you read *any* of it?"

Melanie nodded her head like a good little student while I tried to remember the last time I had even seen the packet. I had a vague recollection of it on the floorboard of the backseat of my SUV. I didn't need to answer the doctor's question. My expression said it all, and I was growing quite accustomed to the sound of her resigned sigh.

"Okay, well here's what we're going to do," she said, setting her steno pad aside as she rose from her chair and crossed to her desk to retrieve another new patient packet. She handed it to me but held tight when I reached for it. "Read it this time."

Her expression said she meant business, and I felt like I was back in high school, awaiting punishment in the principal's office.

"I will, I will," I said, laying the folder in my lap once she finally relinquished it. Alternating waves of anger and embarrassment were pouring off Melanie as her complexion ruddied.

"Because I'm going to be blunt here," said Dr. Whittier, standing over us and crossing her arms. "If you aren't even willing to read this, I can't help but question your commitment to healing this relationship, and I can't see much good coming from future appointments. You're simply wasting your money and all of our time."

7

"I'll read it," I said emphatically. The tips of my ears were burning. "I'm sorry."

I glanced at Melanie, but she had turned away, unwilling to show the hurt reflected on her face. I was blowing this big time, but I couldn't seem to control the raging panic that seized control of me anytime I considered the possibility of Gina's secret being revealed, even in a confidential session with a qualified therapist. I had to consider the safety of my entire family, including my brother's infant daughter, Abbie, and after everything I'd been through, I simply couldn't afford an error in judgment.

Another soft chime sounded, and Dr. Whittier took a step backward, clearing a path to the door. "That's all for today. Next week, the floor belongs to Ms. McGregor, and we'll try this again. By the end of the session, we'll evaluate if there's any merit to continuing our sessions. Agreed?"

Melanie nodded stiffly, gathering her coat and purse before hurrying toward the door. I smiled sheepishly at the doctor and made a great show of setting the new patient packet aside long enough to slide into my own barn coat before tucking it carefully under my arm. Once outside of the office, I turned right and tried to catch up with Melanie, who had already reached the end of the tile hallway. She had foregone the elevators, apparently unwilling to wait for one of the building's two cars to ascend a single floor and veered toward the switchback stairs leading down to the building's lobby. The soles of her shoes tapped out a staccato beat as she descended them with purpose.

"Hey, can you hold up a minute?" I called out, which only encouraged her to pick up her pace, disappearing from the landing as she trotted down the final stairs. I raced after her, finally catching up in the middle of the nearly empty parking lot. I reached out for her arm, but I had no more than touched it before she jerked it away, turning on me angrily.

Hot, angry tears had breached her mascara barrier, blackening the area around her eyes. "Do not *touch* me," she snapped, and I pulled my hand away, startled by her ferocity. "If this is how you're gonna be, what are we even *doing* here? You don't seem to give two shits about fixing us."

I was already shaking my head. "That's not true, Mel. I love you. I've never loved *anyone* the way I love you. I'll read the damn packet. I'll jump through any hoops that lady wants me to jump through—"

She took another step backward, issuing a short exhalation of disgust. "This isn't some series of tasks you get to complete, and I'm not some prize you get to claim! This is about learning how to communicate with each other in a way that's sustainable. You don't even know *half* of the shit you do that just irritates me to pieces."

I blinked.

"And in all fairness, I'm sure I make you crazy about some things too," she conceded. "If we've got any chance at all at making this thing work, we need to learn how to communicate better."

"I get that, Mel—I swear, I do. But do we really need to bring in outside help? I just feel like this is something we can—"

"*No.* Trying to handle this on our own has only gotten us where we are now, which is absolutely nowhere." She dabbed at her eyes, getting mascara on her fingers. She fumbled with her purse, digging for tissues. "Shit. Look what you've done. I look like an idiot."

"You look beautiful."

She shook her head. "Stop," she warned. "That isn't what I need from you."

"Just tell me what you need," I implored. "If it's even remotely possible, it's yours."

She smiled at me sadly. "I need you to be able to make statements like that without automatically attaching a qualifier to them. I need you to say you're willing to move heaven and earth for me without worrying if it's possible, because it's that kind of commitment—that kind of effort that I need."

I stood there working my mouth soundlessly, terrified of saying the wrong thing again.

She turned her eyes skyward and dabbed at the mess of mascara with a tissue. "I've gotta go. I've got a child waiting at home for her dinner. Just read the damn paperwork this time."

"I will," I promised sincerely.

She got her keys out of her purse and approached the driver's door of her silver Mazda, unlocking it. She opened the door and paused. "One last thing."

"Yeah?"

"I can't believe I have to actually spell this out for you, but you *do* know that I'm not going to say anything specifically about Gina's—situation, don't you? I understand the risk completely. What I know stays between you and me. Period."

I was almost light-headed with relief as her words lifted a tremendous source of anxiety from me. "Thank you."

"The fact that I actually had to say it out loud is at the very heart of our problems," she added. "I could have been there for you for all of these months, if you'd only been able to—never mind." She ducked into her car, pulling the door closed behind her. The engine cranked and engaged, and she backed around me before easing down the gently sloping blacktop lane that wound through a thatch of leafless trees leading back to the city streets. It was after five o'clock on a Tuesday evening, and the sun was casting long shadows as it dipped into the western horizon.

I crossed the lot to my red Hyundai SUV, unlocking it and carefully placing the new patient folder in the passenger seat. There was only one other car in the lot, a sporty white Lexus hardtop convertible, parked in a section nearest the doors and reserved for the facilities' practitioners. I admired it from afar, realizing Dr. Jillian Whittier must be raking in some serious dough to afford such a sweet ride.

My gaze wandered to the second floor, where I caught the doctor observing me coolly from her office window. Our eyes briefly met before she disappeared behind her curtain, and I couldn't help but wonder if my disdain extended to all counselors or was specifically reserved for her. Something about her just rubbed me the wrong way. I got into my car and headed home.

······•••••◦◯◦•••••····

I awoke to the sonic whoop of smoke detectors and the smell of pizza burning in the oven.

I had popped a frozen Red Baron into the stove before reclining on one of the two leather couches in my living room and resting my eyes. I hadn't even managed to turn the television on before nodding off, and now I was scrambling to my feet, trying to locate my cell phone which was adding to the cacophony of obnoxious noise that had my cat's fur standing on end as he darted from room to room.

"Sorry! Sorry!" I yelled apologetically at the phone as I put the call on speakerphone and laid it on the counter beside the oven. "I was trying to cook!"

I assumed it was my security company following up on the alarms, but the response through the speaker was unintelligible. I grabbed a kitchen towel and pulled the blackened husk of pizza from the oven and tossed it like a frisbee into the sink, turning on the exhaust in the hood while I fanned the air wildly with the towel. I crossed the room to lift the window above the sink and blasted the smoldering carcass with cold water from the faucet. After what felt like an hour, the smoke detectors hiccuped and quieted, leaving only Dexter's guttural cries for help to fill the void.

"Hello? *Hello? Morrow!* Are you there?"

It wasn't the voice I expected. It was Doug Boggs, former classmate, and current employer at Boggs Investigations. I leaned against the counter, leaving the call on speakerphone.

"Sorry about that," I said. "I was fixing dinner, and I forgot to set a timer. What's up?"

"I'm gonna need you to be in the office tomorrow morning," he said, and I groaned inwardly. I wasn't currently on any active investigations, and I had just finished a server upgrade and data migration project from my own IT consulting business. I was looking forward to a few days off.

"Why—what's up?" I managed, flailing the kitchen towel toward the open window to encourage more of the sullied air to exit the building. Dexter appeared in the open archway to the kitchen, his tail full and whipping about wildly. He issued a lengthy hiss before launching into a quick lap around the living room, then darting up the stairs.

"New client," said Doug, and I could hear the mushy nub of cigar working its way around his mouth. "She's due in at ten. I've only talked to her briefly, but Ma will be up to see to the contracts. I just want you to do a basic interview to determine her needs."

I scowled at the phone. This was a first. Doug was a control freak. I was never the one to do initial interviews. *"Ooo-kay."*

"What's the matter? Don't you think you can handle it?"

"Well, sure I can," I said. "You've just never allowed it."

"I've got a conflict tomorrow," he said. "I can't be in two places at once, and we could really use this case."

"What's the conflict?" I asked.

"None of your damned business," he snapped. "I write the schedules, and this is where I need you to be. Are we clear?"

"Fine, fine," I said, waiting a beat before asking, "It's Lucy, isn't it?"

Lucy Graves is an officer with the Lawrence County Sheriff's Department, and the surprising former love interest of a man I had always assumed was asexual. She was also the mother of Doug's little girl, a fact only recently discovered, and let me tell you, the dust was still settling all over the place.

He ignored my question. "The client's name is Rochelle Pendleton."

"Is this another 'cheating spouse' thing?"

"Not at all," he said. "It actually sounds pretty interesting. She claims to have a paternity issue she needs resolved with her son and a father who won't claim him and wants nothing to do with him."

"Let me guess, she's looking to collect child support payments?"

"I wouldn't know," he said. "Maybe. But Ms. Pendleton's not hard up for cash. She's agreed to double our going rate if we can handle the matter quickly and delicately."

I had to admit it sounded better than our normal cases. "Okay, sure. I'll be there."

"Now, this is only an initial interview," he said. "I want more details before I commit to anything, so don't go making any promises. I don't want you actively working this case until we have a chance to discuss. If we take the case, I might take the lead. You aren't exactly known for your delicacy."

"I can be tactful," I said defensively.

"Oh, yeah? Give me one time you've been tactful."

I wasn't prepared for a pop quiz. I struggled to produce an example, and the silence only stretched out.

"That's what I thought. Be there at ten. We'll talk in the afternoon."

I disconnected the call and crossed the room to close the window, looking at my ruined dinner floating in the sink. I grabbed a bowl from the cabinet to the left of my sink and perused my choices of cereal that were neatly lined up on the counter, opting for Honey Nut Cheerios.

As I poured cereal into the bowl, I had to admit I was pleased that Doug was considering a case that on the surface was infinitely more upscale than our norm.

Of course, on the surface, an iceberg is just a pretty sculpture of frozen water. You can't see the danger lurking below until it's entirely too late.

CHAPTER TWO

I had barely blinked before the damned alarm clock was screaming bloody murder, or at least it felt that way. It was only six-thirty, and the sun was still a half-hour away from peeling back the layers of night. It didn't seem fair that I should have to rise before the sun, so against my better judgment, I whacked the snooze bar and slipped right back into the deepest slumber.

Next thing I knew, it was almost seven-thirty, and I was running late. Sure, I didn't have to be at the office until ten to interview our new client, but I had been very diligent about re-establishing my morning routine. As much as I detest the early hours, I have to admit I feel loads better for the entire day if I force my way through the agony of that first hour.

I had been giving myself a pass on my three-mile morning jog for far too long. I had gotten soft in the midsection and was tired of lying to myself about what I saw in the mirror—it was disappointing. I expanded my routine to five miles and was rewarded for my efforts with painful shin splints that sidelined me almost immediately. Undeterred, I resumed a brisk walk as soon as humanly possible, cutting it back to three miles before increasing first the length and then my stride. I was nearly back up to a full jog.

Anything was preferable to the oppressive emptiness of my own home.

Even Dexter agreed with me. He was expressing his discontent on my furniture, relentlessly sharpening his claws until property damage was achieved. I was the object of his persistent scowl, and he had taken to darting up and down the stairs whenever I tread on them, his motive looking more and more like murder every day.

It was amazing how quickly I had grown accustomed to the sounds of others milling about, and even as I slipped into my tennis shoes and stepped out into the frigid February morning, I couldn't keep those ghosts from following me. What used to be my time to clear my head had become a time to think about what I'd done, and even a couple of months hadn't lessened the scrutiny I subjected myself to. I went through the motions of stretching on my porch before jogging down the wooden stairs and to the end of my drive, turning west once I reached Orin Way.

The time between Thanksgiving and Christmas had been the worst.

I had insisted Melanie keep her house key, sure that we could eventually work things out, and when she hadn't argued, I had taken it as a good sign. I should have known better. Every time I came home, more and more of Melanie's things were gone. Obviously, she knew my schedule. She was purposefully avoiding me.

I called her.

A lot.

She swept me off to voicemail most times. When she did occasionally answer, she was irritated already, like my calls were an intrusion, and it broke my heart to realize they were. I didn't know how to fix this, and as hard as I tried, I only seemed to make things worse. We tried dinner a couple of times, but they ended badly, always with me trying to apologize for something I didn't understand, and Melanie making sure the one thing I *did* understand was that I had said the wrong thing.

Again.

Imagine my surprise when just before Christmas, Melanie called me, asking me what my plans were for the holidays. It would seem that neither of us were in any real hurry to tell our families of our current plight, and they were all expecting us to make an appearance to exchange gifts. I knew Mom had gone all out on a Demon Academy mega-playset that Jasmine had been eyeing for months, and Melanie's sister, Cheryl, wanted us on hand for the unveiling of the big "surprise" her husband Craig had teased during our Thanksgiving stay. I have to admit, I was curious about that one, myself. The entire trip had been an exercise in awkwardness as we barely spoke while alone in the car but did our best impression of a happy family while we were there. Never one to miss a beat, Mom knew something was off, but I smiled and lied right to her face, compounding that transgression by fibbing about a pressing case with Boggs Investigations that required us to make yet another hasty retreat.

I felt sorriest for Jasmine. She kept our dirty little secret like a trooper, leaning into our act a little too completely. With more than a little guilt, I wondered exactly how long it took to really screw up a child, and I believe the thought was on Melanie's mind, too. On the return trip to Grove City, she kept peeking in the mirror to the back seat where her daughter was enjoying the Christmas haul she had raked in from both my family and hers, and she practically scared me to death when she broke her silence, asking if I had any interest in couples counseling. A friend of hers from work had a recommendation, and I said yes without a second thought.

The second thoughts came later.

······•••••◦◦•••••······

I made it to the office with ten minutes to spare, my hair still damp and cold against my neck. I parked my SUV next to Loretta's bright yellow Volkswagen station wagon, slung the strap of my laptop bag over my shoulder, and let myself into the rear entrance we shared with Charley Morse, the taxidermist who occupied the first floor. His door was closed, and his space was dark, contrary to the hours of business posted on his door. Charley pretty much came and went as he pleased, unconcerned with losing customers. After all, his business *was* pretty specialized. I, for one, was just fine with his absence. He was a bit of a talker with a corny and morbid sense of humor, and he always wanted to show off his latest work. I was too short on time to stand around *ooh-ing* and *aah-ing* over someone's dead parakeet.

I trotted up the narrow staircase to the outer door of Boggs Investigations, twisted the knob and nearly knocked myself out running into a door that didn't budge. I grabbed for the stair rail to steady myself as my laptop bag slid off my shoulder and into the crook of my arm.

"What the fuck?" I muttered, my nose still stinging from its impact with the door. Why would the door still be locked? I was *certain* I had seen Loretta's car in the lot…

A short burst of white noise was followed by Loretta's crisp voice. "Please identify yourself by facing the camera to your upper right, and kindly state your business for being here."

She nearly made it through the whole spiel before erupting into laughter.

Following her directions, I looked up and saw a new piece of electronic surveillance mounted near the corner of the foyer's ceiling, its red electronic eye observing my every move. Scowling, I straightened myself and prepared to hammer on the door, but just as I reared back, I heard an electronic *click!* Cautiously, I tried the doorknob again, but this time, the door swung inward.

I stepped into our upstairs suite to find Loretta sprawled across her desktop, laughing herself into tears. "Come here, come here, come here," she said, waving me over while she struggled to catch a breath. She angled her monitor in my direction just in time for me to catch the high-definition playback of my altercation with the door. As "video-me" struggled to keep from falling down the stairs, Loretta's laughter and tears began anew. She pushed away from her desk, leaning back in her task chair as her ample midsection hitched and heaved. I prayed with everything I had that the rollers on her chair would drop off the chair mat and flip her to the floor, but the fates were not on Team Dwayne today.

"Very funny," I said, unable to produce even a clever retort. "We can't be doing that during business hours. There's no landing out there. A client could seriously get hurt."

"Oh, *pffft*," she said, saturating a tissue with tears and runaway mascara. "I don't leave it like that during business hours. In fact, I only activated it when—when I—when I saw you pull into the lot." And she was gone again, guffawing from somewhere deep within the very bottom of her black, heinous soul.

"You'll be deleting that, by the way," I said as I crossed to my own desk and set my laptop bag on its cluttered surface.

"Oh, yeah, I'll get right on that." More laughter.

I scowled at her. "If you don't, I will."

She straightened in her chair, finally regaining a little composure. "No, Mr. Man, in fact you will *not*. You can't. Even *I* can't. It's part of the new security system."

"What new security system?"

"It's the Big Brother 5000," she said, sorting the paperwork back into the tidy piles she had disrupted while rolling to and fro across her desktop, howling at my expense. "Dougie had it installed yesterday." She retrieved a nondescript white card from the center drawer of the desk and held it out to me. "Here. You'll need this."

I took the card and examined it with more than a little disbelief. I'm fairly certain Doug Boggs was the last man on earth to finally get a smartphone. His disdain for modern technology was a known commodity. It had taken me months of dogged persistence to get him to agree to internet-enabling the office, and even then, he still held on to his ancient fax machine—*just in case.* While the office had been equipped with a basic alarm system that covered the doors and windows and was disarmed by individual codes entered into an increasingly desensitized keypad, the key card in my hand suggested a major investment had been made without any request for my input at all. Doug's complete and total disregard for my IT background was frankly offensive. I glanced around the room, noticing the sleek new cameras that had been mounted in various corners, ensuring every square inch of floor space was covered.

"You've *got* to be kidding me," I finally managed.

"Not even slightly," said Loretta. "Didn't you hear? Someone broke into Charley's downstairs while we were in Vegas." She referred to a most unusual training seminar we had attended the previous week as part of our ongoing commitment to becoming a better team. Personally, I felt our odds hadn't improved all that much.

"*Ewww,* no," I said with an involuntary shudder. "Why in the world would someone break into a taxidermist's?"

"Beats the heck out of me," she said. "I reckon Charley might keep some petty cash on hand or something, or maybe there's some black market for dead animal innards—I don't know. I'm guessin' the burglar didn't know what taxidermy means, 'cause I heard he was in a full-fledged panic by the time the police arrived. He thought he was being attacked by some sort of specially trained wildlife. But the burglar could have just as easily come up the stairs and invaded our space, and next time, he might have gotten away. This new system doesn't miss a thing. Besides the maglock on the door, it also monitors the windows, not just for entry but also glass break. The video runs 24/7 and uploads to off-site storage on one of them clouds."

I crossed back to the short side of her "L"-shaped desk and leaned in, examining the control panel on her screen. "I'm sure there's a way to manage the content somewhere in there. Here, let me—"

I reached across for the mouse, and she slapped my hand. "You'd best keep your hands off my stuff."

"But Loretta, I can see a 'delete' icon right below the video. If you'll just—" I reached for the mouse again only to receive another slap. *"O-o-o-w! Shit*, that hurt!"

Her eyes narrowed as she covered her mouse protectively. "Keep it up with the potty mouth, and I'll be slapping it next." She cleared her throat and relaxed a bit in her seat. She clicked the 'delete' button and was immediately provided a prompt to enter an administrator password. "See? It's password protected to prevent unauthorized folks from deleting what they don't care for, and Dougie's the only one who has it."

I stared for a long moment, fully aware she was fibbing, and waiting for her to crack. Doug was notoriously bad with information like this, and it wasn't the sort of control she would willingly relinquish; she still kept track of her son's birth certificate and other important papers, for heaven's sake! Still, her poker face was unyielding, so I moved on.

"So, that video just stays there until the end of time?"

She scowled. "Of course not! Storage may be getting cheaper, but it ain't free. It's managed by an automated retention policy that prevents tampering, and ours is set for ninety days."

"Sounds expensive."

She shrugged, examining her zebra-striped nails. "Meh. I negotiated a little bit of a partnership with Be-Safe Security. Boggs Investigations has agreed to be a flagship installation location, and for our trouble, we get a hefty monthly discount."

"And what exactly does 'our trouble' entail?"

"Pffft." She made that leaky tire sound again, which I was beginning to find insultingly dismissive. "They may *occasionally* bring prospective customers by to have a gander at our setup and Be-Safe becomes our default recommendation for security services to our customers."

"And what kind of services do they offer?"

Her penciled-in eyebrows knitted together as my questions exceeded her patience. "Well, I don't know every little thing that they do! What's with the twenty questions?"

I shook my head in disbelief. "How can we possibly recommend their services if we don't know what those services are? And exactly what kind of reputation does this 'Be-Safe' have? Are they reputable, or are they gonna drag our name through the dirt? Who owns them? Are they local or corporate? How large are they? What's their rating with the Better Business Bureau? How—"

"Enough!" she barked, covering her ears with her hands. "I do not have to answer to the likes of you, a moron that doesn't even have the good sense to keep from running face first into a locked door. I—"

"Excuse me?"

The voice was sharp, female, and sounded from directly behind me. Loretta and I stopped bickering and turned our heads towards the door in unison. A petite young woman around my age was standing just inside the suite, her hand resting on the doorknob as if she hadn't decided if she was going to stay. Dressed in jeans and a simple pink cotton top, her face was free of cosmetics and framed by wavy, shoulder-length chestnut hair.

"Are you two gonna be all right, or do I need to call the police?" she asked, her crooked smile hesitant at best.

I felt color flooding into my cheeks as Loretta averted her eyes and began thumbing through the stacks of paper on her desk.

"I'm so sorry about all that," said Loretta, her shift in tone jarring as she donned her most professional persona like flipping a switch. She skirted by me with a manila file folder clutched in one hand and approached our leery client, extending the other in greeting. "You must be Ms. Pendleton. I'm Loretta Boggs, office manager here at Boggs Investigations. Won't you please come in?"

"Are you sure I'm not interrupting something?" she asked, reluctantly letting go of the doorknob to take Loretta's hand in her own. "You two seemed to really be going at it."

Loretta barked a donkey-esque bray of laughter. "Us? Oh, shoot, *no!* It's just like family here, ain't that right, Dwayne?"

My smile was more of an apologetic wince.

"Yeah—sure."

I plucked the file from Loretta's hand, and for a fraction of a second, I thought she wasn't going to let go, but then she released her iron grip. I extended my other hand and tried on a smile I hoped wasn't too frightening.

"Good morning, Ms. Pendleton. I'm Dwayne Morrow. I understand you spoke with my partner, Doug Boggs, yesterday."

I hoped she missed the dark look Loretta sent my way at the word, 'partner.' It was almost physically painful to refer to Doug as my boss, even if it *was* technically the truth.

"It's Rochelle," she said, taking my hand and another pensive step into the room. "Mr. Boggs asked me to drop by to discuss the particulars of why I'd like to engage your services."

"Of course. Why don't we have a seat at the conference table?" I suggested, waving her farther into the office and around to the left where a small, round table with four chairs was centered between the windows along the front wall. I would've liked a little more privacy, but real estate was at a premium in our miniscule suite, and the only real privacy to be found was in Doug's tiny office and the bathroom. Between the two and right out in the open was my own tiny, battle-scarred desk, catercorner from Loretta's L-shaped station—entirely too close for my comfort.

I pulled a chair away from the conference table for our guest, and she sat, nodding appreciatively. I nabbed the laptop from the bag on my own desk before positioning myself across from her and turning the computer on.

"Bear with me while I bring our new client form up," I said, waiting for Windows to load and my computer to connect to our private network. I looked up to find her eyeing and no doubt evaluating her surroundings. "Would you like something to drink? Coffee? Tea? Water?"

"A glass of water would be nice," she said. "My throat's a little scratchy—it's a little bit dusty in here."

"Sure thing," I said, ignoring the dig at our lack of good housekeeping. She wasn't wrong. "Loretta, would you mind getting Ms. Pendle—uh, Rochelle a glass of water, please?"

I was grateful the client's back was to Loretta, saving her from the withering look that came my way. "Why, of *course*, *Mis*-ter Morrow." She bowed ever so slightly before flipping me off and heading toward the small kitchenette that occupied the corner formed from the outer wall of Doug's office and the back wall of the suite.

I opened our new client template in Word. "You can either dictate your personal info to me or you can enter it yourself," I said. "Whichever you prefer."

She reached for the laptop, and I slid it across to her. Her typing was hunt-and-peck, and her tongue slid to the corner of her mouth as she focused on the screen.

"So, what brought you to Boggs?" I asked. "If it's a former client's recommendation, we have a referral program, and I want to make sure they get credit."

Her fingers froze over the keyboard, and she lifted her eyes briefly to mine before returning them to the screen. "No, nothing like that."

"I hope it wasn't the television ad," I said, involuntarily shuddering at the memory of that whole debacle. "We had to pull that because it erroneously overstated our capabilities in a couple of ways."

She shook her head. "Nope. No commercials. I don't really watch much TV. I found you on Google."

"Oh, of course," I said, as if it wasn't the most natural thing in the world. Google has virtually replaced the Yellow Pages with its ability to connect people and services, complete with GPS navigation assistance, and none of that surprised me. However, one thing still did. "There are quite a few private investigators listed on Google. What made you choose Boggs?"

If I wasn't mistaken, a shadow of guilt crept across her expression as her eyes flicked up to mine, and she seemed grateful for the interruption when Loretta sidled up next to me with a glass of ice water extended in her hand. "Here you go, darlin'."

She leaned forward and placed a napkin emblazoned with the Omelet Hut logo on the table for use as a coaster. Apparently, our miniscule operating budget remains in balance by cribbing and repurposing paper products from other local businesses. My shudder of mortification was barely discernable.

"Thank you," she said with a slight smile before shifting her focus back to the keyboard, pecking out her next response. Loretta continued to hover beside me, rocking on the balls of her feet expectantly until I shot her a pointed glance.

"That'll be all, Loretta," I said with a tight smile. I was rewarded with a sneer, but she turned and headed back to her desk. "So, where were we? Oh, yes. What made you choose Boggs?"

Rochelle sighed, sliding my laptop back to me as she had finished completing her section of the form. "Honestly? I've already tried most of the investigators with the best reputations and the biggest ads, but none of them will take my case. I'm just working my way through the ones who are left."

I smiled. "I see. And Boggs comes pretty high in the alphabetical order of things." She shrugged apologetically, but I could only laugh. "Hey, I asked. You're just being honest. Nothing wrong with that. Mr. Boggs told me your case involves the paternity of your son, is that right?"

"Yes and no," she said, fiddling with her hands and avoiding my gaze. "It's a little more complicated than that."

"How so?"

"Does the name Parker Ghant mean anything to you?"

I blinked, stiffening in my chair. "As in *Senator* Parker Ghant?"

"That's the one," she said, her smile slight but wistful. "I worked for his re-election campaign when he was running for office last time. I truly believed in everything he promised, and I've never met a man with such magnetism. People just flocked to him like—I don't even know what to compare it to."

"His entire family is a political dynasty in Ohio," I said absently, tugging at my bottom lip as my mind began to race.

"I was surprised at how approachable he always was," she continued. "He seemed genuinely interested in what I had to say. He stopped by my desk once or twice a week during lunch. He'd just pull up a chair and shoot the breeze, you know? Just like any normal guy might. Pretty soon, once or twice a week became almost every day. I was worried that people would start to talk, but he laughed it off, calling me his 'work wife.' He even made a point of introducing me to his actual wife, Cassandra, fairly early on, and while we weren't exactly buddies, we got along well enough. For months and months, there was never even a hint that he was looking for something more than friendship."

"Until?" I asked the obvious while my mind continued to churn along a parallel track.

Her smile was melancholy. "The night he won his seat in Congress. The campaign staff held quite the victory party. Champagne was flowing, and everyone was just so caught up in the euphoria. I don't know how closely you follow these things, but his opponent, Victor Slade, was right on his ass. The race was impossible to call for most of the evening."

Politics weren't really my thing. I shrugged my shoulders and motioned for her to proceed.

"Cassie wasn't there for the celebration. Her mother had a massive stroke earlier in the week, and she had flown to Atlanta to be with her. Her prognosis didn't look good, and Cassie's sister had called the family in."

"But Parker stayed," I said.

She nodded, almost defensive when she said, "Cassie practically demanded that he stay through election night." She paused before sighing deeply. "I'm so torn. In some ways, I wish she had asked him to go with her, but at the same time, I wouldn't have it any differently."

A moment passed before I realized she had stopped talking. My attention had wandered out the window, and when I looked back at her, she was staring at me, bewildered and more than a little angry.

"Am I *boring* you, Mr. Morrow?" she asked pointedly. "I'm getting the distinct feeling that you've already decided against taking my case, but unlike your competitors, you don't even have the courtesy to hear me out."

"I'm sorry, Ms. Pendle—Rochelle," I said. "That's not it at all. I'm just—"

"Well, what *is* it, then?" she demanded, folding her arms across her chest.

I sat there with my mouth working, but I couldn't seem to manage any actual words. I was still reeling from the mention of Senator Parker Ghant.

He was one of three Congressional representatives responsible—either directly or indirectly—for the accident that removed my sister, Gina, from our lives.

CHAPTER THREE

"Is everything all right over there?" Loretta asked pensively from across the room, acutely attuned to the abrupt shift in atmosphere. I had zero doubt that she was eavesdropping on every single word.

I recovered as quickly as I could. "We're fine, Loretta," I called, my voice a tad higher than normal.

Rochelle studied me dubiously. "Are we?"

I took a deep breath and shifted into damage control mode. "I am so sorry, Ms. Pendleton—Rochelle. I've had a lot on my plate lately, and without needlessly going into a bunch of details that wouldn't mean a thing to you, your story just sent my mind down another path. Please forgive me. I'm not normally this unfocused. You've got my full attention, I promise."

"Are you sure?"

I nodded, sitting forward in my chair. "I just haven't had my morning coffee yet. Are you still okay with your water?"

"I'm fine."

I smiled, holding up a forefinger to pause her interview while I called, "Loretta? Would you get me a cup of coffee, please? Black."

"You know where the kitchenette is, *Mis*-ter Morrow," came the pithy reply.

"*Loretta!*" I twisted in my seat and shot her a venomous glare.

"Fine."

Loretta grumbled like Popeye as she ambled over to the coffee maker and filled a mug that, if I was not mistaken, was emblazoned with Frisch's Big Boy. She returned with it, setting it just outside my easy reach before focusing sugary sweetness on our guest. "Are you still good, dear? I could probably rustle up a donut or something if you're hungry."

Rochelle's smile had finally softened. "I'm fine. Thank you." She waited until Loretta had retreated to her desk before whispering, "Are you two *always* like this?"

"Honestly? Yes. We're a bit like oil and water," I admitted with a disarming smile, stretching to retrieve the Big Boy mug. "Her son and I go all the way back to grade school together, and we haven't always gotten along. Loretta's a protective mama bear. She holds grudges like nobody's business. But we're all learning to work together. It's a process."

The snort from Loretta's area confirmed the foregone conclusion that she was still completely eavesdropping, and it only widened my smile.

"So, please," I said, taking a sip of the scalding hot brew. "Continue with what you were saying."

For a moment, I wasn't sure she was going to continue. She fiddled with her phone, swiping its screen to unlock it before tapping this, that, and the other icon. Finally, she looked lovingly at the screen before laying the phone on the conference table and sliding it toward me, turning it so I could see the screen. Staring up at me from within a field of stuffed animals sat a rosy cheeked, bright eyed toddler with chestnut hair and a wide grin that showed every single tooth he had managed to accumulate up to that point of his life.

"This is my Joey," she said, the pride evident not only in her face but her voice as well. "He turned three this past August."

"He's a cute kid," I said, my mind already doing math that only required counting to nine. "Senator Ghant is his father."

She retrieved her phone, dimming its screen and tucking it away, but not before taking another loving look at her son. She nodded. "The product of one night of indiscretion and entirely too much champagne. It should have never happened, but I'm so glad it did. I can't imagine life without my—"

Her voice thickened, her words choking off as she struggled to keep her emotions in check. I scrambled for a box of tissues that sat on a lateral file cabinet to my left, handing her a few to dab at her nose and eyes. I was relieved to see they were simply labeled, 'Kleenex,' and hadn't been co-branded and pilfered from yet another of our neighboring businesses. I diverted my eyes until she got herself back under some semblance of control.

"I'm sorry," she said before laughing shakily, her eyes still glistening. *"Woo!* I promise myself I'm not gonna cry every single time, and yet every single time, I'm a big ol' liar." She took a deep, steadying breath.

"You're fine," I assured her. "Continue whenever you're ready."

She cleared her throat and tried again from a different angle. "When Parker found out I was pregnant, he was done. He wanted nothing more to do with me or our baby, and I had no intention of disrupting either his family or his career. It was a careless thing that happened in the heat of the moment, and we were both consenting adults. I just felt like letting him know was the right thing to do, you know? He completely wigged out, offering me money to 'take care' of things—"

"Wait a minute," I interrupted. "'Take care' of things? Wasn't 'pro-life' a big component of the senator's campaign?"

Her smile was tight. "It was—and he still votes along those lines. I learned pretty quickly that Parker wasn't the man I believed he was. His official positions are completely arbitrary when his career or image are in jeopardy. He even offered me a ridiculously large lump sum payment in exchange for a non-disclosure agreement, but those things were never a consideration for me. I was an only child born into a wealthy family, so money was never an issue, and I was perfectly happy to raise my little boy on my own. What hurt was realizing he never really valued anything about our friendship, and I really liked him. Frankly, it's humiliating to have fallen for his act."

"Your parents were supportive?" I asked.

"I lost my mom to cancer when I was a teenager, but yeah, my dad's been great, all things considered."

I raised an eyebrow. "All things considered?"

"He was diagnosed with dementia last year," she said, her face clouding over again. "I had to move him into assisted living for safety reasons. I just couldn't be there all the time."

I sat back in my chair, sympathetic to her situation and thinking about my own father's perceptible decline since the loss of my sister. "I'm sorry. That has to be hard."

"It is," she said, managing a slight smile. "But he has more good days than bad, and he's on some promising new medicine that's supposed to slow the disease's progression. Of course, it comes with its own set of side effects that we won't even go into, but we're getting off track."

Her phone had reappeared in her hand, and she stared lovingly at the picture of her child ensconced in stuffed animals, tears collecting in the corners of her eyes once more.

"This is about your son," I prompted.

She nodded, and her eyes locked onto mine. "He's dying."

"He's—" I started to repeat her words as a question but caught myself halfway there. I was as good in these kinds of situations as I was at funerals, and Lord only knew what might come out of my mouth if I didn't slam the brakes on. Just like the moon pulls at the tide, tactful condolence pulls my foot straight to my mouth.

Her tears were flowing freely now, but she was determined to proceed, her voice threatening to fail her at any moment. "He has acute myeloid leukemia. He's always been on the sickly side, but it took a while to work through all the normal issues that sometimes affect babies, you know? Do you have children?"

I shook my head, still not trusting myself to speak.

"These first years are the worst, because babies can't even remotely tell you what's wrong. Non-stop crying is dismissed as colic, and as a mom, you're both frustrated and relieved. You're getting no sleep, but at least the problem is within the range of normal. But it's just the first symptom." She took a moment to pluck another tissue from the container and dry her eyes before taking a sip of water and clearing her throat. "From Joey's unhealthy pallor to his excessive naps, I knew something wasn't right, but for a little while, I was terrified to have extensive testing done. But when he started bleeding from his gums, I—"

Her voice choked off again as she buried her face in a handful of crumpled tissues, unable to contain her sobs any longer. I nearly jumped out of my chair as Loretta breezed past me, skirting around the conference table to pull up a chair next to Rochelle. She sat beside our potential client, offering a much-needed shoulder to cry on, and Rochelle clung to Loretta as if for dear life. Loretta cooed and shushed, saying only what little needed to be said as she rocked the woman gently, calming her within minutes. It was a shocking display of maternal instinct of which I would have never thought Loretta capable, and I was in equal parts appalled at my own inadequacy and relieved that someone else was able to provide this poor woman some relief.

I waited patiently and quietly, averting my eyes until the hitching of Rochelle's shoulders subsided, and she gradually extracted herself from Loretta's comforting embrace. She straightened herself in her chair and made use of a few more tissues while Loretta remained attentive at her side.

"So, tell us what Boggs Investigations can do for you," I said, taking a sip of my coffee.

"Joey's case is not terminal," she said, dabbing at the corner of her eye. "He has decent odds of beating this thing with chemotherapy and a bone marrow transplant. The donor tissue needs to be a match, and the closer the match, the more likely the transplant will succeed in producing healthy new blood cells."

"But you and your father aren't a match," I said, and she nodded.

"Unfortunately, we're not. Siblings and half-siblings tend to be the most likely donor candidates."

I was beginning to see the big picture. "And Parker has other children."

Rochelle nodded. "He and Cassie have three, a son and two daughters, and Parker has two older sons from a previous marriage. I can't help but be hopeful that one of them would be a match for my Joey."

"So, why do you need our help?" I asked.

"I can't get close enough to Parker to even ask," she said, exasperated.

"Have you considered going through the court of public opinion and giving your story to the media?"

Her eyes fell away as she chewed on her bottom lip.

I leaned in, ready to provide not only encouragement but the means, as well. "Listen, I've got a friend who works for *The Dispatch*. His name's Brady Garrett. Maybe you've heard of him?"

She was already shaking her head. "I can't."

"Of course, you can," I said. "It isn't like Senator Ghant is giving you any choice. I'm sure I could arrange for Brady to—"

"No," she said, still shaking her head.

"Look, I get that you're trying to keep this whole thing low key," I said, dogged in my persistence. "But you've got ample leverage to at least bring the senator to the table to talk things out. Even the threat of going public might—"

"*I said no.*"

Her three short, sharp words stopped me in my tracks, and I sat back in my chair, completely at a loss. *"O-ka-a-a-y,"* I said, and she sort of deflated.

"I'm sorry. It's not that I wouldn't. It's more like I can't," she said.

"I don't understand—" But then suddenly I did. "You took the settlement and signed the NDA."

She nodded, looking pitifully ashamed of herself.

"But *why?* I thought you said it wasn't about money."

"It wasn't," she said. "But at the time, it seemed like *something* to do. Parker wouldn't take my calls or speak to me directly. I thought that just maybe this might hurt him, if only just a little. Violating that NDA will open me up to all sorts of financial trouble, and with Dad's medications and Joey's ongoing treatment, I don't know how much of that storm we can weather."

Loretta gave Rochelle's hand an encouraging pat but kept her opinion to herself while I was left to navigate an interview with no viable path forward. Finally, I sighed, throwing my hands up in defeat. "So, what exactly are you asking us to do here?"

"I'd like for you to find a way for me to talk to Parker, one-on-one or even with his wife present. In fact, it might even be better if Cassie were there. Surely, she would understand the position I'm in."

I shrugged. "Doesn't necessarily mean she'll be sympathetic towards it."

"I don't know. She might. Especially when she understands that I'm not trying to tear her family apart or destroy Parker's career. The problem is Parker's team. They're Super Bowl champions at running interference. It's literally what they're paid to do. They are the reason none of the other firms I've contacted will stay on the job. They excel at putting fires out before they get started, and apparently, everybody's got a price. I can't get past them to plead my case, and as rude an awakening as it was when Parker turned his back on me, I just can't believe he would be *that* coldhearted. Do you think you can help me?"

I took another sip from my coffee, mulling things over. It wasn't my decision to make. Doug had given me explicit instructions to conduct an informational interview only, and I was doing my best to stay in my lane, despite the overwhelming sympathy I felt for Rochelle's plight.

I wish I could say that there wasn't any self-interest involved, but that would be a lie.

This was an opportunity to investigate Senator Parker Ghant without violating the promise I had made to my sister to leave things alone. I already suspected he was capable of far worse than what Rochelle could ever imagine. Maybe by helping her, I could also help myself and my own family. My brain was working at the speed of light to rationalize taking this case on the spot without giving Doug cause to fire me when the sound of Loretta's voice startled me from my reverie.

"Of course, we can, sweetheart," she said, offering a sympathetic smile. "Why don't you come with me over to my desk, and we'll get that pesky contract out of the way. Sound good?"

"Oh, my God! Thank you! *Thank you!*" Rochelle said, relief washing across her face like the tide breaking. After she and Loretta stood, she embraced Loretta tightly, fresh tears of gratitude streaming down her cheeks. I sat there and watched the exchange in stunned silence, my mouth hanging open. Loretta had taken a terminating offense off the table for me and placed it squarely on her own broad shoulders.

I could've hugged her myself, and if you ever tell a soul, I will deny it 'til the day I die.

••••••●◉◎●••••••

"What in the hell is *this?*" I asked, smiling broadly as I stepped out into the parking lot. It was a little past noon, and the sun was high in a cloudless blue sky on this deceptively cold February afternoon.

Brady Garrett hung his head out the driver's side window of a cherry-red Dodge Charger that idled across the way, grinning like a goon. "Isn't she *sweet?*" he said, dangling an arm through the window to lovingly stroke the door. "C'mon. Get in. You've gotta see how she handles."

As much as I hate to admit it, Brady Garrett is the closest thing I've got to a best friend. He's a reporter for *The Columbus Dispatch*, and when we first met, I was pretty sure he was a serial killer. We've come a long way since those days, and maybe I've just fallen victim to his unquestionable charisma, but I've decided that as much as he can grind my gears, he isn't such a bad guy. He has an incredible ability to meld into any crowd, and he damn near always gets the girl with his dimples, perfectly straight teeth, and one-liners that reek of skeeze from clear across the room. It's truly beyond my comprehension, but whatever.

I wondered what had prompted Brady to invite me to lunch out of the clear blue nowhere, but now I saw. He wanted to show off his newest toy. I circled the car, trying to suppress my amusement as I nodded appreciatively at the car's sleek lines and shiny black tires. There wasn't a speck of dirt or grime to be found, and I had to admit, she was a beauty. I opened the passenger door only to be assailed with the intoxicating scent unique to new cars, rolling in waves from its black, leather interior. I inhaled deeply and started to get in.

"Hold up, there, buddy," he practically barked. I froze with my foot in the air. "Can you check the bottoms of your shoes, please? I know there are floormats, but they're black carpet, and everything shows like you wouldn't believe."

"Umm—sure," I said, examining the bottoms of my shoes before deciding to slide them off. I lowered myself onto the seat and fastened my seatbelt, holding my shoes in my lap.

"Geez, Dwayne, you didn't have to do all *that*," Brady said, but the relief on his face was palpable.

"Didn't I?" I asked rhetorically. I wasn't really upset. I might have been just as protective if this beast were mine. I mean, sure, I was happy with my recently acquired secondhand Hyundai SUV, but it didn't exactly make heads turn as it zipped by. "What happened to the Saturn?"

"What Saturn?" he asked, and we both laughed. "I was on my way back from Anyssa's last weekend when it threw a rod on 71. I can't really complain. I've had that car forever. It was time."

"Anyssa's, hunh? You two are still going strong, I take it. Is all this to impress her?"

He shot me a knowing look. "I impressed her before she even knew I *had* a car."

"Yeah, yeah, whatever," I said, grinning. "Are we going to lunch, or are you going to make me lose my appetite?"

"We're going, we're going," he said. "I found this great little place on Dublin Road that you're gonna love. Are you buckled in?"

"Yes, sir," I replied.

He eased the car gently around the parking lot so as not to kick up and dust or gravel and pointed us toward Broad Street. Spying a break in traffic, he cut the steering wheel right before launching us at warp speed toward the interstate, reminding me in no uncertain terms why I always drove whenever we shared a ride.

I just closed my eyes and prayed.

"Holy *shit*, Brady!" I said, clutching the armrest as he careened to a stop between two parked cars. "You're gonna total this thing before the week is out if you keep driving like that!"

37

"Oh, *pffft*," he said. "You're such an old lady. She handles like a duh-*ream*. If you're lucky, I'll let you take her for a spin sometime after I've gotten her broken in."

"This old lady wants to live. You'll let me drive her back to my office after lunch," I said, unbuckling myself and opening the passenger door. I tossed my shoes to the pavement outside. "Otherwise, I'm calling for an Uber."

"Yeah, we'll see," he said, spot-checking his look in the rearview mirror and running his fingers through his dark, curly mop of hair before exiting his side of the car. I awkwardly stepped back into my shoes in the narrow space between the passenger door and the sleek Tesla that Brady nearly sideswiped beside it. My heart was still racing as Brady tagged the key fob and the car responded with a series of thunks and beeps, indicating it was locked, its security system armed.

"What's so special about this place?" I asked, shielding my eyes against the sun and looking at the restaurant's signage. Tapscott's Bistro and Tap Room. It occupied the corner wedge of an L-shaped strip mall whose other storefronts included DeFazio's Pizza, Ruth Anne's Hallmark, and a UPS Store.

"Great food, nice atmosphere. Come. You'll see."

I followed along as we passed through a vestibule into a darkened chamber where we were embraced by an assortment of appetizing aromas. A young woman with a blonde pixie cut manned the hostess stand. She wore a form-fitting black minidress and lit up like a Christmas tree when she spotted Brady. "Mr. Garrett! It's so nice to see you again!"

"Karyn!" he exclaimed, pronouncing her name 'Car-In' as he leaned in and gave her a quick kiss on the cheek. "It's *always* lovely to see you. I've brought a friend along to sample your exquisite cuisine. This is Dwayne Morrow."

She turned her megawatt smile on me where it faltered for just a fraction of a second. "Nice to meet you, Mr. Morrow. You know, I have the strangest feeling I've heard your name somewhere before, but I—"

Out of the corner of my eye, I caught Brady tersely shaking his head, but he stopped when I gave him my full attention.

"What?" I asked, smiling warily. "Am I missing something?"

"Nothing at all," said Brady. He turned to Karyn. "Dwayne's just got one of those faces that looks like everyone else. We hear it all the time."

I blinked. "We do?"

Karyn was quick on the uptake, recovering her composure and sliding her smile back into place. "Let me show you fellas to your table. If you'll follow me?" She grabbed a couple of menus and headed into the dimly lit interior.

"What was all that?" I whispered to Brady.

"Nothing," he replied. "I assure you."

"Slow down," I grumbled, fighting the sensation I was walking through a haunted house. My eyes hadn't fully adjusted from the bright sunlight, and I could barely see where I was going. "Did they forget to pay the electric bill?"

"It's called ambiance, you rube. Look it up," Brady said through his teeth, smiling and nodding at the vague shape of patrons on both sides of the aisle. It was astounding the number of people this man knew.

Karyn guided us to a booth near the back of the restaurant and handed us each a laminated menu. "Your server will be with you shortly, guys." She winked at Brady before turning to walk away, her sashay giving him something to ogle as she returned to her post.

"I thought you were with Anyssa," I reminded him as I eyed the double-sided menu.

He sighed, scowling at me before glancing at his own menu. "You're a non-stop buzzkill, did you know that? Anyssa and I are not mutually exclusive, and I've told you that, so you can stop with the guilt trip. I recommend the Cajun wings. They're amazing."

"Yeah, no," I said, discounting the recommendation. I have zero tolerance for spicy food and wings are too messy. I always end up with the sauce all up in my hair and occasionally in my eyes. I scanned the other options, which leaned heavily into Mediterranean and Cajun profiles. "I guess I could play it safe with a burger, but the muffuletta looks interesting."

"Best in town," our server said, startling me with her sudden appearance at our tableside. "If you know what you'd like to drink, I can get that while you decide. My name is Melanie, and I'll be your serv—"

Her words froze on her lips as recognition set in, and my mouth fell open. Brady's Cheshire grin was accompanied by a pair of waggling fingers. "Hey, Mel! Imagine running into *you* here."

CHAPTER FOUR

"*Dammit*, Brady!" Melanie hissed, lowering her voice while shooting daggers across the table with eyes that barely acknowledged my presence. "Why would you bring *him* here?"

"I was illustrating to my buddy that there are better options for lunch than Burger King," he said, still clearly pleased with himself. "The food here is out of this world, although I have to say, the service is usually a bit friendlier."

"You knew I didn't want to get into this with him, and especially not *here*," said Melanie, hands on her hips, and jerking her head in my direction.

"*Hey*," I said. "I'm sitting right here. Why are you waiting tables? What's going on?"

She took a deep breath and examined the ceiling before letting out a long, slow whoosh, finally giving me the courtesy of her attention. "I lost my job. As of the end of January, A-1 Fertilizers was no more."

I was shocked, fumbling for an appropriate response while doing some quick math in my head. It was already practically the end of February. "What the—? I mean—*wow*. Geez, Mel, I'm sorry. I know how much you loved that job, but were you ever gonna tell me?"

She sighed, tossing Brady another quick and dirty look. "What's to tell? A shitty thing happened, and I dealt with it. End of story. It's not really any of your business."

"Not my business? That's bullshit! If it affects you, it affects me, too." I couldn't help it; my voice was beginning to rise, and the patrons around us were beginning to tune in as evidenced by their dim shifting shadows.

"It really doesn't," she countered. "I'm not going to come running to you every time life throws me a curve."

"But maybe I could've—"

"Stop it," she said, urging me to be quiet with her hands. "I don't want or need some knight on a white horse riding to my rescue, okay? I have to be able to count on *me*. Can we just drop it for now? *Please?*"

I just stared at her with my mouth hanging open.

"What would you like to drink?" she said, focusing on her order pad.

"I'll take a Diet Pepsi, please," Brady said brightly, utterly unruffled.

She didn't even wait for my reply. "And a Pepsi for you." Of course, I was fairly predictable. "Right. Be right back, gents." She receded down the aisle, disappearing into the gloom.

I scowled at Brady across the table. "You knew about this."

"Well, *duh*, mi compadre. Don't get me wrong, the food here is every bit as good as I've said but watching you and Melanie do this weird little dance has gotten physically painful to watch. I hate it when Mom and Dad fight."

I sighed, pushing my menu away. "Me, too. I just can't see any reason she should have kept this from me. I could have at least listened to her vent, you know? A shoulder to lean on."

"Sounds to me like she's tired of leaning," said Brady. "She wants to stand on her own two feet."

My scowl only deepened. "What the hell is that supposed to mean?"

"Can you take it down a notch?" he asked, smiling and nodding at the folks seated across from us. Apparently, I was getting loud again. "There's nothing wrong with being able to take care of yourself, you know. Melanie's spent her whole life relying on someone else to do her thinking for her. This is something she needs to do."

42

"And when did you become such an expert on Melanie?"

"She and Anyssa talk. Anyssa and I talk. And now I'm talking to you," he said. "Do you see the common denominator, here?"

I'm sure I looked like I wanted to choke him.

"*Communication.* It's this thing where you don't just talk—you *listen*. And not just to what you want to hear, but to the stuff that's hard to hear, too. Understand? I mean, cripes! This is like Therapy 101. Are you getting *nothing* from your sessions?"

I was about to serve up a smartass vulgarity, but our drinks arrived, delivered by a gangly red-haired fellow who was built like a pencil. "Who had the Diet?" He looked pointedly at me before Brady raised a finger, and he proceeded to distribute the glasses.

"What happened to Melanie?" I couldn't stop myself from asking as I twisted around in my seat looking for her.

"She handed you gentlemen off to me," he said with more than a hint of irritation. "My name is Jerrod, and I'll be picking up the slack. Have we decided what we'll be having for lunch?"

Brady must have felt I had experienced enough shock for the day, returning me to the Boggs office with considerably more consideration than he had demonstrated on our way to the bistro. Melanie had managed to avoid us for the remainder of the time we were there, and I ain't gonna lie—my nose was still more than a little out of joint over the whole thing. I was shocked when Brady insisted on picking up the tab. He must have really felt sorry for me.

He nosed in next to the rear entrance and shifted his shiny new toy into park, giving the engine a little gas just to listen to its throaty response.

"Thank you again for lunch," I said, unfastening my seatbelt and opening the passenger door. I dropped my shoes out into the parking lot. "And thanks for—you know, bringing me up to speed or whatever. I can only imagine how long Mel would've let that go on."

"You're welcome, but I have to admit, it wasn't strictly out of the goodness of my heart," he said, and I turned to squint at him.

"Yeah?"

He nodded. "Anyssa and I are having a get-together at my place on Saturday, and we wanted you both to come—even if it's not together. I've been waiting and waiting for Melanie to tell you, but she was running my clock out, so I decided to force the issue. I didn't want you two getting into it at what is bound to be an incredibly celebratory evening for me."

I eyed him suspiciously. "A new car *and* you picked up the tab for lunch," I said. "What's going on here, Garrett?"

His grin was even wider than usual. "Channel 10 hired me as on-air talent. Not only will you be reading my incisive and illuminating stories, but you'll also be able to watch me deliver them in glorious high definition."

I can't say I was entirely surprised. Cameras love Brady—all cameras. I don't think I'd ever seen a bad picture of him. Even when he's caught off guard, he somehow manages to save face at the last moment, and frankly, I'm more surprised he hadn't made the move sooner, considering his generally vainglorious nature.

"You're giving up reporting for *The Dispatch?*" I asked.

"Nope. I think I can manage both, at least for a while. I'll be fact checking candidates and their platforms as the election year progresses, and if all goes well, I might make the transition to television completely once the elections are over. We'll see."

"Well, congratulations, buddy," I said, genuinely pleased for him. No reason one of us couldn't have our lives in order. "I'm happy for you. What time on Saturday? And what should I bring?"

44

"Come any time after six, and you don't have to bring a thing. Just try and negotiate a cease-fire with Mel before then, okay? It's only Wednesday, so that should give you plenty of time. The one thing we will absolutely *not* permit is for either of you to bring the drama. The night is all about me, and I will not have it any other way."

"Understood," I said, getting out of his car and slipping back into my shoes. "And speaking of drama, I'm late for a conference call with Loretta and Lord Boggs. Say a little prayer for me."

"Will do," he said as I closed the passenger door. He maneuvered his car to the edge of the lot, careful not to kick any gravel up into his wheel wells, and eased onto the pavement of Broad Street at which point he buried the pedal, peeling out as he fishtailed out of sight.

I shook my head, saying a little prayer for him, too.

······•••••◦◦•••••····

The conference call was already underway as I eased into our suite. Loretta's painted and arched eyebrows framed the dirty look she sent my way, silently mouthing, *"You're late."* It occurred to me—and not for the first time—her passing resemblance to John Wayne Gacy when he was entertaining guests.

I shrugged, dropping into one of the ugly yellow bucket chairs in front of her desk. Doug's baritone boomed from the tinny speaker of our conference phone, filling the room with the monosyllabic pablum of his day, but before I could catch any of its meaning, Loretta interrupted him. "Well, we can talk about that after I get home, son. Dwayne's *finally* back from lunch, so we can get our meeting started."

"It's about time," he groused. "I've got better things to do than sit around all day waiting for you to wander in."

"I'm sorry, *team*, but it's just a few minutes. What's the big deal?"

45

"The big deal is that the world doesn't revolve around you, much as you'd like us to believe it does. Some of us have other engagements to keep. When I schedule a meeting, I expect you to be timely."

"Fine, fine," I said. "Let's get this party started, then."

"How did the appointment with Ms. Pendleton go this morning?" It was fairly obvious Doug was eating something, and I was glad we were spared the visual. He still hasn't mastered that whole 'chew with your mouth closed' thing no matter how frequent or blunt the reminder.

"I think the meeting went a little farther than you intended," I said, smirking at Loretta as she squirmed in her chair.

Doug sighed. "Dammit, Dwayne! I specifically told you not to make any promises! What is *wrong* with you? You can't seem to follow even the simplest instruction."

"*Whoa*, there, partner," I interrupted. "This isn't my doing. You want to take it from here, Loretta?" I stared at her pointedly.

"Dougie, I just couldn't help myself," said Loretta. "The poor thing was practically hysterical, and I can certainly see why. This is a matter of life or death for her little boy, and I just couldn't turn her away like everyone else has done."

I forced myself to suppress my giddy anticipation as I waited for Doug to remind his mother who was in charge of this whole operation, but I really should've known better. "Well, Ma—I suppose if you felt strongly about it—"

"Oh, come *on!*" I interrupted. "If this had been me, you'd be reading me the riot act."

"Not necessarily," he hedged, working another bite of whatever into his mouth. Loretta was practically aglow with vindication as it was obvious there would be no repercussions for her.

"That's horseshit, and you know it. You were already chewing my ass before you even knew what happened."

46

"Well, you *have* overstepped your authority on more than one occasion," he said. "I've come to expect it from you."

I folded my arms across my chest and hunkered down in my chair, sulking. "The least you could do is suspend her for a few days."

"Can we just move this along, please?" said Loretta. "I want to be on my way home before rush hour turns the outerbelt into a parking lot. You know how these big city drivers get my heart to palpitating."

"Of course we can," Doug said, sympathetically. I threw my hands in the air, defeated by pervasive despotic nepotism once again. "How about a little background on Ms. Pendleton's situation?"

Loretta took the lead, bringing him up to speed with what we knew while I doodled onto a notepad what we didn't. When she finished, silence stretched out until I wondered if the call had dropped.

"Well, then," Doug finally said. "What does Ms. Pendleton expect us to do without violating the NDA she signed?"

"She didn't know her boy was ill when she signed that thing," said Loretta.

"Doesn't make it any less binding," I said.

"Dwayne's right," Doug said. "Now I understand her need for diplomacy. Again, what does she expect us to do?"

"She's convinced herself that Senator Ghant will listen to her if she can just get an audience with him," I said. "His security detail isn't having any of that."

"So, how are we supposed to get around them?"

"That's exactly what she's hiring us to figure out," I said, barely refraining from adding 'Einstein' to my reply. Believe it or not, I've been consciously working on my sardonic nature. Baby steps, baby steps…

"*Hmm*," was Doug's only reply, and I could almost hear his mental gears grinding. Granted, this was significantly different from our usual cases, so

I didn't really expect him to have an immediate plan. I took the opportunity to consult my notepad and throw out some suggestions of my own.

"The first thing we should do is run a quick background check on our client," I said, immediately earning a scowl from Loretta.

"On Ms. Pendleton? Why would you want to do a thing like that?" she asked. "If you ask me, it's just a waste of time and money."

I tutted at her easy dismissal. "Not so fast, there. I, for one, am tired of finding out that the client is withholding as much as they're sharing. We've been bitten on the backside more than once by not doing our due diligence all the way around. I can start with that right away."

"Agreed," said Doug. "But assuming that the background check goes smoothly, what next?"

"We try and get a sense of the Senator's daily routine. We might be able to intercept him by cozying up to one of the people who works for him," I suggested.

"Or maybe we could corner him at a public event," added Loretta. "I can check out his campaign website to see where he's going to be speaking. It's an election year, so I would think he'll be out there a good bit."

"Good, good," said Doug. "It sounds like a place to start. Dwayne, you handle the background check, and Ma, go ahead and pin the Senator's schedule down. My business down here isn't progressing as quickly as I'd like it to, so I will probably be out of pocket until next week, but we can touch base again late tomorrow afternoon to decide next steps."

"So, how *is* Lucy?" I ventured, unable to help myself. I watched storm clouds gather across Loretta's face. She still struggled mightily with the sudden title of 'Grandma.'

"Difficult," Doug said. "And how are things with Melanie?"

I chuckled. "Touché. Well, I hope you get it all sorted out soon."

"Right back at ya, buddy," he said before shifting back to business. "Hey, Ma? One last question about the Pendleton case."

"What's that, son?"

"What did you mean when you said you couldn't turn her away like everyone else had done? How many agencies has she already approached before trying us?"

"All of 'em, I think," she said, studying the black-and-white gloss of her fingernails. "None would stay on the case."

"Hmm. I wonder why?"

It was a question that wouldn't linger for long.

......•••••◔◔•••••.....

Loretta gave me a quick tutorial on arming the new security system before she bustled down the stairs in her quest to beat traffic on her way out of town. I settled in at my desk and started perusing public records for any additional details about Rochelle Pendleton that might serve as red flags, but after about an hour-and-a-half of work and my daily Wordle puzzle, I hadn't learned anything startling that might discourage us from pursuing the case.

I was scrolling through a series of images taken at campaign headquarters during the last election night when I discovered one of Rochelle Pendleton sharing a laugh with Parker Ghant. Despite her earlier assertion that they were only friends, it was impossible to ignore the adulation in her eyes as she stared up to a man whose values she truly believed in, and for his part, Parker was ruggedly handsome and exuded charisma. I'm sure he secured the votes of many of his constituents based on his looks alone. For all I knew, this picture might have been taken the same night that Joey was conceived.

I studied his face more carefully; I possessed a piece of the puzzle that I was unable to share with my teammates, and wasn't that becoming a recurring theme with me? Ghant, along with two other members of

Congress, were directly tied to what had happened to my sister, and this case might be exactly what I needed to figure another outcome for Gina that didn't involve spending the rest of her life hiding out in protective custody. The two cases weren't even remotely related, save for this one undeniable connection, and if I could find legitimate cause to tarnish Ghant's reputation beyond recovery, he might just cease to be the threat he currently was to my sister's safety.

With one crooked politician down, there would only be two more to go.

I pored through the photos, examining the man and the company he kept, hoping to find something useful while drifting into a daydream I desperately wished was real. It was all too easy to imagine the look on my parents' faces as they opened their front door to find Gina safe and sound on their front porch, escorted home by her private-detective-in-training brother who was now a national hero, having single-handedly exposed a necrotic arm of corruption that had been festering at the highest level of government for—

There was a well-dressed man in a custom-tailored dark suit standing just inside our office door. He was staring at me, and I started visibly. I had zero idea how long he'd been standing there.

"Holy shit! I mean—*gah!"* I jumped to my feet, grabbing at my chest, and chuckled uneasily. "Excuse the language, but clearly, I didn't hear you come in. Is there something I can help you with? Our office manager has gone for the day, but—"

"It's Mr. Morrow, isn't it? Dwayne Morrow?" he asked, shooting a finger pistol in my direction as he cast an easy, cockeyed grin my way that raised all the hairs as one on the back of my neck. He was tall, broad-shouldered, and coming from a guy who is also both of those things, that's really saying something. I felt somewhat diminished in his presence.

"Um, yes," I said, hating the way my voice sounded. While I knew Loretta hadn't armed the security system when she left, I was pretty sure the door was supposed to chime or something when it opened. Then again, we hadn't heard Rochelle Pendleton when she arrived earlier, either.

He crossed the room with self-assurance, extending a giant hand in my direction. "Do you have just a minute? I promise I won't take up any more of your time than necessary." His unsettling grin remained in place, and I was fairly certain the question was entirely rhetorical.

"Sure," I said, taking his hand and submitting to his vice-like grip as he casually asserted his dominance for a few seconds longer than was necessary. I motioned to the ugly orange bucket chair across from my desk as I sank back into my task chair, casually massaging the blood back into my throbbing hand. "I was just on my way out, though, so—"

He called my bluff with a simple tilt of his head, his bemused grin belying the dark twinkle in his eye. "Just a moment of your time, I promise," he reassured. His hands remained in close proximity to his midriff, and I halfway expected him to produce a weapon based strictly upon body language.

I cleared my throat and tried to get a grip on myself. "You have me at a bit of a disadvantage," I said. "You know who I am. Who are you?"

"Mr. Green," he said, his slate-gray eyes twinkling, and I sincerely doubted it was his real name.

"No first name?"

"Mr. Green will be fine," he said. "It has come to our attention that your firm is taking a case from Rochelle Pendleton into consideration. Is that true?"

I couldn't have hidden the surprise from my face if I tried, but I gave it my very best shot. "I'm not at liberty to discuss the identities or affairs of any of Boggs Investigations' clients with you, Mr.—*Green*. Even if I could, what makes you think I would?"

His grin tightened, and he leaned forward in his chair, linking his jumbo fingers together and casually cracking his knuckles. "This isn't attorney-client privilege, Mr. Morrow. What I'm asking you isn't technically out of bounds."

I frowned, considering his point. "It may not *technically* be out of bounds, Mr. Green, but it's most certainly ethically out of bounds. What is your issue with this—um, I'm sorry, what was her name again?"

Disbelief competed with disappointment for control of his features. "Pendleton. Rochelle Pendleton. *Please*, Mr. Morrow. Do we really have to play these games?"

It was my turn to smile. "I don't have any idea what you're talking about, Mr. Green. Can you please get to the point? As I said earlier, I was just on my way out."

In the end, disappointment won out as his smile dropped away. "I heard you were a smart man, Mr. Morrow. I hope I haven't been misinformed. I would advise you strongly against accepting this assignment from Ms. Pendleton. My employer isn't about to have his good name dragged through the mud by a former colleague with an eye on revenge. I would think long and hard about your own vulnerabilities here. I mean, you're trying to grow your firm's reputation, right? One wrong step, and my employer will ensure that never happens."

"And just who is this employer you represent?" I asked.

He answered by way of standing to fetch something from his inside jacket pocket, and I just knew I was seconds away from being murdered. I scrambled to my own feet and backed away as he brought his hand back into view, but where I expected to find a weapon, he only held his clenched fist over my desktop. He opened his hand, releasing a square object that fell face-first to its surface before turning on his heel and walking away.

I picked it up and turned it over as he exited the suite and descended the stairs.

It was a gaily colored refrigerator magnet, resplendent in red, white, and blue, with *'Don't Think Ghant Can't!'* emblazoned in a semi-circle around Parker Ghant's smiling face.

CHAPTER FIVE

I wasted no time crossing the office and pressing my ear to the door, waiting until I heard the exterior entrance open and close at the foot of the stairs before locking the door. I powered down my laptop and quickly gathered my things while giving my uninvited guest ample time to drive away. Even so, it took me two attempts to get the new security system armed as my hand had a bad case of the jitters, and I kept fat-fingering the keys. I would have loved the opportunity to review the security footage and grabbed a screenshot of Mr. Green, but Loretta had only shown me how to arm and disarm the system. She hadn't gone as far as setting up any sort of user access for me yet, which wasn't entirely surprising considering my determination to delete what would inevitably be her latest submission to *America's Funniest Home Videos*.

The sun had dipped low in the sky, casting long shadows across the parking lot. I surveyed the area from the relative safety of our entrance, making sure the coast was clear before hauling ass to my SUV and checking its interior before piling inside. I locked the door with the press of a button and sank into the driver's seat, only then aware of the accelerated pace of my heart thudding behind my sternum.

No doubt about it, the entire incident had me shook.

I found myself watching for a tail as I worked my way down Broad Street to the interstate, but I seemed to be on my own, merging into traffic heading south on I-270. It occurred to me that if Mr. Green—or whoever he was—could find me at the office, he could just as easily find me at home, so the likelihood of being followed wasn't all that great.

But how could he have known about our involvement in the first place?

It would appear that Ghant's men were keeping a close eye on Rochelle Pendleton's whereabouts, a rather discomfiting notion considering we were supposed to be living in the land of the free. I couldn't figure any other way unless I *really* wanted to get paranoid and consider the fact that I had just been searching my laptop for public records about Rochelle and the senator moments before Green showed up. After everything that happened to my sister, I couldn't completely discount the possibility, however delusional it may seem.

I shivered uncontrollably and bumped the heat up a few degrees.

I wondered if Doug or Loretta had been approached? I thought Loretta was a more likely target as she had been present during the meeting, but when I tried her cell, it just rang and rang before finally going to voicemail. I disconnected without leaving a message. There was no real reason for alarm; her aging VW had none of today's modern conveniences such as Bluetooth, and Loretta double-fisted the steering wheel whenever she drove. She had gotten her license somewhat late in life, and driving didn't come naturally. She kept her phone buried in the bottom of her purse so as not to tempt her into foolishly partaking in distracted driving, which was not only smart but strictly illegal in Ohio. I tried Doug's cell, too, just to dot my i's and cross my t's, but he shuttled me off to voicemail after one ring. I would try again after dinner. I was eager to let them know what happened. I wondered if our client had any knowledge of this 'Mr. Green' and if he had ever tried his not-so-subtle intimidation on her.

I was finally beginning to relax as I traversed the hard-packed dirt and gravel lane that was Orin Way. My two-story farmhouse loomed in the distance, and I looked forward to settling in for the evening with my cat to watch some Netflix. Maybe I'd order a pizza from Donatos. I hadn't been to the grocery in over a week, and I wasn't looking forward to cobbling dinner together using expiration dates as the determining factor.

I was almost to the driveway, fairly deep in my own thoughts when my brain suddenly caught up with the signals my eyes were sending. I slammed on my brakes, cutting the wheel sharply to the right and bumped up onto the lawn, narrowly avoiding the ancient oak tree whose currently naked limbs provided ample summertime shade to this patch of land stretching between my oversized barn and the road. I quickly switched off the headlights, killed the engine, and hunkered down in the seat, my heart galloping. I was partially hidden from view by the hulking framework of the barn, but if I leaned my head out my window and craned my neck, I could see most of the wraparound porch and the frontage of my house.

The front door stood open with only the storm door keeping Dexter inside. The curtains were drawn wide and every light on the first floor was on, my living room in full view from the street and lit up like a Broadway stage. It might be my imagination, but I could have sworn I saw a dark figure dart across the rear of the room and beyond my line of sight.

Fuck.

I had gone to great lengths to fortify my personal fortress of solitude after a crazed serial killer had taken to depositing body parts at my front door the previous year. I had also taken self-defense a little more seriously, investing in a handgun and training in its responsible use and storage, courtesy of Vince Holland, a crusty old bastard who operated a shooting range Melanie and I frequented near Plain City. He had sold me a lock box to store my gun in the trunk of my then-car, which had subsequently been totaled. For no real reason, I hadn't had my SUV fitted with something similar, and this wasn't the first time I was kicking myself over my procrastination.

I quickly dialed 9-1-1.

"9-1-1, what's your emergency?"

"I've got a prowler inside my house," I whispered reflexively, automatically triggering the dispatcher's concern.

"Are you in any immediate danger?" she asked.

"No," I said, clearing my throat and allowing myself a little more volume. It wasn't like my intruder could hear me at this distance. "I'm calling from inside my car, and I'm parked beside my barn. I don't think anyone saw me pull in."

"Can you confirm your address for me?"

I rattled it off as I heard her fingers busily entering the information on her keyboard. "All right, I have a car that's less than five minutes away from your location. My advice to you? Start your car and drive away. Give the officers a chance to check things out, and we'll let you know when it's safe to return. Can you do that?"

"Sure," I said. "Thank you."

I disconnected the call and put my foot on the brake, my finger moving toward the push-button ignition where it hovered over the switch before slowly dropping away. This was horseshit, and I was beginning to feel heat building around my eyes. How many times was I going to let someone scare me out of my own house? Frankly, the whole thing felt entirely too coincidental. Having just endured Mr. Green's scare tactics at the office, this felt like a second act, designed to take my fear to the next level, to show me that there wasn't *anywhere* beyond their reach, and I just wasn't in the mood.

Why wasn't my security alarm going off? While I didn't have all the fancy cameras that were features of our new system at the office, my alarm should have been screaming bloody murder. I checked my text messages and call history to make sure I hadn't somehow missed a message from my alarm company, but there was nothing to find. Of course, if they had somehow gotten the code to my system...

I shook off the thought, refusing to let paranoia take hold. I switched off my automatic dome light before opening my driver's door and easing out into the night. I hurried around the front of my SUV and pressed myself to the side of the barn where I couldn't be seen from the house. I slid forward inch by inch until I reached the front of the barn, and I peeked around the corner toward the house.

Dexter's furry black head was visible in the lower pane of the storm door, raised on his haunches to peer inquisitively out into the night. This was an unusual vantage point for him, and he had seized upon utilizing it, curious cat that he was. His head turned suddenly, his attention drawn toward something inside the house, and he was suddenly gone. My heart stuttered in my chest as visions from old thrillers came unbidden, the ones where the family pet makes the ultimate sacrifice in a boiling pot of water as a lesson in compliance to its recalcitrant owner.

Next thing I knew, I was closing the distance between the barn and my front porch, my eyes darting from one lighted window to the next, fully expecting to be spotted at any moment. I heaved a sigh of relief once I'd mounted the stairs to the porch, pressing myself flat against the rough siding that fronted my house, apparently undetected. I eased toward the storm door, craning my neck to cautiously peek inside through its top pane of glass.

The living room was empty, as was the open hallway leading back into the brightly lit kitchen.

I eased the storm door open and slipped inside, closing it gently behind me. My gun was in a locked drawer in my desk, and I eyed the closed door to my den. It seemed impossibly far away with two couches, a coffee table, and a whole lot of floor space between me and it, and for all I knew, the intruder might still be inside. The wooden block of big, sharp kitchen knives was in plain sight, straight ahead along an unobstructed path. While I'd rather have my gun, a knife was better than nothing, right?

For shit's sake, Dwayne! Make a decision!

I hurried through the living room, past the stairway to my left, and had just entered the kitchen when an enormous thud sounded from the second floor, jostling the hanging light suspended over my dinette table. Adrenaline surged through my veins as I grabbed the butcher knife from the block and hurried back to the entrance of the kitchen, flattening myself against the pantry door that was adjacent to the stairway. Galloping footsteps raced along the length of the upstairs hallway before screeching to a stop at the landing just above my head. My ragged breathing was so loud in my own ears I felt sure the intruder had heard me and was likely creeping down the stairs one at a time. Sweat trickled down from my armpits as my ears strained to isolate the random creak of a stair riser—anything that might betray my uninvited guest's location.

The suspense was killing me.

I had very nearly talked myself into going on the offense when there was a squeal, and the footsteps thundered down the first length of stairs above my head, skipping the last few to jump to the landing at the midpoint before cutting left to tackle the final length. Something about all of this niggled at my memory, but my knuckles were white from gripping the handle of the butcher knife, waiting for my intruder to finally make an entrance.

Dexter suddenly shot down the stairs, spinning out at the bottom with his claws scrambling cartoonlike against the hardwood floor before he finally gained purchase, banking a hard right to disappear into the living room. I only had time for a startled yelp as I realized the source of my déjà vu.

"Jasmine—?"

I stepped out in front of the stairway just as Melanie's daughter leapt from the third stair, her muted giggling morphing into an ear-shattering scream. I barely managed to fling the butcher knife aside before her airborne weight hit me full force, knocking the wind out of me as I fell back

59

and into my dinette table, promptly destroying one of its chairs as I crashed through it.

"POLICE! FREEZE!"

Our heads turned in slack-jawed unison toward the front door as two officers squatted just inside the room, their feet planted, and guns leveled in our direction.

Jasmine promptly burst into tears.

·••••●●━◦◦━●●•••••·

With a heavy sigh, I dropped down onto the wooden glider on my porch and patted the seat beside me. "Have a seat, kiddo."

We had just seen our police friends off after a seemingly endless round of identity verification that proved we were who we said we were and there was nothing illicit going on. Officer Dempsey seemed intent on phoning Melanie since I wasn't technically Jasmine's father, but Jasmine somehow talked him out of it, explaining that her mother had started a new job and was already a bundle of nerves. She would hate to upset her over something so silly, and wasn't it apparent that they lived here? After all, she knew the alarm code and would be happy to show the officers her room, if they'd like. Officer Parker was both the older and the more level-headed of the two, and he reined his partner in at this point.

I just kept my big mouth shut and watched the little sociopath go. I mean, who lies like that? To be completely honest, part of me was jealous while the other part wondered if I'd ever be able to believe another thing this child told me. Her skill set bordered on the pathological.

After they were satisfied that Jasmine was in no danger, I was chastised for not listening to the police dispatcher's instructions to leave the premises until officers had arrived on scene. I might have been killed if it had been a real burglar, and I didn't need anyone to tell me what might have happened had I not had the reflex to toss the butcher knife aside as Jasmine threw herself upon me from the stairs. The bitter taste of bile still lingered at the back of my throat as I considered alternate outcomes. I got a second reprimand for not being aware of the child's schedule and was urged to "get my head in the game" before they had finally taken their leave.

Jasmine perched on the edge of the glider. "Are you mad at me?"

"I'm too relieved to be mad," I said. "But this isn't going to become a habit. My heart can't take it. How did you even get here?"

She shrugged, absently kicking her feet in the open air below her knees. "I took the bus."

"Jasmine! The closest bus stop is almost two miles away on Georgesville."

She shrugged again. "It isn't *that* far. I knew Mom was working until late, and I wanted to see Dexter. It's been weeks."

As if on cue, Dexter began a two-handed assault on the other side of the windowpane behind us, reminding us he was still there and not even slightly amused at the interruption in his evening's entertainment. Jasmine booped his nose through the glass, eliciting a silent meow and a broad sideswipe of the windowpane as he tried in vain to get some attention despite the transparent barrier.

I stared at her, frowning. "Your mother would have never okayed this."

She refused to meet my eyes. "My mother never okays *anything*. And what's the big deal? It's not like I'm with some stranger."

I sighed. "You're only twelve, Jasmine. You've got no business walking all this way by yourself. What if something had happened? No one would have even known where you were going."

"Fine," she snapped, pushing off the glider to her feet. "If you don't want me around, I'll get my things and go."

"Hey, hey," I said, snagging her arm and urging her back to the swing. "I didn't say that, and by now, you should know I'd *never* say that. I'm just saying you could have called. We could have worked out transportation that wouldn't have had you hoofing it along a busy four-lane road. I'm guessing it probably wouldn't have been on a school night, but we would have made it happen."

"*Really?*" she asked, finally fixing me in a stare that felt uncomfortably defiant.

"Well—yeah," I said. "I think so."

She snorted softly before shifting her attention to her feet. "I hate this."

"You hate what?"

"*This,*" she repeated, her arms flung wide to dramatically indicate the whole damn world. "Everything was going so well. It felt like—I don't know."

She had my full attention. "Go on. It felt like what?"

Her mouth opened and then closed as she deliberated her reply before finally changing course. "I think Mom wants to move back home once our lease is up."

"Why would you say that?" I asked, startled by the possibility.

"Because nothing has gone the way she hoped. The apartment sucks. The walls are flimsy, and the neighbors fight all the time. The husband keeps hitting on Mom, and I mean right in front of his wife. It's awkward." Jasmine's fingers were interlocked in her lap as she fidgeted beside me. "I probably shouldn't tell you this, but she doesn't seem to be in any hurry, and I don't know why—but she lost that job she loved so much at the fertilizer place last month, and she's gone back to waiting tables. I think she's embarrassed."

"I actually found out about that just today," I said.

She looked at me, surprised. "Mom finally told you?"

My chuckle was half-hearted. "Oh, no. Brady took me to lunch at her new workplace. It was his not-so-subtle way of forcing the issue. Right now, I'm not sure who your mom wants to throttle more, me or Brady."

"Well, good. At least she can't blame me for spilling the beans. I'm just so sick of all these secrets."

I couldn't have agreed more. Such wisdom from the mouths of babes.

We rocked quietly for a few minutes with only the chirp of crickets to disturb the evening's tranquility. Stars twinkled overhead in a cloudless sky, and the temperature was beginning to drop.

"Do you think you and Mom will ever work this out?" asked Jasmine, and I could tell from the tone of her voice she was afraid of the answer. She counted on me to be straight with her, and I wasn't about to let her down now.

"I hope so," I said. "I love your mom. And you're alright, too, you know—when you make an effort."

She managed a slight smile. "Yeah? You're not so bad yourself."

I returned her smile, patting her arm.

Jasmine's face clouded over again. "I just don't get it. We were so happy here. I know she loves you, too, even if she won't admit it. She's just so freaking stubborn. It's almost like she enjoys it when we're miserable."

"Well, I don't know about *that*," I said, for lack of anything more insightful.

"It sure feels that way," she said, sulking. "She cries herself to sleep most nights."

"She *what?*"

She shrugged. "She thinks I can't hear her, and I pretend like I don't, but you know—thin walls."

Ouch.

I hated that I was the cause of Melanie's heartbreak. I resolved then and there to give our counseling my unqualified attention with no more worrying about what might be divulged over the course of our sessions. How could I expect Melanie to ever trust me again if I didn't trust her first?

Frankly, we were doomed if we couldn't break this stalemate, and no amount of counseling could fix that.

"Everything is going to be fine," I said, wrapping an arm around Jasmine's thin shoulders and pulling her in for a hug. It was a risky thing to say, but I didn't actually promise, so it felt honest, if only on a technicality. I sounded far more confident than I felt.

"I hope so," she said, her voice cracking slightly, and I knew I wasn't fooling anyone. This kid had been dealing with disappointment her entire life. She was too damn smart for her own good.

She rested her head against my shoulder, and we rocked in silence again until my stomach gurgled, reminding me I hadn't had dinner yet.

"How about you say goodbye to Dexter and grab your things, and then we'll go have dinner? I can drop you off at the apartment afterward."

She nodded her head. "Okay."

She slipped from beneath my arm and went inside, where Dexter met her at the door, greeting her enthusiastically. I had to fix things with Melanie. I just had to.

The thought of her moving back to Lymont was more than I could bear.

"Fu-u-u-dge," I said, course-correcting my language on a dime. We were nearing the back of the apartment complex's parking lot, and Melanie's rusty silver Mazda was parked beneath a paltry streetlight in one of her two assigned parking spots. "Your mom's home."

While I knew Melanie trusted me with her daughter, I wasn't at all sure what our current protocol was. Would she be okay with me taking Jasmine to dinner without getting approval first? Who knew? Navigating a landscape of eggshells was exhausting.

"What?" said Jasmine, checking her phone for missed calls or texts. "It's barely eight. She was supposed to close tonight. I didn't expect her until ten. I'm surprised she hasn't blown up my phone." She sighed. "You can just drop me here if you want. I don't want to give her any more reason to be mad at you. I can tell her I was at a friend's here in the complex."

I looked at her skeptically. "I thought you didn't have any friends here in the complex."

"I don't."

I chuckled, pulling in beside Melanie's car. "I've got a better idea."

"What's that?"

"The truth," I said. "I hear it's entirely underrated."

She rolled her eyes and unfastened her seatbelt, hopping down from the passenger seat to retrieve her backpack from the backseat. I waited for her at the end of the sidewalk and escorted her to the last small apartment on the right. The picture window that looked out over a semi-private patio was brightly lit behind closed blinds. The front door stood open behind its screen door, and as we approached, I heard voices inside, one of which was decidedly male.

Hmmm.

Jasmine pulled the door open, interrupting Melanie mid-sentence and announcing, "I'm ho-o-me."

"So, I see," Melanie said, her eyes registering a flicker of surprise as I appeared in the door frame behind her. She returned her attention to her guest who sat smiling on the couch. "This is my daughter, Jasmine, and my—my—"

"No introductions necessary," I said tightly. "Hello, Mr. Green."

CHAPTER SIX

"Mr. Morrow!" he said, his inflection a damn good approximation of genuine surprise. He stood, extending a hand. "Twice in one evening. What an extraordinary privilege."

"Cut the shit," I said, my tone causing Jasmine to instinctively step behind her mother. Melanie eyed us warily, unsure of what exactly was unfolding in her living room. I kept my eyes locked on Green. "What in the hell are you doing here?"

"Why, I'm just canvassing the neighborhood, and this is my last stop," he said, smarmy smile firmly in place. I eyed the stack of flyers on the sofa cushion beside him, Senator Parker Ghant's ruggedly handsome face projecting confidence in full color. "I understand that Ms. McGregor is new to our district. I want to make sure she's registered to vote and has all the information she needs to help keep our good senator in Washington."

"Get out," I said, stepping aside to clear a path to the door.

"Dwayne!" Melanie was flustered, her cheeks splotchy as she shot me an angry glare. "You can't just come in here and throw someone out of my apartment." She looked at Mr. Green apologetically. "I'm so sorry, I—"

"Melanie, trust me, this asshole isn't here just *canvassing*," I said. "And now he's leaving. Aren't you, Mr. Green?"

"Stop it, Dwayne," she said hotly, and Green didn't even try to hide the amusement on his face. "If anyone's leaving, it's you." She grabbed my arm and turned me towards the door.

"It's alright, Ms. McGregor," Mr. Green said, collecting his stack of flyers from the couch. "I didn't mean to cause any disharmony between you folks. It's late, and I can always come back later. Why don't I just leave you with one of these informational flyers for you to peruse? It's a quick and dirty cheat sheet to bring you up to speed on Senator Ghant's political experience and where he stands on all of the hot button issues that are especially important to women voters."

"Emphasis on *dirty*," I muttered, and Melanie actually pinched me. *Hard.* "Dammit, Dwayne—*enough.*"

"It's truly alright, ma'am," he said, with a tip of his head. He continued to dangle the flyer within reach.

"Well—if you're sure," she said, accepting it and giving it a cursory glance. She folded it into quarters and tucked it into the pocket of her black slacks. "I can't apologize enough for Dwayne. He's not normally this—surly. But to be completely honest, I just got finished working a long shift, and my feet are killing me. Another time would probably be better for me, too."

He favored her with another Velveeta smile. "Of course." He looked at me, raising an eyebrow. "If you'll excuse me, Mr. Morrow?"

I took another step backward as he crossed the room toward the door. "Maybe I should see you to your car," I said, managing a single step before Melanie's hand clamped down on my arm, holding me in place.

"Don't you dare," she hissed, earning me another bemused smirk from the bastard as he passed in front of me and stepped out onto the stoop.

"If I find myself back in the neighborhood, I'll make sure and stop by. I'd love to share more of Senator Ghant's initiatives with you," he said. "When it's more convenient, of course."

"I'd like that," said Melanie, stepping in front of me and taking Mr. Green's outstretched hand for a quick shake. He casually sauntered down the sidewalk towards the parking lot, not the least bit concerned that I might be following.

Melanie closed the door and turned around, her eyes ablaze. Surprisingly, she focused on her daughter first. "You're grounded," she said flatly. "Go to your room."

"What did *I* do?" Jasmine whined, stomping the floor.

"You went to Dwayne's house without my permission, that's what. In fact, before you storm off, I'd like your bus pass, please," she said, holding out a hand expectantly.

Jasmine looked blindsided. "But how—?"

"Mother Knows Best," interrupted Melanie, waggling the display of her cell phone in her other hand and deftly reopening another old wound between us.

Mother Knows Best was a tracking app that gave peace of mind to innumerable parents, lending them the ability to locate wayward children with just a few flicks of a finger. She had also installed it on my phone without my knowledge or permission, which I still considered an invasion of my personal rights.

Okay, *fine*—it saved my life once, but she should have asked before installing the damned thing. It was about the *principle*. I have since removed it.

"Right now, it's the only thing keeping me sane," she continued, impatiently flexing the fingers of her outstretched hand. "Bus pass. *Now.*"

Jasmine retrieved it from a lanyard around her neck and placed it into her mother's open palm, sighing heavily.

"Not only could I tell that you went to Dwayne's, but I also know you've already had dinner. I followed your little bobblehead icon all the way to

Donatos, where you spent the better part of the last hour. Sound about right?"

She nodded sullenly. "So, how long am I grounded?"

"Until you're twenty-three," said Melanie, bopping her daughter lightly on the top of her head. "I don't know. We'll talk later. Go on to your room, and if you've got any homework, you'd better get busy. I need to talk to Dwayne for a minute."

Shit. My turn.

Jasmine broke rank long enough to give me a quick hug and an apologetic smile before scampering off to her room. As her door slammed shut, Melanie focused a most withering gaze in my direction.

"Do you want to tell me exactly what the fuck that was?" she asked, her arms folded across her chest as she struggled to keep her voice low and steady.

"I do," I said, eyeing the room warily while remembering Jasmine's earlier words. "But not here. The walls are thin."

She shook her head and sighed. "I'd say you need professional help for your paranoia, but we see how well *that's* going."

"C'mon, Mel. Just humor me." I opened the door and nodded toward the enclosed patio outside.

"Fine," she said, taking a step toward the door before wincing and cupping the small of her back.

I was at her side in an instant. "What's this?"

"Oh, it's nothing," she said, inhaling sharply as she massaged the area just above her right glute.

"Doesn't look like nothing," I said, trying to figure the best way to provide assistance without it seeming like some lame attempt at grab-ass. My hands hovered uselessly over the area like I was some sort of spiritual healer. "What happened?"

"I fell in the kitchen at work," she said. "The floor was wet, and my shoes don't have the right kind of soles. I tried to tell them it wasn't a big deal, but they made me go home anyway. I'm sure it cost me a chunk in tips."

"You should have gone to Urgent Care," I said. "You might have broken something."

She straightened up and laughed. "Yeah, like my bank account. No thanks. I'll be fine. After you."

She indicated the open door, and I stepped outside, waiting for her to join me on the dimly illuminated square of concrete that was shielded from neighbors' prying eyes by six-foot wooden slat privacy fencing.

"So, what's this all about?" she asked, ignoring my invitation to sit on one of the matching plastic molded chairs squatting on her patio.

"It's about Gina," I said, cutting to the chase and keeping my voice low. It certainly got her attention. "I should probably start at the beginning, and it's way too early to say how it's going to end, but this has absolutely nothing to do with paranoia. Do you believe me?"

Her eyes found mine and held. After a lengthy moment, she gave a single nod, her curiosity finally beginning to outweigh her irritation with me. "I do."

I smiled at her. "Thank you. Now, would you please humor me once more and take a seat? I'm having a hard time focusing when your back is clearly killing you. This is going to take a few."

Reluctantly, she lowered herself into one of the chairs. I took the other, pulling it around to position us practically knee-to-knee as I began relaying my morning to her and everything that had happened since.

Melanie sat in contemplative silence with her fingers steepled beneath her nose as she processed what I told her. The silence seemed interminable, and it was taking all my self-control to keep from breaking it, but there wasn't anything more to add. She was either going to believe me or not, and if she didn't, I wasn't sure where to go from here.

She shifted in her seat and retrieved the flyer from her pocket, unfolding it to stare down at the senator's megawatt smile staring back at her. "Senator Parker Ghant. Are you sure?"

I sighed. "Of course, I am. That night plays over and over in my head— it haunts my *dreams*. I'm not likely to forget any of their names."

I was referring to Ghant and two other well-known politicians who Gina had named when she had captured photographic evidence linking them to some sort of top-secret project that harvested school-age children who were identified as talented and gifted by some undisclosed criteria. They were being trained in secretive, regional military academies all across the country for a future in which democracy played no part. These politicians and the cronies who worked for them had threatened the safety of my entire family if Gina didn't surrender her pictures, and in the end, they had put a hit out on her, forcing a horrific highway accident shortly after our brother's wedding. Her car had collided head-on with a gasoline tanker, leaving behind only the charred metal husks of the vehicles' twisted frames.

Only Gina hadn't been inside her car.

To the best of my knowledge, she was currently in protective custody, unable to reveal herself, even to her own family—at least until these politicians were exposed for who they truly are. They had managed to recover her photos, and their belief that she was dead was the only thing keeping me and my family safe. The only reason I knew this was because Gina had risked a visit, imploring me not to investigate any further or tell anyone else what I knew. Of course, I was in an ambulance under heavy sedation, so parsing truth from fiction had taken time. The whole exchange played out as a recurring nightmare in frequent rotation, but those names were permanently etched into my mind.

"It seems a little convenient that this case is pretty much bringing one of them right to your door, don't you think?" Melanie asked, leaning forward while wincing from the motion. "Do you think this Pendleton woman is on the up-and-up?"

"I've only done some preliminary digging, but from what I can tell, yes, she's telling the truth," I said. "I think this might just be the universe finally giving me a break."

"How do you figure?"

"If I can find some other way to completely discredit this monster, I could be that much closer to bringing my sister back home where she belongs," I said, unable to keep the excitement out of my voice. "One down, two to go."

Melanie's brief bark of laughter was less enthusiastic. "Slow it down, there. You sound like you're already getting your priorities out of order. You've got a client to represent, and the situation with her son is just heartbreaking—I mean, not that yours isn't, but—"

"I know, I know," I said, saving her the trouble of trying to explain. "It's a matter of life-and-death for Joey—I get that. But I can't help but get a little excited, you know? It gives me an opportunity to dig into the guy without it being directly related to what happened with Gina. And it's not like we solicited Rochelle's business. She came to us. The fact that I work for Boggs is kind of incidental to the whole thing."

"Rochelle?" she asked, raising an eyebrow.

"Oh, come *on*, Mel. It's her name. She's pretty much our age. Our generation doesn't exactly stand much on formality."

"So, what's the deal with Mr. Green?"

"Intimidation, most likely," I said. "Boggs wasn't the first PI firm Rochelle attempted to engage. In fact, I don't think we were even in the top ten. But all the other guys have backed off. I suspect our 'Mr. Green,' or whatever his real name is, may have paid them all preemptory visits, too."

"Do you think Rochelle might recognize him?" she asked, and I couldn't help but smile. She looked at me curiously. "What?"

"I miss this," I said, resting my hand on her knee. "I miss puzzling through things with you. We've always been a good team."

She looked away uncomfortably, shifting her knee out of reach, so I cleared my throat and sat back in the hard little plastic chair that was rapidly putting my butt to sleep.

"Anyway," I continued. "That's a really great thought. I've been meaning to call Loretta and Doug to let them know about Green's office visit and to see if anyone has tried to approach them. I kind of doubt it because Doug's been dealing with something down home all week. Loretta typically only works in the Columbus office Monday through Wednesday, and she was driving back home tonight, but I'm hoping she's able to access our new security system remotely and capture some stills of Green's face that she can forward to me. I have a couple of late morning appointments with IT clients, but I'm hoping to touch base with Rochelle again in the afternoon. We really don't have a game plan yet."

Her eyes landed on mine again. "Be careful."

"I will. And you need to let me know if that guy comes sniffing around again," I said. "I don't know what he's up to, but it isn't anything good. I wouldn't let him back inside."

She got to her feet, wincing the whole while. "I will take that under advisement."

I was up like a shot, despite the pins and needles tickling my backside and thighs. "Are you sure you don't want me to take you to Urgent Care? I really don't mind. It's not like I've got anything else to do."

She waved my concern away. "I'll be fine. I just need to get off my feet and stretch out for a bit. But first, I have to deal with that willful child of mine."

I placed my hand gently on her arm to detain her for just a moment longer. "Hey, Mel? Try to take it a little easy on Jaz, okay? I know she can't be doing things like this, but she's really having a hard time with what's happening here."

"Yeah, well, who ever said life was fair? I'm having a hard time with it, too."

"We *all* are, Mel, but—" I paused, struggling for the right words. I didn't want to divulge exactly how direct Jasmine had been with me. "Jasmine feels like she's caught up in something where she has zero say. Just as soon as she gets a new normal, it gets ripped away."

The muscles in Melanie's jawline clenched, and I knew I was in dangerous territory, but I figured I'd come this far; I might as well finish my thought while I still had the floor.

"And I honestly wasn't trying to derail your workday today. I had no idea what Brady was up to when he brought us there for lunch."

I was relieved when she smiled. "I know. That guy's a regular ol' Cupid, it seems. Did he tell you about his new gig?"

"Of course, he did. He had to show off his fancy new ride, too. And I thought *you* were a bad driver." I rolled my eyes and pulled a face that made her laugh.

"Hey! I take offense to that. You drive like a deceased grandmother."

We lingered, smiling at each other under the moonlight, and I wanted nothing more than to pull her to me and kiss her glistening lips. I decided not to push my luck.

"Did he invite you to his party on Saturday?" I asked.

"He did."

"Are you going?"

She shrugged. "I don't know. I don't know any of his work friends. It would be nice to see Anyssa again, but it would probably be awkward."

"So, why don't we go together? At least we'd have *somebody* interesting to talk to."

"I don't know if that's such a great idea," she said. "Our conversations seem—*safest* when we have mediation."

"We've done alright tonight."

"After a *very* bumpy start." Her smile turned wistful. "I'll let you know."

She limped to her stoop and let herself inside, closing and locking the door behind her.

I smiled all the way to my car. She hadn't said no, so for all intents and purposes, I had myself a date!

································

By the time I got home, it was too late to call Loretta, whose strict requirement for beauty sleep wasn't a point I cared to debate. When I tried to reach Doug, his phone went straight to voicemail. I left a terse, "Call me," and then followed it up with an identical text. By the time I was nodding off to reruns of *The Big Bang Theory*, he hadn't done so. With a stretch and a yawn, I headed upstairs to my bedroom, Dexter stealthily padding along behind me.

My Thursday morning started off bumpy at best.

I had set my alarm clock for PM instead of AM, and if it hadn't been for Dexter's insistence upon being fed, I would've slept right through my morning appointments. As it was, I missed my morning run, and I was racing to get ready, completely frazzled to discover my water tank had bitten the dust some time since the previous morning. I hoped I'd get by just reigniting the pilot light, but the damn thing was blinking a bunch of red error codes on its control panel and under the paltry light in my dank basement, all I could tell for sure was that something was very wrong. Even a brief shower under ice cold water felt endless, my shampoo seemingly made impervious to rinsing simply by the difference in temperature. By the time I emerged, my nipples were diamond chisels, and my teeth were chattering. I'd have to get a plumber out in the afternoon, despite the rate such emergency service commanded. Homeownership can be quite a bitch, but then again, so can a man with excruciatingly tender teats.

As I headed north on I-270 to my first customer in Hilliard, I called Loretta and told her about the unexpected visitor who had stopped by the office after she had left for the evening, asking if anyone had tried to contact her.

"No, it's been quiet here," she said, yawning. "In fact, it's been a little *too* quiet."

"Yeah?"

"Dougie didn't come home last night, and he wouldn't answer his phone, no matter how many times I called," she said, clearly miffed, and I could only imagine how high that number climbed. "I finally got a short text telling me he'd see me sometime today. *Sometime.* I don't like what that woman is doing to him."

She didn't need to invoke Lucy Graves' name for me to catch her meaning. Other than his mother, Lucy was the only other woman in Doug's life, even if it wasn't exactly amicable.

"Now, Loretta," I chastised. "You're going to have to face it. Your little boy is almost a middle-aged man."

"Oh, up yours."

"I'll agree with you on one thing, though," I said. "It hasn't been easy to get hold of him lately. He didn't return my calls *or* send me a courtesy text, so I guess you win. I think he should know about this Mr. Green and his mob-like tactics, so can you fill him in whenever you do finally speak to him?"

"Sure."

"One more thing," I said, activating my turn signal as I eased into the rightmost lane to take the Cemetery Road exit.

"What?" she asked impatiently. "My programs are about to start."

"That fancy new video system we got?"

"I am *not* deleting that video," she said. "You can just give it up right now, mister."

"No, not that," I said. "Can you access the system remotely?"

"Of course I can," she said, and it sounded like I had offended her personally. "This is a top-of-the-line system. It can do anything you'd want."

"Can you get screen grabs from the recorded video?" I asked.

"In high definition."

"Awesome. I'd like you to log in and get a couple of screen grabs of this Mr. Green's face and email them to me. I'm planning to visit our new client this afternoon, and I'd like to see if she recognizes this joker."

She sighed like I'd asked her to move furniture. "Fine. It might take me a few. I'm still learning all of the controls."

As I was asking a favor, I ignored the opportunity to belittle her level of training. "That's okay. I'm heading into a customer site of mine and will be tied up for an hour or so. Thanks. I appreciate it."

She grumbled something surly and disconnected, just as I merged into heavy traffic on Cemetery Road. I crawled along for several blocks until I reached Leap Road and turned right. Immediately on my left was a long strip mall anchored by a Kroger on the end closest to me. My appointment was with Bonnie's Bundts, a mom-and-pop bakery specializing in mini-bundt cakes, and owned and operated by an ornery old bird named Ginny Rockwell. I had no fucking clue who Bonnie was. I was installing a new mini-PC and configuring web-based software they had purchased to manage their custom orders and point-of-sale transactions. I had barely nosed my car into a slot at the storefront when my phone rang. Seeing Loretta's name on the Caller ID, I sighed, wondering what part of my instructions were too difficult for her to follow.

"What, Loretta?"

Her next words stopped me in my tracks.

Pinching the bridge of my nose, I asked, "What do you mean, 'there *is* no video?'"

CHAPTER SEVEN

"I don't understand," said Loretta, and I could hear her heavy handing her mouse in the background. "The video of you from earlier was crystal clear. Maybe—"

I waited for her to finish her thought while Ginny waved at me with a big smile from behind her storefront glass. I sent us down a short path of charades, holding a finger up and pantomiming being on the phone to which she gestured pouring a cup of coffee while raising her eyebrows to officially ask if I was interested. I shot her a big thumbs-up before mouthing 'black' and pointing to my dark hair. She winked and disappeared into her store.

"Maybe what, Loretta? Did it just stop recording?"

"No," she said, flustered. "I logged out and back in, but I'm still getting the same thing." She suddenly guffawed.

"What's so funny?" I asked.

"Um, nothing—it's just that darn video of you. It still plays perfectly fine. But the video from later—it's almost like it's overexposed or something. Everything except the very edges around the screen are like looking into a black hole—well, I guess it's more of a *brown* hole. I'll have to call the company, I guess. Maybe the camera is bad."

"After *one day?*" I was incredulous. "What kind of discount dollar store did this equipment come from? What about the live feed? You can still access that, right?"

"Of course I can," she groused, taking personal offense to any criticism levied against her precious security partnership. A flurry of keystrokes and mouse clicks indicated she was changing her view. "Well, hey. The live feed looks fine. Hold on—let me check all of the cameras." More clicking. "Huh."

"They're fine?"

"Seem to be," she said before finally admitting, "I should probably have the system checked out, just to be safe."

"I have a feeling this was the handiwork of our Mr. Green," I said, not fully understanding how he might have managed to scramble video, but the concept wasn't unheard of. It suggested a level of resource that was more than a little unsettling. I caught myself examining the parking lot around me to ensure I wasn't currently being tailed. "Still, that's probably a good idea."

"I'll call them right now," she said. "And if they're able to access the video from last night, I'll send you those screen grabs."

"I won't hold my breath, but thanks," I said. "And Loretta?"

"Yeah?"

"Don't answer the door to any strangers while you're there alone, okay? Rochelle Pendleton told us most of the other investigators she tried to hire wouldn't even take her case, and those who did dropped it in very short order. Someone's trying to intimidate us. You need to be careful."

She tutted at my concern. "I've been going to self-defense classes twice weekly, remember? *You're* the one that needs to be careful."

She disconnected before I could even respond, and yet she wonders why I have such a difficult time being civil. *Sheesh.*

⋯•••••●⦶⦷●•••••⋯

By three-thirty, I had finished with both of my own customers and was racing home to meet a plumber I'd persuaded to drop everything and look at my water tank. He was from a local outfit called Root-em Toot-em, a company with exactly zero reviews on Yelp. That should've been a gigantic red flag, but I was desperate. My nipples still weren't talking to me after the Cold-Water Challenge they had endured without consent that morning. Every other plumber I tried was booked until the following afternoon, and commanded a steep diagnostic fee, while virtually assuring me that at least parts, if not a whole new water tank, would need to be ordered before I'd have hot water again. Iggy from Root-em Toot-em undercut 'em all, had availability, and sounded confident he could have my existing tank operational in one visit. He claimed to carry a wide variety of replacement parts in his van and could handle anything manufactured in the last three decades.

My confidence began to wane as his unmarked, rust-pocked white van bumped up into my driveway, lurching to a stop beside my Hyundai, halfway in my drive and halfway in my front yard. Its frame continued to bounce on blown suspension for a nauseating moment after it had been shifted into park, and I could smell weed just as soon as Iggy opened the driver's door.

"Mr. Miller?" he called, squinting to where I stood on the porch.

"Morrow," I corrected, cursing my damned luck. He was a young kid with gangly arms covered in what appeared to be self-inflicted tattoos—the kind where spelling was phonetic at best. His thick, dark hair fought to escape the ballcap he wore backwards on his head, and his broad smile revealed more than one gaping void where once upon a time there had been teeth. His grimy t-shirt hadn't been white in some time, and his jeans were threadbare and on life-support, hanging low on his hips and held in place by a length of rope that had been fashioned into a belt. I reluctantly bridged the distance, meeting him in my front yard. "It's Iggy, isn't it?"

"My friends call me Ig," he said, offering a filthy hand, which I reluctantly took, using all of my self-restraint not to recoil visibly. Maybe— just *maybe*—this kid might be able to resolve my hot water problem. "Well, let's see what we've got."

I started to lead him to the front door but altered course towards the rear once the first wave of his body odor permeated the cloying sweet scent of cannabis that clung to his every fiber. Access to the basement was closer from the back door, and there was no sense sullying any more of the air inside my house than necessary. I led him down the rickety stairs, turning on the few bare bulbs that were mounted to the floor joists above. Dexter followed us closely, keen to be involved in whatever was going on. Iggy stood before the water tank with his hands on his bony hips, looking at it like he was observing an alien aircraft.

"Well, *huh*," he finally said, and just like that, he took my last shred of optimism with those two simple words.

"Is there any hope?" I asked futilely.

He half-snorted. "Well, sure—I mean, I guess so. Let me get my tools and see what I can find."

"Feel free to come and go as you need to through the back door, just keep an eye out for my cat," I said, retracing our path to the stairs and climbing them to emerge in the kitchen. "He's an indoor cat, but that doesn't mean he won't try to escape."

"Yo, gotcha, dude," Iggy said, opening the back door wide just as Dexter darted like lightning out into the back yard. "*Awww*, oops—"

I sighed, shaking my head as I grabbed a bag of cat treats from the counter and headed outside.

82

I deposited Dexter into my office, taking the unopened bag of treats as I closed the door behind me. He yowled his disapproval at my deception, and I yowled right back, mocking him. Like I should *reward* his insubordination.

As if.

At least now, I had relieved Iggy of at least one responsibility beyond his capabilities. I wasn't particularly hopeful about the other as I heard him clunking around downstairs doing God-only-knows what. I opted to sit on one of the sofas in my living room where the noise wasn't quite so loud and conduct a little business.

First, I checked my email to confirm that Loretta hadn't somehow been able to miraculously retrieve a still from last night's security video. Nothing from her, just a suspicious shitload of advertising for the various plumbing repair services in my area. It was almost as if all those cookies encountered while Googling my options had collected my personal data and sold it to— well, *everybody*. I held on to the emails. I suspected I might still need them.

Next, I called Rochelle Pendleton.

She answered after several rings, sounding a little breathless. "Well, hey, Mr. Morrow! I didn't expect to hear from you this late in the afternoon."

I glanced at my watch and was surprised to find it was nearly four-thirty. "Please—it's Dwayne. I hope I didn't catch you at a bad time," I said. "I really meant to call you earlier, but the day has sort of gotten away from me. I've got a repairman in the house as we speak."

"I'm sorry to hear that," she said. "And it's not a bad time at all. We had a doctor's appointment this afternoon for Dad, and I was just getting Joey back into the house and settled. I'm eager to hear what your team has decided is the best plan of attack."

"Oh," I said, caught a little off guard. It hadn't occurred to me that she might want a progress report. I can't imagine she'd be thrilled to know I had spent the majority of my time checking out *her* credibility while Loretta had simply gone home; Doug was too busy with his own affairs to come out and play at all. "Um, we're still discussing that. I'm still waiting for a little input from Mr. Boggs. He prefers to be hands-on with all our cases."

"Oh," she said, unable to hide the disappointment in her voice. "Okay. That makes sense, I guess. So, how can I help you?"

"We had a little—weirdness happen last night," I said.

"Yeah? Like what?"

"A visitor who went by the name of Mr. Green," I said. "Does the name mean anything to you?"

"Um, no, I can't say it does. Should it?"

"He was there on behalf of Senator Ghant," I said. "He was there to scare us off."

There was a long silence before Rochelle finally spoke again, and she couldn't have sounded any more despondent. "I suppose that's it, then."

"I'm sorry?"

"Isn't this the part where you tell me that Boggs Investigations can no longer pursue my case? I've heard at least a dozen versions of it. What's your excuse going to be?"

I blinked. "No excuses necessary. We're not going anywhere."

A short silence this time. "Really?"

"Really. I just wanted to know if you ever heard of the guy. Maybe you recognized him from your days with Ghant's election team."

"Oh," she said, before devolving into a slight fit of giggles. "I'm so relieved. I was just sure—well, never mind. But still, I can't say the name means anything to me."

"I'm fairly certain the name is bogus," I said. "It sounds pretty generic, like someone has a thing for *Reservoir Dogs* or—"

"*Clue!*"

"Beg pardon?"

She chuckled. "Clue. You know—the board game. Miss Scarlet, Professor Plum—"

"Ah," I said as the dots connected. "Yes. Well, I had really hoped to pay you a visit with some stills from our video feed to see if you recognized his face, but that doesn't seem to be an option. Our brand new, state-of-the-art security system went wonky during the exact time he visited."

"How convenient," she said, not sounding the least bit surprised. "I swear, it's like Parker is untouchable. He always had a team of muscle that ran interference for him."

"Unfortunately, at this point, I'd need the assistance of a police sketch artist to see if his likeness means anything to you," I said, chuckling ruefully while she said nothing in response. "That was a joke."

"Maybe not," she said. "What are you doing for dinner?"

"I haven't gotten that far. I'm still awaiting the grim prognosis of my water tank. Why do you ask?"

"Well," she said. "I'm not a police sketch artist, but art is my passion. I'm not half bad with charcoal sketching when I apply myself. Maybe with your description—" She tapered off to let me fill in the blank.

"Are you sure?"

"I was just getting ready to start dinner for the fam. There will be more than enough for everyone. I make a pretty mean chicken marsala."

My stomach growled loudly, reminding me I hadn't eaten since scarfing down a mini-bundt cake courtesy of my first customer of the day.

"It sounds like heaven," I said. "I've got your address from your file. I'll be there as soon as I can."

We disconnected just as the scent of Iggy blossomed, forecasting his imminent arrival. I hurried to meet him in the kitchen where he looked positively forlorn.

"This doesn't bode well," I said, disappointed but already resigned.

"Dude," he said. "That thing is *beyond* dead."

85

•••••••——◦◦——•••••••

I'll give him this, Iggy didn't want to take any sort of payment since he was unable to realize his promise of same-day service. He also worried about making it home with what little gas remained in his gas-guzzling Econoline, and while it technically wasn't my problem, the thought of him living in his van in my driveway felt like more of a realistic possibility than I cared for. I forced him to accept a fifty which was less than half of what his competitors charged as a non-refundable diagnostic fee. I considered it the cost of my own learning curve. He eagerly offered to install a "slightly used" model he could almost certainly get from his stepfather who operated some sort of salvage yard down on McKinley Avenue in Columbus, but I politely declined. My existing unit was powered by natural gas, and I'd never get another night's sleep if I knew he had touched those gas lines. I spent the next half-hour online ordering a new unit from Home Depot and scheduling its installation for the following Wednesday. I figured by the time it was installed, I might smell every bit as ripe as the Igster, but what could I do?

Next up, I texted Melanie to see if her back was feeling any better. I was surprised when my phone rang almost immediately in response.

"Hey," I said. "I didn't call because I figured you'd be at work."

"I'm supposed to be," she said. "I had to call off. I could barely get out of bed this morning."

"Aww, *Mel!* Why didn't you call me? I would've taken you to a doctor myself."

"And that's exactly why I didn't call," she said. "This isn't the first time I've thrown my back out. All I need is a steady supply of Aleve and some bed rest. I'm scheduled off tomorrow and Saturday, so that should give me plenty of time to recuperate. I already feel a lot better."

86

I sighed, knowing it was futile to argue the point any further. "Is there anything I can do to help? Maybe bring dinner for you and Jaz?"

"Already got it covered," said Melanie. "The little one is currently doting on me and has a cookie sheet of Pizza Rolls in the oven."

"She's a sweet kid."

Melanie snorted. "Yeah, right. I'm pretty sure this isn't entirely selfless. She's trying to put a swift end to her grounding, but I've got some disappointing news for her. She's a repeat offender. How's your day been?"

I groaned. "I've had better."

I regaled her with my water tank drama, which had her giggling inappropriately at my misfortune. I didn't realize how much I missed that sound, and my heart ached, longing for a do-over that could never happen. I shifted gears before melancholia had a chance to creep into my voice.

"Interesting update on our mysterious Mr. Green," I said.

"Yeah?"

"Apparently, he has the ability to scramble video signal. I asked Loretta to try and get me a screengrab of his face, but all the footage was ruined. In fact, I'm on my way to our new client's to see if she can sketch his likeness based on my description."

"She's an artist?" Melanie sounded surprised.

"Mmm-hmm. Rochelle claims competence with a pencil and thinks it's worth a shot. I'm really curious if she recognizes this joker from her time working on the senator's election campaign."

"And if she does?"

"Maybe she can give a little background on how he's connected to the senator's inner circle. He couldn't have rubbed me more the wrong way if he tried. And before you call me paranoid, that business of showing up at your apartment was no accident," I said. "That was for maximum effect."

Melanie was quiet for a moment. "I have to admit, I halfway expected him to turn up here again today."

The hairs on the back of my neck prickled. "He hasn't, has he?"

"No, but the whole thing *was* pretty weird."

"If he does come back, please don't answer the door," I said. "And make sure Jasmine knows better, too."

"Oh, *Dwayne*—"

"I'm serious, Mel. Humor me until I have a better idea who this guy is. Please?"

She sighed. "Fine. But it's mostly because I don't want to get out of bed."

"I can live with that," I said, my relief palpable. Our conversation had gone better than many of our recent exchanges, so I decided to stick my neck out a little further. "Hey, about Saturday night. What do you think the odds are that you'll be feeling well enough to—"

"You can stop right there, mister," she said. "I still haven't decided if us going to Brady's together is such a great idea, regardless of how much better I feel."

"But you're still thinking about it?"

"Yes. Back off. I'll let you know."

We disconnected, and I couldn't help but smile.

She didn't say no.

I released Dexter from the captivity of my office, receiving a disgruntled hiss for my trouble. He scrabbled across the floor for his food dish, and I added a little bonus for his inconvenience. He accepted my offering without acknowledgement, tending to the business at hand while turning an icy cold shoulder to me. I sighed, wondering if he was really worth all the trouble, but I was already scritching between his shoulder blades before I stood, so I guess there's the short answer.

I grabbed my phone, keys, and wallet, and headed for the front door, my empty stomach urging me along toward a home-cooked meal that sounded absolutely delightful. I was halfway through the door before I stopped, checking myself, and returned to my office. Stepping behind my desk, I unlocked the second drawer from the bottom where I had begun storing my gun and its ammo. I double-checked that the safety was engaged and that the gun was loaded, pocketing a spare clip just in case.

I was done making *that* particular mistake.

······•••••⊝⊖••••••······

I guess it doesn't matter how many passes I take around this big ol' sun of ours, I'm never fully prepared when confronted with someone else's casual affluence in the real world.

Following my GPS to the address Rochelle had given, I wound my way out Route 42 toward Plain City, veering off on a network of rural gravel lanes that intersected with little to no warning. The sun had completely set, and long expanses of flat farmland were broken up by fields of weedy overgrowth and woodsy groves of elderly trees, their bare branches pointing upward to a moon that was nearly full.

As I closed in on my destination, an eight-foot stone wall sprung up on my right, covered in crawling ivy and kudzu. I squinted, looking for an ingress when Lady Google abruptly announced I had arrived, startling me. I inched forward until I came upon a break in the wall defended by a no-nonsense wrought iron double gate, deterring accidental interlopers. It was inset under an ornate, stone archway that proclaimed 'The Pendletons' in a tastefully chosen font, and there was a speaker box mounted to the left side of the drive for visitors to announce themselves. I pulled up and depressed the button. I was just beginning to wonder how much time was reasonable before pressing it again when a red light on the panel came to life, and I realized I was on camera.

"Oh, hey, Mr. Mor—I mean, Dwayne. Sorry it took so long. I'm up to my elbows in the kitchen. Let me buzz you in. Just follow the drive all the way back. The main house is at the end of the drive."

"Okay," I said, for lack of anything better. *Main house?* What *was* this place?

There was a buzz, and the gates began a slow swing inward. I crept through before they changed their minds and found myself on well-maintained acreage with a gravel drive that wound gently towards the back of the property. The 'main house' was nowhere to be seen, but I hadn't traveled very far before I spotted a small cottage to my left, its windows dark. It couldn't have been more than a handful of rooms, but it was quaint with a look reminiscent of a gingerbread house, its frontage edged by empty plots of dark, rich soil that would likely teem with flowers in a few short months. As I progressed down the drive, I had to wonder how many landscapers it took to maintain a property this size. All of the shrubbery was neatly trimmed, and the grass had been shorn a uniform length before winter. I passed a latticework gazebo several hundred yards to my right before finally rounding a bend that offered a first glimpse of the palatial manor Rochelle Pendleton called home. It was three stories of red brick opulence, tucked behind a wading pool that was currently empty. I pulled my SUV into the circular drive near the grand entrance. It was the only vehicle on premises, and I could only assume Rochelle utilized a garage I had yet to discover. Only a handful of lights shone through the grilles of the ten-foot-tall windows, and I felt dwarfed as I ascended the stairs. The entire manor seemed built for people much taller than me. A motion-activated security light flicked on, momentarily blinding me before I had a chance to find the doorbell.

It didn't really matter.

The door flew open, and I found myself face-to-face with a wild-eyed man wearing a burgundy brocade smoking robe cinched at the waist.

"If I've told you once, I've told you a *hundred fucking times!*" he shrieked. "Get off my *goddamned property!*"

Raised in his white-knuckled fist was a fireplace poker, reared back, and he appeared more than ready to plant the business end in the top of my skull.

CHAPTER EIGHT

"*D*addy! Daddy! Daddy!*"

Rochelle's hand seized her father's wrist just as I thought my eyes couldn't get any wider. He was startled by her touch, and the poker fell from his grasp as his eyebrows shot up in surprise.

"Please, don't hurt our guest," said Rochelle, shooting me an apologetic glance. "I asked Mr. Morrow over for dinner."

Mr. Pendleton looked from his daughter to me and back again. "Margaret?" he finally managed, uncertainty causing his voice to tremble. "Is that you, dear?"

"It's me, Daddy," said Rochelle, rubbing her father's arms as she turned him away from the door. She nodded for me to come in. "It's Shelley. Okay? Look at me, daddy. It's Shelley."

She kept his focus on her face by gently cupping a hand underneath his chin as his expression shifted through a sequence of disparate emotions, finally landing on comprehension.

"*Shelley*," he said, embarrassment registering all the way to the tips of his ears. "Of course it is. I thought I heard someone at the door."

"You did," she said, releasing his chin and wrapping her arm around his frail shoulders. "Mr. Morrow is trying to help us with Joey. I invited him to dinner. Dwayne, this is my father, Gerard Pendleton."

He turned to look at me, his expression souring. "I don't like the looks of him," he muttered as I shifted uncomfortably on my feet.

I aimed for my most congenial smile and slowly extended a hand. "Dwayne Morrow, sir. I'm very pleased to meet you."

He recoiled like I had offered a piping hot bowl of the plague. "Keep your filthy hands to yourself. I know your kind. *I know your kind,*" he hissed before turning back to his daughter. "I need the facilities, Margaret. Did they tell you where they were?"

"Yes, Daddy," said Rochelle, guiding her father to the hallway from which she had come at the rear of the foyer. "Follow me."

Her face offered a slightly more protracted apologetic, *"Yikes!"* and she held up a forefinger so I would stay put while she tended to things. I was fine with that. I didn't want to upset or confuse her father any more than he already obviously was. They wandered out of sight, his confusion lessening with each of her patient, soothing responses.

I took a moment to examine my surroundings.

Dark paneled walls stretched to high ceilings where intricate, hand-painted tiles were inlaid. A burnished, wrought-iron chandelier was suspended by chains extending all the way to the topmost ceiling, and peering up, I could follow the handrail of a spiraling staircase that wound all the way to the top. Where the staircase opened out into a field of Minton tiles in the foyer, a rather incongruous white plastic baby gate had been fitted to block access to the upper levels, and I suspected it was as much for Rochelle's father as it was for her three-year-old son. A set of closed doors were side-by-side to my left, effectively piquing my curiosity and discouraging it at the same time. The heavenly smell of dinner wafted through the air, and my stomach voiced its embarrassingly enthusiastic approval. I was startled and extremely happy Rochelle wasn't there to witness. It was every bit as menacing as a large dog growling.

After a surprisingly short time, Rochelle hurried back into the foyer, her high cheekbones flushed with mortification. "I am so sorry about that," she said. "He's almost never like that, and it never lasts for long. Are you alright?"

"Yeah, he just caught me by surprise," I said, unable to suppress a nervous little titter. "I thought you said your father was in a facility."

"He is," she said, nodding. "But when he's doing well, and I don't have too much on my plate to keep an eye on him, I sometimes bring him home for the weekend. As I mentioned earlier, his new meds have been doing wonders. This was—well, an unfortunate surprise. Are you sure you're okay?"

"Really, I'm fine," I said. "Who's Margaret?"

"That was my mother," she said, tucking an errant strand of hair behind her ear. "I've been told I'm her spitting image."

"Must be hard."

She shrugged. "It is what it is. I was just getting ready to take dinner up."

"Are you sure dinner is a good idea? Me being here seemed to be what upset him. I don't want to make things more difficult for you."

She shook her head. "It'll be fine. He already had his dinner a couple of hours ago. He starts fussing if it's much past five, and he would have never eaten my chicken marsala anyway. He's kind of fixated on Apple Jacks at the moment, and as long as he's eating, I let him have whatever makes him happy. He's at the mercy of the nutritionists where he lives most of the time. I can't imagine occasionally bending to his whims does any real harm. I took him back to his room, and turned on *Everybody Loves Raymond*. He loves Peter Boyle. He'll be out like a light in minutes. Come on back."

The dining area sat in the central section of a grand expanse that occupied the entire back corner of the house. Four sets of double French doors spaced equidistantly along the back wall opened out, but onto what I couldn't tell. Gauzy cream curtains were drawn across the glass panes, obscuring whatever lay beyond. The room's open concept design turned a museum-like space into cozier areas. I say 'cozier' because each zone still presented with the opulence of a home far beyond my means. I sat at the head of a long rectangular walnut dining table that could easily seat twelve while Rochelle took the seat to my left. The room flowed into the kitchen behind her, and it was a space suitable for a team of professional chefs with industrial grade, stainless steel appliances built into the walls and central island, and enough counter space to prep innumerable dishes. An aluminum hood hung from the ceiling, hovering over a cooktop integrated into the island, and the counters themselves were constructed of a material I was unlikely to find while perusing my neighborhood Lowe's.

To our right was a comfortable living area with matching, overstuffed off-white sofas arranged in an "L" around an oval, southwestern-themed area rug. A gentle fire was the centerpiece of the far wall, and above its mantel, an enormous widescreen television transfixed the young toddler who was currently bouncing on his feet in his playpen in the corner, thoroughly entertained by the latest antics of Bluey and his friends.

My fork clacked onto my empty plate as I swallowed the last exquisite bite of tender chicken, and I couldn't suppress my slightly orgasmic groan of pure ecstasy.

Rochelle giggled, her own fork suspended midair. "You like?"

"Me like," I nodded, dabbing at the corners of my mouth with the cloth napkin she had neatly folded at my place setting. "This was incredible. Where did you learn to cook like that?"

She shrugged as if it was no big deal. "About a billion years ago, I dreamed of becoming the female Gordon Ramsay. I majored in Culinary

Arts at Columbus State and had my sights set on my own television show where I would rescue failing restaurants across the United States but without all the histrionics and f-bombs."

I tutted. "I hate to break it to you, but the American people seem to love those histrionics and f-bombs. They've made Mr. Ramsay quite the star."

"Oh, well," she said wistfully, pushing her own plate forward. "Life had other plans for me anyway. Would you like some more? There's plenty."

"As much as I would love to, I'd explode all over your lovely home," I said, gently laying a hand on my straining stomach. "But thank you. Joey sure seemed to approve." I indicated the empty highchair beside her where her adorable son had voraciously mowed his way through his portion of finely cut chicken and pasta. He turned at the sound of his name and burbled something unintelligible before returning his attention to Bluey.

"Yeah, there's nothing wrong with his appetite," said Rochelle, taking the bite from her fork before rising to gather our plates.

I stood and took the plate from her hand. "Let me get this," I said. "Please. It's the least I can do after you fixed that amazing dinner."

"Oh, *no*, I couldn't—"

"I insist," I said, stacking her plate onto mine and scooping all of the silverware up to deposit on top. "I know my way around a dishwasher. If you'll point me to where you keep the storage containers, I'll put the leftovers in the fridge while I'm at it."

She indicated a pantry door along the back wall. "Thank you, Dwayne. Just set the knives in the sink—they aren't dishwasher safe. I'll use the opportunity to put Joey to bed and grab my sketch pad and pencils. I'll be back in a jiff."

She crossed the room and scooped her little boy into her arms, and I waved bye-bye as she carried him out into the hall. His five-little fingers waggled back at me, and he grinned with every little tooth he had. He really was a cutie pie.

We had kept the dinner conversation light while Joey was seated at the table; it felt unseemly to discuss anything case-related with his innocent ears tuned in.

I took the dishes to the double basin sink, rinsing them off and loading them into a high-capacity dishwasher manufactured by a company I'd never heard of, but I knew it cost more than I'd ever pay. Next, I scavenged for Tupperware and sealed away the leftovers, setting them aside as I rinsed the cookware and added it to the dishwasher rack.

I stood transfixed before the open door of the cavernous refrigerator with the containers in hand, never having seen such a well-organized icebox. I wasn't sure if the contents were organized by food type, alphabetization, or some other cryptic cipher, but there was a definite system in place that was far beyond my comprehension. My usual M.O. was to stash things wherever there was any free space and close the door before they could jump back out at me. From there, it usually stayed put for weeks before turning into something fuzzy and unidentifiable before I finally relegated it to the trash, where I probably should have put it in the first place. I wasn't great with leftovers. But these leftovers were of a different caliber. They demanded preservation, and in this brightly lit, spotless appliance, finding space wouldn't be an issue. Despite a bounty of refrigerated goods, there was ample room for more, and the plethora of free space was oddly overwhelming. After a quick round of eenie-meenie-miny-moe, a decision was made, and I moved on.

I had just finished hand-washing the knives and put them in the dishrack beside the sink when Rochelle returned with pencils clutched in her hand and her sketchpad tucked beneath her arm. I froze when I realized she had changed into something a lot more comfortable, and I could feel the tips of my ears beginning to glow.

She sent me a sly wink and motioned me over to the sofa. "I hope you don't mind, but I changed into my jammies. Joey had a pretty big whoopsie all over me when I was changing his Pull-Ups, and I figured I might as well be comfortable. Have a seat, and we can get started."

She sat with her bare legs crossed at one end of the sofa that divided the living and dining areas, and I sat stiffly at the other, leaving ample room between us. I wasn't sure what kind of signals she was sending out, if any at all. I've never had a good sense of these things. But in my mind, all I could think about was what Melanie might say if she were to walk into the room, and we already had enough issues without me having to defend these optics.

I smiled nervously and cleared my throat, waiting for some direction. "So, how do we do this?"

Rochelle reached behind her to the end table and turned on a lamp before flipping to an empty page in her sketchbook. "Let's start with the basics. You said he called himself Mr. Green?"

"Yeah, but I'm pretty sure that's not his real name."

She jotted it at the bottom of the page anyway. "How old would you say he is?"

"Around my age."

"Skin color?"

"About the same as mine."

"Hair color?"

"About like mine."

Rochelle sighed, grinning crookedly at me. *"Dwayne*—at this rate, I'm drawing a picture of you."

"Well, I don't mean *exactly* like mine," I said, color creeping into my cheeks. "It was shorter, almost shaved at the back. He parted it on the right side and used some sort of pomade or gel to keep it in place."

She tucked her tongue in the corner of her mouth as her pencil flew across the page. "Describe the general shape of his face."

"Square."

"Dwayne."

"What? I don't mean his *whole* face, but his jawline was really pronounced, and so was his chin."

She dusted the page with an eraser before making some adjustments with her pencil. "We call that *chiseled*," she mumbled, teasing me.

"I'll try and keep that in mind."

We proceeded feature by feature until she had constructed a whole face, and when she showed it to me, it was startlingly close.

"His eyes were shiftier," I said, scooting closer to get a better look.

"Shiftier? What does that even mean?"

"You know—not so round. His eyelids were heavy. And his pupils were smaller—sort of beady."

She made a few more adjustments and showed it to me again. "Is this closer?"

I studied the picture. It was almost right, but something was missing, and I couldn't quite put my finger on it. Rochelle suddenly gasped and pulled the sketchpad back into her lap, her pencil a blur as she added another detail without any prompting from me. She swiveled the pad back in my direction.

"How about this?" she asked expectantly.

I slowly began to nod. She had modified the shape of his lips to be fuller in the center, narrowing at the corners, and further defined his chin, adding a somewhat prominent cleft to its center. It was spot on. "That's him," I said.

Rochelle emitted a sharp, victorious bark of laughter.

"I take it you know him?" I asked.

She nodded, still grinning at her handiwork. "It's Kevin Moody. He's Parker's right-hand man. They go way back—like all the way back. He's a former student from back when Parker taught school in West Virginia."

And suddenly, she had my full attention. "West Virginia?"

"Yeah, I don't know. Some private military school out in the middle of nowhere in West Virginia, but that was years ago. You might have heard about it. It was all over the news last summer when it burned down."

"I remember."

Understatement of the year. I was there when it happened. The Academy was at the very heart of why my sister was presumed dead. When I had gotten a little too close to the truth of its top-secret operation, its Powers That Be had initiated a self-destruct sequence that destroyed the facility before any damning evidence could be collected about it and the powerful people behind it, one of whom was Parker Ghant.

Rochelle was staring at me, and I realized I must have zoned out. *"Hmmm?"* I asked, snapping back into the present.

"Are you alright?" She leaned in, laying her hand on my arm, her concerned eyes searching my face.

"Yeah, sorry—I'm fine. So, you know this Kevin Moody?"

"I wouldn't say I *know* him, but yeah, he leads Parker's security team. I never had much interaction with him, and frankly, that was perfectly fine with me. He always gave me the creeps. He seemed to enjoy his job just a little too much, if you know what I mean. It makes sense that he'd be running interference now."

"Do you think he's dangerous?" I asked.

"Oh, yeah. Once, I saw him knock a reporter out with his own camera. The poor guy had to have his jaw wired shut, and the whole while, the smile never left Kevin's face," she said, shuddering at the recollection. "He *enjoys* hurting other people. The whole team can be scary, but Kevin's the worst."

"How many are on this team?" I asked.

"Last I knew, there were four, all hand-picked by Parker and all graduates of his precious Academy. If it weren't for some superficial physical differences, I would swear they were cloned in a lab. At times, they're like robots—very mercenary."

I chewed on my bottom lip, hesitant to ask what felt like a big favor, but she seemed eager to assist. "I don't suppose you could sketch the others, could you? It might be helpful to know who I might be running into next."

She flipped to a clean sheet in her sketchpad. "Of course. I hope you don't mind hanging out. It might take a little while."

"If it's not too much of an imposition."

Her smile went all the way up to her eyes as her finger traced a path along my arm. "It might just take all night."

Hoo, boy. Even *I* couldn't miss the unspoken offer hanging in the air between us. I had only just started stammering when my phone rang, providing a much-needed distraction. I fumbled it out of my pocket, and saw it was Doug Boggs, finally returning my call.

"If you'll excuse me, it's Mr. Boggs. I need to take this," I said, extracting myself from underneath her roving finger. She smiled and nodded as I wandered back to the kitchen, the phone already pressed to my ear. "It's about time."

"Well, *pardonnez moi*," said Doug, slaughtering the French expression with his Southern Ohio twang. "I wasn't aware that I reported to you. You've got Ma all upset, and she's been blowing my phone up all day. I'm trying to deal with some important business of my own here. What in the Sam Hill is goin' on?"

I counted to ten to temper my response before my inner smartass managed to autoreply, but *man*, it was hard. I filled him in on my dual encounters with 'Mr. Green,' the mysterious effect he seemed to have on the surveillance footage from the office's new security system, and how the whole thing had led me to our client's house, where she had managed to identify the man from sketching my description.

"And now you're pretty much up to speed," I said. "Your mom said that no one from the senator's team had been in contact with her, at least not as of when I spoke to her this morning. No one's been in contact with you, either?"

"I don't think so," he said. "But I haven't really been taking calls, and I haven't had a chance to check my voicemails."

"I noticed," I said, dryly. "Your voicemail has been full for as long as I've known you. Don't you ever check it?"

He was silent for a conspicuous moment.

"You don't know how, do you?" I challenged, needing zero confirmation that I had just correctly answered my own question.

"If it's important, they'll call back."

I scoffed. "Didn't really work for me, did it? You know, we really need some sort of bat-signal or something, some way I can get your attention if I really need it."

"I'd never get a moment's peace."

I scoffed even harder. "Trust me, I'd only use it if I had to. But this guy is something else, and believe it or not, I was a little worried about you and Loretta. I didn't want either one of you to be blindsided by him or someone like him showing up at your door."

"All right, all right. Point taken," he conceded. "How about 'The goose flies at night?'"

"What?"

He sighed. "'The goose flies at night.' It could be our code."

"That's overly complicated and stupid. How about 9-1-1?"

"I *guess* that could work." He was sullen.

"How are things going with Lucy?" Since I had him talking, I figured I'd try and sneak the question in.

"We're not talking about this," he said. "I'll look for a status update tomorrow afternoon. Keep up the good work."

He disconnected before I had a chance to reply.

Rochelle was smiling at me from the couch, and in that moment, I realized a subtle solution to my predicament. I called Melanie.

For a scary moment, I didn't think she was going to answer, and she sounded groggy when she finally did. "'Lo?"

"Hi," I said, projecting my voice just a skosh so Rochelle couldn't help but hear. "I just wanted to check in and see how you're doing."

"Dwayne? *Seriously?* It's almost ten. I was already asleep."

I looked at my watch, startled by the time. "Oh, geez, I'm sorry. I didn't realize how late it was—I mean, not that it's particularly late. You're never in bed by ten. Are you okay?"

"No, you goon," she said, clearly irritated. "As you well know, I wrenched my back. I took some muscle relaxers and was trying to get some extra rest."

I inhaled through my teeth apologetically. "I'm sorry I woke you. I'm still at Rochelle's and have some new information about our mysterious 'Mr. Green.'"

"Can't it wait until tomorrow?" she said, stifling a yawn.

"Well—sure, I guess. I just thought you might want to know, and I wanted you to know where I was—you know, just in case you were looking for me or something." So much for subtlety. I was pacing the kitchen and stammering away like a moron.

"I don't need to know where you are every second of the day. You made that plain when you uninstalled the app from your phone, remember? Good night."

Ouch.

"Well, yeah, but I—um, good night—" The line went dead. "—sweetheart."

I plastered a phony smile across my face and turned back to the living room, prepared to explain who Melanie was but was surprised to find the sofa empty.

"Rochelle?" I called out, raising my voice slightly while trying to avoid waking her child or her father. As I crossed to the couch, I felt a distinct draft waft in from the hallway. I backtracked to the foyer, where I saw the front door was standing wide open. Rochelle stood on the stoop, scanning the dark grounds. I eased up behind her. "What did I miss?"

She turned to me, panic in her eyes. "I caught a chill coming from the front of the house, and when I went to check, the door was like this. Joey's asleep in his crib, but I can't find Daddy anywhere. It's nearly freezing, and I think he's wandering around somewhere out here. I've got to find him!"

CHAPTER NINE

I'd love to say I'm amazing in a crisis, but by now, you already know that I'm a lousy liar. Too often, I act before I think, and I was already halfway out the door when Rochelle called out, "Hold up! Where do you think you are going?"

"To try and find your father, or at least I thought I was," I said, still caught up in the urgency and perplexed by her reticence.

She had entered a small cloakroom beside the doorway and was rummaging through coats hanging in shadows. "No," she barked forcefully, and I backtracked into the foyer. "He doesn't know you, and after seeing how he reacted earlier, I can only imagine he would try to hide from you if he saw you coming."

"Okay," I said, realizing she was very likely correct but a little stung by the tone of her rapid-fire direction. "How can I help?"

She had retrieved a long, beige woolen overcoat and was working her arms into its sleeves. "Will you stay here with Joey? His room is just down the hall and to the right. I don't want to take him out in the cold, and it would take too long to get him dressed anyway. Hopefully, I'll only be gone a few minutes, and he'll sleep right through this. You shouldn't have to do anything."

"Well, sure," I said, stepping away from the door. "Should I call the police or the EMS?"

"No," she said, pausing to offer a beleaguered smile. "I don't want to blow this all out of proportion, and I'm sure he's out there. Somewhere. I'll find him." She patted herself down, double-checking the pockets with a hint of panic on her face until she spotted her cell phone on an accent table between the entrance and the cloakroom. She scooped it up and slipped it into her pocket. "I'll be right back. Call me if you need anything."

"Okay, I—" She was already through the door and sprinting across the yard. "—will."

I sighed, closing the door gently behind her. The temperature had dropped several degrees since my arrival, and the chill was beginning to pervade more than the foyer. I shivered, hugging my own arms tightly before turning back towards the living room.

I froze.

Three-year-old Joey Pendleton stood in the mouth of the hallway in his powder-blue Bluey PJs, suckling a forefinger while staring up at me with wide, curious eyes.

···•••••◦◦••••••···

We sat side-by-side on the sofa, sizing each other up.

I was far more subtle, keeping my eyes mostly adhered to the fireplace while stealing an occasional glance at the child, but the boy was too young to realize that staring was impolite, and he continued to bore holes through me while suckling that darned finger, like he might miss something if he looked away, even for an instant. I would have assured him he wouldn't, if I had even the faintest idea of how to communicate with the lad. I had exactly zero experience with children his age.

Initially, I had tried depositing him in his playpen, hoping the assortment of toys that surrounded him would occupy his little mind. I had barely sat back down on the couch before he started fussing, calling out for his mama.

I tried to explain that she would be right back, but that was no comfort at all, and soon, he was chucking his toys one-by-one towards the fireplace with alarmingly good aim. As I was retrieving him from the playpen, I was struck by the certainty that he would need his Pull-Up changed, and that was so far beyond my comfort zone that my pulse began to race. I gave him a quick sniff and prayed that the Pull-Up was still under capacity as it didn't seem bloated and Joey's jammie bottoms were dry. It was at this point that I deposited him on the couch, instigating his current stare down, and for the life of me, I couldn't imagine what he thought was so interesting. Still, it seemed to calm the child, and the cries for his mother tapered away.

In fact, I started to notice a grin blossoming on the boy's face as my attention invariably wandered back in his direction. On my latest pass, he leaned forward and unexpectedly barked, *"GAH!"* It startled me so much that I visibly jumped, eliciting the most heartfelt guffaw from the child's very center. I scowled at him, and his giggling hit new squealing heights. Soon, the whole thing had devolved into some deranged version of peek-a-boo, and we were both practically in tears from laughing so hard.

Eventually, we ran out of gas, and I realized he had inched himself closer to me during our nonsense. "I'm Joe," he said, suddenly very earnest.

"I'm very pleased to meet you, Joe," I said, taking his little hand into mine. "I'm Dwayne."

"Dane," he repeated.

"Close. Let's try that again. Duh-way-ne," I said, enunciating clearly.

"Dane," was his response.

"Duh-wa-a-a-yne."

"Dane."

I sighed, scowling at him through narrowed eyes. "Fine. Dane it is."

He giggled before stifling a yawn. "Story?"

His eyes were hopeful, but again, I was completely out of my league. I sucked regret through my teeth before saying, "I'm sorry, little guy, but I don't really have any material prepared."

It was his turn to scowl, and let me tell you, it was a ferocious one. "Story." No longer a question, it was now a demand.

"O-o-kay," I said, wracking my brain for something that might entertain a toddler. I could tell him about my water tank woes, but even *I* wasn't interested in hearing anything more about that. I took my phone out of my pocket, hoping I'd missed a text from Rochelle with some sort of update on her search for her father, preferably including an imminent arrival time back at the house, but there was nothing.

"Kitty," said Joey, smiling and scooching closer to my side. He touched the phone's display, where a particularly regal picture of Dexter filled the home screen.

"You like kitties?" I asked, and he nodded his head enthusiastically. "Well, alright then. Let me tell you a story about a boy named…Dane, and the cat named Dexter who let Dane live with him."

"Dex-ter," he repeated. Of course, he got the *cat's* name right.

Inspiration struck. "Hey, here's a thought—would you like to see some more pictures of Dexter?"

Joey's head bobbed up and down enthusiastically, and he was practically in my lap by now. I unlocked my phone and opened the picture gallery, scrolling through my collection of His Nibs doing all the things he does best. I had the child's complete attention, and soon enough, he had worked the phone into his own hands and was flipping through the pictures at his own pace.

I had only begun to relax when the little booger, bored with the activity, threw my phone across the room, where it faceplanted on the hardwood floor about two feet in front of the fireplace.

"UH-oooh," he said, giving Macaulay Culkin's infamous expression some serious competition.

"Uh-oh? *Seriously?"*

He blew a raspberry at me and dissolved into giggles that shook his tiny little body. I managed to maintain my scowl for all of five seconds before the corners of my mouth started to twitch, and soon enough, I had my own case of the giggles. We sat side-by-side cackling like a couple of fools until my throat suddenly caught, and the reality of this little boy's circumstance came crashing down around me.

This impish little boy with the high-pitched giggle and crooked grin was living with a condition that would prove terminal if a bone marrow donor couldn't be found, and he had absolutely no idea of his precarious position—nor should he. The world is filled with men and women doing awful things with malice aforethought, many of whom would live to retirement and beyond, spreading their stain like an unabated cancer while this little boy's expiration date was already just around the corner. My heart ached in a way I can't describe as I couldn't help but question any grand design that could be so unspeakably cruel. I looked away, forcing a laugh that carried none of the genuine frivolity we had just shared, but my eyes were clouding, and I'd be damned if I was going to upset the little guy by sitting here and bawling over the injustice of it all.

"Hey, I've got an idea," I said, discreetly dabbing at the corners of my eyes and standing to retrieve my phone. I turned it over to discover the bumper on its protective case had been soundly defeated; a crack ran from the top of the screen to the bottom, like a jagged bolt of lightning. Should I have expected anything different? Not with the way this day had been going. I nabbed the television remote from the end table and sat back beside Joey, who was watching my every move with intense scrutiny. "Let's see if we can find you something on TV," I suggested, and those were the magic words. He nodded enthusiastically, clapping.

"Bluey!" he commanded as I turned the device on.

"Alright, let's see what I can find," I said, navigating the onscreen menu. We were in luck! The DVR had multiple episodes of the show primed and ready to go.

As soon as I selected an episode, Joey's little forefinger found its way back into his mouth, and he zoned into his favorite cartoon world. He inched closer, leaning over and using me a bit like a pillow. I glanced at my watch and was startled to find that it was after eleven o'clock. It felt like hours since Rochelle had gone after her father, but I hadn't noticed the actual time when she had gone outside. Joey's surprise appearance had thrown me for a loop. I tried not to worry, but I seem to have picked up a little of that proclivity from my dear sweet mother. I was aware the property was gated, which provided some comfort, but I had absolutely no idea how much acreage was contained within those gates nor how long was *too* long to be reasonable.

My arm was falling asleep, and I looked down to discover that Joey had done the same lying on top of it. And I had to pee.

Oh, well. I wasn't about to awaken the child. I laid my head against the back of the couch and closed my eyes, intending only to give them a quick rest.

I promptly fell asleep.

"Dwayne."

I snapped to consciousness with a snort as Rochelle's face loomed in front of mine. Startled to realize that Joey was no longer beside me, adrenaline coursed through my veins, and I sat up, almost headbutting Rochelle in the process. *"Joey."*

She smiled, placing her hands on my chest to keep me from leaping to my feet. "He's in bed," she said quietly. "So is Dad. Thank you for taking care of my little boy. He almost never gets up after I put him down for the night. I'm really sorry—"

"*Pffft*," I said, stifling a yawn. "It was no big deal."

"Yeah?" She picked up my phone from beside me on the couch and showed me its cracked screen. "I don't recall it being this way before. Joey's got an arm like he's throwing for the Buckeyes. Did he do this?"

"Well—not on purpose," I said, hedging. "I was showing him pictures of my cat, and he got a little—enthusiastic. No worries. I've got extended coverage. Where did you find your dad?"

"In the last place I thought to look for him," she said, taking the seat formerly occupied by her son. "He was in the guest house near the front entrance. I'm surprised it took me so long to think of it. Joey and I used to stay there before it became clear that Dad needed live-in assistance. I think he got there on muscle memory, but I was just so frantic about him being out there in the cold, it never occurred to me. We've always kept a key under the mat, so he was able to let himself in, and he remembered enough to disable the alarm, or else I might have found him a lot sooner."

"Did you have any trouble getting him to come back with you?"

She shook her head. "He was back to his old self by the time I got there, although he didn't remember taking the walk. This is the first time something like this has happened, but he was just so agitated earlier—"

"By me," I acknowledged, and she shot me a sympathetic look. "I'm really sorry about that. I don't normally have that effect on people."

"Don't be silly," she said. "Unfortunately, his behavior is only going to get more erratic. I may not be able to do these weekend visits much longer without hiring a caregiver to tag along."

"I really am sorry that you're dealing with, you know—*all* of this," I said sincerely. "It's really late. I should get out of your hair."

"It's *beyond* late," she said, grinning, her hand still resting on my arm. "It's after midnight. You may as well just spend the night."

I can only imagine the expression on my face as I scrambled for the right words to extract myself from the situation. She let me dangle in discomfort for a long moment before laughing.

"I know you've got a girlfriend," she said. "Your earlier call wasn't exactly subtle."

Heat flooded into my face as I looked at her sheepishly, keenly aware that whatever came out of my mouth next would likely only serve to embarrass me more.

"I wasn't inviting you into my bed, I promise," she said, giving me a Girl Scout salute before following it with a wink. "Although I ain't gonna lie, I'm tempted. You're one of the good guys. Your lady is lucky to have you."

I snorted, fairly certain I was about to burst into flames. "I'm not sure she would agree with you."

"Well, that would be her loss," she said, breaking the moment when she stood. "I've got plenty of guest rooms, and you're already half asleep. It's the least I can do."

"No, really, I was going to look into getting a hotel room anyway," I said, fighting another yawn. "The hot water tank in my house bit the dust this afternoon—that was why the repairman was there earlier. Turns out, he can't fix it, and I won't be able to have a new one installed until next Wednesday." I started to say something about cold showers but realized the inappropriateness in this moment. "I'm hoping to find a place that's pet friendly. Dexter holds grudges like you wouldn't believe when I leave him on his own too long."

"Well, that's complete nonsense," she said. "You can use the guest house until your repair is done and bring your cat over tomorrow morning. It's just sitting there empty, and I won't take no for an answer. I've told you where to find the key, and I'll text you the alarm code, and it's the same code for the gate—your phone *does* still work, doesn't it?"

I gave it a quick once-over, making sure I could unlock it and access the messaging app. "Seems to. Are you sure? I don't want to be an inconvenience."

She held up a hand to stop my protest. "The bedroom linens have been fairly recently changed. There are fresh towels in the closets. I won't hear another word."

•••••••�○◎●•••••••

I have to admit, I slept like a rock, although I woke up completely disoriented. The bedroom faced the west, so there was no morning sunshine to blind me in the wee hours. If I hadn't set the alarm on my phone, Lord only knows how long I might have slept. I hadn't realized the pitiful condition of my own mattress until I had slept on a deluxe model like this. I'd have to ask Rochelle for details, even though I was fairly certain its cost was well beyond my budget.

The bathroom was clean and modern, and I took full advantage of the spacious walk-in shower with its oversized showerhead and seemingly endless supply of hot water. What many showers lack is adequate water pressure, but I actually had to turn the pressure down; the water was stinging my feet as I luxuriated beneath its steady stream. I wasn't crazy about the shampoo and body wash, either. It was a little too floral and distinctly feminine, but as the old saying goes, beggars can't be choosers.

It was only after I had toweled off that I realized I had nothing to change into.

Shit.

I rifled through the empty drawers of the dresser before inspecting the closet. The only thing I found was a white terrycloth robe two sizes too small for me. I could barely cinch its belt around my waist, and I was one wrong move away from peekaboo time. I really hated the thought of putting my dirty clothes back on and was trying to summon the courage to make the drive home in the robe when my phone rang.

It was Melanie.

"Hey," I said. "How are you feeling this morning?"

"Much better," she said. "Where are you?"

"I'm sorry?" The question wasn't difficult, but it caught me off guard.

"You're never up this early," she said. "After I got Jasmine off to school, I swung through McDonald's and grabbed us breakfast. I thought we could talk about Brady's party. I'm standing on your front porch, and you're not here. Judging from the racket your lunatic cat is making behind the front window, you haven't been here for a while."

I chewed my bottom lip and weighed my options. There was always the truth. They say the truth will set you free, but as I currently was without underwear, I sincerely doubted this was the sort of freedom to which that old idiom applied. Still, considering the fractured state of our relationship, lying could be deadly.

"No," I said. "I didn't come home last night, but before you start thinking something happened that didn't, let me explain."

Utter silence.

"Are you still there?" I asked, halfway convinced she'd already disconnected the call.

"Mmm-hmm."

My explanation erupted like a dam bursting. "Rochelle's dad got loose in the yard, and he has dementia, and he was already scared of me so I couldn't look for him, so I stayed in the house to watch her little boy who was already asleep, except that he wasn't by the time Rochelle left, and I had to occupy him until his mother got back with his grandpa, but by then, we had both fallen asleep and it was already after midnight, and my hot water tank is busted, but there's an empty guest cottage here and Rochelle insisted that I stay—in fact, she and Joey used to live there until they moved into the main house to keep a closer eye on her father, but it's empty now, and Rochelle offered it to me until I got my water tank replaced, and how could I say no to such a generous offer, especially when I was practically dead on my feet?"

More silence, but I could hear her breathing this time. I suspected she was counting to ten—maybe twenty.

"Are you still there?"

Melanie sighed. "Well, that certainly was a mouthful."

"Nothing happened, Mel. I swear." They were the same words used by every cheating partner in the history of *ever*, and I hated their feel as they slipped through my lips. *I* wouldn't have believed me, and I knew what actually happened.

"You're a grown man," she said coolly. "You don't answer to me."

"But I'm telling you," I said. "You can ask Rochelle."

That brought a laugh. "I most certainly will not. What is the matter with you? If this woman is actually a client of yours, exactly how professional is it going to look when you ask her to provide an alibi for you to your girlfriend? In fact, I can hardly wait to hear what Doug has to say on the matter."

Hmm. That was a thought that hadn't occurred to me, either. I could already hear Doug skewering my lapse in judgment as Loretta lapped it up. Probably my best option was to get that hotel room after all.

"You're right," I said. "It was a dumb idea. I'll find a hotel room that will allow cats. I was just so tired, and I wasn't thinking straight. But nothing happened. Fixing us is my top priority. You've got to believe me."

Again, with the silence.

"Are you still there?"

"Mmm-hmm."

"You *do* believe me, don't you?" I just couldn't let it go. I had to know.

After another moment of uncomfortable silence, she said, "Lord help me, I do. And Lord help *you* if I'm wrong. A story that long-winded and ridiculous could only be true, especially when it's coming from you. You can't lie for shit. Your lies are always acts of omission, and this most certainly was not that."

Relief washed over me despite the underlying jab, and I practically giggled. "Thank you."

"Besides," she said before muttering something under her breath while I fought to keep my robe tied.

"I'm sorry, I didn't catch that," I said. "Besides what?"

She sighed heavily. "As much as it pains me to say this, I think you should probably stay put in Ms. Pendleton's guest house, at least for the time being."

I blinked, not quite sure I heard her correctly. "Excuse me?"

"It would appear our Mr. Green has been here."

"Wait—*what?* He's been to my *house?*"

"Unless you've suddenly decided to hit the campaign trail for Senator Ghant, I believe so," she said. "There's a sign in your yard and a stack of propaganda on your porch swing. I have to admit, there's something about the way this guy operates that rubs me the wrong way."

"Now you believe me about Green?"

"I never said I didn't believe you," she said.

"You sure acted that way the other night." I was a little sullen.

"I was mad at you and the way you were acting," she said. "I don't need some big protector making my decisions for me. But maybe Ms. Pendleton does. Thinking about how Mr. Green acted last night and seeing all this— frankly, it feels a little threatening. He left you a note. I'd read it to you, but I'd rather you see it for yourself. Hang on and let me send a pic."

I waited for notification of an arriving text to sound in my ear before pulling my phone away to look at the picture Melanie had just sent. Taped eye-level to my front door was a page from a personalized memo pad bearing the letterhead, "From the Desk of Senator Parker Ghant" rendered in an appropriately pompous font. The message, handwritten with penmanship that was practically smirking, was short and to the point:

Mr. Morrow—
So sorry to have missed you!
We still have so much to discuss.
I'll be in touch again.
Soon.
Mr. Green

CHAPTER TEN

A cat's vengeance is a curious thing.

I scurried through the front door struggling to keep my borrowed but entirely too-small robe cinched against an unexpectedly rigorous breeze that threatened my dignity with seemingly deliberate frequency. I thanked my lucky stars once again for the seclusion my considerable tract of land afforded me. I could only imagine the show I would have just given my neighbors, if I had any. I closed the door and turned, rooted in place by shock.

Perched along the back of the leather sofa nearest me and striking a most decidedly sphinxlike pose, Dexter scowled through narrow slits, one ear cocked, his self-satisfaction apparent. Scattered throughout my living room were the shredded remnants of an entire 32-pack of toilet paper rolls. I could barely see the hardwood floor peeking through the two-ply catastrophe that was my penance for leaving the little monster to his own devices for too long.

"That's *it*," I threatened, pointing a forefinger at his smug face. "It's dry food for you until further notice."

He yawned and looked away, unchallenged by my bluster. Admittedly, I was a little less than intimidating when it took everything I had to keep my robe from gaping wide. I took a few deep breaths to calm myself and began to prioritize my day, or what little was left of it. First up—clothes. I dashed up the stairs and quickly dressed myself, snagging a few wardrobe changes including something I could wear to Brady's party on Saturday night. I carefully rolled the items to prevent them from wrinkling and stuffed them into a well-worn duffel bag that was my go-to when traveling.

Once downstairs, I swept all of the expensive toilet paper into a large pile and tried to figure a way to salvage at least *some* of it, but Dexter Scissorhands' work was quite thorough. No single scrap measured much larger than a postage stamp, and I didn't have a fucking clue what he'd done with all the cardboard tubes that served to mount the rolls to the dispenser. In the end, I hauled it all out to my recycle bin.

By the time I had assembled a 'to-go' box of litter and enough food to keep His Nibs satiated for our long weekend away from home, I couldn't locate the actual cat to place him in his pet carrier. We had enough history on the road together that he recognized all the tell-tale signs of impending travel—*not* his favorite thing. His response was to tap into that curious talent all cats seem to possess and pull a vanishing act while my back was turned. After twenty minutes, some inventive pejoratives, and an untold escalation of my blood pressure, I found him lurking in the bottom of my clothes hamper, feeling entirely too smug and superior. Can a cat even smirk? I'm fairly certain that's what he was doing. I scooped him into my arms, reading him the riot act all the way to his carrier before plopping him inside and latching the top.

Once in the car, I warned him to behave himself as I headed back to the Pendleton property, only to have him challenge my authority in the most nerve-shredding, guttural way possible, yowling almost non-stop for the next thirty minutes. I found myself driving faster and faster the louder he got, but I was handed a tiny slice of mercy in that I didn't get a speeding ticket en route.

I used the security code Rochelle had given me to pass through the gate, making a beeline for the guest cottage to unload my things and release the little beast from the confines of his carrier, at which point the yowling stopped and all was forgiven. He found himself in uncharted territory, and his intense exploration of the premises was immediately underway.

Whatever.

A small writing table sat underneath a window along the eastern wall of the bright, cozy living room, and I unpacked my laptop from its bag, using the table's surface as a temporary workspace. I sifted through a handful of emails, mostly junk, and touched base with my appointments for the day. There was only one—a standing touchpoint with Doug and Loretta at three o'clock to report progress on the cases we worked, including the Pendleton case. I had both new information and questions to ask, so I opened a Word doc and started getting my thoughts in order.

I fished the note from Mr. Green—aka Kevin Moody—from my pocket. Melanie had left it and the campaign material on my porch, weighed down by an ashtray I just couldn't seem to part with. I added the campaign material to the recycle bin before folding the note and tucking it into my pocket—once I was finally wearing pants again. Now, I flattened the note on the table and re-read between its precisely slanted lines, imagining the sneer on Moody's face as he left the items for me to find, knowing full well their likely impact. I wished I could call his bluff, but I'd be lying if I didn't admit I was a bit unsettled.

A brisk tapping sounded at the front door, and I nearly jumped out of my skin. Maybe I was a little more than a bit unsettled. I pressed my eye against the peephole in the door to find Rochelle standing on the stoop with Joey in one arm and her sketchpad in the other. Both were wearing brightly colored and insulated winter outerwear, their cheeks rosy beneath snug knit caps. I opened the door, greeting her with a smile. "Good morning," I said.

"Good *afternoon*," she corrected, and of course, she was right. My morning had passed before I was even fully awake. "I hope I'm not disturbing you, but I just wanted to make sure you were getting along okay." She turned to her son. "Joey, this is Mr. Morrow, remember? You met him last night."

"Dane!" he responded, clapping and grinning before leaning into his mother, suddenly shy.

"Ah, yes," I said, reaching out to tousle his hair. "Dane. And how are you this morning, little buddy?" I stepped back, motioning for them to come in from the cold.

"Go-ood," he said before his eyes widened and his mouth formed a perfect little circle. *"Dexter!"*

I turned to find Dexter observing us from the kitchen alcove, his curiosity piqued by the sound of strange voices. He peeped and tilted his head, venturing a few more steps into the room as Rochelle lowered Joey to the ground, plucking the knit cap from his head. "Oh, my goodness, he just loves kitties," said Rochelle. "Is it okay for me to let Joey roam?"

"Of course," I said. "This is your property. Let the little guy go. I've never known Dexter to hurt anyone—well, other than occasionally hurting my feelings. In fact, I think he prefers Jasmine to me—Jasmine is my girlfriend's daughter."

Joey's patience was tested as Rochelle worked his arms free from his coat, finally allowing him to toddle off towards Dexter, softly chanting the cat's name. We observed for a moment as Joey gingerly sat beside him and reached out to stroke the top of his head. He squealed as Dexter ducked beneath his hand, bringing his nose up to catch the scent of this tiny little human. Having apparently passed the "smell test," Joey was then allowed to place his fingers between Dexter's ears, where he gently scritched the top of Dexter's head.

"He's sweet," noted Rochelle.

"Meh, he has his moments. I want to thank you again for offering me the use of your guest house. I wish I could offer you some sort of discount on

our services, but Doug would never go for that. I'd be happy to pay you out of pocket," I said, reaching for my wallet.

She waved it away. *"Please.* It's just sitting here empty. In fact, it makes me feel a little bit better knowing you're nearby while Kevin is skulking around and up to who knows what."

"Has he ever threatened you?"

"Not directly. But after what you told me last night, I'm fairly certain that he and his buddies are the reason I can't get anyone to stay on this case for longer than two minutes."

I crossed to the writing desk and retrieved the note he had left, handing it to Rochelle. "I'd say you're right. He tried to pay me another visit this morning, but I wasn't home. He left this on my porch."

She read it, frowning as she handed it back to me. "I don't really know what to say. I'm surprised you came back."

"I'm not intimidated that easily," I said. "In fact, I'm really pretty pi—" My eyes drifted to her son, and I automatically censored myself. "—peeved that he's now invaded both my place of work and my personal residence. Whatcha got there?" I pointed to the sketchpad she had set aside while freeing her son from his winter wardrobe before pulling her own coat and cap off.

"You asked me to sketch the other guys in Parker's security detail just before everything kind of went off the rails," she said. "And again, I'm so sorry about that."

"Oh, please don't apologize," I said, offering her a seat in the living room of her own guest cottage. It felt as awkward as it sounds. Still, I joined her on the cream-colored camelback sofa that was a little too stiff for my own comfort. "How is your father this morning?"

She sighed, shrugging. "It wasn't his best visit ever," she admitted. "He woke up agitated, and it only went downhill from there. It was surprising because mornings are usually his most lucid times, but, well—not today. I went ahead and took him back to Golden Angels so his doctors could assess him sooner rather than later. I'm hopeful that it's just an adverse reaction to the new medication we thought was working so well. I guess we'll see."

"I'm so sorry," I said. "It's got to be tough."

"I'm just taking it one day at a time," she said, her eyes misting over. "It's really all I *can* do at this point."

We sat in uncomfortable silence for a moment while I avoided looking directly at her and saying something profoundly stupid, as was my greatest talent. I didn't know how to segue into another topic without sounding like a complete cold-hearted bastard, so I was relieved when she wiped her eyes and shivered, forcing a small laugh.

"Enough of that," she said, reaching for her drawing pad and pulling it into her lap. "Why don't we go over these sketches?"

"Sure," I agreed. "Let's see what we've got."

She opened her sketch pad to the image she had rendered the previous evening. "You've already met Kevin Moody, or whatever it was you said he called himself."

"Mr. Green."

"Right. Next up is Danny Pizzatti," she said, flipping the page to show me a face that looked like it belonged behind the counter in a deli somewhere. Dark hair, heavily lidded eyes, and a thick unibrow that looked like a plus-size caterpillar catnapping at the base of his ample forehead.

"Is he even awake?" I asked, and Rochelle chuckled.

"Yeah, he's a bright one," she said sarcastically. "But he isn't part of Parker's team for his brains. He's five-and-a-half feet of pure muscle. I've seen him get the best of guys way bigger than he is. I know *I* wouldn't want to tangle with him."

"Duly noted."

She flipped to the next page. "And this is Alvaro Martinez."

Martinez could have easily been a model with chiseled features that suggested his Latino heritage, with bright, intelligent eyes and a knowing smirk that suggested he knew something you didn't—even as rendered in charcoal. Rochelle was really quite talented.

"Looks like a smooth operator," I said, committing his face to memory.

"Well then, I've captured his essence," she said with grim satisfaction. "I don't think I quite got his eyelashes right. His are somehow even longer—but never mind that. He is every bit the ladies' man you might expect someone so pretty to be. I'd say he wrote the book on love 'em and leave 'em, but that's a really old book, isn't it?"

I grinned. "The oldest."

"If I had a dollar for every time that he hit on me—well, suffice it to say, I'd have quite the supplemental income."

"It didn't bother the big boss?"

She chortled. "Why would it? Like I told you before, it wasn't like Parker and I were together or anything. Just that one night." There was something wistful in the way she said it that caught my attention. Her eyes drifted over to where Joey continued to lavish Dexter with gentle adoration, and there was no doubt this child was the sun and the moon in his mother's eyes. "It's not like Alvaro was aggressive—just persistent. I don't think he was particularly accustomed to women telling him no. He always had a joke at the ready, and they were always so *awful*."

"Yeah?"

She nodded, unable to suppress a grin. "Two men walk into a bar."

I could've waited for all eternity, but nothing else was forthcoming. Rochelle just sat there looking like the cat who ate the canary. "Okay, I'll bite. *And—?*"

"And nothing. It was a crowbar."

I literally winced. "Oh, that's *bad*. It's not even corny."

"I warned you. Worst part is, they really tickled Alvaro's pickle, and he was giggling before he even got the last part out, the highest-pitched, most ridiculous guffaw you've ever heard in your life. It was like a donkey braying with hiccups. It was *impossible* not to laugh right along with him." As if to prove her point, Rochelle got a sudden case of the giggles, finally tapering off when I didn't join in. "I guess you'd have to hear it for yourself—but again, never mind that. Somehow, I doubt this is the type of information you were looking for."

"Not exactly," I said kindly. I really didn't mind. Rochelle was drawing vivid pictures with her words as well as her hands, and I was willing to grant her a little latitude. She was engaging. "So, what is Mr. Martinez's superpower?"

"He's good with all the communications and tech stuff. He kept Parker on schedule, or at least mostly on schedule. There are times when Parker does exactly what he's gonna do, and no one can control that. And while Alvaro has a lot more personality than his colleague, Danny, he's every bit as capable of handling physical threats. In fact, he's damn scary when he gets serious. I only saw it a couple of times."

"That seems to be a common trait," I observed, reaching for the sketchpad. "Who's our last contestant?"

I flipped the page, and all the air seemed to rush right out of the room.

Staring up at me in shades of charcoal was none other than Michael Arthur.

It was a face that periodically haunted my dreams, and I hoped to never see again, at least not in person. He was the man responsible for luring me on an ill-fated trip to West Virginia the previous summer, a trip I barely survived. He had presented himself as my sister's boyfriend, eager to uncover what was really behind the car crash that had supposedly taken Gina's life. I was so shaken and hellbent on revenge that I swallowed every single lie he told without question, allowing myself to become trapped and

125

used as bait. Memories of my time in that town flashed before me in vivid Technicolor—the bright lights of the Ferris wheel, the discordant jangle of carnival music piped over loudspeakers, the smell of cotton candy and corn dogs wafting through the air. A fortune teller's tent. *Hattie.*

I pinched the bridge of my nose and tried to shake the images away, but they clung like leeches, my heart beating faster, my head feeling lighter. I had grievously wounded Michael with an inadvertently well-placed bullet to the loins. He had survived, only to disappear while being transported to his designated place of incarceration. It was the general consensus that he had been taken out by his own kind, his knowledge of the inner workings of the Academy too dangerous for a man in custody, a man who might crack under interrogation. The uncertainty only left me unsettled, leaving open a doorway into my nightmares, if only a crack.

Like it was coming from the bottom of a well, Rochelle's voice slowly pierced the dense fog that had shrouded my mind, and I realized she was staring at me with nothing short of alarm on her face. She reached out and grabbed my arm, breaking the spell.

"I'm sorry—what?" My voice was like sandpaper.

"Do you need me to call the squad? You don't look so good."

I managed a meager smile and shook my head. "No—I'm sorry. I'm fine. I didn't mean to scare you. It's just—I know this guy." I pointed toward the sketchpad, not quite trusting myself to look at it again.

"Let me get you some water," she said, and she was already moving toward the kitchen.

I didn't object.

I was thoroughly embarrassed by this involuntary reaction I was having. Was this what PTSD felt like? I'd likely never know, based on the level of trust I currently placed in the practitioner counseling Melanie and me. Rochelle bustled back into the room, shoving the offending image aside as

126

she handed me the glass. I drank almost half of it greedily before wiping my mouth with the back of my hand and taking a deep breath.

"Thank you," I said, smiling sheepishly before drinking the rest.

"Are you sure you're alright?" She was unconvinced, her concern still evident.

"Really, I am," I said, and my voice was steadier this time. I cleared my throat. "It just took me by surprise. I've had some prior dealings with the Academy, specifically this guy. They weren't exactly pleasant."

"Do you want to talk about it?"

"*No.*" I said it so abruptly she jumped, and I held up an apologetic hand and tried again. "No, but thank you. Old news."

She looked dubious. "Well—okay. I have to say, I'm a little surprised. Out of all of Parker's flunkies, I always thought Kevin Moody was the scariest, but admittedly, I never had much contact with Duncan, and he—"

"Whoa, whoa, whoa," I interjected, my world tilting slightly sideways again. "*Who?*"

"Duncan," she repeated, reaching for the sketch before thinking better of it. "Duncan Moore. The guy from the picture I drew. What's wrong?"

I shook my head, making a mental note of the name. "He called himself Michael Arthur when I knew him, but then again, I guess I didn't really know him at all. Do all of these guys have fake IDs?"

"I couldn't say," she said. "I'm just telling you what he was going by when I knew him. Are you sure it's the same guy?"

I fought the urge to shudder. "Yeah. I'm sure."

"Towards the end of my time on Parker's campaign, he transferred to a new position, but I really don't know anything about it. Odds are fair that he's been replaced by someone else by now, but it hadn't happened before I left, so I can't really help you with that. Sorry."

"Don't apologize! Three out of four is way more info than I had before. I appreciate your help," I said, picking the sketches up from where they had fallen onto the floor, keeping the one of Michael Arthur/Duncan Moore buried below the others. "Do you mind if I keep these to share with my team?"

"Absolutely," she said, her smile returning. "They're all yours. Maybe you can avoid trouble if you see it heading your way. Do you have any ideas on how you plan to approach Parker to discuss our little situation?"

"We've got a conference call scheduled this afternoon, and I'm sure that will be on the agenda. These will definitely help. You're really very talented."

Her cheeks brightened. "Thank you! It's one of those gifts I inherited from my mom—well, that and my love for peanut butter." She glanced at her watch. "Listen, I should really get out of your hair. It's almost time for Joey's nap, and I'm sure you've got a million things to do. I just wanted to get these to you as quickly as possible."

"And I surely do appreciate it," I said as we both stood. "Before you go, can I ask you one more question?"

"Sure. Fire away."

"I know you said you signed a non-disclosure agreement with Ghant when Joey was born, and that violating it could be financially—well, difficult. It's also just as plain as the nose on my face how much you care for your little boy and will do anything for him. What happens if we can't find a way to get to Ghant?"

She inhaled slowly through her teeth. "If push comes to shove, I'll go public. But you *are* going to try, right? I really don't want to be responsible for derailing either his career or his family life."

"You love him, don't you?" Maybe I was pushing it, but there was a certain something that reflected in her eyes whenever she spoke of the man, and I had to ask.

Her only response was a sheepish shrug as she called her son over and began bundling him up.

I spent the next couple of hours with Google, going down a couple of rabbit holes before hitting paydirt on Duncan Moore. My reaction wasn't nearly so visceral when pictures of a more youthful version of the man I had known as Michael Arthur appeared onscreen. Apparently, this was his actual name. He was some sort of high school football prodigy in his hometown of Beavercreek, Ohio, setting records when he was only a freshman. I created a folder on my laptop and started saving all the information I could find into it, articles that lauded his achievements, an interview that named his parents, Oscar and Elise. I planned to forward it all to Loretta, who currently was the only one with access to our specialized software that could do a deeper, more focused dive than I could ever accomplish flailing about on Google. She held the only seat license that Boggs Investigations was willing to purchase, and she'd sooner go out without her makeup on than share her password.

Before I knew it, it was five minutes after three. I dialed into the conference call using the speakerphone on my cell and laying it flat on the writing desk beside my computer.

"You're late," said Loretta, by way of greeting.

"I was working," I said. "I lost track of time."

"*Hmmm.*" Her disdain was palpable, and I could already imagine her noting my employee record with yet 'another occurrence' of the tardies. I expected that by now, my employee record occupied its own entire drawer in one of those industrial filing cabinets back at the office.

"Is Doug even here?" I asked.

"I am." His voice boomed through the speaker, and the wet sound of the unlit cigar in the corner of his mouth was crystal clear. "So good of you to join us."

"I really *was* working," I said, hating the fact that I had to justify my every minute. "Quite a bit has happened since we spoke last night, and I—"

"Well, hold up just a sec, Dwayne," said Doug, interrupting me. "Before you get started, I thought we should take a minute and introduce the latest member of the Boggs team. In fact, she's with us on the call right now."

My mouth flapped wordlessly for a moment before gaining traction. "Wait—what? We hired someone?"

"Yes. In fact, I'm fairly certain you've met before."

My mind automatically went to Officer Lucy Graves, Doug's maybe-lady love and mother of his young daughter. But why would someone as seemingly successful as Lucy trade her career in law enforcement for a position on Doug's ragtag team of misfits?

"Hi, Dwayne."

It wasn't the voice I expected.

It was Melanie.

CHAPTER ELEVEN

"*M*elanie?" I couldn't even begin to mask my perplexity before plunging ahead with the worst question possible. "Is this some kind of a joke?"

"*Really?* That's the very first thought to pop out of that pointed head of yours?"

Melanie was *not* amused. I could practically feel the temperature in the room drop, and she wasn't even in it. I mentally kicked myself as I scrambled for some after-the-fact tact.

"I mean, you just started working at that tap room. What happened to that?"

"They let me go. They're terrified I'm going to file Workers' Comp, not that I was even considering it because I wasn't wearing the right shoes, and—what does it really matter, anyway? It's not like it was my dream job. I thought you might have actually been a little excited. Weren't you just saying that you missed puzzling things through with me?"

"Well—yeah, of course, but—" I stopped before I could dig myself in any deeper, taking a breath before trying a different approach. "It's just that I didn't even realize Doug was looking to expand the team, so you can imagine my surprise when—"

Doug cleared his throat loudly, interrupting me. "Much as I would love to listen to you kids go on bickering, I got more important things to attend to here, so can we get back to our meeting?"

"Um, sure," I said. "By all means, go right ahead."

"Thank you," said Doug. "Not that the administrative affairs of Boggs Investigations are any business of yours, but Melanie called me this afternoon with an interesting proposal. Apparently, this Mr. Green approached her in an effort to get to you, is that right?"

"Kevin Moody," I corrected automatically.

"Kevin who?" asked Doug.

"Kevin Moody," I repeated. "That's his real name. It's part of the info I was able to glean from Ms. Peterson last night. But yes, he was at Melanie's when I took Jasmine home."

"Okay, fine. Melanie says you argued in front of him before sending him on his way."

"*Mel,*" I whined. I rankled at the thought of Doug and Loretta having intimate knowledge of our personal disagreements, but Melanie was quick to defend her disclosure.

"It occurred to me that Mr. Green, or Kevin Moody—whoever he is— knows we're broken up. It's public knowledge. And while he pretty accurately figured that paying me a visit would make you crazy, the only thing he saw from me was anger and irritation at the way you were acting."

"I really hope you're going somewhere with this," I said. "I'm not exactly comfortable sharing all this with these two."

"Oh, get over yourself, mister," Loretta interjected, unable to remain silent for one second longer. "It's not like we didn't *all* know this young lady would tire of your shenanigans sooner or later. She's smarter than that."

"Well, thank you, Loretta, but I honestly don't need your help," said Melanie, not unkindly. "My point, Dwayne, is that he would never suspect me of trying to help you in any way. I was thinking that Monday, I might just find myself in the campaign office of one Senator Parker Ghant, volunteering to help in his reelection efforts."

"*No.*" My response was automatic and came out much sharper than intended.

"It isn't your decision to make," said Melanie.

"It's reckless. *Crazy.* I don't know why you would want to take such an unnecessary risk," I said. "These people are dangerous."

"What could happen to me in campaign headquarters?" she asked. "My thought is this Ghant seems to be a real womanizer. Maybe if I flirt a little, bat my eyes—"

"*No.*" The room was heating up fast, and I was dangerously close to speaking my mind, which rarely works in my favor. It would seem I had already lost control of the situation as Melanie plodded forward.

"—maybe I can get close enough to talk to him about Ms. Pendleton and her son. I might be able to—"

"How could you bring this to Doug without talking it through with me first?" I demanded, my mouth working independently from my brain.

"I tried to discuss it with you this morning when I stopped by your house, but you weren't there, remember?" She was getting angry, too. "You were spending the night with your client."

"*What?*" Loretta screeched. "Please tell me my ears are mistaken. Please tell me you did *not* take advantage of that poor young woman."

"Of course not, Loretta," I said. "I mean, I *did* spend the night, but not like that."

"Oh, Lord," said Loretta, selectively hearing what she wanted. "Fire him, Dougie. I told you he would be the end of us. He's got the morals of an alley cat, and what has he really brought to the table, anyway? Fire him before he damages our reputation beyond repair—"

"Enough!" barked Doug with an admirable amount of authority. "What Melanie suggested is a fine idea. If there's a possibility we can make an end run around the senator's front line, we should take it, and I think the idea of a woman appealing to the man's decency makes a certain sort of sense."

"But why does it have to be *my* woman?" I demanded, recognizing my poorly chosen words almost immediately.

"Oh, you did *not* just call me *your woman*," Melanie said. "What kind of neanderthal is steering your go-cart, buddy?"

I took another deep breath, trying to grab the reins of my mouth before I managed any irreparable damage—if it wasn't already too late. Unfortunately, I couldn't just spill my reasoning in this open forum. It had taken me far too long to share the details of everything that had happened in West Virginia with Melanie. I didn't intend to ever divulge those details to Doug and Loretta—not ever.

"I'm sorry, Mel. That all came out wrong."

"Talk about an understatement. That's the first sensible thing you've said so far."

I sighed. "It's just that I don't think the senator *has* a sense of decency. I truly believe Ms. Pendleton is deluding herself that the man doesn't know exactly what is going on, and it's at his own direction. For whatever reason, she's clinging to the memory of the man she thought he was, not the one he actually is. I think when push comes to shove, she's going to be in for a rude awakening."

"That may be the case," said Doug. "But I still think there's a chance we can arrive at that conclusion with a lot less trouble if we try Melanie's idea. What harm could come of it?"

I bit back every argument that came to mind, finally saying, "We can talk more about this privately, Mel. Okay?"

She grunted noncommittally.

"Good, then. It's settled for now," said Doug. "Let's move on with our meeting. Ma? What did the security company have to say about the disruption of services?"

"They've never seen anything like it," said Loretta. "They're assuming it was faulty equipment but are hard-pressed to explain the odds. I mean, one faulty camera—okay. But two? Either way, they're replacing both of them with a different model—at no cost to us, of course."

"All right, then. Dwayne? Would you like to enlighten us with whatever you were so eager to report earlier?"

I brought them up to speed with a lot less enthusiasm than I had begun and told them I'd send pics of the sketches Rochelle had made. They found it all interesting, but without being able to underscore the relevance of these men's connection to the Academy, I couldn't fully express the reservations I felt. At least Melanie was picking up some of what I was putting down, reading between the lines once I mentioned that Senator Ghant had been an instructor at the facility. Her tone was noticeably less challenging when she spoke next.

"I think it's a good idea for you to keep an eye on Ms. Pendleton until I have a chance to assess the situation on Monday," she said. "I don't care for the way this Moody guy operates. Every single thing he does is a thinly veiled threat."

"And that's exactly why I don't like the idea of you getting involved," I said, keeping my voice calm.

"I get that," she said. "And we can talk about it later."

I blinked. "We can?"

"Sure," she said. "Right after we're done with this call, if you'd like."

"I'd like that a lot."

Doug cleared his throat even more loudly than before. "As much as I'd like to stick around and listen to you patch up your little differences, I got a boatload of other things to do."

"Sorry, Doug," said Melanie, which was more charitable than what I was about to say.

"It's alright, let's just not make a habit of it. My only real concern about bringing you aboard is the two of you working together. You've got to keep it professional," he said. "I'd like to welcome you to our team. I think you have the potential to fit in real nice, especially with some changes I imagine are coming up on the horizon."

"Changes?" I asked, unsettled by the prospect of what *that* might entail. "Exactly what sort of changes are we talking about here?"

"Never you mind for now," he said. "Does anyone else have anything they'd like to discuss?"

No one did.

"All right, then. Everyone have a good weekend, and we'll touch base again on Monday."

· • • • • • ● ⊖ ⊝ ● • • • • · ·

"I really don't like this, Mel," I said, doing my very best to choose my words carefully. I was really getting sick of the taste of my own foot. "These people are real trouble. Did they really let you go from Tapscott's?"

Her sigh was audible through the phone line. "Why would I make up a thing like that?"

"I didn't mean it like that," I said. "It's just that I'm pretty sure it's not legal for them to retaliate against someone for filing a claim with Workers' Comp. Maybe you should, you know? Take a little extra time to rest your back and get paid while doing it."

"Would you just stop it, please? Ohio's an at-will state, which means they can let me go at any time with or without cause, as long as it's not illegal, and I was still early on in my probationary period. They'd never admit they let me go for the reasons I suspect. In fact, they told me they just got a little

136

overzealous when hiring, not that any of us spend a lot of time standing around without any customers to serve. It would be a completely uphill battle, and quite frankly, I'd rather just move on."

"Well, how about your writing? I thought you wanted to write children's stories—and that other thing you were working on."

I was, of course, referring to a romance novel I had inadvertently gotten a peek at while we were participating in a mystery weekend the previous summer, hosted by Brady's current flame, Anyssa Williams. It appeared to be somewhat based on our own lives, and not necessarily in the most flattering way. After our past few tumultuous months, I could only imagine the direction it had probably taken since I'd seen it last.

"Dwayne." It was a mild reproach. My mouth never really *does* know when to quit. "It could be years before I ever realize any profit from my writing, and that's if I ever do at all. I need to be able to pay my bills and take care of my child. You're just grasping at straws."

"Still," I said, reluctantly admitting defeat. "I wish you had talked with me about it first. Not that I could have changed your mind—"

"Clearly."

"—but it wouldn't have been such a jolt. You know I can't go into all the details with Doug and Loretta about what happened in West Virginia. It just knocked me off my axis a little."

"Believe it or not, I *do* understand, but I also think my plan just might work. Regardless of what these guys may be capable of, they don't just kill people willy-nilly. After a while, it would start to stand out," she said.

"We'll just have to agree to disagree on that one," I said. "But I'm done arguing over it."

"Good," she said. "And honestly, I did intend to speak with you about it first, but I didn't want to do it over the phone, and when Doug called me this afternoon, I just thought I should go ahead and discuss it with him."

"Doug called *you?*"

"Uh-huh. I mean, he wouldn't bring me on if this one little mission was all there was, would he?"

The surprises just kept coming.

"I'm not following," I said, feeling like the stubbiest little crayon in the box. "Why would Doug call you?"

"Loretta is looking to cut back the hours she's spending at the West Broad office. I think the commute is getting to be too much. He's looking for someone who can handle the clerical functions of the office, and he thought of me. I only mentioned my idea about joining Senator Ghant's campaign after the offer was already on the table, and he liked it."

For the tiniest of moments, my elation at the thought of Melanie supplanting Loretta's overbearing presence in the office made me forget all about my concerns. In fact, I'm pretty sure I giggled a bit. "Are you serious? Don't mess with me, Mel."

"I am. I think there's more to the story, and I think it has more than a little to do with Lucy Graves and their daughter—Loretta's granddaughter, that is. But I wasn't going to press the issue. The timing is perfect for me, and so are the hours. The only real concern I have is whether we can work together. We still have a lot of unresolved issues we're trying to deal with in counseling. It's probably not the best idea I've ever had, but I'm willing to give it a go if you are."

"I am," I said with no hesitation. It seemed like a golden opportunity to reverse some of the damage I had done to our relationship—or quite possibly ruin it completely, if I couldn't avoid putting my foot in it every time I turned around. I gave myself some optimistic odds at fifty-fifty. I decided to shift gears while we were on stable ground. "So, what have you decided about Brady's party? Will you be joining me, and what time can I pick you up?"

She laughed. "Not so fast, mister. I'm going, but not with you."

"But I thought—"

"Dwayne. We can't be seen out in public together if we're trying to project the image of being at odds. As far as we know, that Moody guy might just show up or something. Lord knows he's shown up everywhere else. I'll be going by myself. It's not like my invitation was contingent on going with you. As a matter of fact, Anyssa invited me even before Brady invited you."

I almost bit my tongue as all of my concern about her foolish plan came crashing back into the forefront of my thoughts. I realized that working together was going to present a whole new series of challenges, but I wasn't quite prepared for one so immediate.

"Fine," I said. "I guess I'll see you there, then."

"But not too close, okay? We have to keep up appearances."

I grumbled something unintelligible before disconnecting, wondering what in the world I had just agreed to.

······●●●●●●◉◉●●●●●●···

A row of red brick buildings cast elongated shadows over the alley, shrouding it in darkness. None were taller than three stories, but their shadows seemed to stretch on for miles. Darkened industrial windows stared down without blinking, giving the illusion these buildings were abandoned when most likely it was only past normal business hours. The moon was full overhead, the only other source of light coming from a streetlamp at the far end of the alley. The one above my head was only jagged glass, a probable victim of vandalism. To my left was a handful of empty gravel lots skirting the rear of businesses that faced the other direction. Weathered clapboard fencing separated some of these lots, and I had the distinct feeling I had been here before but couldn't for the life of me place it. The asphalt below my feet was in a sad state of disrepair, cracked and pitted and crumbling around the edges.

A faint trace of music wafted through the air, discordant and jangly, like a stylus clinging for dear life to a groove etched in warped vinyl. It came from my left, and as my eyes adjusted to the gloom, I noticed a pale neon halo pulsing ever so slightly above the tops of those buildings. I was just about to investigate when I caught a flicker of motion out of the corner of my eye.

A slender shape perched on the edge of the dumpster nearest me, worn canvas tennis shoes abnormally bright in the moonlight. I only caught a quick glimpse before the shape pulled its feet up and over the rim, dropping into the metal container with a hollow thud. My world tilted one way before overcompensating in the other, and I staggered to the building closest to me, placing a steadying hand on its cold, rough surface.

No. This couldn't *be.*

I was in Briarstaff, a town I had hoped to never see again.

Cold sweat glued my shirt to my back, fat droplets trickling down between my shoulder blades, and my throat felt too thick to speak. Once I felt like I had recovered my balance, I took a couple of tentative steps toward the dumpster, only then noticing the rusting IGA cart parked at its side and filled with assorted oddities.

From deep within the dumpster, I caught a hint of a sweetly misinterpreted lyric to an old Olivia Newton-John song.

"Have you ever eaten marshmallows?"

"Hattie," I croaked, my heart clutching hard in my chest.

I wanted to turn and run, but my feet seemed to have their own agenda, carrying me even closer to the dumpster. I was terrified of what I might find inside. I stumbled over something small and looked down to discover one of the canvas shoes underfoot, its brightest white sullied by a large crimson splotch that could only be blood.

There was sudden movement to my left, and I looked up to find Kevin Moody approaching from the far end of the alley, his features distinct as he crossed beneath the streetlight. His signature shit-eating grin was firmly in place while not even coming close to reaching his dead eyes, and his gait was unhurried, only sure and steady. Michael Myers from *Halloween* sprang to mind; he never had to run to catch his victims either.

I was frozen, stupidly watching him bridge the distance. My feet felt like they were glued to the pavement, and I looked down to see what held them in place. It was nothing more than gravity, but it took everything I had to get them to budge. First my left foot, then my right, and with each attempt, movement came a little more easily. I looked back up only to gasp.

Kevin had already cut the distance in half, and he was no longer alone.

He was flanked on each side by Alvaro Martinez and Danny Pizzatti, and they made quite a formidable impression with their matching ghoulish smiles and unblinking stares, all of which were focused on me.

I managed a few steps backward before turning to run and was startled—first by my feet, which actually cooperated, but more so when my pursuers decided to match my pace. I burst out of the alley and into an empty side street, the slap of their footfalls loud in my ears. I didn't dare look back as I veered right and raced up the slight incline toward the main drag, where the multicolored neon glow was noticeably brighter. The faint music morphed into a familiar carnival refrain, and there was only one thing it could be.

The goddamned Apple Festival.

On some level, I knew this was a dream—it had to be, but I was at a loss for how to get myself out of it. I could almost feel hot breath on the back of my neck as the footfalls grew louder—closer. As I approached the corner I now recognized as belonging to Briarstaff Savings & Loan, I could see several of the vendor tents across the main street, none of them occupied, but all of them open for business, including an enclosed tent at the farthest end. Outside its closed flap and pinned to its fabric wall was a large sign that read, *"Reading in Progress! Do NOT disturb!"* The street was entirely empty, save for occasional pieces of refuse that skittered like tumbleweeds across the pavement, moved by a breeze I couldn't feel against my own skin. The Ferris wheel whirled away at a speed that seemed excessive considering none of its seats were occupied, and I was getting winded, my legs beginning to cramp. I risked a glance over my shoulder and was shocked to discover that the street behind me was empty. Kevin and his friends must have abandoned their pursuit.

I gave myself a minute to catch my breath. Leaning forward and resting my hands on my knees, I inhaled deeply, keenly aware of the redolence of fried goodness hanging in the air. This was the most realistic nightmare I had ever experienced. I straightened up, my back popping as I did so, and turned around, running directly into Michael Arthur—er, Duncan Moore— whatever the hell his name was.

Like his comrades, his eyes drilled holes through me. Blood soaked his trouser legs, emanating from the amateur vasectomy I had delivered once upon a time with a lucky shot from a gun I had barely been able to hold steady.

"Well, *hello*, Dwayne," he said, baring his teeth rather than smiling. "I've been waiting for you."

I sat straight up in a bed I didn't recognize, my heart hammering in my chest, as I shook the last of the nightmare away. Its clammy sweat had followed me into the waking world, and I kicked the covers to the floor, sending a startled cat flying with them. With a disgruntled hiss, Dexter darted through the door and into a darkened corridor I suddenly realized was in Rochelle's guest house.

I slipped out of bed as my pulse stabilized and was astounded to discover that my legs ached as though they had actually taken part in my nocturnal sprint. Cottonmouth had also transcended the dreamscape, and my tongue felt thick in my mouth. I padded down the darkened hallway on my bare feet, wearing only boxer briefs. My skin was a cool sea of gooseflesh as the perspiration began to dry.

Dexter was already in the kitchen when I arrived, sitting expectantly by his empty food bowl. I reached for his cat treats, prompting his usual starvation wail. "It's too early for breakfast, bud, but I guess I owe you a little something after that rude awakening," I said, sprinkling a handful of treats into his dish. "Sorry about that."

All was apparently forgiven as he dug into the stinky little morsels, a low rumbling interpolating with the sound of enthusiastic swallowing. I scritched between his shoulder blades before rummaging through the cupboards until I found a tall drinking glass. I dispensed cold water from the door of the fridge and drank the entire glass in one long swallow. I refilled the glass and wandered into the darkened living room, taking a seat on the stiff couch, and setting the glass beside the lamp on an end table. I didn't bother switching on the light. I was already going to have enough trouble finding sleep again.

I leaned back and closed my eyes, marveling at the vividity of my night terror. I couldn't recall ever having one quite like it, and frankly, I hoped the whole experience was just a one-off, but I had my doubts. This case was picking at scabs that weren't even close to being healed.

It was my last thought before I drifted back into a mercifully dreamless sleep.

I awakened with sunlight in my eyes, streaming in through the partially open slats of the window blinds. Dexter had parked himself beside me on the couch, curled up as cats are wont to do. I realized I really had to pee, and my teeth were chattering as I stood and stretched. I had fallen asleep upright and without covers, and my boxer briefs weren't doing very much by way of keeping me warm. I started to head back to the bedroom I was using when a flash of color caught my eye through the blinds. I crossed the room and peeked outside. Not three feet in front of the porch, a sign was planted in the yard and facing the house. Parker Ghant's smiling face stared directly at me from above a slogan that was becoming all too familiar.

Don't Think Ghant Can't!

CHAPTER TWELVE

"It feels like you're getting worked up over nothing," said Rochelle, and my jaw practically hit the floor. She continued to focus on the eggs she was scrambling while Joey jabbered from his playpen by the television.

"He was *on your property*," I repeated, waggling the sign in front of me as evidence. "You don't find that disturbing?"

"It's not like this is Fort Knox," she said, shifting her attention to the strips of bacon frying in another skillet and giving each piece a casual flip. "Are you sure you don't want any breakfast? I can always make a little more."

I sputtered in disbelief. Food was the furthest thing from my mind—well, almost. It did look pretty tasty, and it smelled wonderful. I pushed the thought away. "Does your security gate extend around the entire property?"

"It does," she said, scooping some of the eggs onto one half of a plastic divided plate featuring Bluey—who else? "Would you mind handing me the apple juice from the fridge?"

"I should check for forced entry," I said, absently fulfilling her request as she crumbled some bacon into the other half of the plate.

"Fill that, will you?" she asked, nudging a matching sippy cup my way with a greasy knuckle. She turned to the toaster on the countertop behind her that had just ejected a couple slices of golden-brown bread and began slathering butter on each piece. "I'm sure it's fine, but by all means, if it makes you feel better, go right ahead. I mean, who would cut through iron bars when it would be far easier to defeat the lock on the gate? Are you sure you don't want some of this?"

I stood there with my mouth hanging open as she washed her hands in the sink. I couldn't believe how calmly she was taking this breach of security. I mean, what was the point of securing the property if someone could just waltz right in? Of course, Kevin Moody wasn't just anybody. He had worked some kind of magic on Boggs' brand-new security system, so it wasn't very hard to imagine him knowing how to bypass the more antiquated electronics at the gate.

I realized she was staring at me with a sly grin on her face.

"Are you just going to stand there, or are you going to pour my son his juice?" She nodded toward the sippy cup before carrying the plate to where Joey's highchair was positioned at the long dining table. She then crossed into the living room to extract her son from his playpen, making *nummy-nummy* noises the whole while.

I sloshed some juice in the sippy cup and screwed its top on, meeting her at the table. "I'm really at a loss here," I said, setting the cup in front of Joey's eager fingers. "Why doesn't this bother you?"

She sighed, buckling Joey into his chair before heading back for her own plate. "The alarm system on the house is much more advanced. If anyone had gotten anywhere close to the house, the police would have been alerted immediately. The doors are solid steel with reinforced door bolts that go into the ceiling and the floor. Short of a battering ram, no one's getting inside. We even have a panic room, if you can believe that. Dad was always big on security."

"And yet, you seem utterly unconcerned," I said, flopping down into an empty chair at the table.

"Well, I'm not exactly *happy*," she acknowledged, setting her plate down before taking her own seat. "But it's not like we don't know who did it."

I was back to sputtering. "That's my whole *point!* You said it yourself—these guys are scary. Who knows what they'll do?"

She blew on a bite of egg before popping it into her mouth. "It's not me they're trying to scare."

My head was dangerously close to exploding. "Are you even *listening* to yourself?"

Joey smacked his lips and giggled. "Dane is *funny*."

"He sure is!" agreed Rochelle brightly, prying the nearly empty sippy cup out of his hands and replacing it with a plastic safety fork. "Now eat your eggs, honey. We've got things to do in a little bit." She turned toward me. "Look, Dwayne, I get what you're saying, but they're just pulling the same old stunts to try and scare you and your team away from me. It's worked with everybody else, so why not?"

"And it doesn't bother you, like, at *all* that they were on your property?"

"Well, I'm not exactly thrilled, but I'm not scared. Are you?" She stared at me expectantly while nibbling on a corner of toast.

"Let's just say I'm unsettled," I said, scowling.

"Please don't tell me this is all it's gonna take for your team to drop this case," she said. "Not after you've gotten my hopes up. I don't even know what—"

"I didn't say that," I interrupted, my hand sneaking over to steal one of her pieces of toast. "It's just that I know a little bit more than you about the type of person this Academy produces."

"Really? Is that why you got so weird when I mentioned it last night?"

"I wouldn't say I got *weird*, but—"

"You *did*," she insisted, putting her fork down and giving me her full attention. "Tell me all about it."

I squirmed, having already said too much. "I'm sorry, I really can't," I finally said. "It's part of an ongoing investigation, and I'm not at liberty to discuss it."

She deflated in disappointment. "You sound just like a TV show."

She wasn't far off. That's exactly where I'd gotten it.

"I'm sorry," I said. "But I really can't. Just trust me when I say that these guys aren't just scary—they're dangerous. What makes you so sure that they won't get tired of chasing away all the people you've been trying to hire and just deal with the problem at its source? And by that, I mean you."

"Pffft." She waved my concern away dismissively, but I could see a hint of doubt in her expression. "Parker would never allow them to hurt me."

"You don't know that," I said, reaching over to rotate Joey's plate so he could access the food he had pushed to the far side. "It's wishful thinking on your part."

She reflected on that for a moment as she continued to pick at her breakfast. Finally, she pushed her plate aside. "I really don't believe that's true, but even if it were, I'm not scared. I keep a gun in my nightstand. I can take care of myself."

"Let's hope it doesn't resort to that," I said. "Listen, we're working on the details for a plan to reach Senator Ghant through his campaign headquarters. We hope to have something in place by Monday, but in the meanwhile, I'm glad that I'm here to keep an eye on things. I really don't like the thought of you and Joey out here all by yourselves."

She slowly nodded. "Okay, I'll admit it—I feel a little better knowing that, too."

"That being said, we're not in the business of bodyguarding, so I wasn't exactly prepared to stick to you like glue twenty-four seven."

"If it's a matter of money, I'd be happy to—"

I held up my hand. "It's not. You're already doing me a huge favor by letting me use the guest house while my water heater is down. I don't mind the extra time, it's just that I've got a prior engagement this evening, and I'd have a really hard time getting out of it."

"No worries," she said, wiping Joey's mouth with a wet wipe. "I have a few errands to run this afternoon, but I've got a friend who's been bugging me for forever to spend some time with her out on Buckeye Lake. I can give her a call and take her up on it. In fact, we'll probably just stay through the weekend. It might be nice to get away from everything, even if it's only for a couple of days."

Relief washed over me. I was going to ask her if there was any place she could go where she and her son wouldn't be alone, but without being able to share my rationale for being so concerned, I was fully prepared for her to fight me every step of the way.

"That's great. You do that. I'll let you and little mister here get back to your day." I tousled Joey's hair, and he blew an exuberant raspberry at me.

Kids are so weird.

·······•••••◦◯•••••·······

Dexter remained firmly underfoot as I tried to dress for a party I was less than enthusiastic about attending. It's funny how easily yes slips out when an invitation is extended, yet when the day finally arrives, it is front loaded with nothing but anxious dread.

Maybe it's just me.

I knew from experience that once I arrived, I would have a much better time than I anticipated. It did nothing to quell my unease that the khakis and powder-blue Henley shirt I had brought to wear were entirely too casual.

"What do you think?" I asked Dexter. He peeped and wound his way around my ankles, leaving a swath of black fur in his wake. I sighed, wishing

I had the foresight to include a lint brush and wondering if I had time to make another quick jaunt to my house for a change of clothes.

I didn't care so much about what Brady thought, but I didn't want to embarrass myself in front of Anyssa. I had only seen her a handful of times since our time on her island, and I wouldn't want to be the guy she had to explain to her friends.

The screen of my phone lit up with Melanie's smiling face, and the opening of Chris de Burgh's "The Lady in Red" began playing. Cheesy? Perhaps. But I couldn't bring myself to change the ringtone. It would feel like I was giving up on us. I put the call on speakerphone.

"Hey, you," I said. "What's up?"

"Just checking in to make sure you're still going," she said. "I figured by now you'd be making a wreck of yourself, overanalyzing everything including whatever it is that you decided to wear."

She knew me too well.

"Please tell me they didn't say it was black tie or some stupid shit like that," I said, and she laughed.

"No. I would avoid jeans and Pepsi T-shirts, but anything above that should be fine," she said before quickly adding, "No halter tops, either."

"Nuts," I said, smiling. "And I'm back to square one. Are you taking Jasmine to stay with Billy at the Caudills?"

"No," she said. "Sarah was here this morning to pick her up. We decided a weekend with her grandmother and her little half-brother was in order."

"That's great, Mel," I said. "I'm glad you've come around on the whole issue."

"Yeah, well, I'm working on it," she said. "It's still hard to see my late husband's face on that little boy. It just reminds me all over again of what a fool I was thinking Ryan could have ever been faithful."

"He was an idiot," I said, and I meant it, but fidelity was never a part of my former best friend's DNA. "I'll bet Jasmine was excited."

"Oh, yeah. She couldn't get out the door fast enough. She's really enjoying this new role of big sister. I think she likes having someone to boss around."

I grinned. "I think she likes the responsibility—the connection to her dad. She's a good kid."

"Except when she's running off without permission to some strange guy's house out in the country, that is," she teased. "But I'm sure she'll be a big help to Sarah. Give her a little bit of a break, you know? It's been a lot of years since Sarah had to deal with that kind of boundless energy on a non-stop basis. She looked tired."

"Sarah?" I laughed. "That woman has more energy than I ever have on a good day."

"Maybe. But I'm sure she'll appreciate the opportunity to spend a little time doing whatever it is *she* wants to do for a change. She's more than earned it."

"Agreed. So, what time are you planning to arrive?" I asked, picking at the fur that clung like static to the cuffs of my khakis. "I thought maybe we could—"

"Dwayne. Like I told you before, we can't just hang out together all evening. I don't want to take a chance on compromising the perception of our current status. It could make my plan for infiltrating Ghant's headquarters seem entirely suspect."

"I'd be okay with that."

"Dwayne."

"Fine," I grumbled. "You can't blame a guy for trying. Am I even allowed to acknowledge you're there?"

"Well, sure. I mean, we're both friends with Brady and Anyssa. It's plausible we could be civil to one another. Just—you know, don't stand so close to me. I'll see you there."

As her smiling face dimmed from my screen, it was impossible not to realize the perfect 80s song by The Police to replace my current choice as her ringtone.

···•••••●◯●•••••···

My nerves weren't settled much by the assortment of cars parked in Brady's front yard, most of which were fancier than mine. He had actually hired a valet in an effort to control parking and maximize his minimal space while leaving enough of the long driveway open so folks wouldn't get blocked in. I didn't care for anyone else operating my vehicle, but I grudgingly handed my keys to a uniformed kid who looked like he should be delivering newspapers—if that was even still a thing anymore. I watched in horror as he whipped my car around and into a tight spot between a Lexus and Mercedes, stopping mere inches from the bumper of an emerald-green Jaguar. I rummaged through my wallet, wondering what might comprise an appropriate gratuity when the kid smiled and shook his head.

"Please, sir, no tips. Mr. Garrett is providing this as a complimentary service," he said, pivoting to attend to the latest car to arrive, also nicer than my own. *Ooh la la!* It would appear that Mr. Garrett spared no expense in this glorious celebration of himself.

I sighed, taking one last look at my slightly rumpled khakis which still bore remnants of Dexter's fur around the ankles and wondered if my anti-perspirant was still holding out. Inside, I was pit stains down to my knees. I approached the front door, and before I even had a chance to ring the bell, it swung inward.

"Dwayne! I'm so glad you were able to come," said Anyssa, smiling warmly. She wore a brightly patterned off-the-shoulder designer print that popped against her flawless, light brown complexion, and her hair was swept up into a matching wrap. She reached out and took my hand into

both of hers and surprised me by pulling me into a hug. I wasn't great with the touchy-feely, but I tried not to stiffen entirely. "Come in, come in!"

She stepped back to allow me to pass into Brady's living room, which was already teeming with activity. Small clusters of smiling strangers engaged in quiet conversation while soft jazz whispered in the background. Brady's functional living room furniture had been removed and replaced with a smattering of matching barrel chairs scattered about the room and glass-topped end tables for guests to deposit their drink glasses when they grew weary of carrying them. I didn't recognize a soul, but at least they hadn't dressed above me—at least, not by much.

"Mel isn't with you?" asked Anyssa innocuously, looking around as if she might have somehow missed her. Bless her heart. She was rooting for us to work things out almost as much as I was. It was good to have a cheerleader on my side.

"No," I said. "I know she's coming, though. She should be here any time, I would imagine."

She tilted her head sympathetically and patted my arm. "Hang in there. She'll come around eventually."

"I'm trying," I said.

"Well, I'm glad you're here to help Brady celebrate his big promotion, but I've got to mingle. There are drinks in the kitchen and a buffet table is set up in the game room downstairs. That's probably where you'll find Mr. Bigshot holding court. Help yourself to anything and everything, and feel free to wander around. I'm sure we'll get a chance to chat later."

I smiled and nodded as she started working the room with an ease I couldn't even imagine. She was the picture of grace and elegance, and for the life of me, I couldn't imagine what she saw in Brady, but I guess opposites attract.

I worked my way through the tiny gatherings, nodding and avoiding eye contact, as I forged a path toward some liquid courage in the kitchen, where an overbearing guy with a sad toupee was in the middle of regaling a group of hostages with what he believed to be the funniest story *ever*. Their polite laughter told another story, and most looked relieved when I broke his momentum by asking if I could slide past him. He was blocking access to the whiskey on the counter that was calling my name. I poured myself a healthy tumbler, and excused myself, apologizing for the disruption.

I was surprised to see party guests milling about on the elevated deck that lay beyond the sliding glass doors at the rear of the kitchen. While it was unseasonably warm, it was *February*, after all, and it was colder than I would have thought comfortable until I spotted a quartet of propane patio heaters anchoring each corner, casting an orange glow across the deck. Upon closer inspection, I realized this was the "smoking room" for those who hadn't yet managed to kick the filthy habit, and I stared at them with a longing that would only deepen once I had consumed my drink. As an ex-smoker, I was that rare breed who could cave to a single cigarette while enjoying adult beverages without completely falling off the wagon.

"Hey, matey!"

A large hand clamped down on my shoulder, startling me, and I nearly dropped my drink. I turned to find Jacko Pierce grinning at me like a goon. He was a big, good-natured co-worker of Brady's from *The Columbus Dispatch* who had assisted me with a case in which Brady had nearly gotten himself killed. As payback, I gave him the exclusive when things had finally broken, and it had given his career quite a nice boost.

"Hey, Jacko, good to see you," I said, offering my free hand, which he shook the very life out of. "Been a while."

"I'll say," he said, his Australian accent reminiscent of the late Steve Irwin. I half expected him to say, *'Crikey!'* at any given moment. "You've been keeping a low profile here lately. What's it been, three whole months since someone tried to kill you?"

He was sarcastically referring to my last real scrape in Southern Ohio this past Thanksgiving, when I was featured yet again in a handful of articles that managed to garner a little more attention than I was comfortable with.

"What can I say? I'm lying low." I tossed back half of the whiskey in one gulp, my eyes watering as its fire crept down my throat. "How have you been?"

"Eh, you know, trying to find my way out of the shadow of Mr. Garrett, but he's making it pretty difficult. This is a really huge deal for him, you know, especially with this being an election year and all. We'll be seeing his grinning mug on the telly so much this fall we're likely to be sick of it."

"Oh, I'm pretty sick of it already," I said, grinning. "I don't suppose you've seen him, have you? I should probably say hi or something."

"Last time I saw him, he was trying to impress some of the brass from WBNS with his supposed pool skills. His smack talk is miles ahead of his game, but I guess it never hurts to let your new bosses hand you your ass in a round of friendly competition."

I nodded, smiling. I started to step away but stopped. "Hey, Jacko?"

"Yeah?"

"Say, *'Crikey!'* for me."

"Piss off, you fucking Yank," he grinned, waving me off. "I'll catch you later, mate."

I worked my way through the thickening crowd to the top of a set of stairs I had never before descended. A chair rail had been installed to follow the outer edge of the U-shaped staircase, providing access to the game room for Brady's son, Billy, who was born with spina bifida. In the handful of times where I had found myself in Brady's house, we never had reason to explore the lower level, and I was surprised at the level of noise wafting up from below. Most of the party guests had migrated down, and I guess that made sense as that was where the food was being served. I descended the stairs to the sound of billiard bills breaking and smooth jazz continuing

155

to provide a soundtrack through hidden speakers that were apparently installed throughout the house.

The entire lower level was one big Berber carpeted playroom, with a pool table at its far end and a couple of vintage arcade games against the wall—Galaga and Street Fighter II. Brady's house was built on an incline, so it was no surprise to see another set of sliding doors opening out onto a paved patio beneath the deck on the upper level. A centrally located fire pit provided heat for the folks milling about outside while plenty of others lined up to fill plates with an assortment of tasty finger foods and desserts from a pair of banquet tables that were positioned as far away from the pool table as possible. My stomach grumbled, reminding me I hadn't eaten since snagging that single piece of toast from Rochelle at breakfast, so I polished off the last of my whiskey and swapped my empty glass for a plate that wouldn't remain empty for long, joining a line that moved like molasses.

As my patience was tested by a wafer-thin woman who couldn't seem to decide what she could allow herself to eat, I heard Brady's voice above all the others, telling his own animated story punctuated with manufactured laughter I had learned to distinguish from the real thing a long time ago. He was playing to his crowd, and they were responding in kind, tittering and guffawing at whatever inane hilarity he was espousing.

I followed my ears and spotted him, standing by the pool table, his cheeks a little rosier than usual, most likely from the adult beverage he sported in one hand. I started to lift a hand to wave when my eyes locked onto the familiar face he was entertaining, chuckling at the last delightful thing Brady had just said.

It belonged to Senator Parker Ghant.

156

CHAPTER THIRTEEN

I turned around so quickly I bumped into the lady in front of me, causing her to lose the single Korean meatball she had finally decided upon. She looked at me crossly, but before I even had the chance to apologize, a hand clamped down on my elbow, pulling me back.

"Is there a problem here?"

"Hey! What's with the manhandling? Let go of my arm—" My words dried up as I found myself staring into Danny Pizzatti's square, unsmiling face.

"Are you alright, Mrs. Ghant?" he asked the woman behind me, and I couldn't believe my lousy luck. A zillion people at this party, and who should I run into? And *of course*, the senator and his wife were traveling with his security detail.

"I really *am* sorry, ma'am," I said, trying not to sound as foolish as I felt. "I wasn't paying attention."

She glared at me from below salt-and-pepper bangs, her face a perpetual pucker. "I should say *not*," she huffed, inching away as if I might just pluck the dazzling emerald necklace she wore from around her neck. Miniature replicas of the pendant were embedded in each of her oddly elongated earlobes, and I could only imagine their combined appraised value.

"Cassie? Darling? Are you alright? Did this man hurt you?"

It appeared I had caught the senator's attention after all, and he placed a steadying hand on his wife's arm while regarding me with suspicion. Brady was right on his heels, chuckling in that annoyingly high-pitched, phony key he utilizes when things aren't even remotely amusing. He was working to diffuse the situation before it could escalate any further, and I was the object of his unamused scrutiny.

"Dwayne—*buddy*," he said through clenched teeth. "What's going on here?"

"I-I-I—" I was a stammering idiot.

"Did you say, *'Dwayne?'*" the senator asked Brady before turning his attention back to me. "Dwayne Morrow?"

"Um, yes—sir?" I squeaked, hating the tremulous sound of my own voice.

Ugh. He was an elected official, not fucking royalty. Why was I getting so tongue-tied?

He grinned, aiming a forefinger at me. "I recognize you from the news a while back. You helped track down that serial killer that had our good state in such an uproar."

It was a statement of fact, and he somehow managed to convey a warmth that didn't even come close to reaching his eyes. I realized my discomfort came from the fact that he knew *exactly* who I was, and considering his association with the Academy, my skin was crawling. He was undoubtedly aware that I was currently working for Boggs Investigations who, in turn, was working for Rochelle Pendleton, but he wasn't intimidated by my presence, only amused. I took the opportunity to step back, clear my throat, and get a grip on myself.

"That's right, Senator," I said. I turned to his wife who still regarded me as if I stood before her with poo on my shoe. "Again, please accept my apologies, Mrs. Ghant. I'm clumsy on a good day, but that's not really an excuse. Please forgive me."

She nodded tersely but wasn't letting go of the disdain any time soon.

"Of course," said Ghant, nodding slowly as his eyes bore through me. "I guess I realized Brady documented some of your antics, but I didn't realize the two of you were friendly."

"Well—I don't know if I would say *friendly*, but we're acquainted," said Brady, distancing himself from me at the speed of sound, while I registered silent umbrage at having my investigative work dismissed as mere *antics*.

"Well, it's nice to finally meet you," the senator said, extending a hand which I took without reservation. I watched his bodyguard tense out of the corner of my eye as we each refused to react to the other's unnecessarily aggressive grip. Ghant cocked his head, his bottom lip jutting out in a slightly pouty moue. "Such a shame about your sister—Gina, wasn't it?"

Every muscle in my body tensed as a wave of hot anger swept through me, threatening to blur my vision—but not before getting the satisfaction of seeing the good senator wince at the sudden increase of pressure I was applying to his hand. The move wasn't lost on Danny Pizzatti—or Brady either, for that matter. Before either could react, I released the senator's hand.

"Yes," I said, smiling tightly. "How good of you to remember."

Brady's utter discomfort would have been comical in any other situation, and the pointed looks he sent me guaranteed I wouldn't be on the short list for any of his future soirees, but that was perfectly fine with me. His relief was palpable when Anyssa inserted herself into our tight circle, her smile capable of thawing even the iciest frost.

"I'm so glad you were able to drop by, Senator Ghant," she said. "I imagine you'll be seeing a lot of Brady's face on the campaign trail."

"It's my pleasure, Ms. Williams," he said. "And I should certainly hope so! I have a great respect for our news media and their obligation to keep the public well informed. I'm looking forward to any and all opportunities to discuss the issues that are most important to me and my constituents, and I'm not afraid to answer the tough ones, so please don't hold back."

His chuckle was a manufactured sound bite used like punctuation, and I couldn't help but notice his wife looked as irritated at the sound of it as I was.

"Oh, I won't," Brady assured him, issuing his own insincere chortle. "I plan to come out swinging."

They did some weird sort of bob and weave boxing pantomime that caused everyone nearby to titter, with the exception of Danny Pizzatti, but I couldn't imagine tittering was a thing the thick-necked thug could do. Smiling would be a stretch. In any event, the tension had finally diffused, and I just wanted to escape before I did anything else to embarrass my hostess. I wasn't really concerned about humiliating Brady, but I sincerely hoped to never make Anyssa apologize for my aberrant behavior.

Fortunately, the senator seemed prepared to call it a night. He clapped his hands together and looked towards his wife. "Cassandra, darling? Are you nearly ready?"

She looked longingly at the Korean meatball that had gotten away, but nodded meekly, turning away from the table, and taking her husband's outstretched arm.

"Oh, Senator Ghant—what's your rush?" asked Anyssa while Brady shot me another dark look. "You and your lovely wife only just arrived."

"We'll have to beg your forgiveness, Ms. Williams, but we're on our way to a prior engagement. We only had a minute to stop by as this was on our way, but I didn't want to miss the opportunity to stop in and wish your young man congratulations on his new position with one of Central Ohio's foremost news teams." He turned to Brady. "I really look forward to speaking to you again in the near future."

"Of course," said Brady, taking the senator's hand and pumping it. "Any time. Thank you so much for stopping by. Let me walk you out."

Ghant waved him off. "Oh, heavens, no. You have other guests to attend to. We can certainly see ourselves to the door."

"Please allow me to get your coats," said Anyssa, not waiting for a response before heading toward the stairs. Mrs. Ghant followed while Danny paused, waiting for the senator who had once again turned his attention to me.

"It was very nice to meet you, Mr. Morrow," he said, baring every single one of his pearly white teeth while his eyes locked onto mine. "And no hard feelings. After all, accidents happen all the time."

I could only stare as Ghant caught up with his wife and Anyssa on the stairs, Danny shadowing his every move. The senator's threat wasn't even remotely subtle. Was I the only one picking up on it?

Apparently so.

Brady's hand clamped down on my arm and he dragged me to a quiet corner near the bottom of the stairs. "What in the hell *was* all that, man? You practically pushed that poor guy's wife onto the buffet table. Is that some sort of Southern Ohio party game?"

I pulled my arm free. "Fuck off, Brady. It was an accident, and I barely bumped her. I tried to apologize—"

"By wrenching the senator's hand off his arm?"

"Hey, I didn't start that pissing contest. I just finished it."

Brady's eyes widened in disbelief. "Are you even *listening* to yourself? This isn't some junior high dance you're rumbling in. This is my home, and these are my guests. Is there something going on between you and Senator Ghant that I should know about?"

"Of course not," I said a little too quickly, and I had already averted my gaze.

I'd never survive a casino experience. Brady's inner intrepid reporter went on point, his eyes lighting up like Christmas.

"There *is!*" he said, putting a forefinger in my face. "Spill it, Morrow. You know how I am when I get my teeth into something."

I managed my own manufactured chuckle. "There's nothing to get your teeth into here, I promise. I just don't care for the guy. I don't agree with most of his stances, and he just rubs me the wrong way."

Brady was already shaking his head. "There's more to this than that. I can tell."

Well, of course there was, but I wasn't about to enlighten him. While it had been a difficult and costly decision to delay discussing Gina's situation with Melanie, I felt absolutely zero inclination to share with Brady. He would be the very last person Gina would want me to take into my confidence. Next thing I knew, the entire thing would be Brady's latest headline, and I wouldn't put my family into that sort of jeopardy. Unfortunately, it only made my disdain for the senator seem disproportionately irrational since I couldn't come up with a good reason for feeling the way that I did.

"There's really not," I said, forcing myself to look Brady in the eye. Okay, *fine*—his bushy eyebrows. I hoped it was close enough. "And like the good senator said, don't you have other guests to attend to?"

His dubious gaze lingered, before he finally looked back into the crowded room. "I'm a little afraid to leave you unchaperoned. I've got new colleagues everywhere you turn, and this is not the kind of impression I wanted to make hosting my first big gathering. I mean, look." He pointed toward the staircase. "There's award-winning meteorologist Ashley Barone coming down the stairs now. If you hurry, you could probably clothesline her before she reaches the bottom!"

I tried to cover my smile, but I was a little too late.

"It's not *funny*, man! I'm trying to impress these people, not make them regret giving me this opportunity. What happened back there was *not* cool.

I mean, at least when Melanie was around, she could make you act somewhat civilized, but—"

"*Whoa,*" I said, stopping him cold. "What did you just say?"

He winced, regretting his poor choice of words immediately. "I'm sorry. I didn't mean to say that."

"Yes, you did."

"Well—not out loud, anyway." He grinned sheepishly. "Honestly, I *am* sorry. You know I'm really rooting for you two to work things out—me and Anyssa both are. Why do you think I dragged you up to Tapscott's the other day?"

"To show off your fancy new car and brag about your fancy new position."

"Sure, but that wasn't my *only* motivation. In fact, shouldn't Mel be here by now?" He took another glance around the room. "She *is* still coming, isn't she?"

"As far as I know," I said. "But she doesn't exactly run her agenda by me anymore."

He threw an arm around my shoulders and led me back out into the crowd. "Let's get you a little something to drink. You're depressing as hell like this. Just promise me you won't pick any more fights with my guests, okay?"

I scowled at him. "I'll do my best."

I spent the next hour or so milling about Brady's house, smiling and nodding while forcing myself to keep tabs on how much whiskey I was sipping. Eventually, I would need to make the long drive home, and I certainly didn't need a DUI to make life any more difficult. I bounced from floor to floor trying to people-watch while melding into the background and never staying in any one place for too long. I nodded and mumbled pleasantries at folks I'd seen on TV and other party guests but had no clue how to insert myself into huddles that felt like they were formed by invitation only. People kept coming through the front door while no one seemed to leave, and although Brady's house was more spacious than I had previously realized, it was beginning to get more than a little claustrophobic inside. More concerned about embarrassing myself again than I cared to admit, I eventually wandered out onto the elevated deck. It wasn't nearly so congested, and I breathed in a long, relaxing lungful of secondhand smoke, enjoying the feel of the cool night air against my face.

I fished my phone out of my pocket and was just about to call Melanie to find out what was keeping her when I changed my mind, phoning Rochelle instead. Melanie would probably rankle at me following up on her, and after my earlier unsettling encounter with Parker Ghant, I wanted to make sure that Rochelle and Joey had arrived at her friend's safely, if only for my own peace of mind. I wasn't nearly so sure Rochelle enjoyed the impunity she imagined from Ghant's potentially diabolical machinations. If only I could get *her* to believe it.

"Dwayne!" she said, answering the phone brightly. "I really didn't expect to hear from you tonight. Didn't you have somewhere to be?"

"I'm still there, just waiting for it to end."

"Yikes—is it a work thing?"

"It feels like it," I said, eyeing an abandoned pack of cigarettes that had been left on one of the patio tables. "It's a dinner party."

Rochelle laughed. "You poor thing! Is the food not to your liking?"

"No, it's fine," I said, picking up the pack only to be disappointed to discover it was empty. I crumpled it and tossed it into one of the small waste receptacles beside the sliding doors. "It's just not my sort of thing. I have to admit, it hasn't been without its surprises."

"Oh, yeah?"

"Mmm-hmm. I ran into the good senator and his wife—quite literally, in fact."

She was surprised. "Parker? *Really?* I didn't realize you were in the same social circles."

The thought of me in *any* social circle brought a smile to my face. "Neither did I. The party is for a buddy of mine who's celebrating his new position with 10TV. He'll mainly be doing election coverage in the fall, so I guess he's in the process of ingratiating himself to all the candidates. I was just as surprised as anyone when I nearly knocked Cassandra Ghant onto the buffet table."

Rochelle gasped but couldn't hide her amusement. "You *didn't.*"

"Not on *purpose*, but yeah, I kinda did. I'm pretty sure I came uncomfortably close to experiencing Danny Picante's—"

"Pizzatti's."

"—full wrath. It got a little heated, but I managed to talk my way out of it."

She was instantly on alert. "But you didn't mention me—or anything about the case, did you?"

"Of course not," I said. "I didn't completely lose my mind. You asked for discretion, and that's what you'll get, even if I don't fully understand why."

"Good," she said, her relief evident. "I can't expect you to understand, but I just couldn't do that to Parker's family. I'm sure he'll do the right thing once he realizes what's at stake."

I shook my head. Her stubborn devotion was years in the making. I wasn't going to change anything over the course of one measly phone conversation, so I jumped topics.

"I was just calling to make sure you and Joey made it to your friend's alright."

"Yep, we got in around five. Joey's down for the night, and Lauren and I are drinking margaritas while bingeing Channing Tatum movies on Netflix. This weekend is exactly what I didn't know I needed, so I guess I should thank your paranoia for that."

"I'm not going to apologize for exercising caution," I said. "Until we complete our assignment, or you fire us, I'm your guardian angel from Boggs Investigations, so I appreciate your cooperation. Will you stop by the cottage and let me know when you and Joey are headed back to the house?"

"Of course," she said. "I wouldn't want you to lose any sleep."

"Thank you."

"No, thank *you*," she said. "Even if I *do* think your concern is a bit extreme, it's nice to know someone is watching out for me and my little guy. We'll see you on Sunday."

We disconnected, and I sighed, wondering exactly what it was going to take to get those rose-colored glasses off her face. Maybe Melanie could get through to her, woman to woman.

Melanie.

I still hadn't seen any sign of her, and it was nearly nine o'clock. Melanie was never late for anything—that was always my thing, and I couldn't help the worry that was beginning to niggle within. My finger hovered over my screen, hesitating for only a second before I surrendered to the urge to call.

Her smiling face lit up my screen as the call began to ring. Once. Twice. The third ring was cut short as I was shuttled off to her voicemail, where a generic female voice informed me, "The person you are trying to reach is currently unavailable. Please leave your message after the tone."

Beep!

I disconnected, frowning at her image as my screen faded to black. Worry that began as a niggle was beginning to sour in the pit of my stomach. I considered calling her right back, but stopped myself, realizing how irritated she would be if her dismissal had been intentional and for legitimate reasons I couldn't for the life of me imagine. Instead, I opted to send her a short text.

Call me when you're free.

I proceeded to stare at the phone, willing it to ring when my eyes were drawn to the latest party guests arriving. Anyssa was greeting them and partially obscuring my view in the process. I slipped my phone back into my pocket and pulled the sliding door open, stepping into the kitchen. I had barely made it through the door when Brady appeared at my side, grabbing my arm and leaning in.

"Is that who I think it is?" he asked conspiratorially.

I slowly shook my head. "I don't know. It almost looks like him, but— did you actually *invite* him?"

"I wasn't planning to, but Anyssa said it would be rude if I didn't. Is that his *mother* on his arm?"

"No, not his mother," I said, weaving my way through the room with Brady right behind me. Anyssa was in the process of taking their coats, and they hadn't noticed me yet. "Doug? Officer Graves?"

I was practically gaping. Doug was the cleanest shaven I had ever seen, and his clothes not only fit, they *matched*. This wasn't some OshKosh B'gosh ensemble. Lucy wore a sleeveless, spaghetti-strap dress, and her strawberry blonde hair, usually pinned at the nape of her neck, flowed in loose waves around her freckled shoulders. She smiled, something I wasn't sure I'd seen before.

"You can call me Lucy—at least for tonight. You should close your mouth before something flies in."

My mouth snapped shut, and I directed my attention toward Doug, still marveling at how well he'd cleaned up. He was like the end product of a reality show makeover. "I'm just surprised to see you. You didn't mention anything about coming to town on our call this afternoon."

Doug raised an amused eyebrow. "I didn't realize I was under any obligation to clear my schedule with you."

"Well, of course not," I stammered, struggling to find anything to say that wouldn't come out the wrong way, and it wasn't helping that Brady continued to goggle with his bushy raised eyebrows and widened eyes. "I just—I just—it's good to see you both."

"That's better," said Lucy, smiling and lightly patting my cheek. "You look so much better without your foot in your mouth. Would you mind if we actually came in, or shall we spend what's left of the evening blocking the door?"

"By all means, come in!" said Anyssa, startling Brady out of his reverie with a warning look I suspected she was perfecting. Collectively, we stepped back into the room, giving Doug and Lucy a little more space. I couldn't imagine what I might say next and was relieved when Lucy stepped in to fill the void.

"Clearly, this comes as shock to you all, so let's get this over with," said Lucy. "Doug and I have decided to pick up where we left off a long time ago. We don't know if it's going to work, but we owe it to ourselves to find out."

"And to our little girl," Doug added, sliding an arm around Lucy's waist and giving her a quick squeeze. "Speaking of which, maybe you should give Ma a quick call and check in, babe—see how Brianna's settling in."

"I'm sure she's fine, hon," she replied, but she was already fishing her phone out of her purse. "But since I know you'll worry all night—"

This was *The Twilight Zone.* So many questions, none of which I could ask. Last I knew, Loretta hated this woman with a passion. She even disavowed her own granddaughter, clinging to denial and insisting on paternity tests that failed to convince despite their conclusive results.

99.99% was apparently not conclusive enough. As I listened to Lucy's light banter with Loretta, punctuated by laughter that actually sounded sincere, I realized my own cell phone was ringing from the vibration in my pants.

I retrieved it from my pocket, relieved to see Melanie's face smiling up at me through my cracked screen. "Hey, Mel. I was just starting to get a little worried—"

"Dwayne," she interrupted, and she was clearly upset.

I stepped away from the group. "What's wrong?"

"I need you to come," she said, and every muscle in my body tensed up. "It's Sarah."

"Sarah?" My voice sounded miles away in my own ears. "What's going on?"

"She had a heart attack. I need you to *hurry*."

CHAPTER FOURTEEN

Two hours and the same number of speeding tickets later, I raced into Lymont Memorial, entering through Emergency as the main entrance had closed at eight. I wound my way through a labyrinth of nearly empty corridors, in search of the elevators. Cardiac care was on the second floor, and as of Melanie's last text update, Sarah was still in surgery.

After getting turned around a time or two, I finally found the family waiting room, spotting Melanie a split second before she saw me. Relief flooded her weary face, and she rushed into my arms, fighting to keep from crying in front of Jasmine, who was busily occupying her half-brother, Jordan, in a quiet corner of the waiting room. From the looks of her red-rimmed eyes, it was a fight she'd been having for some time.

"Any updates?" I ventured.

"Not a word. She's been in surgery for hours," said Mel, stepping back and regaining a little composure.

"What happened?"

Melanie cast a cautious glance towards the children before easing me out into the hallway and keeping her voice low. "Jasmine called me as I was getting ready for Brady's party. She was so hysterical I could barely understand the words coming out of her mouth. She said Sarah wasn't feeling well the whole way home, and once they got to Brenner Hollow, she asked if Jasmine would mind watching Jordan while she laid down for a bit.

She was in the middle of teaching him Candyland when she heard a big crash in Sarah's bedroom. She found her grandmother lying on the floor unconscious."

"Oh, my God," I said, and we both looked at a girl who you'd never guess had gone through such trauma only hours before.

Melanie couldn't keep a few errant tears from spilling at this point. "I've never been so proud of that little girl in my whole life. She had the presence of mind to call 9-1-1 and start CPR until the squad could arrive, all while keeping Jordan as calm as she could, too. Her hysterics didn't come until later. I swear, if I have to work five jobs, I'm buying that child the pony she's always wanted. If it wasn't for her, Sarah would be dead. Now, I can only pray that she makes it through this surgery."

"*Shh*," I said, pulling her back into my arms, kissing the top of her head. "Everything's gonna be just fine."

She pushed away from me. "You don't *know* that."

"Okay, you're right, I don't," I admitted, never big on making promises I couldn't keep. "But whatever happens, we'll get through this. I'm here for you and Jasmine. Where are Joe and Ann?" I was asking about Sarah's parents, the Savitches.

Melanie shook her head, wiping her eyes. "They've been in Gatlinburg this week with Sarah's brother and his family. I've been dragging my feet about making the call. I'm hoping I'll have better news to share soon. *Dammit!* How long before we hear something?"

"I thought I heard voices. Niles, reinforcements have arrived."

Cordelia McGregor stood in the entrance to the waiting room, her words slightly muffled behind the mask she wore over her nose and mouth. Immaculate in a cream-colored pantsuit and low heels, she looked as out of place as she probably felt. She had cut her hair since the last time I had seen her; her jet-black, shoulder-length bob was undoubtedly inspired by Vogue commander-in-chief, Anna Wintour, and I had to admit, she wore it well.

She motioned with a latex-gloved hand into a corner of the room I couldn't see, and soon enough, Ryan's father, Niles, appeared at his wife's side. He had taken protective gear to the next level, a plastic shield covering his masked face, its strap causing what little hair he had left to stand on end.

"Dwayne," he said, nodding. "I'd shake your hand, but—" He flashed his own latex encased hands in my direction.

"No worries," I said, tossing an inquiring glance at Melanie. I could almost understand Niles being here, but Cordelia? She and Sarah had been sworn enemies from the moment Cordelia had stolen Niles' heart. Between you and me, Niles and Cordelia were much better suited for one another, but I'd never let Sarah hear me speak that particular truth.

"Jasmine called her grandparents after the squad came," said Melanie, filling in the blanks. "Niles and Cordelia brought the kids in and waited with them until I could get here. I was just north of Chillicothe when I called you. I haven't been here very long myself."

"Are you ready, darling?" Cordelia asked her husband, nudging him towards the hallway.

"Wait a minute," said Melanie, holding a hand up. "You're *leaving?*"

"Well—yes, dear," said Cordelia. "It's not like our being here will make any difference. Besides, I absolutely *detest* hospitals."

"You've *got* to be kidding me," said Melanie, turning her back on her former in-laws and struggling to keep her voice low before wheeling around to invade Cordelia's personal space. *"Nobody* likes hospitals! Has it occurred to you that this is more than just an inconvenience for you? We don't know how much longer Sarah's going to be in surgery or if she'll even pull through. I don't think these kids need to see this unfold in real time. Don't you think it might be a good idea to at least *offer* to take your grandchildren with you? They certainly don't need to be here."

"Ni-i-les," whined Cordelia petulantly, clinging to her husband's arm with flawlessly manicured talons.

I watched Melanie's hands tighten into fists, her knuckles whitening. When she spoke, her tone was low but steady and more than a little scary. "I can count on *one hand* the number of times that Jasmine has spent the night with the two of you. Tell me, would you even *recognize* Jordan in a line-up? I'll give you a hint. He's the one who looks just like his *fucking father*. Do you even remember Ryan? He's the one we put in the ground not so very long ago."

"Now, Melanie," said Niles, holding up a hand in protest. "There's no need to get ugly. Cordy's just tired. She's not used to being around children."

"Well, maybe she'd be a little more comfortable if she gave it a try once in a while," snapped Melanie as if Cordelia wasn't standing right in front of her. "Look, I don't expect you to hang out, but I really could use a little help here. It's not like you'd have to do much. I mean, Jasmine actually enjoys taking care of her brother. It's so late, I'm sure they'll be asleep in no time."

"Of course," said Niles, nodding even as Cordelia shot him a dirty look. He crossed over to where the kids sat on the floor and kneeled down to their level. "How about it, kids? Wanna spend the night with Papaw Niles and Mimsy?"

Jasmine's uncertainty was clear as glass as she looked to her mother and finally spotted me. She was in my arms in an instant, her pent-up emotions releasing in a tidal wave of body-racking sobs. "Oh, Dwayne, it was *terrible*."

"I'm so sorry, sweetheart," I said, my throat tightening. "I hear you saved the day. I didn't know you knew CPR."

Her broken chuckle was heartbreaking as she tried to staunch the flow of tears. "We studied it in health a couple of weeks ago. I'm surprised I even remembered what to do. Me and Keaira spent the entire time laughing about everyone making out with the CPR dummy in class. We were so *stupid*."

"Hey," I said, looking into her face. "Every kid makes fun of that dummy. The important thing is you knew what to do."

"But she still might not—might not—" Her face crumpled, and this time, Jordan's followed suit, not fully aware of what was upsetting his sister but unhappy about it just the same.

"*Shhh*," I said, hugging her and motioning to Jordan. He toddled over and put his arms around his sister, and I pulled him into our circle. "Listen to me. I want you to go with your Papaw and Mimsy back to their house and keep right on watching after Jordan. He's not old enough to understand what's going on, but he's picking up on all of our concern, and it's upsetting him. He's already been through so much. I need you to be strong for just a little longer. Can you do that? I won't tell you not to worry because you will anyway, but Sarah's getting the very best care as we speak. Your mom and I will stay here, and we'll let you know the minute we hear something."

She nodded, snuffling as Melanie handed her a couple of tissues. After tending to her own face, Jasmine shifted to Jordan and dried his eyes. "Let's go, Bub," she said, taking his hand into hers, and he had already calmed considerably.

Melanie leaned down, kissing both children on their cheeks before addressing Cordelia and Niles. "Thank you. I know it's not what you hoped for, Cordelia, but I trust that you're enough of an adult to not let that affect the way you treat the children, and believe me, I'll know if it does."

I could imagine Niles' wince behind his mask. "Of course not, Melanie. We're more than happy to have them over. After all, it's just for one night."

I gaped at the man's utterly poor choice of words. Could he not hear himself? The veins in Melanie's temples were beginning to throb. Cordelia, still in a bit of a snit, led her husband and grandchildren away from the waiting room and toward the elevators.

"*Mimsy?*" I asked, and Melanie rolled her eyes.

"She can't see herself as a grandma, but then again, neither can I," she said. "And it has absolutely nothing to do with whatever she decides to call herself. I hope I'm not making a mistake putting the kids in their care."

I chuckled. "I guarantee they'll be on their best behavior. I'm fairly certain Cordelia's a little scared of you. The kids will be fine."

She sighed, eyeing the empty seating in the waiting room. We were the only unfortunate souls to occupy the room at this hour, and exhaustion hit us both like a wall. We dropped onto one of the uncomfortable vinyl couches, and Melanie tucked herself beneath my arm, resting her head on my chest. I knew better than to read too much into this; Melanie needed someone to lean on, and I was more than happy to oblige. Sarah was like a second mother to me, and I wouldn't allow myself to imagine the dark turn this could take.

"And now we wait," she said. "Dwayne? I know you're not particularly religious, but—"

"I'm already praying," I said, and I wasn't fibbing. I had been pleading with the Big Guy upstairs since tearing out of Brady's driveway.

···•••••◦◦•••••···

"Mrs. McGregor?"

The voice came from afar but jolted us to consciousness in an instant. Melanie struggled to an upright position as I wiped away a stream of drool I was embarrassed to find leaking from the corner of my mouth. I had only intended to rest my eyes and was surprised to see that it was nearly two-thirty in the morning according to the clock mounted to the wall across from us. A doctor stood over us in scrubs, his surgical mask pulled down to reveal his Middle Eastern features partially obscured by a thick five o'clock shadow.

"I'm Dr. Nassar," he said, startling me with his South Shore drawl. "I've got an update for you on your mother-in-law. May I speak freely?"

His eyes shifted in my direction as we stood, and Melanie nodded, taking my hand, and gripping with more force than she realized.

"Sarah is in recovery. She had severe blockage in all of her coronary arteries, requiring a quadruple bypass."

"But you *were* able to correct it?" Melanie asked, and I had to pull my hand free from her vice-like grip. The bones were beginning to grind together.

The doctor nodded. "The repair was successful, yes, but she's not completely out of the woods yet. The next forty-eight hours will be critical. She had an adverse reaction to the anesthesia, and we almost lost her a couple of times."

"Oh, my God," said Melanie, as she blinked back fresh tears. "Can we see her?"

The doctor's smile was kind as he shook his head. "Not just yet. She'll need some extra time in recovery until we're certain the anesthesia is no longer a concern, and then she'll be moved to our cardiac care unit for the next few days. Most likely, she won't even be lucid until tomorrow morning, so you should take this opportunity to try and get some rest yourselves. This is going to be a long, slow recovery, and Sarah's going to need all the help she can get."

"Of course," I said. "We'll do anything we can."

"I just don't know how to thank you, Dr. Nassar," said Melanie, taking his hand into both of hers. "I don't know what I would do if anything happened to her."

"I'm just happy to be able to bring you a little bit of good news," he said, smiling before his face turned solemn. "A condition like Sarah's doesn't always end well, and she's still got a big fight ahead of her. If I were you, I'd keep those prayers coming."

...•••••◗◖•••••...

While Melanie kept her promise to her daughter, calling to update her despite the lateness of the hour, I checked my own phone, which I had silenced prior to entering the hospital. I was surprised to find a handful of missed texts and calls, two of which were from Doug Boggs, but the rest were from Brady. He hadn't bothered with voicemail—who does anymore?—so I scrolled through the string of texts that started landing around eleven with a new one arriving every half hour or so.

Wow u really know how to kill a party. Let me know when u make it to Lymont.

Pick up ur damn phone, man. U should be there already.

Starting to feel ignored.

Any word yet?

Ur worrying Anyssa to death. Asshole. CALL ME.

Listen, call whenever u can. Don't worry about waking us up. We won't be able to sleep til we know what's going on.

At this point, I was smiling. As a reporter, it was in Brady's nature to be persistent, but that was typically when he had something to gain from it. This entire night was supposed to be about him, and yet here he was fretting over a woman he had never even met. I mean, surely, he wasn't worried about me—was he?

177

Realizing it had been over an hour since his last text, I decided to play it safe and send him one of my own instead of calling.

Sarah made it through surgery but it's still touch and go. I'll call you in the morning.

I was about to slide my phone back into my pocket when it vibrated in my hand, startling me. Brady's smug countenance grinned up at me from the screen.

"Hey," I answered, rubbing my bleary eyes.

"You don't follow instructions for shit, dude," he said, sounding as awake as ever. "I said *call* me."

"I didn't see the point of waking you if you'd fallen asleep like a normal person," I said. "Sorry."

"How bad is it?" he asked.

"Bad enough," I replied before summarizing the doctor's earlier report. "Sarah's damn lucky Jasmine was there and knew what to do. Otherwise, Jordan would have been living his worst nightmare all over again."

I shuddered at my own flippant observation. It hadn't even been a year since Jordan was discovered alone with the corpse of his overdosed mother. That poor kid was probably fractured in ways it would take years of therapy to fix.

"She's a great kid," Brady said. "How are you and Melanie holding up?"

"Been running on E for miles," I said, stifling a yawn. "Melanie's delivering an update to her daughter, and then I think we're going to find someplace to crash for a little while. The next couple of days are going to be rough."

"I'm sure. Is there anything we can do to help out? Feed that mangy cat of yours?"

I inhaled sharply through my teeth. *Dexter.* He was all alone in Rochelle's guest cottage and would be expecting his breakfast by mid-morning. I had left him a guilty little bonus in his bowl before leaving for Brady's party, and he had plenty of water, but by noon, he'd likely be shredding the most inconvenient things to show his displeasure.

"Are you still there, buddy?"

"Yeah, sorry," I said. "It's just that I've been staying at a client's guest cottage while working her case, and Dexter is currently home alone."

"Can't she feed him?" he asked. "I know he's not the friendliest cat in the world, but I've never known him to refuse food."

"She's out of town for the weekend. I guess I'll be making a return trip in the morning. Thanks for reminding me. I have a feeling I'm going to be living out of my car for a while."

I realized that Melanie had ended her call with Jasmine and was waiting for me patiently.

"Listen, man, I should go. We need to try and catch some Zs while we still can," I said.

"Of course, of course," said Brady. "But hey, listen—before you go, I wanna ask you about something."

"Sure," I said, fighting another yawn. "What's that?"

Brady paused, gathering his courage before plunging ahead. "All that business tonight with Senator Ghant and his wife—it's not my imagination, right? There *is* something going on there."

I groaned, rolling my eyes. "I should have known. *Jesus*, Brady!"

"What?" His utterly shocked response grated like cheese, and it didn't take much imagination to picture the righteous indignation on his face. I'd seen it before. Plenty of times.

"This was never about your *concern*."

"Of course, I'm concerned! Anyssa and I both are. It's just—" His voice trailed off, dangling bait I wasn't about to take.

"Good night, Brady."

"Fine," he said. "I'm sorry about that. My timing was bad, and it could have waited. The concern is real. You know that."

I let silence be my answer, and you might have thought he'd be smart enough to leave it alone, but no. His Spidey sense was in overdrive.

"But come *on*, man. I know when I smell a story, and—"

"Good *night*, Brady."

I disconnected the call and watched his goofy dimpled face dim on my cracked screen. I was too tired for outrage. I'd yell at him later.

I turned to Melanie. "We should probably go pick up the kids and try to get some sleep."

"I've got a better idea," she said as we ambled toward the elevators like zombies. "Why don't we leave the kids with Niles and Cordelia for the night? Jordan's already asleep, and now that Jasmine knows that Sarah is out of surgery, I think she'll be able to fall asleep, too. I hate to disturb them."

The elevator arrived, and we had it all to ourselves.

"Where do you want to go? There isn't much to choose from here in Lymont. We might do better if we go over to Portsmouth," I said.

"I've still got my key to Sarah's," she said. "We could save ourselves some money and just crash there."

"You don't think she'd mind?"

I realized it was a stupid question as it left my mouth, and Melanie laughed. "She'd insist."

The elevator doors opened onto the ground floor, and we followed the signage pointing us towards Emergency.

"I suppose you overheard about Dexter. I'm going to have to make a quick trip home tomorrow morning, but I'll either bring him back or get him moved back down to my house where Brady can take care of him until we return," I said.

"You don't think Brady will mind?"

I snorted. "I think Brady will do whatever I ask, at least for a little while. Senator Ghant and his wife were guests at his party, and we sort of had a little incident."

"Oh, no," she said. "You didn't blow the case, did you?"

I shot her a look. *"No.* Why is that your first thought? It's just that Brady picked up on the friction between us. Obviously, it's not something I can talk about, especially not with him. Don't ever tell him I said this, but he's pretty damn good at his job."

We walked in companionable silence for a moment, the empty corridor surreal in comparison to what I'd expect to find at Riverside or Grant in Columbus. The only hint of activity came from the end of the hall, where the entrance to Emergency was located. A stout security guard sat near the exit, prepared to direct any new arrivals to a walkthrough metal detector near his desk.

I nodded to him as we approached, heading towards the exit door that was already sliding open when a familiar voice caught my attention, carrying across the waiting room of the ER. I paused, following the source and doing a double take once I found it.

"Mom?"

CHAPTER FIFTEEN

The security guard had to slow me down as I marched through his sensor without much regard for protocol, setting off a symphony of audio-visual alerts. The sight of my mother and Aunt Eunice huddled together in this particular setting was a jolt I hadn't expected. Needless to say, they were just as surprised to see us.

"Dwayne? Melanie? What are you doing here?" Mom asked, her maternal worry never far from reach. "Has something happened?"

"I was just about to ask you the same thing," I said, scanning the scant few others who occupied the waiting area as my exhausted mind struggled to process what I saw before me. Mom had never learned to drive, leaving that anxiety-inducing task to Dad. In Dad's absence, Aunt Eunice occasionally filled the role. It took longer than it should have to do the math, but once I arrived at an answer, a fresh wave of dread washed over me. "Where's Dad?"

Mom exchanged a nervous glance with my dad's older sister before placing a hand on my arm. "I'm sure it's nothing," she said, an attempt at reassurance that did anything but. I flashed back to the previous Thanksgiving when I first noticed the toll my sister's supposed death was taking on a man who had always seemed virtually indestructible. It was a stunning realization, and my mind went racing in a million different directions, all of them dark.

"It's nothing?" I stupidly repeated, gawking at them both. "What's nothing?"

"He just had a little spell earlier, that's all," Mom said, continuing to downplay things while Aunt Eunice's face told an entirely different story.

"What kind of spell?" I asked.

Mom sighed impatiently. "It was just a little bout of confusion. It only lasted for a few moments, but it was enough that I thought he should be checked out. I didn't think it was a good idea to let him drive, so I called your Aunt Eunice and asked if she could bring us in. Honestly, by the time we got here, he was back to his old self. They've taken him back for testing," she said. She turned to Melanie and proceeded to change the subject. "So, why are you two here?"

"It's Sarah," Melanie replied. "She had a heart attack."

Mom's eyes widened as her hand flew to her mouth. "Oh, no! Is she going to be alright?"

"She made it through surgery, but it's really too soon to tell," said Melanie. "We're certainly praying."

With those three magic words, Melanie set Aunt Eunice's head to earnestly nodding. She was undoubtedly mentally updating the Midland United Methodist prayer chain in her head, and by the wee hours of morning, a fair amount of Lymont's church-going populace would be apprised of Sarah's current plight. I hoped she wouldn't mind. Aunt Eunice's intentions were good.

Four years older than my father, Aunt Eunice was one of his seven sisters, and a test to be passed—whether you signed up for the class or not. At barely over five feet in height, she had a headful of tight, rust-colored curls courtesy of Clairol, and her leathery skin belied the age suggested by her trim physique. Gifted with a metabolism that allowed her to eat anything without gaining an ounce, she reveled at the opportunity to share this fact with others less fortunate, including my mother. Heaven forbid you call her skinny, an enviable attribute to most but an utter insult to Aunt Eunice. She was *tiny*. Outspoken and conservative, she had thrown herself into the community service of her church after her abusive, alcoholic husband, Vance, had left her for a younger salesclerk at Vincente's Department Store, a woman who happened to share Uncle Vance's predilection for hard liquor. My aunt referred to her only as The Grand Whore, and at this point, I couldn't even remember her actual name anymore. My mind keeps going to 'Jezebel,' but that can't possibly be right. I was maybe ten at the time, so the details are a little fuzzy, but after a particularly violent altercation in which Uncle Vance tried to strangle my aunt into eternal silence, she had taken refuge in our house for a short while. The family thought she was lucky to escape with her life, and Dad was instrumental in convincing her to file for divorce, but Aunt Eunice never cared to talk about that. She preferred to play the role of abandoned wife and generally wronged woman. It played better to a crowd, evoking greater sympathy.

"I don't believe we've met, dearie. I'm Todd's sister, Eunice." My aunt extended a delicate hand to Melanie while giving her the not-so-subtle once over. "You must be that widow woman who's been seeing my favorite nephew," she added, managing to insert a hint of judgmental disdain without batting an eye. I should also note that I am *not* her favorite nephew. It's just a toss-away term she uses for whichever nibling was in front of her.

"Pleased to meet you, although I sure wish it was under better circumstances," said Melanie, unfazed by my aunt's bluntness. "I'm Melanie. Melanie McGregor."

A nurse appeared out of nowhere, mercifully interrupting what would have likely been an unpredictable and awkward exchange. "Mrs. Morrow?" she asked, querying the room.

Mom moved in her direction. "I'm Jo Morrow."

"Your husband's been returned to his triage room, and he's asking for you," she said with a smile before turning to activate the automated security doors. Mom followed without a single look back, and I scrambled after her.

"Can I see him?" I asked.

The nurse looked to my mother expectantly, but to my astonishment, Mom shook her head. "I don't think so, honey. Your father didn't want me to worry you or your brother until we know if there's anything to even worry about, so why don't you and Melanie just go on? I promise to keep you posted."

She disappeared behind the secured doors before I could even respond. Melanie placed a hand at the small of my back. "Are you alright?"

I was completely stunned. My mouth flapped ineffectually before I finally found words. "I guess I'll have to be."

"Listen," said Aunt Eunice, sidling up to us conspiratorially. One thing's for certain, she was never at a loss for words. "I'm glad we have a few minutes to talk privately. I think your mother is in state of denial."

"How so?"

"This isn't the first little episode your father has had," she said, whispering despite the fact that we were virtually alone. "It's just the worst."

"What happened?" I asked.

"You know how close me and your father are," she said. "Over the course of a normal week, I see him, what—three or four times, easy. He's been having these spells where he just suddenly loses his train of thought. It only lasts for a second or two before he's back. He's never been like that, and it's hard not to notice after you've seen it a few times. I was going to mention it to you or Matt next time I saw you, but you hardly ever come down anymore, especially since Gina—well, never mind that."

I was grinding my teeth and losing patience. I mean, it wasn't like she didn't have my phone number, but she couldn't stop herself from taking that nasty little jab. If she didn't spill some beans and fast, she was liable to face a second round of attempted strangulation.

"What happened *tonight?*"

"You know how your folks are," she said. "Todd is early to bed, early to rise—always has been, but your mother's a real night owl, watching all those trashy movies they show once decent folk have called it a night—"

I rolled my hand to hurry her along. I had no patience for her commentary on Mom's television viewing habits.

Aunt Eunice cleared her throat. "Apparently, your father got up around midnight and was wandering through the house, not really sure where he was. When he came across your mom watching television in the family room, he—uh—didn't exactly seem to recognize her."

"Did he hurt her?"

"Oh, heaven's no!" Aunt Eunice said, waving that particular concern away. "Your father's not a violent man. He was just confused. He thought your mother was Nancy."

I stared at her. "I'm sorry, he thought she was *who?*"

She sighed impatiently. "Nancy. Obviously, it startled your mother, so she called me, but by the time I arrived, Todd had already come around. It took both of us to convince him to—"

"Wait, wait, wait," I said, holding up a hand and squeezing my eyes shut. "Who is this *Nancy?*"

Aunt Eunice blinked back surprise. "Well—she was your father's first wife, of course. Surely, you knew that."

· · · · • ● ⊖◯ ●• · · · ·

The fuck I did.

Melanie and I drove to Brenner Hollow in complete silence as I struggled to process a world turned upside down. Once Aunt Eunice realized she'd stepped into something big, she clammed up tight, refusing to divulge any details and instead, referring me to the very people who had perpetuated this whole coverup for my entire life. Never *once* had there ever been a mention of a previous marriage in all my thirty-five years on this planet. Oh, sure, I knew my parents had a long-standing policy of never really discussing anything substantive in front of the children, and in their eyes, we would never be old enough to hear about whatever skeletons might lurk in the family closet, but this was beyond anything I could have ever imagined. When had Dad and this Nancy woman been married, and for how long? What caused them to split, and—oh, God. Was Mom "the other woman?" Were there little half-siblings out there I knew nothing about? My head was filling with so many random questions, I'd need to make a list before I next saw my parents. That is, if I could ever look at those people again.

"Dwayne!"

The urgency in Melanie's voice snapped me out of my reverie, and I gasped, slamming on the brakes just in time to avoid slamming into the largest deer I'd ever seen. It stared at me from the middle of the narrow road, not even slightly intimidated by our sudden approach. In fact, it looked irritated that we had interrupted its leisurely moonlit stroll. I honked my horn, and it finally scampered off, allowing us to proceed.

A nervous, high-pitched giggle escaped my lips, and I looked at Melanie and grimaced. "Sorry. You alright?"

"Other than drowning in the deep end of an adrenaline pool? *Sure*," she said, patting her chest. "One more good scare, and they'll have me in a bed beside Sarah at Lymont Memorial. Slow it down, will you?"

I complied. Neither one of us had any business driving. We were both in that zone just beyond exhaustion. Thankfully, Sarah's house was just around the next bend.

It seemed strange to see Sarah's Jeep parked in front of the darkened ranch house, knowing she wasn't inside. Of course, at this hour, she'd be asleep, most likely sacked out on her couch in the living room, having fallen asleep to never ending reruns of *Blue Bloods*. She never could get enough of Tom Selleck, and in my head, I could almost hear her tossing off one of her frequent, lusty comments about a man she had mooned over for decades. Despite the utter cringeworthiness of it all, I'd have given anything to hear one of her risqué propositions right then. My chest tightened at the thought I might never hear one again.

I parked beside Sarah's car, and we got out, Melanie fumbling in her purse for her keys. We trudged like the undead to the front door, and I used the flashlight from my phone to help guide Melanie's hand toward the lock. In the middle of navigating a crisis, it hadn't occurred to Jasmine to turn the outside security light on, something Sarah never failed to do. Living alone in the middle of a wooded hollow could get downright creepy at times, and pushing back even a little of the darkness diluted the innate spookiness of the setting, not that Sarah would ever admit to it. I couldn't recall ever seeing her scared of anything. For us, however, standing in the shadows where the only illumination came from the streetlamp at the far end of her drive and from the full moon overhead, it only added to the desolation shrouding the place.

The key turned, and Melanie pushed the door inward, prepared to silence an alarm that never sounded. Of course, Jasmine hadn't thought to set that either, but who could blame the poor kid? Her hands had been rather full. Melanie bypassed the light switch, following the ambient moonlight spilling into the living room from the double doors that led out onto Sarah's small deck. I followed along behind her, through the small dining room and into the living room where we dropped side-by-side onto the couch and stared at the ceiling fan which wobbled in a slow, lazy circle.

"Are you okay?" Melanie asked, her fingers tracing a path down my arm. "That was quite the bombshell."

I could only shake my head, adrift in a sea of emotions, with anger and guilt fighting to control the ship. The sense of betrayal was overwhelming. Okay, technically they hadn't lied, instead committing the greatest act of omission of all time, but either way, I was furious at being left in the dark for so many years. I had a right to know my family history without having to extract it one piece at a time, like long-impacted wisdom teeth. I couldn't wait to share my discovery with my brother, Matt—and it suddenly occurred to me that he might already know. It was doubtful, but at this point, I had already been shaken to my very foundation, so maybe it was best to keep that possibility in mind. At the same time, I still didn't know what was going on with Dad, and I felt guilty for even being angry at all. I should be prioritizing these things, getting to the bottom of what was causing Dad's worsening fugue states, and offering Mom the support she had yet to realize she needed. And all of this on top of what was already going on with Sarah.

"*Ugh*," I finally managed. "My family sucks."

Melanie smiled, taking my hand into hers. "No, they don't. I mean, come on. You've met *my* family. I can't imagine that any of this was done with the express purpose of hurting you."

"It's like I have to question every single thing I've ever believed in my life," I said, content to wallow in self-pity. "I mean, it's one thing to shield your children from a little ugliness in the world, but when does it end? When are we ever old enough to know *anything?* I honestly don't see how you're doing your children any favors pretending to live in a Brady Bunch world where real problems don't even exist. That's part of the reason why Ryan and I hit it off so well. Everything was so *real* here. Sarah and Niles were in the middle of an ugly divorce, and they didn't hold anything back.

According to my folks, divorce was something that only happened on TV. Or in Europe. Seeing it unfold in real time was eye-opening."

"Well, I'm certainly glad their total misery was a valuable learning experience for you," said Melanie sarcastically, letting go of my hand.

I sighed. "I didn't mean it like that. It's just—they both treated me and Ryan like adults who could handle a little uncomfortable truth. It was refreshing."

"And you were all of what, thirteen?" asked Melanie, and I nodded earnestly. "That is within a year of my own daughter's age, and I've got more than a little experience with children at that age than you do. I might suggest that Sarah and Niles *should* have exercised a little more restraint in front of you guys. Maybe that's why Ryan spent his whole life desperately seeking approval, because part of him felt he should have been able to keep his parents together, you know? Like he was never quite good enough for them."

I cast her a dubious look. "You've been watching *way* too much Dr. Phil."

"Okay, maybe, but that isn't really my point. Look, being a parent doesn't come with some sort of guidebook. I mean, sure, there are tons of books in the library written by some of the world's foremost experts on how to be a picture-perfect parent, but honestly—who has time to read all that shit? You're too busy working, keeping house, worrying about bills— all while trying to keep your relationship with your partner alive, if it hasn't already died. Life's exhausting before you even *have* a child. So basically, at that point, we're all just winging it and doing the best we can. Your natural instinct is always to protect—well, unless you're a complete monster like my father, but for the sake of argument, I'm going to consider him a statistical aberration. So, maybe your parents haven't used the best judgment here. I'm not going to challenge that point, because it's understandably upsetting. Still, I don't think it was a malicious act. I mean,

190

think about your parents. They clearly still love each other, and after all the years they've been together, that's *huge*. They love you and your brother, too. There are a whole lot of kids out there that don't get that kind of support. I'm sure they had their reasons for not disclosing this little tidbit of information, but there's not really a whole lot of point to making yourself crazy guessing. You'll have an opportunity to get your answers, but that's after we know your dad is well. You need to focus."

I continued to stare at the ceiling fan, resisting the urge to pick at Melanie's sound reasoning. It would have been an act of unnecessary and misdirected belligerence. Looking away, my eyes landed on the open box for Candyland in the far corner, its contents spread wide, and I could almost picture Jasmine patiently teaching the game to her brother before all hell broke loose. The very thought made me ashamed of myself for being so affected by news that was pretty much ancient history. Oh, yes, there were conversations to be had, but it wasn't like they would change anything. Melanie was absolutely correct. I needed to focus on what was truly important.

"Enough about me," I said, suddenly embarrassed by my own self-absorption. "How are you holding up?"

She shrugged. "By a thread. I don't know what I'm gonna do if Sarah—"

"*Shhh,*" I said, taking her hand back into mine. "Don't even."

"I'm glad we're here," she said, looking around the darkened living room. "I don't know if you knew this, but Ryan and I lived here for a little while when Jasmine was first born. We weren't making enough money to afford a place of our own, and Sarah wouldn't take no for an answer. She put us in Ryan's old bedroom, the one that Jasmine uses when she's down. It was a tight fit, but I don't know that I've ever felt any more at home than when I was right here."

I smiled as a ton of bittersweet teenaged memories washed over me. "I know what you mean. It's been a second home for me for as long as I can remember. I spent almost as many weekends here as I did at my own house. It always felt safe. Of course, Sarah worked lots of long hours back then, and we kind of had the run of the place to ourselves. We did lots of things we shouldn't have back then."

"Yeah? Like what?"

"Oh, I don't know," I said, suddenly sheepish. "Stupid shit."

"I wish I could see how the two of you were back then."

"I'm sure there's pictures somewhere, but trust me, you're not missing much. Even now, I'm not entirely out of my awkward phase."

She smiled, closing her eyes for just an instant before her face squinched up, and tears started flowing.

"Hey, hey, hey," I said, pulling her close. "What's this?"

Melanie's body hitched as I rocked her, giving her as much time as she needed to collect herself. When she finally spoke, it was punctuated by great, gulping hiccups. "I don't know what I'm going to *do*. I'm going to have to call Doug and turn down the position he just offered me—which I'm sure makes *you* happy. But now I don't have a *job*, and the rent is due in ten days, and—and—and—"

"*Shhh*," I said, continuing to gently rock her. "We'll figure this out together. What makes you think I'd be happy about you not working for Boggs?"

She pulled back, fixing me with a knowing look.

"Well, okay, maybe I wasn't thrilled about it at first, but I was warming to the idea. The thought of spending my days with you has a certain appeal."

She shook her head, starting to get upset all over again. "You don't get it. I don't see how I'm going to be able to work at all. Even if Sarah comes through this, she's got a long road ahead of her. Who's going to take care of Jordan while she's recovering? Niles and Cordelia?" She snorted derisively. "It was all I could do to get them to step up for one night."

"What about Joe and Ann?" I asked, referring to Sarah's parents, and Melanie looked at me like I was a moron. Admittedly, it wasn't my greatest idea.

"At their age? No. Besides, that poor boy has been through so much this last year. I would hate to shuttle him off to another strange environment. At least if he's with me, he'd have Jasmine there as a familiar face."

I found myself smiling as I watched Melanie process the shitty hand she'd been dealt, the tracks of her tears glistening in the moonlight. It hadn't been very long ago at all since she had wanted nothing to do with a child who was conceived during one of Ryan's numerous extramarital affairs, refusing to let Jasmine spend time with her half-brother once she'd learned of his existence. Melanie's change of heart had been gradual, but this was a leap that was nothing short of miraculous.

It wasn't long before she caught me staring.

"What?" she asked, dabbing at her eyes.

"You are the strongest woman I know," I said, gently using my thumbs to dry her eyes. "Stop worrying. We'll get through this, whatever it takes. You're not alone."

Her eyes searched mine, struggling to take me at my word. She leaned in, tentatively finding my lips with her own, igniting a fire that needed absolutely zero accelerant. She slid a leg over and straddled me, our bodies grinding together as our hands found favorite haunts on autopilot. Our mouths barely allowed us to come up for air as we surrendered to a hunger borne of months of abstinence, and we were suddenly on the floor wearing significantly less than we started with.

Melanie suddenly gasped and pulled back. "Stop—*wait*," she said, her ragged breath warm against my neck.

"*What?*" I was practically whimpering.

"We can't do this here," she said. "We're in Sarah's living room."

"Would you prefer we use her room or one of the kids'?" I asked, nibbling her neck and letting my fingers do some walking.

"Oh, *ewww*. Good point," she groaned. "Carry on."

CHAPTER SIXTEEN

"*G*et up, get up, get up, get up!*"
Melanie's fingertips punctuated each command, jabbing at the tender flesh just below my collarbone. I squinted against the bright sunlight pouring in through the panes of the double door leading to Sarah's deck, momentarily unsure of where I was or why I was there, but keenly aware that I was butt ass naked.

"*Unnh?*" I managed through a mouth of cotton.

"We overslept," said Melanie as she slid into her jeans, tossing articles of my clothing at me as she located them. "Get dressed."

I was suddenly wide awake and scrambling. "Did something happen? Is Sarah alright? Is my Dad—"

"I don't know. I only woke up because I heard someone out on the deck. It was old man Runyon, delivering Sarah's mail and getting a free peep show in the process. Scared the shit right out of me. I thought it was Niles and Cordelia with the kids."

I slipped into my boxer briefs. "What time is it?"

"Almost eight-thirty. We've got to go."

"Relax," I said, yawning. "It's not the end of the world. If something happened, surely they would have called us."

Melanie laughed sardonically. "My battery died sometime overnight, and I left my charger in my car."

"Well, I'm sure they would have called me if they couldn't get hold of you. How about Sarah's landline?" I asked, rummaging through the pockets of the khakis I had yet to put on with increasing urgency. My phone didn't seem to be in any of them. I turned my attention to the couch cushions, digging underneath them in case my phone had slid out of my pocket the previous evening.

"She got rid of it last year," said Melanie, running a brush through her hair before pulling it into a ponytail. "Are you *serious?* You can't find your phone?"

I shrugged at her helplessly. Her panic was contagious, and I was getting tangled up in my own pants legs trying to get them on.

"Oh, my God," she said, her eyes rolling to the heavens. "Coming here was a mistake."

I flinched as her words struck me like a physical blow. She was already out the front door before I could even manage a reply.

My phone was in the center console of my car. Three missed calls from Niles' cell that started landing just after seven before repeating every half hour. There was a single text from my mother informing me that she and Dad were back home, and everything was fine. She'd call me later.

I guided the car back to civilization as Melanie used my phone to return Niles' call while hers recharged on my car adapter. After a terse initial exchange, it soon became evident that there was nothing new with Sarah—it was only Niles and Cordelia's impatience to get back to their daily normal that had prompted the calls. They were eager to unload the children, which earned Niles another blistering observation from Melanie, who finished by telling him we would be visiting the hospital before collecting the children, and he would simply have to adjust his daily normal. The kids wouldn't be allowed into Sarah's room, even if we had wanted to take them with us, and it was a point he grudgingly conceded.

Normally, I would have relished the opportunity to listen to Melanie light into her former father-in-law, but I was too busy being sullen and feeling stupid. I really thought we had turned a corner the previous evening, putting an end to our months of separation by mending fences both spiritually and physically, but apparently, I was mistaken. I kept my thoughts to myself, and my eyes focused on the road as I turned onto the highway headed back into Lymont.

After a few miles driving in silence, Melanie asked, "Aren't you going to call your mom?"

"No," I said flatly.

She shot me a surprised look. "Don't you want to know what happened with your dad?"

I shrugged. "Mom's text said everything was fine."

"Well, what about—"

"It can wait."

I could tell she was staring at me from the corner of my eye, but I didn't want her to see my disappointment. I kept my eyes on the road as we approached Lymont, and we continued in silence until we pulled into the hospital parking lot. Once I had found a decent parking spot and pulled in, Melanie unfastened her seatbelt and shifted in her seat to look at me.

"Is something wrong?" she asked, reaching out to touch my arm.

I flinched, pulling my arm away. I couldn't help the look I shot her.

"*What?*" she asked, eyes wide and sounding genuinely perplexed. "What could I have possibly done in the time it took to get from Sarah's to here?"

My throat was tightening, and my eyes dropped to my hands, shaking my head. "Last night didn't feel like a mistake to me," I finally muttered, hating the sound of my own insipid voice, and it didn't help one bit when she threw her head back and laughed. I stared at her in disbelief. "It's not

197

funny. You know how hard I've been working on us. It was a cruel thing to say. If you—"

She pressed her fingers against my lips, staunching my free-flowing vulnerability as it poured forth like water through a burst dam. "Stop it, already. You misunderstood me." Her smile was sweet and apologetic. "I said going to Sarah's was a mistake. It was too far away from the hospital and from where the kids were staying, and once we realized we had been incommunicado for *hours*—well, I felt guilty. But trust me, it's a mistake I would make all over again."

She leaned in to kiss me, and my elbow landed on the horn, startling several nearby birds into flight and drawing attention from a couple of passersby in the lot. We giggled our way through a quick smooch before settling back into our seats.

"So, we're okay?" I asked, determined to land on a definitive current status for our relationship. After all the months of trying to rebuild trust and having my ass dragged into couples counseling, it almost felt too easy.

She nodded. "We are. But we'll take our lessons from this whole debacle and learn from them, won't we? No more keeping secrets—at least not big ones."

I gave her the Boy Scout salute. "I do solemnly swear. But that last little caveat is a little more wiggle room than I thought you were comfortable with. What gives?"

She shrugged. "I'm learning that a relationship requires give and take from both parties. I am willing to concede that we both deserve a modicum of privacy, even from each other. I was being a bit of a hard ass on that point."

"What changed your mind?"

"You were just so sweet last night," she said, taking my hand and stroking my fingers. "You knew exactly what to say and just when I needed to hear it, and for once, you didn't put your great big foot in your mouth.

You better have meant what you said. I don't know how I'll ever get through this without you."

I grinned. "A restraining order couldn't keep me away."

"Honestly, though, it was this thing with your parents that really got me thinking."

I blinked, not expecting that at all. "How so?"

"Your mom and dad are genuinely nice people," she said. "They clearly love each other and have done a great job raising you, your brother, and your sister. I'm sure there's a good reason for not disclosing your dad's first marriage. It's a secret they felt was worth keeping, and you should really hold off on passing judgment until you hear what that reason is. It got me thinking about your reasons for not telling me about Gina, and I think I finally get it. They must have a really good reason, too."

I scoffed. "I can't even imagine."

"So, stop imagining. The cat's out of the bag, so talk to them. Do you really think it's going to change who they've been for your entire life?"

I sucked air in through my teeth.

Cat's out of the bag.

Dexter.

"That reminds me, I have to go and get my cat. I didn't leave enough food and water for him. I only thought I'd be away for the evening. We'd better get moving. I'd like to see how Sarah's doing before I take off, but I'll be back just as quickly as I can. Will you be alright without me for a few hours?" I asked.

"I'll manage," she said. "Promise me you'll think about what I said about your parents."

"For you? Anything."

Sarah was sleeping when we arrived, but we were told she had a good night and had woken up briefly. For someone who had always seemed utterly invincible, it was difficult to see her in such a vulnerable state. She was intubated and hooked to about a zillion different monitors, all of which contributed to an eclectic display of vital data that was mostly meaningless to my untrained eye. Lots of blips and drips with IV lines running to assorted bags of fluid suspended from a metal rack at the head of her hospital bed. She was only allowed two simultaneous visitors, and only for brief periods of time.

Sarah's parents had arrived that morning. Joe was in the process of notifying other family members while Ann had sought out the hospital chapel to have a tearful word with God. I felt better that I wouldn't be leaving Melanie alone when I left.

"I should probably head out," I said as we returned to the ICU waiting room. "Is there anything you need me to do before I go?"

"Nope, I'm good. Since Joe and Ann are here, I think I'll take the opportunity to reclaim the children from Niles and Cordelia. I'm sure they'll be thrilled to get back to their own lives. Joe and Ann offered to take them back to Sarah's, and then we can take shifts here at the hospital so Sarah will always have someone near, but the kids won't have to spend their time here. I might be able to get Jasmine in, but Jordan's too young, and frankly, I'd rather Jasmine not see Sarah while she's in ICU. Seeing her on all those machines was kind of freaking *me* out."

"Same here. I'll be back as soon as I can."

She stood on her tiptoes and kissed me. "Be careful. No speeding tickets this time."

I wrapped my arms around her waist and grinned. "Cruise control all the way, baby. Did I ever tell you that I love you?"

"Not nearly often enough."

·····•◦◦•·····

I sat across from my parents' house on Topenga Avenue with my engine idling.

I had decided not to wait for the folks to decide when they were ready to talk about the ginormous elephant Aunt Eunice had unleashed into the room, and by showing up unannounced, they wouldn't be able to shuttle me off to voicemail or exercise any other means of avoidance—or so I thought. When I arrived, I was surprised to see that Dad's car wasn't under the carport. My first thought was that he must have had some sort of relapse, but before panic could fully take hold, I realized it didn't make sense that his car would be gone under those circumstances. Mom didn't drive; she had called Aunt Eunice when she needed transportation to the ER the previous evening. On a normal day, it wouldn't be unusual for Dad to be out and about, doing the things he usually does. Catching up with his buddies over coffee at the donut shop. Bowling a few games down at Sunset Lanes. But this didn't qualify as a normal day, and it seemed a little premature for him to be out so soon after his inexplicable cognitive episode.

Was it possible they were hiding from me? Okay, sure, it sounds a bit extreme, maybe even paranoid, but they knew I was going to be in town until Sarah's condition stabilized, and they knew me well enough to know I couldn't possibly leave this alone for long. I'm not exactly known for my patience. I was pondering if I should just use my house key to let myself in and wait them out when my phone rang. It was Mom.

"Are you just going to sit out there all day, or are you coming in?" She sounded exhausted.

"Um, yeah. I'm on my way."

I disconnected, and by the time I reached the front door, she was already standing there waiting. She looked as tired as she sounded, dark rings circling her eyes and tiny lines encroaching upon the corners of her mouth.

"Are you hungry?" she asked as she turned, passing through the front room and into the kitchen. She was sticking to a safe, familiar script. "There's some leftover Giovanni's in the fridge, or I could whip you up an egg sandwich if you'd rather."

"No, thanks. I'm fine."

"How's Sarah?" She opened the fridge and snagged the orange juice, carrying it to the counter beside the sink. She retrieved a couple of glasses from the cabinet above her head and filled them both, handing me one as if I hadn't just told her I was fine. She couldn't seem to meet my eyes.

"She's still in ICU," I said. "Melanie and I saw her briefly this morning, but she was sleeping. She's got a long, tough road ahead of her."

"*Mmm*," said Mom, nodding as she sipped her juice. "I'm sure."

"Where's Dad?"

"It's *Saturday*," she said. "Where do you think he is? Bowling, of course. One of the teams always needs a sub, and his favorite kind of bowling is when somebody else is paying for it. You know your father."

Did I? I took a drink of orange juice and let that one pass. "Do you really think he should be driving?"

Mom sighed, placing her glass on the counter. "I told you in my text that everything was fine. He's *fine*."

"*Mom*," I said dubiously. "Nothing about what happened last night is *fine*. You don't just suddenly forget your wife of over forty years and think she's some—some—" I couldn't say the words that were clamoring to escape my mouth. "What did the doctors say?"

"His blood sugar was low," she said, as if that should explain everything. "They said there was no reason to keep him overnight and that he was fine to come home, take it easy and get some extra rest. We're to follow up with

Dr. Daehler next week." Dr. Daehler was the same family physician who had brought me into this world. By my rough count, he must be well over a hundred by now.

"What part of 'take it easy and get some extra rest' includes bowling?" I asked. "What if he's out driving and—"

"*Stop it*," she said, finally focusing her eyes on me, and I nearly flinched at her tone. "If your father felt well enough to go, nothing I could say would ever stop him—you should know that. You know your father."

"*Stop saying that*," I said, surprised at the force in my own voice. "After Aunt Eunice dropped her little bombshell last night, I'm not sure I know either one of you. Dad was *married* before?"

Anger lit up my mom's face before she turned away, unable to hold my gaze. "I could just choke that old busybody. What on *Earth* would have possessed her to say that? I swear, that woman thrives on drama like no other."

"So, it's not true, then? He *wasn't* married before?"

She just stared through the small window above the sink, keeping her back to me as she quietly sipped her juice. It was all the answer I needed.

"Oh, my God, Mom! What else haven't you told us? Do we have any half-siblings running around out there that we should know about?"

She whirled around, her anger now focused on me. "Of course not! And don't you dare speak to me in that tone of voice. This isn't *my* secret. It's your father's."

"I'm gonna have to disagree with you on that point," I said. "You've been complicit all these years."

She laughed, and it was an ugly one. "Yes, that's exactly right. I've spent your entire life purposefully suppressing this vital piece of knowledge that means exactly nothing to you. It was over and done before you were even *born*. Where exactly do you get off thinking you're entitled to know every little thing there is to know about us? Your father has spent a lot of time putting this particular piece of history in his rearview mirror, and I don't see the point of dredging it all up now. It has absolutely nothing to do with you, and I'm not going to talk about it. If it really bothers you so badly, you're going to have to take it up with your father, but I'm not sure that now is the right time. I mean, not after last night…"

Oh no, she didn't!

My eyes narrowed as I gaped at her, reeling at the sheer gall. "Wait— first you're telling me that there's nothing to worry about. Dad's fine. It's just low blood sugar. Right? But now you're telling me I better not ask him about his previous wife because he might just be too weak to handle it. Which is it, Mom? You can't have it both ways."

She showed me her back again. "Do whatever you have to do. It's not my story to tell, and I promise you, it's not one your father wants to tell, either." And then she muttered something unintelligible, although I could've sworn she called Aunt Eunice something colorful I'd never heard her say before. It rhymed with 'shunt.' Her hands gripped her nearly empty glass of orange juice so tightly, I expected it to shatter at any given moment.

I sat my own glass down and left without saying another word. Nothing productive was going to come of this.

······•••●●○○●●●•••······

My drive north was uneventful. I followed my own advice and used cruise control to keep my speed strictly legal, especially through South Bloomfield. I could only afford to lose so many points before it had a negative impact on my insurance premium, which was already high enough. The noonday sun was high in a cloudless blue sky, and the temperature was nearly fifty degrees, which would have normally made for a very pleasant drive, but my mind was still churning from the events of the past several hours, and I was starting to find new things to worry about with this ever-evolving landscape, especially with regard to Rochelle Pendleton. I didn't think I could continue to provide the sort of attention her case required, and I really hoped that Doug would understand and take over. I had certainly been bending over backwards to give him all the time he needed while he worked through things with Lucy Graves. Surely, he would understand that family came first. Melanie and I had only just reconciled, and I wasn't about to abandon her now.

Reconciled.

That put a smile on my face. For once, I was actually looking forward to our next counseling session. We could politely tell Dr. Whittier thanks but no thanks—services no longer required. At least I hoped they wouldn't be. My smile faltered a bit. It would be just my luck for Melanie to insist we continue the sessions in order to avoid future missteps. I sighed. We would cross that bridge if and when we came to it. There were more pressing things to worry about, and I started making a mental checklist of the people I needed to call before I left town again.

I took westbound I-270 and passed all my normal exits, heading toward I-70 and Plain City. Dexter was hours past breakfast, and I hoped he hadn't decided to take out his displeasure on Rochelle's furniture. The possibility was more than feasible with each passing moment. There hasn't been a sofa built that can withstand his vengeful claws.

I didn't like the way I had left things with Mom. We rarely had words, and for her to just shut me out was a completely foreign concept. For her to refer me to Dad was equally unheard of. I get along just fine with both of my parents, but if I'm honest, I have a much more open discourse with my mother, not that she volunteers much of anything—*obviously*. It's just that I would feel more comfortable discussing something personal with her than Dad. Dad and I tend to stick to informational exchanges that never include feelings or junk like that. I couldn't even begin to imagine how I might approach this topic with him.

Rochelle's property was coming up quickly on my right, and as I slowed to make the turn into her private drive, I skidded to a stop. Two police cruisers were blocking the open gate, their light bars flashing ineffectually in the bright midday sun. A couple of stern-looking officers stood guard, the taller of the two approaching my car and signaling for me to lower my passenger window with a slow roll of his ebony hand.

"I'm going to need you to pull in and stop your engine, sir," he said, directing me to the space behind one of the cruisers.

I just stared at him, his words not quite penetrating. "What's going on? Is something wrong?"

His hand hovered above his holstered weapon. "Please just do as I say, sir." He nodded toward the space behind his cruiser, and this time I took the hint.

Once I had done as he asked, he said, "Please step out of the car and keep your hands where I can see them. Name?"

"Dwayne Morrow. Am I in some sort of trouble here?"

He ignored my question and took a step back, using his two-way radio to report my name and license plate to whoever was on the other end. The response he received was rapid and unintelligible to me, so I just stood there with my hands hanging at my sides, making sure to keep them in plain sight. His serious expression suggested my level of compliance should be nothing short of absolute.

"What brings you here today, Mr. Morrow?" he asked, studying me intently.

"I work for Boggs Investigations. My firm was retained by Ms. Pendleton to investigate a private matter, and I've been staying in her guest cottage during the assignment," I said, and curiosity was eating me alive. What in the hell was going on? "I'm actually here to get my cat. I had to leave town unexpectedly last night, and he hasn't been—"

The officer was already relaying the gist of my story through his radio. He didn't give two shits whether my cat had been fed or not. He received another burst of rapid-fire instruction, and he nodded, as if the person on the other end could get the visual cue. He turned his attention back to me.

"I'm going to need you to come with me, Mr. Morrow," he said, taking me by the arm and guiding me toward his patrol car. "Detective Burnside would like to have a word with you."

"Do I need a lawyer?" I asked as he deposited me in the back seat and shut the door, crossing over to his partner to bring him up to speed before sliding behind the wheel and starting his engine. He put the car in gear and nosed through the gate, easing forward along the winding drive, and slowing as he neared the guest cottage. He pulled in beside an unmarked SUV and an ambulance whose lights remained conspicuously darkened, its EMTs milling about outside waiting for some sort of direction.

This did not bode well.

The front door of the cottage stood wide open. I could see into the living room, where a couple of plainclothes detectives hovered over what appeared to be the body of a man sprawled just inside the door, the top of his head visible, even from a distance. I couldn't help but recognize his full head of wavy, steel-gray hair; I had seen it just the previous evening.

It was Senator Parker Ghant.

CHAPTER SEVENTEEN

It felt like hours that I sat by myself in the back of the cruiser as the officer who had put me there went to confer with one of the plainclothes detectives just outside the cottage. Another unmarked car arrived on the scene bringing two men I assumed were from the coroner's office, based on what they hauled inside. One of them began documenting the scene with an expensive-looking camera while the other knelt near what I presumed was Parker Ghant's corpse, lips moving rapidly as he recorded his observations into a handheld voice recorder. It was entirely surreal—a silent movie I hadn't paid to see, and despite the gravity of the situation, I couldn't keep my mind from worrying about Dexter. He was an indoor cat, and the front door had been standing open for Lord only knows how long. He might be somewhere inside, hiding from all the bustling activity, or he might be long gone, having taken his leave before the police ever showed up—I had no way of knowing and was helpless to do anything about it. As I suspected, I couldn't just let myself out of the back seat; it could only be opened from the outside, and the cop who brought me here didn't seem to be in any real hurry to return. I didn't even have my phone on me to call and alert anyone. I had left it in the passenger seat of my car when I had been—taken into custody? Was that what this was? It certainly felt like it. If Detective Burnside wanted a word with me, he was certainly taking his sweet time. I was getting a whopper of a headache from the tension building in my neck and shoulders.

Finally, my door popped open, and I found myself squinting up at the detective who had been conferring with the driver of my car. The sun shone just above his left shoulder, making it hard to see him clearly, but he presented as a middle-aged Harvey Keitel with a bit of a pot belly.

"Dwayne Morrow?" he asked.

"That's me," I said. "Is that Senator Ghant?"

He scowled, a little surprised by my directness. "I'm not at liberty to divulge that sort of information, Mr. Morrow. At least not until after we've notified the victim's family. I'm Detective Gabriel Burnside, and I was hoping we might have a little chat."

He extended a hand to help me out of the car as I continued to regard him curiously. "Is this the sort of chat I need a lawyer for?"

His smile didn't quite reach his eyes. "Do you think you need a lawyer?"

"Well, no," I said, not really sure whether I needed one or not. "I only just got back into town and was coming to collect my cat."

"I'm a little unclear on that," he said, consulting a notepad covered in slanted text. "Officer Larkin said you were working for Ms. Pendleton on behalf of some private investigation firm."

I nodded. "Yes, Boggs Investigations." I handed him one of my business cards.

He looked at it quickly before tucking it into a pocket. "Is it customary for you to bring your cat to a client's residence?"

"Not at all," I said, laughing nervously. "I was actually staying in the guest cottage for a few days due to a plumbing issue at my house. Rochelle—Ms. Pendleton insisted."

He quirked an eyebrow at my response. "Rochelle? Were you and Ms. Pendleton close?"

"*No!*" Good Lord, could my voice have gone any higher? "I mean, we really just met. I was here in a strictly professional capacity."

"*Hmmm,*" he said as he made another note on his pad. "Tell me a little bit about this 'professional capacity.'"

I shifted on my feet, hedging. "I'm really not comfortable discussing one of our active cases. I'll have to refer you to my boss, Doug Boggs."

He looked at me skeptically. "Mr. Morrow, this isn't attorney-client privilege we're talking about. I can always get a subpoena."

"I think I'll defer to the side of caution," I said, holding my ground if not his intensive gaze. "I'm not licensed yet and am only working as an apprentice."

He mulled that over just long enough to heighten my discomfort before changing tactics. "You said you were coming to collect your cat. Where exactly have you been?"

"In Lymont," I said. "I went to a friend's dinner party last night in Hilliard but got called away by a family emergency."

"Do you have anyone who can corroborate your whereabouts?"

I felt my first glimmer of relief. "Yes, of course. Brady Garrett and his girlfriend, Anyssa, were celebrating his recent employment with 10TV to cover the elections this fall. I'm sure there are plenty of people who—"

I stopped in my tracks, belatedly remembering my very public incident involving the Senator and his wife. While I had no reason to hide this information, I knew from experience that this was the sort of coincidence that police officers found a little too convenient, even if Detective Burnside hadn't yet acknowledged that it was the Senator's former mortal coil blocking the entrance to the cottage.

The detective was staring at me. "You were saying?"

"Just that lots of people saw me there. Brady and Doug were both there when I got the phone call about Sarah's heart attack—"

"Sarah?"

"Um, yeah—Sarah McGregor. She's my best friend's mom and is like a second mother to me. I left immediately to be with my girlfriend, Melanie, who also happens to be Sarah's former daughter-in-law and was already on her way to the hospital while Sarah was in surgery."

His eyes narrowed as he adopted an ugly smirk. "You're dating your best friend's ex-wife? Sounds like some reality TV circus. How does your buddy feel about all this?"

"I couldn't tell you. He's been dead for a while," I said, unable to keep the sarcasm out of my voice.

Like a fog lifting, enlightenment registered across the detective's face. "That's *right!* You're that IT guy who helped catch your buddy's murderer before almost getting himself killed by the Eviscerator last year. You've been a regular Jack-in-the-Box on the news here lately, popping up all over the place. Never know what you're going to step into next."

Well, that was certainly a novel way of describing my career trajectory, but hopefully it helped lend a little credence to what I was saying.

I nodded. "That's me. Listen, I know this isn't your top priority, but I'm really worried about my cat. Is there any way that I can see if I can find him?"

He shook his head. "No can do. No unauthorized personnel inside until the crime scene is cleared, and it's gonna be a while. I can tell my men to keep an eye out for you. I've got your card right here if we find him."

I didn't like that answer, but what could I do? I needed to get back to Lymont, but not without my cat. Maybe I could ask Rochelle to look around for him. "Are we done here?"

"Almost," he said, consulting his notepad. "You said you went to Mr. Garrett's party last night. About what time did you leave here?"

"I think I left around seven," I said. "You should be able to get the exact time Ms. Pendleton's security company. I used the code to get through the gate."

"When did you last see Ms. Pendleton?"

"Yesterday morning," I said, sticking to a selective truth that didn't include me racing up to the main house with my concerns about Ghant's signage being posted directly in front of the cottage's front door. "Around breakfast time. She was getting ready to head out to a friend's house to spend the weekend. I spoke to her briefly while I was at Brady's party, too. She said they were all settled in and watching some streaming television."

He raised his eyebrows. "A friend? Did you happen to catch a name?"

I sifted through my memory. "Laurie, maybe? I'm not sure. She did say it was somewhere out on Buckeye Lake. You can just ask her. Speaking of which, I'd like to call her to see if she can keep an eye out for Dexter when she gets back into town. That is, if your men can't find him before that. I really don't like the thought of going back to Lymont without having him in tow, and—"

"I'm afraid you won't be able to reach her," Burnside interrupted. "At least not for a little while."

"Why is that?"

"First, she's no longer 'out of town,' if she ever went out of town in the first place. She was in the main house when we arrived. Second, she's been taken into custody and is currently being questioned regarding the crime that's been committed here. Tell me, did you actually see her leave the premises?" His intense stare was back, white-hot as ever and boring a hole through me.

I blinked. *Did* I see her leave? I really couldn't say that I did. I had a few errands to run in the afternoon before I returned to start readying myself for Brady and Anyssa's soiree.

"No, I can't say that I did, but I spoke to her on the phone last night, and she said she was there." I felt an irrational urge to alibi Rochelle, even though I didn't have all the facts.

Detective Burnside scoffed. "Unless she was on a land line, she could have been *anywhere* when you spoke to her, Mr. Morrow. I'll ask Officer Larkin to take you back to your car. I understand that you're eager to get back to your family, but I want you to remain available in case I have any more questions."

"Of course," I said, nodding numbly. What in the hell was going on? Why would Rochelle be back a full day earlier than she had said? I just couldn't see her as a cold-blooded killer, but as I watched the team from the coroner's office cover the face of the yet-to-be-identified corpse, it removed any and all doubt that what we were dealing with was, in fact, murder.

·····•••◉◎•••••····

Officer Larkin dropped me off near my SUV at the gate without a single word. He wasn't much for small talk—or smiling, for that matter, but my mind was sufficiently overwhelmed, and I appreciated the silence. I had a whole lot of calls to make as soon as I was reunited with my phone.

On the way back to the gate, I scanned the expansive lawn for any sign at all of my cat. The panic of his potential escape hadn't fully set in, but I knew it wouldn't be long before it did. When I was a child, every single pet we had allowed to roam outside met a disastrous and untimely fate, and that was exactly why Dexter had been raised indoors. Sure, he darted out occasionally, but I had always been able to recover him quickly, and he had never been outside so far away from his home turf. Standing beside my vehicle, I couldn't quite make myself leave just yet, looking for reasons to extend my stay. I figured I may as well kill a little time by bringing Melanie up to speed. My round trip was clearly not going to be as quick as I had originally planned, and I didn't want to give her anything else to worry about.

She answered right away, sounding brighter than I had heard in some time. "Hey, you! Guess what? Sarah woke up the last time I was in her room. She wasn't up for long, but she definitely recognized me. Everyone says she's doing really well."

"That's great, Mel," I said, enthused by the news but not fully able to match her tone.

"You sound funny," she said. "Is everything alright?"

I sighed, pinching the bridge of my nose before launching into the events of the past hour or so. It sounded even more incredible on the replay, and it took long enough that I was starting to get a little side eye from Officer Larkin and his partner. What kind of person sticks around after being questioned in a homicide investigation? A guy who's lost his cat, that's who.

"Do you think that there's any possibility that Rochelle actually had something to do with this?" asked Melanie.

"My gut tells me no, but I can't for the life of me figure out why she would have come back early. She had told me she was staying with her friend for the weekend. I'd really like to hear what she has to say, but I'm not sure I'll even have the opportunity to talk to her. They've already taken her in for questioning."

"So, what are you going to do?"

"I don't know. I'll have to talk to Doug. I needed to call him anyway to pass the case back to him with all that's going on with Sarah, but this just makes it all so much more complicated. Plus, I don't know where Dexter is. The front door of the cottage was standing wide open, and I haven't seen him. For all I know, he could be hiding under a bed in there, but they won't let me inside the crime scene. Is it wrong that I'm most worried about my cat?" I asked, chewing my bottom lip and feeling guilty.

"That particular cat? Maybe," she said. "But no, I get it. You don't need to rush back here on my account. For now, things seem to be looking better for Sarah, and between Sarah's parents and me, we can manage the kids.

Jasmine actually *enjoys* watching after that little monkey, so all of the heavy lifting is pretty much covered. Find your cat. See if you can get in to see Rochelle. You might be her last, best hope. Lord knows if I was in her position, I wouldn't want you handing my case off to Doug."

"Are you *sure?* It feels like I'm abandoning you in your hour of need."

She laughed. "I appreciate the thought, but in case you hadn't noticed, I'm no longer a damsel in distress. You took care of that last night."

I could feel myself blushing as I grinned like a schoolboy. "Yeah, that was pretty amazing."

"I was talking about what you *said*, you horndog. Geez. What is *wrong* with you?" she asked, and even though I could hear the smile in her voice, my face flushed three shades deeper. "But honestly, what good would you even be? You'd be completely preoccupied with that missing little monster of yours. We'll see each other soon enough."

I nodded, relieved that she had uncomplicated things, if only a little. "Call me if anything changes. I can be there in a heartbeat—or so."

"I will," she said. "Otherwise, I'll talk to you later."

"I love you."

"Right back atcha, hero."

As we disconnected, my eye caught movement near my rear tire followed by a tiny little peep. I knelt down to peer underneath the frame of my car and couldn't believe my eyes. Dexter was crouched behind the tire, his emerald eyes practically glowing in the dim space.

"Dexter?" I called, reaching out a hand, and he responded with another peep, coming out to rub his little black face along my knuckle. I reached down and scooped him into my arms, relief flooding through me. "Oh, thank God."

He tucked in, his rusty chainsaw of a purr engaging immediately.

"You poor guy. Had yourself a little adventure, didn't ya? I don't suppose you happened to see who shot the nasty old Senator?"

215

From the look on his face, I suspected he did, but my feline-to-English translator was on the fritz.

"Ah, well. That's enough fun for one day. Let's get you home, huh?"

For once, he didn't complain as I put him into the car. Apparently, he'd had enough, too. I got behind the wheel and executed an awkward three-point turn, reversing course to head home. I had only traveled a short distance before a cherry-red Dodge rocketed by me, traveling in the opposite direction; based on its curly-haired driver, I had little doubt about its destination. I shielded my face in the hope that Brady would be too preoccupied to notice me as he passed. News about Senator Ghant's murder was about to hit the headlines, and it wouldn't be long before Brady intensified his inquisition about my differences with the late congressman.

It wasn't a conversation I looked forward to.

· · ·•••••◦─◯─◦•••••· · ·

I called Doug on my way home, and for once, he actually answered. I filled him in on the tumultuous events of the afternoon and listened to him chew on what I had to say as well as whatever he was eating for lunch. I don't know why I always seemed to catch him while he was feeding his gob.

"Well, I guess that solves that," he finally said. "Melanie had already called me to tell me she wouldn't be able to carry out her plan to infiltrate Ghant's office, what with everything going on with Mrs. McGregor. I guess our work is done here."

"What? How do you figure? If anything, our job may have gotten a little easier. I'm not sure that a non-disclosure agreement is still binding after one of the parties involved has died."

"Either way, we can't stay tangled up in this," he said. "Firstly, I don't really like the thought of Boggs Investigations being associated with a murderer—"

"*Suspected* murder," I interjected. "We don't even know what's going on yet."

"*Fine*," he conceded. "But what's more important—how's she going to pay?"

His sense of priorities stunned me speechless. I knew for a fact he must be out of Loretta's earshot, or she would be audibly chewing his ass in the background. Loretta had become invested in Rochelle's situation, and I was fairly confident she would back me up on this one.

"What's *more* important is we help Ms. Pendleton find a potential donor for her son," I said once I had recovered my voice. "We're talking about a little boy's *life* here, you moron."

"You know, I've had just about enough of your disrespect," he said, puffing up.

I wasn't having it. "Well, then stop saying moronic things! Are you telling me that you're ready to bail on a client without even knowing what's going on? That's not the sort of reputation you want for Boggs Investigations, is it? Remember that whole 'innocent until proven guilty' thing? We might want to give Ms. Pendleton the benefit of the doubt for at least a few days, but even then, I'm inclined to try and help her with her son. That little boy truly *is* innocent, and if we can do something to help save his life, I feel morally obligated to follow through. Don't you?"

He muttered something unintelligible, but he was having difficulty disputing my point without sounding like a complete and total ass. Finally, he said, "I'll take it under advisement. We'll talk about it more on Monday morning in our meeting. But in the meanwhile, don't do anything stupid."

"I wouldn't dream of it," I said before disconnecting the call.

As it turns out, stupid is a rather subjective term.

We had no sooner cleared the threshold of my front door when Dexter went all squirmy and squiggly in my arms, certain that his food dish in the kitchen must have miraculously refilled itself. When he realized it was empty, he looked at me like I had kicked him.

"Patience, little man," I said, setting my keys on one of my end tables as I snagged the television remote and turned the TV on. I switched it to channel 10 before proceeding into the kitchen to tend to my already yowling cat. You would think he hadn't eaten for weeks, judging from the complaints he was registering, and for the life of me, I can't understand why he thinks winding a perpetual figure eight around my ankles escalates the process of satisfying his craving—it most certainly doesn't. But after all our years together, it's a dance I've learned well, and soon enough, I was pulling the tab on a smelly concoction called 'Fisherman's Surprise!' to place before His Nibs. He dove right in, obnoxiously purring through his noisy mastication. Disgusting.

The sound of Brady's voice on the television caught my attention, and I backtracked to see what I was missing. It was weird to see his shiny red car parked in the very spot I had just vacated, behind the police cars blocking the entrance to Rochelle Pendleton's property.

"—again, folks, we have breaking news for you out of Plain City tonight. Senator Parker Ghant is dead. The senator's body was discovered in the guest cottage of the property you see behind me." Brady swept his arm toward the barricaded entrance to the apparent consternation of Officer Larkin and his partner. Their matching scowls spoke volumes, but technically, Brady and his cameraman weren't on the Pendleton property— they were a few feet in front of it. Sometimes technicalities make all the difference. "This is the residence of Rochelle Pendleton, a former Ghant campaign volunteer during the last election cycle. The police aren't releasing details on Ms. Pendleton's potential connection to the case, but sources indicate she has been taken into custody for questioning. We'll be updating this story as more information becomes available. For 10TV, I'm Brady Garrett."

The channel returned to its regularly scheduled college basketball, and within seconds, my phone rang in my pocket. I fished it out, fairly certain who I would see on the caller ID.

Brady Garrett.

Apparently, he *had* seen me leaving the scene. I knew it was likely. Brady's observational skills are part of what makes him a decent reporter, not that I would ever admit it to his face. I started to shuttle him off to voicemail but thought better of it. If he was sent to voicemail after only a ring or two, he would know I was purposefully avoiding him. I left it ringing on my dinette table as I trotted up the stairs. This had been an exhausting set of days, and I was still wearing the clothes I had worn to Brady's dinner party. I hadn't brushed my teeth and felt utterly gross. I thought a shower was just the thing I needed.

It wasn't until I screamed when the first ice cold blast of water hit my bare ass that I remembered why I was at Rochelle's guest cottage in the first place.

···•••••◦◯◦••••••···

I somehow managed to survive my shower and was busily toweling off when I heard someone pounding on my front door. I grumbled under my breath as I hurriedly threw on some clean clothes and rushed back down the stairs. I knew I wouldn't be able to evade Brady for long, but the number he was doing on my door was beyond excessive.

"Hey, would you knock it off?" I shouted, halfway through my living room. "I hear you, already!"

I glanced at my phone as I passed my dinette table, and saw five missed calls, all from Brady. I sighed. This wasn't going to be fun. I twisted the

219

deadbolt and threw the door open, ready to ream him for the unnecessary aggression when my voice died in my open mouth.

It wasn't Brady Garrett.

It was 'Mr. Green,' and he looked *pissed*.

CHAPTER EIGHTEEN

He tried to jam his foot in the doorframe, but I stomped his ankle with my bare heel. It would've been more gratifying had I been wearing shoes, but it did the job. He dropped a colorful expletive as he backed up, allowing me to step out onto the porch and pull the door shut behind me. I wasn't looking forward to a confrontation, but if one was going to happen, I wanted it to be right out in the open; I wasn't about to let him into my house. Of course, with my lack of visible neighbors, I wasn't sure it made all that much difference, but it was the principle of the thing. I sure wish I'd had the presence of mind to grab my phone.

"Back it up, *Kevin*," I said, watching his complexion mottle as I used his given name. "I don't recall inviting you inside."

He was back in my face in a second, practically bumping me with his chest. "We need to talk," he said through gritted teeth, all of the muscles bunching together along his square jawline.

"Then I suggest you get out of my face and take it down a notch, *Moody*," I said, leaving no doubt that I knew exactly who he really was. He flinched at the mention of his surname, the color along his cheekbones heightening, but he backed off just enough that I was no longer breathing in his exhaust. "What do you want?"

"This whole business with Rochelle Pendleton," he said. "It's *over*, capisce? I don't want to see you or anyone else from that Mickey Mouse outfit you work for anywhere *near* her, do you understand me?"

"Not entirely," I said, determined to stand my ground. "It seems to me that you've got more important things to worry about than Rochelle Pendleton. From what I've heard, you better be brushing up that résumé, buddy—"

His fist lashed out so quickly, I didn't have time to react. My vision erupted in a starry explosion as he connected with my cheek, knocking me back against my own front door. He followed that up with a couple of jackhammer blows to my midsection that dropped me to my hands and knees, gasping for breath. He crouched down to hover near my head, preventing me from finding my feet, even if I could have attempted to stand.

"Enough of your smartass commentary, fuckwad," he hissed into my ear. "Today, we lost ourselves a real American hero."

Now, you'd really think I'd learn to contain my snark at moments like these, wouldn't you? But no. I couldn't contain a short burst of laughter and surprised myself when I sputtered droplets of blood onto the floor of my porch. I had no idea what part of me was bleeding. "G.I. Joe is a real American hero."

I was rewarded with an elbow driven straight down between my shoulder blades, my face bouncing off the porch as my spine shrieked from the amateur hour chiropractic manipulation. He was back in my ear so fast I thought he must be squatting on my shoulders.

"That bitch is going to honor that non-disclosure agreement she willingly signed," he said, his breath hot on my neck while his words formed clouds around my head in the chilly February air. "Senator Ghant's sterling legacy will *not* be tarnished by some skanky campaign groupie who managed to catch the man's attention in one fleeting moment of weakness. Surely, even you can see that she was in this for another payout, but that's not going to happen. Me and my team will continue to ensure that the senator's family remains fully insulated from any and all slanderous allegations from Ms. Pendleton and anyone else like her. I'm here as a courtesy, Mr. Morrow. Consider yourself released from this case, and before you even think about opening that stupid mouth of yours, let me remind you—we know where you live. We know where your *parents* live. We know where that sweet piece of ass you're so heartsick over lives. Ah, yes—doesn't she have a little girl?"

I saw red. I scrambled to force him off me and got another elbow to the spine for my effort.

"It would be a real shame if bad things started happening to innocent people, wouldn't it? I'd think long and hard before divulging any details of what Ms. Pendleton shared with you or what you may have seen while you were on the estate. It isn't in the best interest of any of the people you hold dear."

With that, he grabbed a handful of my hair at the back of my head, pulling me up only to slam my face right back down onto the wooden deck. Another dazzling display of fireworks filled my head before fading to black.

"Holy shit, Dwayne—are you alright? What in the hell—?"

I could hear Brady's voice, but all I could see was a blinding light, and I wondered if my time on Earth was finally over. Was I about to see the infamous stairway to heaven? The hands persistently slapping at either side of my tender face suggested not.

"Knock it off, you tool," I slurred, hazy images beginning to take shape as outlined by the direct sunlight that was peering over the eaves of my covered porch. "Why would you slap someone with an obvious head injury? Are you *trying* to kill me?"

He stopped immediately, his face still a grayish void as he loomed over me. "Oh, my God—I wasn't thinking. Should I call an ambulance? You've got dried blood all over you, and your face is *jacked*."

I grunted, trying to hide from sunlight that was seemingly everywhere. "No, just help me up and onto the swing. I'll be fine." I hoped I wasn't lying. My ears were ringing, and my head throbbed in time with my heartbeat.

"What in the hell happened to you?" Brady asked, carefully helping me to a crouch before angling me sideways and onto the glider on my porch. I settled with another heartfelt grunt as my abdomen reminded me of its woes, too. At least with the sun out of my eyes, the world was slowly swimming back into focus.

"I don't suppose you'd believe I had an altercation with the mailman?"

Brady scowled at me. "Seriously, man. What's going on? Is this related to Senator Ghant's assassination? I saw you leaving the scene when I arrived, and—by the way, thanks for answering your fucking phone, although I guess if you had, I wouldn't be standing here right now."

I sighed, not really up for engaging in our typical banter. "I can't talk about it, Brady. I'm in the middle of a case that's blowing up all around me."

"So, I figured," he said. "I recognized all the signs, beginning with your presence. Why don't you save me the trouble of wearing you down and just work with me for once? Maybe we could help each other out. Let's start with what was going on between you and the senator at my party last night. You can't tell me that I was imagining all that tension."

And here we were, brushing up against all of the things I couldn't divulge even if I wanted to. Current events were hopelessly interlocked with my sister's ongoing situation, and I couldn't trust myself to partially fill in the blanks to a reporter who would smell my omissions just as surely as any predator can scent prey.

"I can't tell you *anything*, Brady," I said to his clear disappointment. "I need to discuss the current status of things with Doug, and I need to get my head on straight before I even do that. Can you just back off a little bit? Are you really calling it an assassination?"

"What else would it be?" he asked. "Senator Ghant was a well-known political figure, and he's been gunned down in a guest cottage where you were temporarily staying. It's only a matter of time before others get wind of that, and the media is going to be all over you. Why won't you just make it easier on yourself and talk to your old buddy, huh? I understand that they took Ms. Pendleton into custody. Any thoughts on why she might want to murder the man she used to campaign for?"

It wasn't easy, but I got to my feet—additional grunting was required. "You really don't take no for an answer, do you?"

He grinned, his pothole dimples on full display. "Of course not. Persistence is more than half of my charm."

"Well, in this case, I'm going to insist upon a raincheck," I said, edging toward my door. "I really do need to discuss this with Doug first. I'd love to talk to Rochelle and get her take on this, but I don't really know how to make it happen."

Brady's eyes lit up. "I can probably help you with that."

I was skeptical. "How so?"

"A guy doesn't get into my position without making a ton of connections," he said. "Let me ask around and find out who is representing her. If she's willing to talk to you, maybe her lawyer can set something up."

"Oh, shit," I said as a new worry took center stage. "Where's Joey?"

Brady's eyebrows knitted together. "Joey?"

My agitation amplified as my worry fully realized. "Rochelle's three-year-old son. The only other relative I know about is Rochelle's father, and he's got dementia. I don't know if there's anyone else to take care of him, and he's not well—"

225

"I'll find that out, too," Brady interjected, the picture of self-confidence, and I narrowed my eyes suspiciously.

"But not without a cost," I said, and the corners of Brady's mouth dipped as he shrugged.

"It's not unreasonable," he said. "I help you, and you help me—when you are able. Otherwise, I'm just gonna keep digging until I get to the bottom of things. I'm sure it would be a whole lot less painful if we just worked together on this."

He had me in a corner I knew all too well. "Fine," I said. "But hurry. I'm not going to be able to rest until I know where Joey is."

Brady nodded, heading toward the end of my porch. He stopped before descending the trio of stairs and turned around. "Are you sure you don't need to go to the hospital? I'd be happy to take you."

The noise in my head was starting to settle, so I carefully shook my head. "Thanks, but no. I'll be fine."

"All right," he said doubtfully. "If you think that's wise, but you better get inside and clean yourself up. You've got a little something—" He used his open hand in an overall sweeping motion to indicate every square inch of me before returning to his fancy new sportscar.

Yikes.

He wasn't kidding. I surveyed the damage in the mirror of my first-floor half-bath while Dexter passed silent judgment on me from behind. I suspected he had watched as I got my ass handed to me through the window overlooking the porch, and he was less than impressed. Whether it was my inability to defend myself or my general lack of common sense for engaging with someone who had tactical military training was up for grabs.

Dried blood trailed down from my nostrils in twin rivulets, surrounding my mouth and collecting on my chin resembling a Klingon beard. An acorn-sized knot was already rising on my left cheek, an uneasy mixture of yellow and green that was already turning purple and black and creeping towards my eye. I hoped it was my imagination, but my pupils looked a little dilated, and I just didn't have time for a concussion. I used a damp washcloth and soap and tidied up what would wipe away as I debated my next steps.

I should really call Doug. He was the captain of this ship, and I had an obligation to keep him apprised of any significant new developments in a case. It was the technicality I had hidden behind when putting Brady off, but honestly, it didn't feel like the right move. If Brady might be able to facilitate a face-to-face with Rochelle, I'd rather not give Doug any more reason to bail on her, and I was pretty sure that was exactly what he'd do. I'd rather see what Rochelle had to say about the matter first. While I found it difficult to picture her as a murderer, I was very curious about why she had cut her trip short and returned home early. She had seemed completely settled in when I spoke to her the previous evening. I was worried about Joey. I could easily imagine his utter confusion if he had been remanded into the care of Children's Services, and I could only hope the stress wouldn't adversely affect his health.

I debated calling Melanie while I changed out of my blood-spattered shirt.

My first instinct was to let her be. She already had enough to worry about between Sarah and the kids without me adding to the pile. I didn't want to be a burden, and I could always catch her up later, when things were a little more resolved. It seemed like the thoughtful and considerate thing to do.

Dexter continued to stare at me from behind, his eyes narrowed.

I turned around, returning his stare. *"What?"*

He cocked his head, and I swear to God, he scowled, his disappointment in me deepening. He uttered one mournful mew, and I suddenly got his point—loud and clear. I was on the cusp of making another of my famous executive decisions to selectively divulge information, and not even twenty-four hours after I had promised Melanie that I would stop doing it. I sighed, stooping to scritch Dexter behind his ears.

"Thanks, buddy," I said, pulling my phone from my pocket.

After several rings, Melanie answered. "Hullo—?" She sounded groggy.

"Hi—were you asleep?" I glanced at my watch, suddenly unsure of how much time I had lost on the porch and was surprised to see that it was almost five. It would be dark soon.

"It's fine," she said, stifling a yawn. "I was just dozing for a few minutes. I didn't exactly get much sleep last night. What's up? Did you find that awful cat of yours?"

"I did!" I said, grateful for a positive lead-in to the conversation. "He was hiding under my car. I think it was the sound of your voice over the phone that drew him out."

She snorted. "Highly unlikely. That cat hates me. Anything more on the Pendleton case?"

I took a deep breath and plunged into the tale of what had just happened. I kept expecting her to interrupt me, but she let me reach the end without interjecting anything. I told the story as concisely as possible without omitting any of the pertinent details. Admittedly, I *may* have downplayed the severity of Moody's attack, but I didn't omit it. Once I finished, silence seemed to stretch into oblivion. I was beginning to think the call had dropped when she finally said, "I want to see your face. I'll call you back on Messenger." And she disconnected.

Shit.

I was already exiting the harsh bathroom lighting when my phone buzzed in my hand. I dropped down onto one of my living room couches, keeping my face as much in shadow as possible with the setting sunset angling through the picture window behind me. I answered the call and aimed for casual nonchalance.

"Oh my God," she gasped.

"You should see the other guy." I trotted out that old chestnut, trying to grin but wincing instead.

"Did you call the police?"

I sighed. *"Mel.* You know I can't do that."

"Well, you can't just let this go! What happens when he comes back next time? He could kill you!"

"He caught me off guard," I said. "I thought it was Brady. I opened the door without checking. I won't make that mistake again." I didn't see the point in admitting I had egged him on by badmouthing his late boss. In hindsight, it probably wasn't my smartest move.

"He's, like, *special ops!* You can't *afford* to make another mistake like that!"

"I won't," I said. "I promise. I'll start carrying my gun if that will make you feel better."

"I think it might. At least you've been training with it."

I frowned. "As opposed to?"

It was her turn to sigh. "As hard as this may be for you to hear, Loretta is right. It's time this team got serious about self-defense. For a guy your size, you get your ass thoroughly kicked an awful lot—no offense intended."

"A little offense taken," I said defensively. "I think I get by okay."

"Dwayne—your right front tooth is an implant. You have a scar from a bullet hole in your shoulder. You—"

"Okay, okay," I interrupted. "You may have a point."

"I usually do," she said. "Now that I'm an official member of the Boggs team, I'm going to make it a top priority to work with Loretta and find us some suitable self-defense classes right away. I can't be worrying about you getting your pretty face busted up all the time."

I couldn't help but grin at the overly earnest expression on her face, even though it still hurt. "Fine."

"Will you at least go get yourself checked out?" she asked.

"Honestly, Mel, it looks a lot worse than it is. I'm fine."

"Sounds to me like you're slurring a bit."

I blinked. Was I?

"I don't think so," I said, focusing on my s. It sounded alright to me. "Of course, as I think you might have noticed, my face is a little swollen. That must be it."

She didn't look convinced, but she let it slide. "I talked to your mom this afternoon."

The change of subjects surprised me. "Where? Was she back at the hospital with Dad?"

"No, but I wanted to let her know I was thinking about them. She told me you stopped by on the way out of town. She said you had words and stormed off."

"I don't know if I would call it *storming off*, but yeah, I wanted some answers."

"Did you get any?"

I scoffed. "Nope. She refused to talk about it. Said I'd have to take it up with Dad, who, of all things, had gone bowling. *Bowling!* He should've been home in bed recuperating. What if he has another of his episodes while he's out driving?"

"Don't go looking for trouble. Your mom said he has a follow-up appointment for more testing next week, but he seemed to be back to his old self, and you know your dad. Short of hiding his car keys, no one's gonna keep him at home when he has places to be."

"I know. It's not going to stop me from worrying."

"Of course not," she said. "I'm worried, too. We'll just have to keep a close eye on things, and lucky for you, I'm in a position to do exactly that."

"Thank you," I said. "That does make me feel a little better. I don't suppose you asked about that whole 'first wife' thing, did you?"

"Oh, *hell* no! Your mother barely tolerates me as it is. I'm not getting anywhere *near* that mess."

I scowled at her. "My mom likes you. I don't know where you get that from."

She scowled right back. "Trust me—I'm a mother, too. We have an unspoken universal language. No matter how old you get, you will always be her baby, and she will always be willing to go all mama bear for you. I may never be good enough in her eyes."

"*Pffft.* You're imagining it."

"I'm not," she said. "And I'll tell you something else. I'm not imagining how upset she is that you two are fighting. You should call her and make peace."

"I'm not the one who's withholding information," I said.

"No, you're the one who's afraid to pose the question to the appropriate party. This is something you should be asking your dad, but you're doing an end run around him because you think it's easier to talk to your mom."

I didn't want to admit it, but Melanie was absolutely right. These weren't the sorts of conversations I had with my father. "Okay, maybe you've got a point there, but I don't want to ask him about it now. What if it upsets him and triggers another one of his episodes?"

"So, wait a little while. What's it going to hurt? You didn't know about this for thirty-five years. What's a few more days? But in the meanwhile, you shouldn't leave your mom twisting in the wind. None of this is her fault, and she's already got enough on her plate worrying about your dad. She doesn't need the added stress."

I slowly nodded. "Okay, fine. I get it. Are you, like, recording this conversation to play for her later so you can collect some extra points?"

"You bet your sweet ass, mister," she said, winking at me. "Every chance I get."

"I love you."

"You better. It ain't easy being seen with a guy whose face looks like yours," she said, and I laughed. Oh, how it hurt. "Seriously—keep yourself out of trouble. I want that gun on you at all times. You never know when you might need it."

"Yes, ma'am," I said, saluting my phone with my free hand. "I'll talk to you soon."

I stared at the cracked blank screen for only a second before bringing up the favorites in my contacts. I tapped on the icon with my mother's smiling face while I worked out an appropriate apology in my head.

·····●●●◦◯◦●●●·····

I have to admit, I felt a lot better after mending fences. Mom told me that Dad had returned from bowling, and nothing unusual had happened. She even passed the phone to him so I could hear for myself that he seemed like himself. He did. We chatted briefly about a little bit of nothing before he handed the phone back to Mom, and she was clearly relieved that I hadn't decided to launch into another interrogation over the phone. Melanie was absolutely correct. There was no reason my questions couldn't wait until we knew what was going on with him—if anything at all.

I went into my den and unlocked the drawer that held my gun. I dug out my inside-the-waistband holster and attached it to my jeans before loading my gun and stowing it in the holster just above my rear pocket. It was bulky and uncomfortable, and I felt a little like I was playing cowboy, but I had promised Melanie. I'm all about keeping promises.

My phone rang, and when I looked at the screen, I didn't recognize the number. There wasn't any Caller ID, but it didn't register as 'Potential Spam,' so I answered it.

"Hi—um, is this Dwayne Morrow?" The voice was timid and female, and not one I'd ever heard before.

"It is," I said. "And who am I speaking with?"

"You don't know me," she continued, and she was practically whispering. "My name is Lauren DeAngelo. I'm a friend of Rochelle's."

Lightbulbs went off in my head. "Yes! *Lauren*. You're Rochelle's friend from Buckeye Lake."

"Yes, well—I guess you might already know that Rochelle's in trouble. She was afraid something like this might happen. She left me your number and asked me to call you if something did. Would you be able to come out here? I'm really not comfortable talking about this over the phone."

"Of course. I'll need the address. When would you like to meet?"

"Would now be a good time?"

CHAPTER NINETEEN

I followed I-270 around the south side of Columbus as the sun began its nightly descent into the western horizon, dragging the temperature down with it. My head continued to throb at a low decibel, despite the trio of Excedrin I had tossed back prior to departing. At least the sun was in my rearview versus my eyes. Traffic was light as I exited onto I-70 east near Reynoldsburg, and I had only just gotten myself up to highway speed when my phone rang though my car's Bluetooth. Brady's cheeky grin smiled up at me from the center console.

"I'm already keeping my end of the bargain, buddy," he said. "I found out who was representing Ms. Pendleton, and he's agreed to meet you tomorrow morning at nine before he heads to church. His name is Leon Mirsky, and I'll text you all the details."

"That was awfully easy," I said, a little surprised. It hadn't even been two hours since Brady had found me beaten to a pulp on my front porch.

"I'd like to claim all the credit, but I was just lucky enough to get hold of him before he reached out to you himself. Apparently, this Rochelle chick thinks rather highly of you, and she had already asked Mirsky to contact you. Looks like she wants to keep your services retained."

"I don't suppose you were able to find out anything about Rochelle's son."

"Only that he's 'somewhere safe,' according to Mirsky. I don't know exactly what that means, but I'm pretty sure it's not Children's Services. It's a question you can ask tomorrow morning."

"Well, good. Thank you."

My sense of relief was short-lived as my eyes kept drifting to a pair of headlights riding awfully close to my rear bumper. The glare of the sunset made it impossible to see through the vehicle's windshield, but my imagination was doing its best to place Kevin Moody behind the wheel.

"Sounds like you're driving," Brady casually noted. "Where are you off to?"

"Burger King," I lied. "Is that alright with you?"

"Oh, yeah, sure. I just thought you might be headed to the ER to get yourself checked out. That guy really did a number on you. I've been worried."

I scoffed. "Uh-huh."

"I am! I'm counting on you for some inside scoop here, and—well, time is kind of critical. I really can't afford for you to lapse into a coma from some untreated head injury or something."

"Nice."

"Well, you know—maybe you shouldn't be driving so soon after. Hey! Here's a thought—why don't I pick you up tomorrow morning? I could safely transport you to your appointment with Ms. Pendleton's lawyer. Maybe I could even sit in?"

"Goodbye, Brady," I said, disconnecting the call as he persisted in pleading his case. What an ass!

The headlights behind me were really beginning to bug me. I tried slowing down in hopes that the other driver might pass, but the car only adjusted its speed, clinging to my backside. Adrenaline was starting to work through my veins, intensifying the throbbing in my head and wreaking havoc on my nerves. The exit for State Route 310 was quickly approaching

235

on my right, and I whipped onto the ramp at the last moment, my eyes flickering to my rearview mirror as I cut my speed.

The headlights followed me right up the ramp.

Shit.

My heart stuttered in my chest as I considered my options. Left and across the overpass was a handful of fast-food restaurants I couldn't quite see. At this time on a Saturday evening, they were likely to be a decent number of eyewitnesses, but there was no guarantee. Visible to my right was a bustling Love's Travel Stop. My gun pressed uncomfortably against my right glute, and while it did provide some level of reassurance, the thought of actually using it on another human being filled my stomach with acid. I had shot someone in self-defense once before, and despite the justification, it wasn't something I would ever take lightly.

I decided that if someone was going to come after me again, it was going to be in front of as many witnesses as I could find, and I turned my wheel to the right, heading for the busy gas station. My tail stuck tight. Fortunately, traffic was light because my steering was getting sloppy as my attention was evenly split between both ends of my car. I wobbled over the center line before correcting course and gunning my engine to extend my lead, abruptly cutting my wheel hard to the left and bottoming out my suspension as I bumped into the travel stop's parking lot. Just as soon as I was under the bright lights of the canopy, I slammed my gearshift into park and nearly tumbled out of the driver's seat, getting caught up in the seatbelt. I landed in a crouch, my hand finding security in the handle of the gun I had concealed at the small of my back.

I whipped around and stood, as ready as I ever would be for a potentially deadly confrontation, and watched as the other car, a bright yellow Kia Soul, rolled right on by without even slowing down. Giddy laughter bubbled up from my throat as my anxiety lifted, and it was only then that I realized I had attracted the attention of quite a few travelers, all of whom were openly staring at me. They had just witnessed a crazy guy with a jacked-up face perform a one-man act of paranoid delusion, and judging from the collective looks on their faces, they were fearful of an Act Two. It only made me giggle more. I held my hands up in surrender.

"Sorry about that, folks," I said. "False alarm. You can go about your business, and I'll just be on my way."

I ducked back into my car and hightailed it back to the interstate. With a crowd that size, someone had surely already called the police.

...........⌒⌒...........

Buckeye Lake is a 3,100-acre body of water about thirty miles east of Columbus. It straddles three counties, Fairfield, Licking, and Perry and is a popular vacation destination during the warmer months. Every fall, the Buckeye Lake Area Civic Association hosts an Annual Tour of Homes, affording folks an approximately two-hour opportunity to vicariously experience life on the lake, with homes ranging from modestly upscale to ridiculously opulent. In February, the population ebbs to its lowest point, with many of the homeowners snowbirding to Florida to ride out Ohio's fickle and occasionally brutal winters.

Some of the more densely populated areas surrounding the lake include the village of Buckeye Lake along its northern coast and Millersport and Fairfield Beach to the south. The address Lauren had given me was in none of the above. It was somewhere along a desolate stretch of road just outside Fairfield Beach, and by the time I had reached the turnoff along Shell Beach Road, the sun had completed its nightly descent, the moon quite full in a cloudless, starry sky. I was close enough to the water that I could smell it through the heated air circulating through my vents. My head still throbbed dully, but I was considerably more relaxed after losing my imaginary tail on the interstate. Traffic had been negligible since entering the lake area, my rearview mirror completely clear for the last several miles.

When the vapid female voice of GPS instructed me to take my next left turn, I had to slow to a crawl to find it, the road little more than an overgrown nick in the weeds leading through dense foliage encroaching on both sides. Random branches ran their fingernails along the sides of my SUV as I slowly passed through, and I sighed, wondering my odds of escaping damage to my car's clearcoat finish. It certainly didn't sound good.

Just as I wondered if I would ever reach my destination, the woods opened up, and I drove out onto a short, sandy beach. A small, silver sedan was parked near an ancient wooden slip that ran alongside a modest little houseboat floating in the lake. The slip was badly in need of repair, and the houseboat didn't exactly look showroom new, either, but it was the only residence in sight, so when Lady Google announced I had arrived at my destination, I took her at her artificially intelligent word.

As I approached the dock, a light flicked on next to the houseboat's entrance, casting a paltry amount of illumination that didn't even begin to compete with the moon's luminescence, but I was very grateful for it. Up close, the deck was in worse shape than it appeared from a distance, several of its planks loose or missing altogether. I watched my step as I crossed to the open door where a young woman approximately Rochelle's age waited, hugging herself tightly against the chilly lake air.

"Mr. Morrow?" she called, brushing her sandy bangs from her eyes as she squinted in my direction.

"That's me," I said, bridging the distance and offering a hand. "And you must be Lauren."

She nodded and flinched as I stepped close enough for the entry light to reveal my battered face. "Oh, my *God!* What happened to you?"

I sighed, already weary of explaining my sorry condition. My hand hung untouched in the air, as if I were contagious. "I just had a little run-in with someone earlier. It looks worse than it is."

She smiled nervously as she finally took my hand for a brief shake. She stepped back to allow me to slip past her and into her compact living space. The ceiling was low, and I felt like I'd need to watch out or risk knocking myself in the head yet again.

"*Dane!*"

My eyes followed the exultant and familiar cry, and relief flooded through me as I spotted Joey Pendleton standing in the corner, his eyes bright, his sweet little face smiling wide. He raced over and hugged my legs, nearly bowling me over as I was unprepared for quite that level of enthusiasm. I stooped and awkwardly returned his embrace. Another little dark-haired boy with big doe eyes observed from the corner, playing with building blocks and looking a little pissed that I had co-opted his playmate.

"Looks like you've got a friend," said Lauren, observing us with a smile. Seeing Joey's reaction seemed to relax her, if only a little. She was still wary, peering through the middle of three narrow ribbons of glass in her exterior door after she closed it and engaged its deadbolt.

"Are you expecting someone else?" I asked, as I nudged Joey back toward his friend and stood.

"No—why? Did someone follow you?" Worry lines creased her forehead, and she continued to hug her elbows against her midriff.

I no longer believed it was from the chill in the air, and I didn't have the heart to tell her the door was far too flimsy to provide any real protection if someone was determined to get inside.

An icy finger of dread trailed up my spine as I flashed back to a night not so very long ago in Lymont. I was conducting my first amateur-hour investigation, delving into my best friend's murder when I found myself in a secluded trailer out on Turner's Ridge on a night not unlike this one—the only thing missing was a raging thunderstorm. Before the evening was over, a young mother lay bleeding out on her own floor as an armed psychopath closed in, determined to stop my investigation before it ever got started. I had somehow retained the presence of mind to get her infant son and myself through a narrow bedroom window and escape. Tonight, it wasn't a maneuver I thought I could repeat—not with *two* little boys and a house that was surrounded on three sides by frigid lake water.

"No. Is that something I need to worry about?" I asked, my voice a little high in my own ears. I didn't think it would be prudent to share my earlier paranoid escapade at the travel stop. She seemed ready to vibrate out of her skin as it was.

Her uneasy titter did little to assuage my escalating nerves. She worked at the creases in her forehead with a shaky hand. "No, I suppose not. I've just been on edge ever since Rochelle took out of here last night, and then everything just went to—" She glanced at the boys before whisper-spelling, "—S-H-I-T. Come on in and sit down." She waved to a small, mud-brown sectional lining the dark-paneled walls across from the boys. "Would you like something to drink? I've got some RC, Diet Coke, Barq's red pop…?"

In the back of my mind, I could see my father genuflecting as he crossed himself against the unholy trinity, none of which was produced by Pepsi—his former employer and current pension provider.

"I'd love some water," I said. "I don't suppose you have any Excedrin, do you?"

"Um—maybe," she said, entering the small galley kitchen behind her and rummaging through the cupboards for a glass. "Looks worse than it is, huh?"

I tried to grin, but it only hurt my face. "Yeah, well…"

She brought me a glass of ice water and offered me a pill bottle. "All I have is ibuprofen. Will that work?"

I was already working at the child-resistant cap. "Thank you." I shook three out of the bottle before remembering I had already taken the same amount of Excedrin only an hour before. After taking into consideration my weight, height, and level of discomfort, I cut back to two, figuring it wouldn't kill me. I swallowed them both with a gulp of water. "So, tell me why I'm here, Ms. DeAngelo."

She paced the small area with a nervous energy that almost made me dizzy, her handwringing compulsive. "Please," she said. "It's just Lauren. I, uh—I'm not really sure where to begin. This just all seems so surreal. I can't believe he's *gone*. I, uh—"

And with that she folded into herself, her shoulders hitching as a tidal wave of tears overtook her. She shielded her face with one hand, turning away from the children and making every effort to contain the sounds of her grief. I stood and approached her cautiously, wanting to console her but unsure of what to do. She was drawn to me like a magnet, crumpling against me as I awkwardly put an arm around her, patting her shoulders. It only lasted a few seconds before she pulled away, wiping away tears and turning aside.

"I'm so sorry," she said, sniffling and unable to meet my eyes. "It's just all been a lot to process. I think I may be in shock. What does shock even feel like? I don't know—"

"It's okay," I said, aiming for a tone that was soothing. The boys had resumed playing with their building blocks and seemed oblivious to Lauren's distress. "Why don't we just sit and talk, alright? I just want to help however I can."

She nodded and crossed to the shorter section of the sectional, perching on its edge like a bird that could take flight at any moment, her emotions raw and barely below the surface. She was upset and scattered, and if left up to her, it might take hours to finally uncover her reasons for calling me out to her boathouse. It felt like a little gentle probing was in order.

241

"You said you couldn't believe he was gone," I said. "He who?"

Her eyes flicked in my direction briefly before settling back on her wringing hands. "Parker."

I was surprised. "You knew Senator Ghant, too? I guess I was under the impression that you and Rochelle were old friends, maybe from high school or college or something."

Her laugh was ironic. "Oh, no. We met back when we both volunteered for Parker's campaign, and if you'd suggested then that we'd ever be friends, I would have laughed in your face."

"And why is that?"

She shrugged, smiling at a private recollection she wasn't inclined to share. "Parker."

"I don't understand."

"I don't expect you would, even if you had the pleasure of meeting him."

It was my turn to chuckle. "Oh, I met him, alright. He and his wife were at a party I attended last night."

"Cassandra." Lauren's face soured as she said Mrs. Ghant's name.

"I take it you don't like her?"

She shrugged again, her bitter expression fading. "I didn't really know her that well. I didn't really *want* to. She would breeze in and out of campaign headquarters occasionally. Treated most of us like we weren't quite the same species. It doesn't exactly inspire congeniality."

"So, why didn't you think that you and Rochelle would be friends?" I asked. "Admittedly, I only recently met her, but she seems nice enough."

"Oh, she is!" Lauren was quick to confirm. "It wasn't her fault at all—it was all mine. I was just being stupid and naïve."

"How so?"

She looked up from her hands, smiling sheepishly. "Parker."

I was sensing a pattern here. I gave her time to compose her thoughts, not wanting to seem overly intrusive. It still felt like she could bolt from the

242

room at any second. Finally, she cleared her throat, still only able to fleetingly meet my eyes.

"You may recall, it was a special election when Parker was elected to the Senate. Senator Rhodes had lost her battle with pancreatic cancer, and he campaigned to replace her."

I nodded, aware of the events but not in any real detail. I've never been overly political, although current events had me rethinking my position. You don't really have much room to complain about how the government is run if you don't participate in the process of electing its officials. It's a freedom that is anything but universal, with some countries operating under the iron grip of dictators and mercenaries. It was something I'd largely taken for granted as an American citizen, and it was beginning to feel like a dereliction of duty.

"I started volunteering time to Parker's campaign in the early spring, a couple of months before Rochelle did. I had attended a couple of his earlier rallies and was just completely taken by his confidence. He championed the same causes I did and didn't seem to reek of the utter BS that most politicians do. He was charming, charismatic, and captivating, and the thought of working alongside him was—well, *empowering*. I was working retail at the time, and you can only fold so many sweaters before it starts to feel like you're wasting your life, you know? I didn't really expect he'd even notice me, so you can imagine my surprise when he started going out of his way to bring me coffee—or to just chat for a few moments. What could a girl like me have in common with a man like Parker?"

It didn't take a genius to figure out where this was going. "You fell in love with him."

Her cheeks flushed bright red, and she nodded. "I really couldn't help myself. Every time I told myself it was all in my imagination, he would do something sweet—something just for *me*. I started looking for excuses to get closer to him, and he seemed genuinely pleased. I had worked for the campaign for about a month when he asked me to go away for the weekend. I couldn't believe my ears. Why would a man like Parker want anything to do with a girl like me? I mean, I'm nothing special. He could have had his pick of *anyone*."

"Anyone other than his wife, apparently," I said, unable to contain my sarcasm. I never understood the mindset of guys like Ghant, but then again, women aren't prone to swoon at the mere sight of me. I didn't think it would matter if they did. I'm just not wired that way. This guy was nothing short of a predator, protecting his public persona while racking up private conquests like he was on a mission. Maybe he was.

"I could point out that Parker's relationship with Cassandra had been over for years, but that only makes me look even more sad and pathetic," Lauren said, and she was focused on knitting her fingers together again, clearly embarrassed.

I took a moment to evaluate her honestly. No, she wasn't the sort to turn heads, but it wasn't like she was hideous. Her sandy, shoulder length hair was sort of shapeless, her thin features a little sharp, but her most unattractive trait by far was her utter lack of self-confidence. She practically vibrated like a human chihuahua, and it was enervating.

"He took advantage of you," I finally settled on, not wishing to offer any reassurance that might be misconstrued.

She snorted. "Don't you think I *know* that? Or at least I do now. So *stupid*." Her knuckles were bone white from clenching her hands together. "I admit, I was slow to catch on—desperate, actually, to remain blissfully in the dark, but once Rochelle came aboard, I was forced to face the facts."

"Ghant shifted his attention to the new girl," I said, and she nodded, wiping away tears that threatened to spill.

"Yes," she said. "And I hated her for it, although it wasn't hard to understand her appeal. With her high cheekbones and perfect figure, she practically made me look like a boy by comparison. She was vivacious and funny, and her family had money. I'm sure they probably traveled in some of the same social circles as the Ghants. Rochelle caught his eye the moment she walked in, and he never looked back. I mean, why would he? On top of everything else, she was initially oblivious to what was happening. Suddenly, I couldn't even get a private conversation with Parker anymore. His security guys always ran interference, and I was helpless as I watched Rochelle fill a role that had *almost been mine*. I was so awful to her. I'm ashamed to say that if something horrible had happened to her, I would have probably celebrated." The muscles in her jaw tightened, the wound still fresh even after all these years.

"But something must have changed," I said. "Rochelle called you her friend, and I can't imagine she would have left her son with someone who wasn't."

She nodded. "It took me quite a while to come to my senses and face facts I didn't want to believe were true, but eventually I got there. I had left the campaign by then. It was just too difficult to watch Parker using the same lines on Rochelle that I had lapped up like the pathetic, attention-starved idiot that I was."

"You're being too hard on yourself," I said. "As I said before, he took advantage of you. He knew what he was doing."

"Doesn't make me feel any less stupid," she said, and there wasn't anything I could say to counter that.

"So, how did you and Rochelle eventually become friends?" I asked.

Her smile was wistful as she snuck a glance in my direction. "It helps when you have something in common."

Raised little voices interrupted our conversation as the boys erupted into a spat over a particular building block that both felt entitled to. Lauren was on her feet in an instant, seizing the source of their trouble. "That's enough, guys. If you can't share the block, then I'll just have to remove it from contention."

They were equally dumbfounded as they stared at her, stunned that she had taken their prized possession. *Something in common.* Lauren's earlier words echoed in my head as I suddenly noticed the similarities between the boys' features.

"Oh my God," I said. "The other little boy is Parker's too."

CHAPTER TWENTY

"His name is Simon," she said, picking up the dark-haired boy and bringing him close.

"Well, hi there, little guy," I said, offering him a hand. He just stared at it dubiously, his bottom lip glistening with drool that was about to runneth over. I pulled my hand back by reflex, hoping it didn't present as the absolute recoil that it absolutely was.

"I found out I was pregnant about a month after Rochelle started with the campaign. I tried to tell Parker, but by then, I couldn't even get through to see him. I resented Rochelle *so much* for taking him away from me. I was stunned when Parker's attorney reached out to me with a non-disclosure agreement and six-figure settlement amount. I wasn't even showing yet. I don't know how they found out I was pregnant."

She carried her son back to the corner where Joey waited patiently and sat him beside his half-brother. They resumed playing, their dispute already forgotten. Some detective I was—I couldn't believe I hadn't noticed the striking resemblance between the two until now.

"So, you took the settlement and signed the agreement?" I asked.

"Of course, I took it!" she said, looking at me like I was absolutely nuts. "I was about to become a single, unwed mother at the ripe old age of twenty-three. I was abandoned by an alcoholic mother when I was thirteen and aged out of the foster care system at eighteen. I had no skills and was

247

living paycheck to paycheck in a one-room apartment on the east side of town. What else was I going to do?"

"I'm sorry, I don't mean to upset you."

She shook her head and looked away, tears collecting in her eyes. "It's okay. You didn't. I just feel so *stupid*—"

"You are *way* too hard on yourself," I said. "It sounds to me like Parker Ghant had a real pattern of taking advantage of his volunteers. You were used by someone who made a habit of preying on vulnerable young women just like yourself."

She smiled at me sadly as she sat back down on the sofa's edge. "But that's just it. I *wasn't* a vulnerable young woman, or at least I didn't think I was. I watched my mother get used and abused my whole life, falling for one idiot loser after another and always believing whatever lies the latest one fed her. I swore I'd never be like her—I was *smarter* than that. I can't believe I fell into another version of the same old trap. I'm just so disappointed in myself."

The tears began to flow again, and there was no stopping them this time. I couldn't think of any words to ease her self-judgment, and I certainly didn't know her well enough to suggest counseling. What kind of hypocrite would I have been to make *that* recommendation after dragging my feet when Melanie had suggested couples counseling? Silence was my only option, and I waited patiently for her to get herself back in check, and after a few long moments, she did.

"Of course, part of the NDA required me to leave Parker's campaign and keep a clear distance from him at all times. I'll never forget the day I packed up my belongings from my desk. One of his square-headed security baboons stood over me while I loaded up a couple of bankers boxes—like I was going to steal office supplies or something—and escorted me to my car without a single word. As we were headed for the door, Parker was across the room perched on the corner of Rochelle's desk, and they were just laughing their backsides off. I'm sure it was completely innocuous, but in that moment, it felt like they were laughing directly at me. Then, for just the briefest second, he looked at me, and I suddenly saw him for exactly what he was." Her face clouded over with anger as the recollection replayed in her mind. "Part of me wanted to kill him right then and there, but I let myself be led off premises quietly, too embarrassed to make a scene. I never was much of one for confrontation. I decided to put the whole thing in my rearview mirror and never look back."

"Deciding to raise your son by yourself must have been a difficult decision," I said.

When Lauren looked at her son and smiled, her whole face lit up. "Not at all. Easiest decision I ever made, actually. With the hush money Parker gave me, I bought this old houseboat and relocated far enough away from the city that I didn't have to face any of the people I knew. It was a chance to start over, and I was determined to be a better mother to my son than my mother ever was to me. It's kind of ironic that we ended up here, you know? It's one of the few good memories I have from my childhood. Mom had actually managed to land a decent guy for a few months when I was maybe seven. His name was Bill Thackery—he always reminded me of Kenny Rogers. He had a summer house here, and we stayed with him for a little while. I fell in love with the lake and actually made some friends who I really loved, but like everything else with my mother, it didn't last for long. She loved her vodka more than anything else." Her smile faded along with the memory.

"I'm sorry," I said. "Sounds horrible." And there I was, offering up my 'A' game in inane sympathetic blather, despite my utter sincerity. I felt a renewed sense of guilt for the recent fight I had picked with my own mother. Regardless of whatever lurked in my father's past, my siblings and I had grown up in an environment that was safe and stable. It's easy to forget that others' experiences vary—sometimes greatly.

She shrugged it off, never really looking for my pity. "I knew that if I was careful with what was left of the money, I wouldn't have to return to work for a while, and I used the opportunity to get myself an actual skill set. I started classes at Columbus State to become a dental hygienist, taking as many classes online as I could. For the first time in my life, I actually started to feel in control of things, you know? I didn't need Parker's help to raise my son—I didn't want it. Let him move on to Rochelle or whoever else might catch his eye. Screw him. I didn't think I'd ever see any of those people ever again."

I glanced at the boys as they erupted into giggles over something they found mutually amusing. "It seems that you did."

"I couldn't believe it when Rochelle showed up at my door," said Lauren. "Clearly, she was pregnant, and by then, Parker had pulled the same routine with her. I couldn't for the life of me imagine why she had come looking for me. I'm still embarrassed at the way I treated her during the brief period we worked together, but there she was, looking for a kindred spirit to commiserate with."

"I'm a little surprised," I said. "Wasn't that a violation of the non-disclosure agreement you both signed?"

"Sure, but who was going to tell? Certainly not me. Simon was all of four months, and as independent as I'd like to believe I was, it was nice to have another adult to talk to. Rochelle didn't seem to harbor any ill will towards me, and for Simon, it was love at first sight. It never mattered that we have such different backgrounds. As ridiculous as it sounds, our common bond was Parker Ghant, and it only grew stronger after Joey was born. Rochelle and I are both only children, but our sons are half-brothers. They deserve the opportunity to know one another, and at this point, Rochelle is like the sister I never had. It's crazy how things work out sometimes, isn't it?"

"Did she know you were pregnant when you left the campaign?" I asked.

Lauren shook her head. "No one did. She was just brokenhearted over being dumped and felt guilty about being the one who had caused me the same sort of pain, even though she didn't realize it at the time. She came to apologize, if you can imagine that. She's very sweet that way. I never once thought about looking her up to apologize for being a complete—" Once again, her eyes skipped to the boys. "—B-I-T-C-H to her when we were working together. She was as surprised to learn that I had just given birth to Parker's child as I was to see that she was only a few months behind me along that very same path. Like it or not, our futures were irrevocably linked, and I literally thank God for that every single day. We've navigated the ups and downs of single motherhood together, and there have been times I don't know what I would have done without her, and I'm sure she feels the same. Especially after Joey started getting sick."

A light bulb flickered through the dull throb of my headache, and I sat up straighter. "Wait a minute. Since your son and Joey are half-brothers, couldn't Simon be a potential donor match?"

Her smile was sad. "That was our very first thought. No such luck."

I took a sip from my water glass as we spent a moment in awkward silence. As enlightening as our conversation had been, it couldn't be the reason why Rochelle had asked Lauren to contact me. I wanted to nudge her to the point, and subtlety was never my strong suit. Also, I wasn't sure exactly how much about Rochelle's case I could divulge to a woman I had only just met. At what point would I be betraying my client's confidence? I wished I had a better handle on the rules that govern this whole investigatory process, but so far, my training had been lacking at best. I opted for a line of inquiry that felt safe.

"Did Rochelle explain to you why she retained our services?" I asked.

"Well, not specifically your firm, but I knew that she was trying to hire someone who could get through to Parker without making a lot of waves." The corners of her mouth crept down as the lines in her forehead tightened.

"You don't look happy about that."

"I wasn't. I thought it was a bad idea, and I told her so. When people like Parker Ghant want you out of their lives, they have ways of making it happen."

"Did Ghant threaten you?"

"Only with the penalties for violating the NDA, but with Parker's political career on the rise, news of his rampant infidelity could seriously derail his momentum. It doesn't take a whole lot of imagination to picture one of his security gorillas running damage control proactively, and I wouldn't want to be on the receiving end of *that*. Have you seen them?"

I nodded, resisting the urge to inspect the severity of swelling in my cheek with my fingertips and instead focused on the boys playing in the corner. Their energy seemed to be flagging and so was mine. "I have. But what would you have done if the roles were reversed? What if it was Simon who needed a donor?"

"Me? I would've gone straight to the press," she said without hesitation. Clearly, she had given the matter some thought. "I would have called up that cute Brady Garrett guy and given him the exclusive of a lifetime. Why would you give a guy like Parker Ghant a heads up? He wasn't concerned with what happened to us. Why should we be concerned with what happens to him? It just feels—*safer* if everything is out in the open."

"You really *are* intimidated by his security guys. What about the NDA?"

"I'd give it all back," she said, her eyes finally landing on mine. "If my son's health was at stake, there isn't a thing I wouldn't do to help him. None of this means anything without him. I've started over once, I could surely do it again."

"But Rochelle didn't share your concerns," I said.

She shook her head. "No. She made peace with the idea that there wasn't a future for her and Parker, and she even acknowledged that he was a chronic womanizer who would never change his stripes, but she couldn't believe that he wouldn't do the right thing for Joey if only he knew about it. Even as she struggled to find a detective agency that would take her case, she refused to believe that Parker was personally involved with any of the interference. She honestly thinks it's just his people circling the wagons to protect his image."

Of course she did. She was still in love with the man. She had nearly admitted as much to me earlier. Love can make you believe almost anything.

"You seem a lot more realistic on the topic, but you were still in tears earlier. Are you sure you're completely over him?" I asked, earning a reproachful glare.

"Of course I am," she said. "I have been for *years*. Doesn't mean I wanted the man dead. What kind of monster do you think I am?"

I held my hands up apologetically. "I'm sorry, that came out wrong. I'm just trying to understand the mindset."

"I wouldn't expect you to unless you were gay, and believe me, he's very popular with the gays."

My smile was tight. So nicely put, although I didn't detect any malice in her tone-deaf labeling. I'd certainly heard worse. I still couldn't imagine she had called me all the way out here just to tell me this. My headache was worsening again, and I just wanted to go to bed. I decided it was time to cut to the chase. "What was so important that you couldn't tell me over the phone?"

"Oh—of course," she said, looking sheepish. "Before she left last night, Rochelle asked me to contact you if anything weird happened, although I doubt what's happening now is the sort of weird she had in mind."

I blinked. "Contact *me?* I don't understand. I mean, what prompted her to leave? I thought she and Joey were spending the weekend here."

"That was the plan," said Lauren. "The boys had fallen asleep for the night, and we were barely into the second *Magic Mike* movie when she got a text, and suddenly she had to go."

"Did she say who it was from?"

"Huh-unh."

"Did she say where she was going?"

"No, she just asked me if I could keep Joey with me while she was gone," said Lauren. "She said she'd call me if she would be any later than morning getting back."

"Did she seem upset? Scared?"

Lauren shook her head and stood, crossing to the tiny kitchen. She grabbed an oversized canvas purse from where it rested beside the microwave and carried it back into the living room. "Quite the opposite, actually. She was sort of excited. Anxious, but excited. She was almost out the door when she asked me if I had a piece of paper and an envelope she could have. It was practically an afterthought. She jotted out a quick note, folded it up and sealed it in the envelope, writing your name and number across the front. She asked me to call, you know—"

"If anything weird happened," I finished for her, and she nodded. "Didn't that strike you as an odd thing to say?"

"Of course it did! She was really starting to freak me out. I asked her what she meant by that, and she just laughed and blew it off, telling me not to worry about it. She actually blamed it on you."

"Me?"

"She said that something happened with one of Parker's security guys that had you extra antsy, and it must have been contagious. She promised me it was no big deal, and she doubted very much that I would have to make that call. She said she was doing it more out of respect for your peace of mind than her own."

She dug through her purse and handed me an envelope with my name and phone number jotted across its front. I turned it over and noted that it was still sealed.

"Aren't you curious what's inside?" I asked. "I could hardly have blamed you for opening it."

She shrugged and went back to wringing her hands. "I was, but honestly? After what's happened, I just want it out of here."

I started to slide my thumbnail underneath the flap, but Lauren reached out and placed a hand over mine. "Please—not here. Just take it with you. I really don't want to know what's inside. My nerves are already shot. I swear—at times, it feels like someone's watching me. I've probably just caught a case of your contagious paranoia, but it feels like the less I know, the safer I'll be. In the meanwhile, I've got to keep it together for Simon and Joey."

"Fair enough," I said, getting to my feet and tucking the envelope into my pocket. "I'll wait until I get home to read it. I'm actually supposed to meet with Rochelle's attorney tomorrow morning, so hopefully he can clear up any other questions that I might have. You've given me lots to think about. I appreciate you calling me."

"Please let her know that I'm worried sick but let her know that Joey's doing fine. I'll keep him as long as she needs me to," said Lauren, walking me to the door.

"I will," I said, stepping out into the cool night air before turning to face her. "One last question—do you think there's any chance at all that Rochelle might have done this thing?"

Lauren scoffed at the thought. "No way. It doesn't even make sense. She was determined not to harm Parker's professional or personal reputation, even as her child suffers a life-threatening condition that could be cured by finding a familial donor. Murdering him doesn't get her any closer to her goal. And besides, Rochelle doesn't have a violent bone in her body. It's more than I can even imagine."

I nodded, thanking her again before carefully picking my way back across the weatherworn planking of the dock. I hadn't even made it halfway to my car before Lauren ducked back inside and switched off the entry light. Standing beneath the stars and shrouded in shadows with only the gentle sounds of the lake lapping at the shoreline, I couldn't deny the creepy sensation of being watched by countless unseen eyes.

I hurried to the safety of my car and began the long drive home.

I had just crossed beneath I-270 west of Reynoldsburg when my phone rang through the car's audio. The emaciated face of Expectra Autopsa grinned ghoulishly at me from the screen on my dash, and I couldn't help but return the favor. Considering the current condition of my face, I'm sure I was plenty scary myself. She was Jasmine's current favorite from the Demon Academy line of dolls, and Jasmine had insisted that I use Expectra's skeletal visage as my contact photo for her in my phone. Who knew that decomposing corpses could be so fashionable? Certainly not me...

"Hey, kiddo," I said, answering the phone. "Everything okay?"

"I don't know," she said cryptically. "You tell me. Is it true?"

"Is what true?"

"Mom told me that you two were back together again," she said, her tone surprisingly flat.

"Um, yeah, it's true. We made up last night." Boy, did we *ever*—my ears burned at the recollection.

A heavy sigh was her only response, and the smile slipped from my face.

"Hold up," I said. "Weren't you just telling me the other night that you hoped we worked things out? I thought you'd be *happy*."

"Yeah, I thought I would too, but..." Her voice trailed off as my confusion deepened.

"But what? Come on, Jaz. Out with it."

"Honestly? I don't trust either one of you at this point. I don't want to get my hopes all up just to have you both change your minds again. The two of you are playing tug of war, and I'm the rope, and I'm just so sick of it. It isn't fair to me, it isn't fair to Dexter, and it isn't fair to Jordan."

Her words landed hard, but it was that last one that caught my ear.

"Jordan? He doesn't even know me," I said, and the icy silence that followed clued me in that I was missing Jasmine's entire point. "Okay, let me try that again. You're right. I guess we haven't been very considerate, and I'm sorry we've made you feel this way. I didn't realize it was weighing so heavy on your mind."

"Yeah, well, with everything that's happened with Gramma, I've had a lot of time to think. You *do* realize that Jordan will be coming home with us, don't you?"

I blinked. Melanie had mentioned caring for the child while Sarah recuperated, but the full implication hadn't exactly registered. "What makes you say that?"

Another heavy sigh, and I could almost feel her disappointment across the line. "Who knows how long it will be before Grams is able to take care of Jordan again? Who did you think was going to do it? Gramma Ann and Papaw Joe? They're too old, and it shouldn't fall on them anyway. Jordan is my brother. He belongs with us. Are you ready for that? It's one thing to put me through all of this, but Jordan's been through enough. If the two of you broke his heart, I don't think I could ever forgive you."

My head was spinning with information I should have gotten from Melanie, not her twelve-year-old daughter, and I felt a little hijacked. Of course, considering the events of the day, I realized Melanie and I hadn't really had much opportunity to talk, but it was a whole lot more to think about than I ever expected. I wasn't really sure what to say that could provide Jasmine some level of comfort. I needed time to process.

"I'll tell you this," I said, massaging my throbbing forehead. "I've heard every single word that you said, and just as soon as I can get back down there, your mother and I will have a long talk about it. We'll figure this out one way or another, but I promise—no more false hope for anyone. I never meant to let you down."

"Okay, good," she said. "See that you don't do it again."

With that, the little turd hung up on me.

⋯•••••●⊖⊖●•••••⋯

By the time I let myself into my living room, my head was pounding in sync with every single heartbeat. I couldn't recall ever having a headache so bad, and my stomach had gotten more than a little queasy. It's a good thing I hadn't eaten anything, or I would have surely been giving it a second look-see at any moment.

Dexter met me at the door, yowling like he hadn't eaten in days. I held my breath while unleashing the scent from one of his favorite flavors of Fancy Feast and averted my eyes as the ground circle of meat contained within plopped into his serving dish. I knew the sight of its congealed gravy would send me straight into dry heaves. I tossed the empty can in the trash and double-checked the locks on all my doors and windows before heading upstairs.

My first priority was getting another few Excedrin into my system, so I tended to that first before taking another good look at myself in the bathroom vanity. The flesh around my left eye was practically purple now, and it was swollen partially shut, the eyeball itself angrily bloodshot. The cheek below it was thoroughly abraded and presented in complimentary hues from the same palette. It was frightening to look at, but at least I was color-coordinated. It wasn't even ten o'clock, and all I wanted to do was crawl into bed.

I turned off the bathroom light as I went into my bedroom, kicking off my shoes and pulling my shirt over my head. That simple act brought a new series of complaints from my battered torso, and I couldn't keep myself from groaning. I unfastened my jeans and slid them down, my forgotten gun startling me when it fell with a thud to the floor between my feet. If it weren't for safeties, I probably would've blown my own damn foot off, and this was why I didn't normally carry my weapon on my person. I picked it up and stowed it away in the drawer of my nightstand before stooping to retrieve my discarded jeans. My thumb crinkled against the envelope I had also forgotten was stored in my front pocket. I pulled it out and perched on the edge of my bed, sliding my thumb under its seal and tearing it open.

Hey Dwayne,

I feel like a complete moron writing a note you're never gonna read, but I can already hear what you'd say if I didn't, and something happened. Parker texted me tonight. He wants to talk. It's my chance to get the help I need for Joey, and I have to take it. He's meeting me at my house, and I wasn't about to worry you with all you've got going on. I've got a really good feeling about this, and I'm hoping I won't need your services for much longer. But IF—ha, ha, ha!— something should happen, I've got some info you should see in the floor safe of the guest cottage. You know the code.

Rochelle

I read the note a second time before turning it over, hoping for maybe just a little more information. Floor safe? Code? I didn't have a clue what she was talking about. I tucked the piece of paper back into its envelope and placed it on my nightstand, turning off my bedside lamp and plunging the room into blessed darkness. I crawled beneath my comforter, angling for a comfortable position and hoping the day's information overload wouldn't prevent sleep from coming. I had to shake this headache. It was impeding my ability to think. My list of questions was getting longer, and morning couldn't come fast enough.

Mercifully, I nodded off in a matter of minutes.

CHAPTER TWENTY-ONE

The cool, gray light of an overcast morning brought short-lived relief followed almost immediately by a fresh wave of panic as I struggled to silence the opening bits of "Funkytown" spilling through my cell phone speaker—it was my default alarm sound. Laugh if you must—Melanie does—but its pulsating disco beat pulls me up out of sleep like nothing else. My headache had diminished greatly, but my left eye was completely crusted over, and I was having difficulty focusing on much of anything.

After finally silencing the damned thing, I unceremoniously booted Dexter from where he was curled near my feet, eliciting a disgruntled yowl followed by a reproachful hiss as he bolted from the room. The short walk to the bathroom was almost a carnival ride, the room ever-so-slightly tilting and swaying as I struggled to keep my balance, but I really had to pee, so my only real choice was to press on, hoping I didn't faceplant in the process—not that anyone would be able to tell the difference at this point. I seemed to recall reading somewhere that the loss of use of one eye could affect depth perception, but this was ridiculous. Wobbling above the ceramic throne, I couldn't trust myself to hit the target, so I plopped my sorry ass down on the cold wooden seat and peed like a proper lady.

With that crisis averted, I grabbed a towel and washcloth from the narrow bathroom closet and turned on the faucet, examining the trainwreck staring at me from the mirror while I waited for the water to get warm. It took way longer than it should to remember the water was *never* going to get warm, and I groaned. A nice, hot shower was exactly what my aching body craved. Instead, I resigned myself to dampening the washcloth and gingerly coaxing the crust from my eye until I could finally open it, if only a narrow slit. The swollen tissue surrounding my eye socket had settled into the deep hue of eggplant, but at least the abrasions on my cheek were a little less angry than before. As I focused on the task at hand, my equilibrium gradually returned, my dizziness fading away.

From there, I opted for a quick and easy whore's bath, unwilling to subject myself to another ice-cold shower. I brushed my teeth and finished up by dragging water through my dark brown hair with a brush, taming the worst of my morning bedhead. I gave myself one last look in the mirror and sighed. Oh, well. It wasn't like I was going on a *date*.

Dexter shadowed me down the stairs, reminding me of my obligation to him as if I could forget. His morning nibbles came as a scoop of dry food, infinitely less likely to start my stomach roiling again. I topped off his water, grabbed my keys and a coat, and made sure I had Rochelle's note in my pocket before stepping out into a decidedly colder morning. Shock of shocks, I was actually a little ahead of schedule!

I hadn't listened to the forecast, but it looked like it might just snow.

· · • • • • ● ⟨◦⟩ ● • • • • • ·

I really didn't know what to expect as I fed the address that Brady texted me into my GPS. I figured I'd be headed to a detention center in downtown Columbus or maybe even the Ohio Reformatory for Women in nearby Marysville, but I found myself gaping at palatial homes on a residential street in Upper Arlington. When my guidance system warned me that my destination was ahead on the left, I slowed to a crawl, watching the numbers ascend on fancy mailboxes until I spotted one labeled, '*Mirsky*.' It would seem that Rochelle's attorney was inviting me to his home, and despite the impressive property, I was disappointed. I thought I would get the chance to hear Rochelle's side of things firsthand, and maybe I still would, but I couldn't really imagine the wheels of justice turning fast enough for bail to have been set, and that was if she had even been formally charged with Senator Ghant's murder. It was Sunday, after all, and to the best of my knowledge, the judicial system ground to a halt on the Sabbath.

Light flurries had begun to fall as I parked in front of the three-car garage at the end of a long cobblestone drive. The house was a stone-faced McMansion with endless windows from all elevations giving a three-hundred-and-sixty-degree view of the expertly landscaped lawn, complete with a topiary garden at its border. Like a moat around the house's foundation, empty flowerbeds lay dormant beneath a sea of dark mulch, waiting for spring to finally arrive, and it was doubtless that no expense would be spared to ensure they were the envy of the entire neighborhood.

I got out of my car and followed the sidewalk to the front stoop. I pressed what appeared to be a fancy Ring doorbell mounted beside an entry door that would have looked more at home on a castle. I couldn't hear any visible chime through the massive door, and if it weren't for the sudden flicker of a tiny blue light on the device, I might have thought it wasn't working. I waved at the camera and aimed to deliver a disarming smile before remembering my face looked like five miles of rough road.

"No solicitors," a flat female voice said through a speaker embedded somewhere in the device.

"Um, I'm not selling anything—ma'am," I said, feeling foolish speaking to the door. "My name is Dwayne Morrow, and I believe Mr. Mirsky is expecting me."

I stood patiently on the stoop, mildly shivering in a coat that wasn't quite warm enough, waiting for a response that wasn't coming anytime soon. I was just about to press the button again when I heard the deadbolt turn from the other side of the door, and it slowly swung inward. Standing just inside the foyer was a silver-haired wisp of a lady dressed in her Sunday finest. She nodded cordially as she stepped back and let me in, closing the door behind me with a shiver of her own.

"Pleased to meet you, ma'am," I said, extending a hand and gradually taking in the opulence of the place. Everything was white, off-white, or blond, and I was afraid to move for fear of mucking something up. "Dwayne Morrow. Um, should I take off my shoes—?"

She briefly clasped my hand and grinned crookedly. "Only if you stepped in something on the way to the door. I'm Vivian, Leon's wife. He's in his office. It's the first door to your left," she said, pointing. "See yourself in and please excuse me. I'm still not quite ready for Sunday services." She headed for a staircase lining the right wall, calling out over her shoulder as she began her rapid ascent, "Watch your time, Leon! We need to leave soon!"

An older gentleman with more than a passing resemblance to Larry David from *Curb Your Enthusiasm* appeared in the designated doorway. "Don't fret, Vivvy. This shouldn't take long," he called out before turning his attention to me. "Good morning, Mr. Morrow. Won't you come in and have a seat?"

A pang of disappointment registered as I sensed I was already being given the bum's rush. I had hoped for a chance to converse with the man and get a sense of Rochelle's side of the story before asking a few questions of my own, but it looked like I had only been penciled into a five-minute slot on his calendar. I compulsorily checked the bottom of my shoes before crossing the corridor and entering what looked to be his home office. I wasn't sure if Mrs. Mirsky was kidding or not, but I wasn't taking the chance on tracking through her pristine hallway.

Stepping through the threshold was like waking up in Oz. His furnishings were rich mahogany with a vibrant Oriental rug covering most of the hardwood floor beneath. Vivid prints of breathtaking cityscapes adorned each of his four walls. He shook my hand as I passed, trying to contain his double-take as he got a better look at my face.

"My goodness," he said, motioning me to one of two matching burgundy seats facing his desk. "I don't mean to be rude, but was there some sort of accident?" He gingerly touched his own face as he rounded the desk to take a seat.

"Something like that, yes," I said, not inclined to waste time talking about my travails. "It looks worse than it is."

"Well, thank goodness for that, because it looks bloody awful," he said, issuing a short bark of laughter. He sat down and pulled out his middle drawer, retrieving an envelope from it and placing it on the desk before me. My name was written on the front, but the penmanship was distinctly different than that which had been on the envelope Lauren had given me. "Here you go."

I just stared at it. "What's this?"

"Ms. Pendleton authorized me to settle her account with your firm," he said, nudging the envelope in my direction. "Go on—it's yours."

I cautiously picked it up and lifted the flap which wasn't sealed. Peering inside, my mouth went dry when I saw the amount. It was double the fee we had agreed upon. Confused, I could only shake my head. I intended to drop the envelope back down on his desktop, but I couldn't quite seem to release my grip on it.

"I don't understand," I said. "I thought that Rochelle might have had some sort of message for me, maybe some instructions, or—oh, I don't know, her *side of the story* or something."

His surprise was evident. "I'm not sure what might have given you that impression. She simply wanted to make sure her obligation was satisfied. Is there a problem with that?"

"But—but—" I stammered, wholly unprepared for this to be the purpose of our meeting. "Can you tell me what happened? Why she went back to her house that night? What evidence do the police have against her? Surely, you don't think she *did* this, do you?"

"Mr. Morrow, you seem to have me confused with Ms. Pendleton's defense attorney, one who I've yet to procure, although I'm working on it. I'm merely representing her until I can find a suitable replacement. I specialize in contract law, family matters and such, and at this point in my career, I'm more retired than anything. I've been Gerard Pendleton's personal attorney for years, and the only one his daughter could think to call when she found herself in trouble. I've never done criminal law, and I'm certainly not about to start now."

I slumped back in my chair. "So, she didn't give you any other messages for me?"

"I'm sorry, no," he said, standing at the sound of his wife's footsteps approaching from the hall. "Now, if you'll excuse me, my wife and I are on our way to church."

Vivian appeared in the doorway with a faux fur wrap over her arm and an expectant look on her face. "Are you ready, dear?"

I got to my feet and tucked the envelope into an inside pocket of the coat I hadn't even had time to remove. "Did she at least say she was innocent?"

He nodded as he led me to the hallway. "Oh, yes."

I was surprised by his tone. "You didn't believe her? Did she say what happened?"

He sighed as his wife grew impatient by the door. "Frankly, Mr. Morrow, it's what they *all* say. I specifically asked Ms. Pendleton not to tell me anything more. Those are conversations best had with her criminal attorney, and I had no wish to get embroiled in the whole matter. Vivvy and I are only in town for a family wedding and flying back to our winter home in Destin in the morning. I hope to find someone willing to take Ms. Pendelton's case beforehand but, if necessary, I can do all that by telephone. Now, if you don't mind, we're going to be late."

"Of course," I said, stepping back out onto a stoop that was beginning to collect a thin sheen of sparkling flurries. They followed me as I retraced my path down the walk to my car, veering toward the garage once we reached the driveway.

I guess our business here was concluded.

· · · · ●●●●●○◌○◌●●●●● · · · ·

I was barely out of the neighborhood when Brady's grinning face appeared on my navigation screen. I answered the call with an irritated, "What?"

After a brief pause, Brady said, "Well, good morning to you, too, sunshine! I didn't really expect you to answer. I thought I'd get your voicemail. Let me guess—you overslept?"

"No, I didn't oversleep," I said. "I'm already done."

Another brief pause. "It's only twenty after nine."

"I'm aware of the time, Brady. This wasn't the sort of interview I expected."

"How so?"

"For one thing, Rochelle wasn't there," I said, turning right onto Fishinger. "For another, Leon Mirsky isn't her attorney, or at least he won't be for much longer. He was Rochelle's father's attorney, and his practice was in contract and family law. He's also pretty much retired."

"I don't get it," said Brady. "Then why did he want to see you?"

"Apparently, Rochelle authorized him to cut me a check to settle her account with Boggs, but even that doesn't make a lot of sense. I'm pretty sure she already paid Loretta. I'm sorry to disappoint you, but I didn't learn a thing. My debt to you is canceled."

"Now, slow down there, buddy," he said. "I'm sure I can still work some of my magic once we find out who's going to be representing her."

"Hmmm," I said, noncommittally. I wasn't feeling particularly optimistic at the moment. I decided to change the subject. "So, if you didn't really expect me to answer my phone, why were you calling?"

"I thought you might be interested in swinging by for breakfast when you were done. Scotty stayed overnight with Billy, and Anyssa is whipping up a feast for all of us."

Scott Nichols was a teen whose mother had been murdered the previous year. It had been my first real case with Boggs Investigations, not that Doug really wanted anything to do with it. Scott was subsequently arrested for the crime, but Brady and I were somewhat instrumental in proving his innocence and identifying the real culprit. Okay, *fine*—Melanie was the one who had actually stopped the real culprit, saving both of our backsides in the process. Scott had since been adopted by Wendell and Nola Caudill, the same elderly couple who had taken Brady and his son, Billy, under their wings after Brady's wife had tragically died in an automobile accident. Their eventual sainthood was pretty much guaranteed.

"Whaddaya say?" Brady continued. "Pancakes, scrambled eggs, and French toast, with bacon and sausage links, too. It's a veritable breakfast buffet."

The gurgle from my stomach was so loud I was surprised Brady couldn't hear it across our Bluetooth connection. I was rapidly approaching the exits for I-270, and my decision dictated which one I would need to take, and I knew which one my belly was voting for. I activated my turn signal and took the ramp for I-270 heading north.

"I'm on my way."

Any evidence of Brady's soiree from Friday evening was gone. His front lawn, which had served as a parking lot for the event, was now covered in a thin blanket of snow that was intensifying as the day progressed. I wasn't aware of any accumulation in the forecast, but then again, I hadn't really caught the news lately. I parked beside Brady's new plaything and made literal tracks to his front door, stomping the snow off my shoes on his stoop.

The smile fell from Anyssa's face when she answered the door and saw my face. "Oh, my God! Brady told me you had been assaulted, but I guess I didn't realize how bad it was. Come in, come in." She stepped back to let me through, and I slipped my shoes off on the mat just inside the door.

"It looks worse than it is." At this point, it had almost become an autoreply. Anyssa reached for my coat as I slipped it off, and I inhaled deeply. The comingling scents of fresh brewed coffee and various breakfast goodies practically had me drooling. "I wouldn't mind it one bit if you had some Excedrin I could swipe."

"I'm pretty sure I do, but wouldn't you prefer ibuprofen or Aleve? I think either one is better for body aches."

"It's not my body that's aching, or at least not so much," I said, trying not to take it personally that my very appearance suggested I must be in a great deal of pain. "I just can't seem to vanquish this headache. It's just a dull throb at the moment, but I'm hoping to keep it from turning into anything more."

She studied my face with concern. "Did you see a doctor?"

"I've seen enough doctors in the last couple of days," I said. "I'm sure it's fine. Sometimes I get headaches when the weather changes, and it's definitely getting colder out there. Did you notice it was snowing?"

"I did," she said as Brady entered the room and deposited a quick kiss on her cheek. "And that reminds me—how's Sarah doing?"

"She's continuing to improve, as far as I know," I said. "I haven't spoken to Mel today, but I'm going to lean on that old adage, no news is good news."

"I've certainly been praying for her," she said.

"We both have," said Brady. "Come on back. Your timing is perfect. The boys have already loaded up plates and absconded back to Billy's room. They're in the middle of some Wizards of Warcraft online challenge that barely allows them enough time to go the bathroom much less eat. Besides, I'm not sure the things we have to discuss would be appropriate for young ears."

Oh, brother—here we go, I thought, cursing my grumbling stomach for temporarily blinding me. I should have seen this invitation as cover for the interrogation that was likely to follow. Never trust a reporter. *Never.*

I followed them through the living room and into the kitchen, noting through the sliding glass door the thin layer of snow that had already accumulated on the patio beyond. Anyssa broke away to rummage through a cabinet while Brady and I continued to the right where three place settings waited on an oblong table in Brady's breakfast nook. Steaming bowls of eggs, gravy, biscuits, and breakfast meats were the centerpiece, and a magnetic one at that. I slid into a chair as Alyssa deposited a couple of Excedrin by my plate.

"There's orange juice in the pitcher, but I could get you some water, if you'd like," she said.

"The juice is fine, but I wouldn't say no to another Excedrin," I said, smiling sheepishly. She deposited another caplet before taking her own seat. I washed the trio of pain relievers down in a single gulp and set about the more serious business of building my plate. I was so hungry, I was about to forgo silverware altogether.

Brady laughed as I dug in. "Wow, you act like you haven't eaten in days. I guess your Burger King run wasn't very filling."

I was confused. "My what?"

"A-*ha!* I *knew* you weren't on your way to Burger King last night!" he crowed. "You were chasing a lead in the Pendleton case, weren't you?"

I aimed for stone-faced but couldn't keep my lips from twitching. "That's highly unlikely. I haven't even spoken to Rochelle yet. What leads would I have to chase?" I shoveled another forkful of biscuits and gravy into my mouth before mumbling, "Everything's delicious, Anyssa. Thank you."

She smiled and nodded, keeping her focus on her own plate to keep from witnessing my ghastly lack of manners. My mother would have been so proud! I didn't know what Brady expected from me. I wasn't any more at liberty to divulge the specifics of Rochelle's case as I had been the previous afternoon.

He sighed, letting his fork clatter to his plate. "C'mon, Dwayne. When are you going to figure out that you can trust me? When have I ever gone to press with something you didn't authorize?"

I had to focus on swallowing before I spat my food across the table. "Well, I seem to recall being in a boatload of hot water with the FBI because of a certain front-page story that implied I had confirmed a recent murder was the work of an active serial killer."

"*Pffft.*" He rolled his eyes, dismissing my recollection. "That doesn't count. We didn't even know each other back then."

"Oh, wait—that's *right!* You were *working* with the FBI to help bring the killer to my fu—" From the corner of my eye, I caught Anyssa watching us like we were a tennis match. "—freaking doorstep! That's *so* much better."

Brady couldn't suppress a cheeky grin framed by those damned dimples. "It worked, didn't it?"

"It got Melanie kidnapped, and I was almost killed!"

"Okay, fine," he said, throwing his hands up in surrender. "It wasn't my finest moment. But it wasn't entirely my idea, you know. Nina Crockett and Arthur Steele contacted *me*, not the other way around. You really need to let that one go. We've worked together several times since then. What if I guaranteed that anything you shared would be completely off the record?"

I narrowed my eyes—well, my *eye*. The left one was already pretty narrowed from all the swelling. "I'm supposed to believe it would make a difference?"

"Certainly! I mean, *seriously*. What harm could it do to bounce whatever you've got off of me? I might just be able to help you. I have before. We're a damn good team, and you can't deny it." Brady chomped on a piece of toast and grinned, giving me another flash of his straight, white teeth. For the life of me, I couldn't understand why his go-to move worked so often and on so many.

"Melanie and I are a damn good team," I countered, returning my attention to the dwindling pile of food on my plate. It was too good to let it get cold.

"*We-e-ll*—" said Brady, holding up his hand and rocking it side to side, earning an instant slap on the arm from Anyssa.

"*Brady*," she chastised, scowling at him. "What is *wrong* with you?"

"What? I'm just saying they *used* to be—"

She silenced him with a raised eyebrow, but it was my turn to grin, even if it hurt a little. "Oh, hey, that's right. With everything that's been going on, I forgot to mention—Mel and I are back together. We, um, made up while I was down there."

Anyssa's face lit up. "Aw, Dwayne! That's wonderful! I always knew the two of you were end game. You'd have to be a fool not to see it."

"I dunno," said Brady, sipping his coffee. "*I* wouldn't have put money on it."

"I rest my case," Anyssa said, rolling her eyes as she jabbed at Brady's side.

"Hey," he protested, pulling away from Anyssa's playful fingers and tossing me a genuine smile for a change. "That's really great, man. It's about fucking time. Now, try not to screw things up this time, alright?"

His words brought Jasmine's to mind, and I hoped I wasn't being premature in making the announcement. I wasn't exactly thrilled that Melanie appeared to be making decisions about the continuing care of Jordan without discussing it with me first—not that I wasn't willing to give the matter some serious consideration. It just felt like things were happening a little out of sequence, and me announcing our reconciliation to our friends probably wasn't the smartest move on my part. I kept my smile from slipping and nodded, ready to change the subject.

"I'll make you a deal," I said to Brady, loading my fork with my last bit of scrambled egg. "Once I find out who's representing Rochelle in the criminal proceedings, I'll see if I can get her permission to share what I know with you. There are potential complications I'd rather avoid by doing things in the proper order."

"And I'll continue to keep my ear to the ground," he said. "If I hear anything worth sharing, you'll be the first to know, starting now. My sources are telling me that she claims to be innocent. She says she found Senator Ghant's body inside her guest house when she got home but it was dark. She didn't realize what she was seeing until she had already picked up the gun that was lying right beside him. That puts her fingerprints on the murder weapon."

"Your 'sources' must be police," I said, realizing the gravity of Rochelle's current situation.

Brady's face turned to stone. "My sources are strictly confidential," he said, holding his scowl for an extended beat before breaking into another cheesy grin. "See? I *can* be trusted!"

CHAPTER TWENTY-TWO

I left Brady's with more than a bellyful of food to digest. My mind was swirling with questions I had no one to ask, and I didn't have a clue what to do from here. I was worried about Joey, but at least he was safe with Lauren and Simon—people he knew. I couldn't stop thinking about Rochelle's poor father, and how confusing it was going to be when his touchstone to this world just stopped showing up to visit. None of it made any sense. Why would Rochelle kill a man she clearly still loved? It would mean willingly abandoning the two people who needed her most, and I just couldn't see it.

I briefly considered discussing the latest turn of events with Doug, but when had *that* ever helped? Learning that Rochelle's fingerprints were on the murder weapon would be the only excuse he needed to ditch the case altogether, even if he had to return a portion of the retainer he had already received, and the thought only raised another question. Why had Rochelle instructed Leon Mirsky to cut a sizable check for services that had already been paid in full? It felt like subtle encouragement to continue the investigation, especially when coupled with the cryptic note Rochelle had left with Lauren regarding a floor safe in her guest cottage, one that I supposedly knew the combination to.

Driving without any real purpose in mind, I wasn't really surprised that I was halfway to Rochelle's house. The snow had neither intensified nor tapered off, and the roads were still clear—at least for now. Trucks were already out in force treating the highways, and traffic was light. I thought it might be a good opportunity to touch base with Melanie.

"Hey!" she answered on the second ring, her voice bright. "I was just getting ready to call you. How are you feeling today?"

"Better," I said, and it didn't feel like too much of a stretch.

"Good," she said. "And you're keeping your gun on you at all times, right?"

"Um—" I involuntarily whistled air through my teeth.

"Dwayne! You *promised!*"

My mind skittered back to the previous evening when my gun had fallen to the floor as I removed my jeans. I had put it in the drawer of my nightstand and hadn't given it a single thought when getting ready.

"I'm sorry! It's been a busy morning, and I haven't quite integrated this new step into my daily routine," I said, looking to change the subject. "I'll do better. I promise. How's everybody down there?"

"Good," she said. "I was able to sneak Jasmine in to see Sarah this morning. I think it did them both a world of good."

"Aw, I'm glad," I said. "What have the doctors said?"

"Sarah's continuing to improve. She's awake for longer stretches, so that's encouraging. I told her you were here earlier, but she didn't really remember it."

"Well, tell her I'll be back just as soon as I can," I said.

"I will, but don't be in any hurry. The weather down here is *bad*. They've already closed Lymont Hill, and I think we're under one level or another of snow emergency. Sarah insisted that I use her Jeep instead of my Mazda because it handles better, and I wasn't about to argue with her. The kids are with Sarah's parents, and I've just been hanging out here at the hospital. How are things up there?"

"Mostly just flurries," I said. "Not enough to keep me indoors."

"Anything new on Rochelle's situation?" she asked.

My chuckle was grim. "Lots, and none of it particularly good."

I spent the next several minutes bringing her up to speed, and it felt good to unburden myself without having to consciously censor my facts. Now that Melanie was officially part of the Boggs team, I didn't have to worry about violating our client's trust, if that was even a thing. I was merely consulting a colleague.

"I'd really like to speak to Rochelle in person, but until she's officially charged and released on bond, I don't know when that will be," I said.

"Do you really think that's gonna happen? Bail, I mean."

I blinked. "Why wouldn't it? Her background check was completely clean. Rochelle doesn't have any prior criminal history. I'm sure the bond will be high, but I get the impression she can probably afford it."

"That's my whole point," said Melanie. "She's a Pendleton. She can afford a lot of things, which makes her a flight risk."

I chewed on my bottom lip. "It hadn't occurred to me, but you're probably right."

"Also, I can only imagine the public outrage if she's released," she said. "Senator Ghant was a very popular man. Memorials are popping up all over the place. Haven't you seen the news?"

"Between meeting with Lauren last night and Leon Mirsky this morning, I can't say that I've had the time."

"Well, I've been pretty much stuck in a hospital waiting room where the only thing to do is watch TV. There's a lot of very upset folks out there saying a lot of very angry things. It might actually be safer for Rochelle to remain right where she is rather than to be out in the open."

I sighed. "God, what a mess. I don't even know where to begin."

"That's easy," she said. "You begin at the beginning."

"Not helpful, Mel," I said, pinching the bridge of my nose. "The last thing I need is another riddle."

"I'm serious," she said. "This all begins with the man himself, Parker Ghant. What do you *really* know about him?"

"Only what Rochelle has told me," I said.

"Well—that's not *all* you know," she said, and I knew she was referring to the fact that Parker Ghant was one of three influential members of Congress who had been photographed by my sister, Gina, during her ill-fated trip to Briarstaff, West Virginia. She caught them conspiring with high-ranking officials within the mysterious Academy in their efforts to derail the runaway train we call modern technology—and that was probably only the tip of the iceberg.

I truly appreciated the fact that Melanie had begun to accept my paranoia as fact.

The Academy had already taken so much from me and my family, and their influence seemed frighteningly unlimited. For all I knew, all of my phone calls were still being monitored—my internet, too, just waiting for someone to slip and reveal something regarding my sister's current whereabouts—not that I could have helped them with that. I had no idea where Gina had taken cover, and it was exactly how she had wanted it. Still, I had diligently avoided digging into any of the three names I knew for fear of repercussion against my family. I found myself choosing my next words carefully.

"You think I should start by digging into the Senator's past?"

"Why wouldn't you?" she asked. "It's the next logical step in helping your client. A man in Ghant's position is bound to have made plenty of enemies along the way, both personally and professionally. If we're operating under the assumption that Rochelle is telling the truth, you might be able to find someone else who had the opportunity and a far better motive. There should be a wealth of information available on the internet, and not just because of his recently deceased status. He's been a public figure for years."

I had to smile. Melanie was telling me that even if I *wasn't* completely crazy and my internet activities were actually being monitored, digging into all things Ghant wouldn't be an automatic red flag for anyone whose job was protecting the interests of the Academy. Frankly, it would be more unusual if I *didn't* check into Ghant's past. There would be nothing to directly connect the activity to my sister.

"What if I come up empty?" I asked.

"Then you break everything down into pieces. Start looking into all the names you know in Ghant's inner circle," she said. "Focusing on the big picture might be preventing you from seeing something small but significant."

"And if that goes nowhere?"

She was silent for a moment. "I'd try to get back into that guest cottage. Are you sure Rochelle didn't tell you the combination?"

"She didn't even tell me there was a safe," I said. "And while I don't relish the thought of being caught trespassing at the crime scene, I feel like that's where I should be starting. Everything I need to know might be waiting for me inside that safe. Why else would she tell me about it?"

"Why wouldn't she tell you the combination? Do you think she trusted her friend, Lauren?"

"She trusts her with Joey, so that's a pretty strong endorsement," I said. "Honestly, I don't know what to think. Maybe the combination is hidden somewhere on premises. Maybe there's a clue somewhere in the wording of the note that I'm just not picking up on."

"You're heading there right now, aren't you?"

She knew me too well, and her timing was incredible. I was just turning onto the road that would lead me to the Pendleton estate.

"I figured it couldn't hurt," I said.

"Well, don't do anything stupid," she said. "You're no good at all to Rochelle if you end up in an adjoining cell."

"I'll be careful," I promised.

"I'd feel a whole lot better if you were carrying your gun," she said.

I didn't really argue with that. I would have felt better, too.

........••••◦◦••••........

As I neared the property, it became increasingly clear that I wasn't going to have any luck getting to the cottage unobserved. A van was pulling away just as I arrived, its occupant having contributed to a growing pile of flowers and wreaths left at the entrance gate. Crosses and laminated headshots of the late, smiling senator were scattered amongst the burgeoning shrine, and another car pulled in just behind me, its puffy-eyed driver hauling another bouquet to add to the pile. When she dropped to her knees and began to pray, I put my car back into gear and circled back the way I had come. There was no predicting the end of this grief parade.

So much for Plan A. I was resigned to an afternoon of monotony that constituted Plan B—fishing in the vast ocean that is Google.

........••••◦◦••••........

Dexter met me at the door, yowling a familiar refrain. If you haven't caught on by now, cats are relatively single-minded in their motivation.

"You little liar," I said, removing my coat and draping it over the back of my couch. I ruffled the short black fur between his ears. "It isn't even *close* to your dinnertime."

I distracted him by throwing a small bouncy ball up the stairs, and he scampered after it willingly, his inner predator invoked and fully engaged. I grabbed my laptop from my office and set up shop on the dinette table where I had a nice view of the snow gently falling in the side yard. While I waited for Windows to load, I went into the kitchen and filled a tall glass with ice water, nabbing a bag of Doritos on my way back to the table. Dexter had stolen my seat, his rubber ball positioned dead center in the middle of my keyboard. He looked from me to the bag of Doritos with an expression that clearly read, "Hypocrite." I grabbed the ball and tossed it back up the stairs, and he nearly knocked my chair over spinning out in hot pursuit. I sat down, opened a web browser, and promptly laid my head on the table.

I hated this kind of investigation.

Digging through page after page of search results was boring and a strain on the eyes. As it was, my headache still lingered as a dull throb, and copious amounts of reading would likely only exacerbate it. I briefly considered more Excedrin but thought better of it for the sake of my liver. I would much rather ask people questions versus Google, but I was completely out of people to interview, and the sky was threatening more incoming snow.

Thoroughly resigned, I sighed and stared at my computer screen, wondering how best to begin.

Begin at the beginning.

Melanie's words echoed in my head, so I typed 'Parker Ghant' into the search bar, hit enter and watched my screen fill with links to every news outlet in the free world's take on Ghant's murder, most of which were accompanied by the same professional headshot he had been using in his current campaign.

I sighed. This was going to take some time.

I went back into my office and grabbed a stack of index cards and an assortment of colored pens. I thought it might be a good idea to give all the players their own card so I could add pertinent details and move the cards around, perhaps revealing connections that weren't immediately obvious. It was the sort of thing that Sue Grafton's Kinsey Millhone would do, and it was more of a strategy than I ever had. I titled the first card 'PARKER GHANT' and underlined his name twice before returning my attention to my laptop to refine my search parameters, adding 'Early Career' to my original query.

The screen filled with another plethora of choices, but at least several of them appeared to be the sort of information I was trying to glean. I clicked on the first one and started reading as the snow continued to collect in my yard.

•••••••●●⊖●●••••••

I had lost track of how many articles I had read when I felt the sudden pinprick of ten razor-sharp claws penetrating my jeans from behind, startling me to attention.

"I *told* you it wasn't time for dinner yet," I said as I gently dislodged his claws from the tender flesh of my backside. He begged to disagree via an elongated yowl before rubbing his length along the legs of my chair. I glanced at the clock on my laptop's taskbar and was startled to see that it was almost five o'clock. I had been at this for hours and had lost all sense of time. "Well, maybe it *is* time, after all."

I followed Dexter into the kitchen, stretching along the way. My eyes were tired, my butt was numb, and I wasn't sure if I was making any headway at all. After depositing another mound of ground protein into Dexter's dish and refreshing his water bowl, I decided it was time for another dose of Excedrin. I couldn't seem to shake the dull throbbing at my temples, although I'm sure crawling the internet hadn't helped. I snagged an ice-cold can of Pepsi from the fridge and made my way back to the dinette table to survey the mess I had made.

The table was littered with more index cards than I realized, my own heavy block letters taunting me in a rainbow of hues. I had learned more about the Ghant family dynasty than I ever cared to know, but had yet to uncover anything meaningful, or at least not to me. Many of the articles I found had contained pictures or videos, all of which I had dutifully bookmarked and saved in a folder on my bookmarks bar for easy perusal, but perusing them hadn't led to inspiration, either. It was just a bunch of campaign speeches and photo ops designed to elevate the senator's image and secure the votes of his constituents—a sea of doting faces smiling in adoration of a man they saw as a modern-day John F. Kennedy. I had even found one from the special election in which Rochelle Pendleton was actually hugging the man, clearly congratulating him on his only just-announced victory.

Hmmm.

I clicked through the saved bookmarks until I found the photo and enlarged it on my screen. It was taken at Ghant's campaign headquarters where the newly elected senator was surrounded by his faithful volunteers in a sea of congratulatory faces and airborne confetti. The adoration for the man was palpable even in a still shot, but the expression on Rochelle's face conveyed something else, and I didn't need a psychic to tell me it was nothing short of unadulterated love.

I started over, scrolling through the photos more slowly this time, focusing on ones taken at his rallies and campaign headquarters throughout his lengthy political career. Fashions changed, and Ghant aged gracefully, but in every single picture, one thing remained constant. A beautiful young woman hovered near the man, a rapturous look on her face as she gazed lovingly into his eyes, and none of them appeared to be either of the women he had been married to at the time. I wondered how many of these women found themselves in the same circumstances as Rochelle Pendleton and Lauren DeAngelo, banished from Ghant's life with their silence bought and paid for. I sent the photos wirelessly to the printer in my office, hopeful that I might somehow be able to identify the women later. I had collected names of individuals who had worked on Ghant's various campaigns as they were referenced in the articles, and maybe one of them would be willing to talk. I scooped those index cards into a pile and set them aside.

I was surprised at how squeaky clean the senator's overall reputation was. Born into an Ohio political dynasty, the man had been a public figure since birth, thanks to his father's own storied career which included procuring significant manufacturing jobs in the northwest corner of the state as well as desperately needed relief for farmers during periods of both drought and flooding. Parker Ghant had taken up where his father left off, championing equal pay for women while pushing for tax incentives aimed to keep corporations from shifting their operations out of state or, heaven forbid, overseas. He was a working man's hero and had somehow managed to elude scandal at every step. He had married his first wife, Elisabeth, straight out of college. They were parents to two boys, Patrick and Phillip, but after eleven years of marriage, they had amicably gone their separate ways. Parker married Cassandra the following year. They had three children in fairly quick succession—Peter, Paula, and Penelope, and I was beginning to gag at all of the cutesy alliteration. His two oldest boys had followed him into the political arena while the others were either in college or in high school, undoubtedly preparing to follow in the obligatory family footsteps. All five bore a striking resemblance to their photogenic father, as evidenced in the handful of family photos that had been released to the public. For the most part, Ghant kept his family sheltered from the prying eyes of the press, and all of the photos seemed staged for maximum impact.

On the surface, they were the picture-perfect American family, but I knew something about Parker Ghant that most people didn't. He was up to his capped teeth in the Academy, a top-secret organization whose elusive agenda included sabotaging pesky modern conveniences such as the internet with its troublesome ability to illuminate travesties occurring in the darkest corners of the world—and sometimes in our very own backyards. He and his cohorts were the reason my family believed my sister was dead, and it wasn't something I could ever forgive or forget. It was nauseating to read article after article praising the man with virtually no dissenting opinions, save for the usual creative wordplay typical of opponents in any run for office, but even that seemed half-hearted, as if all his challengers were already resigned to defeat.

I almost missed the one public record of actual interest.

During Ghant's very first campaign in which he was running for Westerville City Council, a crazed woman named Janet Harper had been arrested for assault at one of his rallies, charging the podium with a knife she had just used to slash her own wrists. She had been taken into custody at the scene, but not before getting blood all over the astonished candidate's face and dress shirt. The black-and-white photo accompanying the story showed a scene of panic as three security guards restrained the shrieking woman, whose own face was contorted by rage. Blood-spattered and eyes wide with fear, it was the first time I'd ever seen Parker Ghant without his trademark smile. Querying on the dates and names involved in the incident, I soon learned that Ms. Harper had been charged with attempted murder but had plead guilty to the lesser charge of aggravated assault contingent upon her successfully completing psychiatric counseling. I found it odd that Ghant hadn't pressed the issue. His family certainly had the clout. It was more like he just wanted the whole thing to go away. Over thirty years later, she would almost certainly be out of jail, provided she hadn't committed any other crimes or passed away in the interim.

With no other leads to follow, I did a public records search on all Janet Harpers in the Central Ohio area, and was rewarded with seven hits, but only one of them was of the right approximate age. Her last known address was just off of Morse Road in northern Columbus, but she either didn't have a phone or the number was unlisted, so there was no way to reach her from the comfort of my own living room. I really wanted to know what Ghant had done to provoke her into doing something so extreme. Of course, there was no guarantee that she would speak to me even if I had found a phone number, and it would have been altogether too easy to simply hang up. It might be more difficult to turn me away if I simply showed up at her door and applied a little charm. Of course, I might just scare the living shit right out of her with my face in its current condition.

I glanced at the clock. It was only a little past six, and the snow hadn't accumulated too much. What could it hurt to make a little house call? The worst she could do is order me off of her property, and I might just learn something that could help Rochelle's case. Otherwise, I was stuck waiting for an opportunity to speak with Rochelle directly, and until her defense was in place, I had no idea how long that might take.

I sighed. Patience is *not* my strong suit.

I powered down my laptop and banded the relevant index cards together before tucking it all into my laptop bag. I went back into my office and collected the printouts of Ghant's adoring female fan club and added them as well.

"Hold down the fort, buddy," I said to Dexter as I slipped into my coat and checked to make sure I had my keys and phone. He sat in one of the dinette chairs, busily grooming a hind leg that was pointed straight at the ceiling, utterly disinterested in anything I had to say. He had been fed and was deeply invested in grooming himself before settling in for a nice, cozy nap. I was more than a little jealous.

I was nearly out the door before I realized something was missing. I placed my laptop bag on the floor and dashed up the stairs to my bedroom where I pulled open the drawer to my nightstand.

I had almost forgotten my gun.

CHAPTER TWENTY-THREE

Traffic was light even for a Sunday evening as I made my way into downtown Columbus via eastbound I-70 and navigated the exchange onto I-71, heading north. I'm sure the inclement weather was a contributing factor, and I passed more than a few city trucks dousing the interstate with whatever solvent they use to keep the roads from freezing over, but the streets weren't really all that bad—at least not yet. My own SUV was all-wheel drive, so I wasn't too concerned about getting stuck somewhere, despite the gently drifting snow that seemed perfectly content to fall all evening long.

I exited onto Morse Road and turned right. I hadn't been to this part of town in ages. At one point, it had been home to Northland Mall, one of the four prime shopping outlets christened after the directional axes of a compass. I smiled at the recollection of riding along with Dad when he picked up Mom from Aunt Jane's after one of her annual pre-Christmas shopping visits. Aunt Jane had lived in the area before later relocating to Cincinnati, and Mom could get all of her holiday shopping done in one fell swoop while visiting with her sister. Aunt Jane would distract us kids by taking us to visit the Mall Santa as Mom and Dad loaded all of the Christmas loot into the trunk of his car while we were away. In the decades since, Northland Mall—along with its sisters, Eastland, Westland, and Southland—have all been torn down, falling out of favor with consumers who prefer shopping in what are arguably considered better outlying neighborhoods with the subsequent openings of the Mall at Tuttle Crossing, Easton Town Center, and the Polaris Fashion Place. With the surging popularity of online shopping, I'm sure their days are numbered, too—Tuttle is already looking more than a little anemic with several of its original anchor stores already calling it quits. In any event, Morse Road barely resembled my recollection from youth. Largely a collection of fast-food restaurants and automobile dealerships, I usually only found myself in the area during presidential election years where I voted early at the Franklin County Board of Elections.

I followed my GPS, turning left into the residential neighborhoods off of Tamarack Boulevard and soon arrived at my destination, parking along the curb in front. Janet Harper occupied the right side of a nondescript brick townhouse that was the third in a row of five identical buildings separated by shared driveways. Interior light glowed through an assortment of blinds, shades, and shower curtains from front-facing windows all down the line, and Harper's neighbor hadn't gotten the memo that Christmas was over months ago. Strings of multi-colored lights still twinkled from where they were mounted around the unit's door and first-floor window. These buildings were far older than me, constructed to be functional and not pretty, and the lack of snow collecting on their rooftops hinted at exactly how well insulated they were.

I grabbed my laptop bag and made sure my gun was tucked safely out of sight in the small of my back but hidden beneath my coat. While the neighborhood didn't seem even remotely affluent, it didn't feel dangerous, either, but I wasn't taking any chances. I traversed a crumbling sidewalk to a cinderblock stoop and knocked on a door that was in desperate need of painting, triggering a round of furious barking from inside the apartment followed by a startling volley of thumps that shook the door in its frame.

Awesome. I was going to have to shoot her dog. That should endear me to the woman.

The next round of barking was even more ferocious but decidedly human as I heard Fido's owner order him away from the door in a chainsaw timbre.

"Stay right there!"

It took me a second to realize she was speaking to me as the barking faded, the beast being shepherded away from the door and chastised the whole while. After an awkward moment of silence, a 100-watt porch light flared to life, and the front door was flung open by a frumpy woman with dirty salt-and-pepper hair framing her scowling jowls.

"Where the fuck's my pizza?" she snapped, placing her hands on her wide hips and giving me the stink eye.

I blinked. "Excuse me?"

She groaned and rolled her eyes all the way to the heavens. "Oh, man, please don't tell me you're here to sell something, or maybe introduce me to the Lord Jesus Christ Himself, or worse yet—vote for some shit-sucking candidate in the upcoming goddamn election. Don'tcha see my sign on the goddamn door? *No solicitation!*" She jabbed a gnarled forefinger at a faded sign on her door that said exactly that before leaning out and squinting at me. "What the fuck's wrong with your face? You look like you got run down by a COTA bus. Look, I don't want no trouble here. You need an ambulance? I'll call 911 and you can wait on the curb, but don't you even think about forcing your way inside. I've got a vicious dog in the other room, and I won't think twice to kick the nuts right off of you so's I can buy enough time to let him loose."

The dog erupted in another fit of savage barking prompted by the tone of his master's voice, and I backed up a step, holding my hands up in surrender.

"I'm none of the above, ma'am," I said, doing my best to offer a reassuring smile that wouldn't betray my escalating alarm. "My name is Dwayne Morrow, and I was just hoping I might have a moment of your time to ask you a couple of questions. I work for Boggs Investigations, and I think you might be able to help with one of our cases."

She crossed her arms underneath sagging bosoms that were testing the limits of a faded Guns N' Roses t-shirt and narrowed her eyes. "What's it pay?"

I blinked again. "Huh?"

"Pay, pay—what's it *pay?"* she said, emphasizing the word so her intent would penetrate even the dense fog of my inexperience.

I fumbled for my wallet and pulled out a twenty. "Why don't we start with twenty for your time and go from there? I don't even know if you're the person I'm looking for."

Her eyes lit up, and she licked her lips, barely hesitating before snatching the money from my hand. "Who do you think you're looking for?"

"Janet Harper," I said.

She grinned, displaying a fractured set of decaying yellow teeth. "Congratulations, that's me," she said, tucking the bill into her cleavage. "Are we through here? My fucking pizza's gonna be here any minute. It's already a half hour late."

I glanced over my shoulder at the empty street behind me. "It's probably because of the weather."

She looked beyond me, and surprise registered on her face. "When the fuck did *that* happen?"

"It's been snowing all day, ma'am," I said before trying to get my inquiry back on track but struggling for a subtle way to approach what was bound to be a sensitive subject. "Have you been following the news this weekend?"

She looked at me curiously. "Ain't got no use for the news," she said. "I stick to my Hallmark movies and maybe some *Dancing with the Stars*. Why?"

I took a deep breath before asking, "Does the name Parker Ghant mean anything to you?"

It was like I had slapped her across the face. She visibly jerked and stepped back, her hand fumbling for the edge of the door so she could close it in my face. "What in the fuck does he want now?" she muttered as she finally got hold of it.

"Nothing, ma'am," I said, hurrying to respond before she could turn me away. "He's dead."

She froze with the door halfway closed, her eyes slowly returning to mine. "Dead?"

I nodded. "Yes, ma'am. And my client is the woman accused of murdering him, but I don't think she did it. It's my understanding that you have—a history with Senator Ghant, and I wondered if you might be able to help me understand the man just a little better."

Her grip on the door relaxed just as a Domino's driver pulled up to the curb and parked behind my car.

"Maybe you should come inside," she said, opening the door wider to allow me entry.

······•••●◉◉●•••······

Introducing the smell of pizza into the tiny room only served to drive Janet's dog into a greater frenzy, restrained though the animal was behind the door of what must be a closet-sized bathroom sitting between the living room and kitchen. I couldn't smell a thing over the deeply entrenched stench of cigarette smoke that had discolored both the walls and the ceiling. Janet dropped the pizza box on a coffee table where the centerpiece was an overflowing ashtray and motioned me over to a broken-down sofa that sat behind it, leaning against the room's southern wall.

"May as well cop a squat," she said, moving toward the bathroom door which was steadily jumping in its frame under the constant assault of her canine companion. I was busy surveying the cluttered room and trying my best to keep the judgment off of my face when I realized she was about to unleash the hound.

"*Whoa, whoa*—wait a minute there," I said, holding up a hand. "Am I about to be mauled?"

She snorted, reaching for the bathroom door. "Bobbie is a lot of noise. She lost interest in you the minute she smelled pepperoni."

She opened the bathroom door, and a black-and-white spotted bulldog raced into the living room, pausing when she spotted me. I wasn't exactly convinced she was through with me when a low growl formed in her throat as she considered her options.

"*Bobbie!*" snapped Janet, slapping her thigh. "Stop that right this instant, or there will be no crusts for you, I promise!"

She dropped down onto the far end of the sofa with a grunt and pulled the pizza box closer to herself, prying up the lid to inspect her order. A half-empty bottle of beer was on the end table to her right, sweating a new ring onto the table's worn wooden surface. The dog seemed to understand, and after one last whimper, she parked herself at Janet's feet, eagerly awaiting for something—*anything* to hit the floor. She looked at me sideways as she lifted a piece of pizza to her mouth.

"You just gonna stand there and watch me eat?" she asked. "Sit down. And don't be eyeing my pizza. That twenty bucks was for information. It'll take another twenty if you're expecting to be fed."

I nodded and perched on the other end of the sofa, resting my laptop bag beside me on the floor. "Thanks, I'm good," I said with a smile, although I had to admit, the pizza didn't look half bad. I hadn't really eaten anything since breakfast at Brady's and my stomach was starting to grumble.

"Well, alright, then," she said, noisily chewing. "Let's get this over with. What is it you came here to ask me? This isn't a time in my life I care to dwell on, and *Big Brother* will be on shortly." She dangled her half-eaten slice of pizza at a 32" HDTV that was mounted crookedly on the wall across from us, and Bobbie nearly went airborne after it.

"Of course," I said, still struggling for subtlety. "I'll try not to take up too much of your time, Ms. Harper, but your—experience with Parker Ghant seems to be somewhat unique."

That earned a chuckle. "My experience? I've never heard it called *that* before. I tried to kill the man, Mr.—whatever you said your name was."

"Morrow," I said. "But please, call me Dwayne."

She gasped with feigned delight. "Oh, yeah? And *do* call me Janet. Now that we're besties, we can braid each other's hair." She chomped another bite from her slice of pizza and tossed the crust to Bobbie who caught it before it could ever touch the grimy green carpet. "What do you want? You've almost used that twenty up, by the way."

"Uh, okay," I said, deciding on a more direct approach. "How did you know Ghant?"

"A billion years ago, we were in some of the same classes at Otterbein, and after graduation, I volunteered to help him when he ran for City Council," she said, and I took a moment to process that. When using public records to locate the correct Janet Harper, it hadn't really occurred to me that she and Parker Ghant were the same age. At fifty-six, Janet looked at least ten years older while Ghant had retained quite a bit of his youthful appeal.

"You were acquainted?" I asked.

Another snort. "You could say that, but it's more to the point to say we were fucking." She grinned at me, enjoying the sight as I squirmed at her lewdness, but the smirk just as quickly dropped from her face. "That bastard ruined my whole life."

I waited a beat before asking, "Do you want to talk about it?"

"Do you want to talk about it?" Her imitation was ugly. "Hell, no, I don't want to talk about it. How can me talking about it possibly help your client?"

"You're the only one I've been able to locate who doesn't seem to think that Parker Ghant walked on water, my own client included," I said. "He seemed to have a real knack for protecting himself from scandal, but I'm having a hard time believing he was as squeaky clean as his public image would suggest."

"You sure got that right," she said, pulling another piece of pizza from the box and dangling it precariously close to her pup's eagerly panting face. "I'm surprised no one's killed him before this. So, how did your client get mixed up with him?"

"She volunteered to work for his campaign for Senate during the special election," I said. "You could say they got close."

She nodded, chewing industriously. "Ah—of course. They were fucking. Did he knock her up too?"

Too?

"As a matter of fact, he did," I said. "He had already moved on to another young, attractive campaign volunteer. I've also met the young woman he was with directly before my client. He got her pregnant, too. Seemed to be a real pattern with the guy."

She sighed, tossing the uneaten half of her pizza slice back into the box, much to Bobbie's apparent dismay. "Goddamned Sperminator. How did he manage to shut them up?"

"He offered them cash, and a lot of it, but only in exchange for a signed non-disclosure agreement."

Janet's face suddenly contorted, and she reached for a pack of cigarettes as hot tears sprang from the corners of her eyes. "How very tidy," she said, her voice tight as she lit a cigarette and lifted it to her lips with trembling fingers.

"I don't understand."

She looked at me with contempt. "Just take a look around, mister. Does it look like I received any sort of bribe to keep my mouth shut? Hell, no! At least these other girls are operating under the delusion they had a choice in the matter. Me? I never had any choices, not from the moment I told him I thought I was pregnant. He freaked the fuck out and sicced his goddamned family on me."

"His family?"

Her nod was a quick jerk as her bottom lip continued to quiver and her complexion began to mottle. I hoped the unpleasant recollection wasn't pushing her into any old behaviors that might manifest in an unexpected and aggressive way. I was keenly aware of my handgun pressing into the small of my back, but took comfort in the fact that she didn't have anything particularly 'stabby' within easy reach. Janet clumsily dabbed at her eyes with a greasy Domino's napkin before clearing her throat.

"You'd think that arranged marriages only happened in places like India, but Parker Ghant's future was set in stone by his father at an early age. Elisabeth Hammond was the daughter of Gordon Ghant's closest friend, and she and Parker were already engaged when all of this happened," she said, taking a pull from her beer. "There was no way that the Ghants were going to accept me in Elisabeth's place, even if that would have been what Parker wanted. I wasn't the 'right kind of people,' if you get what I'm saying. The daughter of a deadbeat mother who hopped from job to job almost as often as she swapped out her partners—"

Her face contorted again as she steeped in memories better left forgotten. Her eyes were fiercely defiant when she looked my way.

294

"I fought *hard* to make something of myself. I earned *scholarships* to attend Otterbein. I graduated with honors, but I was stupid enough to believe Parker when he said that Elisabeth didn't understand him, and it was only *me* that he loved," she said, shaking her head before smacking her own forehead a couple of times. "So stupid, *stupid*."

"Hey, hey, stop that," I said, daring to reach out and touch her forearm. She recoiled like I had burnt her, so I pulled back. "You weren't the only one who fell for that line, and from what I can tell, not even by a long shot. But he didn't try to buy your silence? That sure seems to be his go-to move now."

"I don't think he *had* a go-to move at that point," she said. "I was the first real complication in his perfect little life, and I think his daddy stepped in to handle things from there. Gordon Ghant may have been well-respected, but he was a man to be feared, too. He had connections that weren't exactly public knowledge. Let me guess—you find that a little too hard to believe."

"Not at all," I said immediately. My personal history with the devastation Parker Ghant could cause made it all too easy to imagine him inheriting his ideology from his father. "What happened?"

She stood abruptly, startling me as well as her own dog, who yipped and skittered away. She jerked her Guns N' Roses shirt up to the bottom of her unrestrained breasts, exposing a network of scars across a swath of her distended abdomen.

"He tried to silence me another way," she practically spat, and I'd seen scarring like this before. My sister-in-law, Sheila, bore similar marks from her encounter with the serial killer who had been stalking me the previous year.

"He *attacked* you?"

Janet lowered her shirt and dropped to the couch, her face hardening like a mask.

"Not personally, *no*," she said. "But one night when I was headed to my car after work, I got jumped from behind by a couple of guys who tossed me into a van. They wore masks, so I never got a look at their faces, but the one thing they made sure I saw was their skintight t-shirts and the campaign slogan emblazoned on the front. *'Don't Think Ghant Can't!'* Sound familiar?"

"That was Parker's campaign slogan."

"It belonged to his father first," she said, her voice increasingly bitter. "They say if it ain't broke, don't fix it. They left me for dead in an alley off High Street in the Short North. If it hadn't been for a couple of drunk kids stumbling through on their way home, I'm sure I wouldn't be sitting here now, and if I'm gonna be honest, about half the time I wish I *had* died."

I was speechless. The online articles I had read didn't mention any attack on Janet Harper, but then again, I hadn't dug much further than to try and locate her present address. What else might I have overlooked?

Janet grabbed the saturated Domino's napkin as fresh tears began to spill. "I lost so much that night. Not only did I lose Parker's baby, but an emergency hysterectomy made sure I'd never have the chance to become a mother again." The crooked look she sent my way was unsettling. "I think it kind of broke me a little bit."

"So, that's when—"

"That's right. I was out for revenge, and I didn't care if it cost me my own life in the process," she said. "I intended to murder that bastard that night, but I couldn't even do *that* right. I cut my own wrists before charging the podium, but I didn't expect to get woozy so fast. Next thing I know, I've been committed to a psychiatric facility for rehabilitation. Once I finally got out, I couldn't find anyone who would hire me for what I was trained for. I've spent the last three decades no better off than my own damned mother, hopping from one menial job to the next, and every single election cycle, I get to see that smug bastard's face grinning at me everywhere I turn." She barked out a short laugh. "I guess we're finally done with *that*."

I was at a loss for adequate words but felt an uncontrollable need to fill the empty air with something. "I'm just—so sorry."

It was nearly as bad as any of my inane offerings at a funeral.

Janet shuddered, forcing a tight smile onto her face as she dried away the last of her tears. She reached for another slice of pizza that had to be stone cold by now. "So, there you go. My entire sad story. I don't really see how that's gonna help your client."

"It might," I said, reaching into my laptop bag to extract the pictures I had printed out. "I've been trying to establish a pattern here, and you were the only woman who seemed to have a problem with Ghant. Even my client was trying to do everything she could to keep from complicating the senator's life."

"And her thanks for that was to be accused of murdering the son of a bitch. Nice," said Janet. "What do they have on her, anyway?"

"His body was found in her guest house, and her fingerprints were on the murder weapon," I said.

"Oh, is *that* all?" Janet asked rhetorically, laughing. "I can hardly blame the girl if she succeeded where I failed. In fact, I applaud her. What have you got there?" She wiped her greasy hands on her beige polyester slacks and reached for the printouts I held.

"These are some pictures I found online taken at some of Ghant's campaign rallies throughout the years. If you notice, they all have one thing in common. There's a different doe-eyed woman hanging on Ghant's every word," I said, leaning in to point as she flipped through the pictures. "I wonder if you might know who any of these women are?"

She harrumphed as she pulled one of the pictures from the stack. "Well, here's an easy one," she said. "This one's me."

I stared at the picture, struggling to see the woman before me in this younger version who gazed adoringly at the future senator's smiling face. It was only slightly easier to picture the enraged version who had been pictured immediately after her attempted assassination of the man, but when I squinted, I could see it in her eyes, maybe a little bit around the corners of her mouth.

"Well, huh," I said. It was all I could manage.

"And this here is Doralee Watkins," she said, pulling another picture from the stack and handing it to me. She couldn't have been more physically different from Janet with her pixie cut blonde hair and practically emaciated frame. Their only commonality was that same, lovestruck gaze. "I can't say this surprises me. We both worked on Parker's run for City Council, and even then, she was just as obvious as could be—batting her eyes and laughing that ridiculous high-pitched laugh of hers at every damn thing Parker said." She imitated the sound before rolling her eyes and muttering, "She was always so jealous of me."

I flipped the picture over and reached into my bag to grab a pen. I wrote her name on the back of the printout. "How about any of the others? Do you recognize any of them?"

Janet flipped through the rest of the pages, the slow shaking of her head increasing in intensity as she reached the bottom of the stack. "No, can't say that I do. Of course, by the time most of these were taken, I was a little busy being rehabilitated. Hey, listen, I'm sorry about your client, but I really can't see how I can be of any more help. And if you don't mind, *Big Brother* will be on soon."

"Of course," I said, taking my cue as she stood and stuffing my printouts back into my laptop bag. My eyes landed on a wall-mounted phone in the kitchen beside the rear sliding-glass door. "I don't suppose you have a phone number in case I have any more questions?"

298

"I don't suppose I do," she said, once again smiling tightly. "No offense intended—you seem like a nice enough man, but if I never see your sorry face again, it will be too soon. This isn't a topic I wanted to revisit."

"Of course," I found myself repeating as she escorted me to the front door. "Thank you for your time."

"Yeah? Well, sorry it wasn't helpful," she said, pulling the door open.

"I wouldn't say that," I said, smiling as I turned to say goodbye, but she had already closed the door in my face, the click of its deadbolt immediately following.

I walked back to my SUV, shivering against the cold. At least the snow had tapered off. My mind was churning as I slid behind the wheel and started the engine.

Doralee Watkins.

Maybe it was something, maybe not—but Janet Harper had at least given me another name to investigate.

CHAPTER TWENTY-FOUR

"Look-y here," Brady sing-songed as I shivered on his front stoop. "Two visits in one day. What's the occasion?"

"I was in the neighborhood," I said, pushing past him into his dimly lit living room. "Sort of."

"Well, come right in," he said, waving me inside with an exaggerated sweep of his arm. "It's not like me and Anyssa had a romantic evening planned or anything."

"Oh, God," I said, stopping in my tracks and furtively looking around. "Am I interrupting—"

"*Nah*," he said, grinning. "I'm just messin' with you. Anyssa's not even here. She's giving Scotty a ride back to the Caudills while I get Billy tucked into bed. It's a school night, although I wouldn't be surprised if it got called for weather. Still, it *is* considered customary, even *polite* to call before—"

"Yeah, yeah, yeah," I interrupted, slipping my coat off and draping it over the back of his sofa. "I've got some new information on Senator Ghant, and your house was closer than mine. Where can I set up?" I waggled my laptop bag in front of him.

"Willingly sharing information with me? That's certainly a first," he said. He led me back to the dinette where we had eaten breakfast earlier. His own laptop already occupied the position at the head of the table, and beside it was a legal pad covered in his spidery handwriting.

"Making use of your resources is a little more like it," I said, pulling my laptop out of my bag and placing it on the table in front of the seat to his right. I sat down and powered up my computer. "You wanna share your wi-fi password, or are you going to make use my mobile hotspot?"

He hesitated, his cheeks reddening. "It's 'Brady+Anyssa4EV'—capital B, A, E, and V, plus sign, and the number four."

I stared at him, a smile slowly creeping across my face until my swollen cheek tempered my reaction. *"Seriously?* How very high school of you!"

"Shut up," he said, stepping around the island cooktop and into the kitchen. "It meets the minimum complexity standards, and I change it every month. It gets hard to think of new passwords that I'll remember. I was about to get myself something to eat. You hungry? I've got some wraps left over from Friday's party."

My stomach answered for me, gurgling so loudly he laughed.

"I'll take that as a yes," he said, snagging a handful of Italian wraps and returning to the table with a bottle of beer for himself and a can of Pepsi for me.

"Thanks," I said, greedily digging in while trying not to get schmutz on my laptop keyboard. "Looks like you were working."

He nodded. "When am I not? Trying to compile a tasteful 'In Memoriam' for some old geezer who keeled over from a brain aneurysm last night. Served as both a representative and a senator for Wisconsin since about the time it was admitted into the Union. I think he might have been Abraham Lincoln's pool boy back in the day. Senators are dropping like flies this weekend."

"Nice," I said. "I hope whatever you come up with will be a little more tactful than that."

"Oh, sure," he said absently, focusing on his own screen while I pulled up a web browser on mine.

"Why are you handling obits?" I asked. "I would have thought this sort of assignment was beneath you."

"It is, but we're a little overextended at *The Dispatch*," he said. "A bunch of people are out with COVID, and since I'm already working on the Ghant assassination, I don't mind cobbling something together, especially since the two frequently worked on legislation together."

My fingers froze over the keyboard.

"What did you say his name was?" I asked, my voice distant in my own ears.

"I didn't, but it was Errol Warren," he said, reviewing whatever text he had drafted. "Family went all the way back to the Mayflower, and…"

Brady's words swam out of focus, and it was a good thing he wasn't paying attention to me because I was busy having an out-of-body experience—it wasn't one he would have missed.

Errol Warren.

He was one of two other powerful congressional officials Gina had seen alongside Parker Ghant colluding at the Academy in Briarstaff. Warren and Ghant were two-thirds of the reason why my sister was forced to fake her own death, keeping our entire family suspended in a perpetual state of grief that was slowly but surely chipping away at our father's steely resolve. Senator Amelia Gorham from Pennsylvania was the only surviving member of their clandestine coven, and I couldn't keep my dark thought at bay.

Two down—one to go.

I'm not accustomed to wishing death on people, but in this case, there was no remorse. These people had shattered my family, and if only some equally grave misfortune could befall Senator Gorham, Gina could finally come home. We might be able to return to some semblance of normal. I could feel heat building in my cheeks as Brady's voice slowly cut through my fog.

"Earth to Dwayne, Earth to Dwayne," he said, and of course, he was staring. "Are you in there?"

I forced a smile. "Yeah, sure, sorry. I—uh, just got a little lost in my own thoughts for a second, there. What were you saying?"

He eyed me suspiciously, pushing his laptop aside. "Doesn't really matter. You said you had some new information on the Ghant case. Spill."

I was already Googling the name, 'Doralee Watkins.'

"Were you aware that there was a previous attempt on Parker Ghant's life about thirty years ago?" I asked.

"I seem to recall reading that somewhere. Some psycho bitch went after him at a campaign rally with a ball bat or something."

I looked up from the query results that had just populated my screen. "A *ball bat?* I sincerely hope you double-check every single one of your references before you ever go to print."

"*Pffft,*" he said, dismissively. "It's been a minute since I read whatever it was that I read, but close enough. Lady was a whackadoodle and ended up getting herself institutionalized. What's the relevance? Surely, you don't think after thirty years she came back to exact her revenge."

I nudged my laptop aside and fished the printouts from my bag, thumbing through them until I found the one I was looking for. "No, but I just came from said whackadoodle's apartment—her name is Janet Harper, by the way. She slit her own wrists before trying to gut Ghant and would have died happy if only she had been successful. Here's a picture from around that time." I slid the picture over to Brady, who picked it up to study.

"Kind of cute for a whackadoodle," he noted. "Sure doesn't look like she's about to plant a blade in the guy. In fact, she sort of looks like she's swooning over him."

"*Exactly,*" I said, sliding the rest of the pictures over to him. "See if you can spot the common thread."

He flipped through them, slowly nodding. "Okay—the senator had quite a way with the ladies. What made this Harper lady turn on him? Did he toss her aside for one of these other girls?"

"More or less, but not before he got her pregnant," I said.

"Huh," said Brady, setting the pictures down on the table. "I don't recall mention of any bastard babies in Ghant's biography."

I scowled at his indelicate phrasing. "That's because the baby was never born. Janet Harper was assaulted by a couple of mask-wearing, knife-wielding men who stabbed her repeatedly and left her for dead. She survived, but the baby didn't. She thinks the men were hired by Parker's father to protect his reputation. He was engaged to be married to his first wife at the time, and infidelity doesn't usually play well to a largely conservative crowd."

"That's quite an accusation," said Brady. "Did she have any proof?"

"Nothing concrete," I said. "She said both men were wearing t-shirts with the Ghant campaign slogan emblazoned across the front. Nothing she could use to identify the men involved, but it was more than enough to convince her."

Brady sat back in his chair, tugging at his bottom lip while he deliberated. "It's certainly possible. Gordon Ghant was definitely a force to be reckoned with in his day. His reputation preceded him. His rivals held him in what they called healthy respect, but I suspect it was more like fear. There were always rumors he had ties to organized crime, but it was never proven. He was massively popular with the working class and farmers, so much so that when he died, he lay in state at the Ohio Statehouse to give folks ample opportunity to pay their final respects."

The sound of a key turning at the front door caught both of our attention, followed by the sound of the door opening and closing. A gust of frigid air wrapped around from the living room amidst the noise of feet stomping on the mat just inside the door.

"Babe? I'm home," called Anyssa. "Is that Dwayne's car I see in the drive?"

"It is," he called back. "We're back here in the dinette. I hope your drive wasn't too awful."

She rounded the corner, and we both stood to greet her. "It wasn't bad at all. The snow's stopped, and the road crews have been on top of it. Of course, I drive a *sensible* car, unlike that flashy toy you're so proud of. I think the boys are going to be disappointed if they're really counting on a snow day. Hi, Dwayne. To what do we owe the pleasure?"

She offered me a smile and a quick hug before rubbing her icy hands together and shivering.

"He's freeloading off of our internet," said Brady, taking her into his arms and kissing her deeply while I squirmed and looked away.

"Guilty," I admitted. "I was just hoping to do a little research to see if I will be making any more stops before heading back home. I'll be out of your hair in just a few minutes."

She extracted herself from Brady's arms and moved toward the kitchen. "Stay as long as you like, I'm not trying to rush you. What I really want is a nice big cup of hot chocolate. I'm freezing all the way to my bones. Any takers?"

"No, thank you," I said. "I'm good."

Brady's face squirreled up. "Beer and hot chocolate don't really mix very well, but I know *another* kind of hot chocolate I'm *totally* up for later." He waggled his thick eyebrows, reminding me of one of those lascivious cartoon wolves whose tongues roll down to the floor before trailing halfway across the room.

"*Brady!*" she admonished, barely able to suppress her grin while I did my best not to lose what little of the Italian wrap I'd managed to eat. Brady's skeezy charm was nauseating and entirely inexplicable to me, but Anyssa was clearly eating it up. She crossed to the pantry and extracted a box of hot chocolate mix while Brady and I sat back down at the table.

"So, what were we talking about?" Brady asked, returning his attention to me.

"A couple of dead Ghants," I said, adjusting my Google query on 'Doralee Watkins' to refine the hundreds of unrelated results that came pouring in with just her name alone. I added 'Columbus Ohio' to the request before clicking 'Search' once more.

Brady picked up the stack of photos and began flipping through them again. "Harper wasn't able to identify any of these other women?"

"Huh-unh. They were all after her time with the campaign—well, except for this one I'm looking for." I reached over and indicated the relevant photo. "Janet said Ghant was carrying on with Doralee Watkins as she was being shown the door."

"And now you're trying to locate her, too?"

I shrugged. "It's all I can think to do. Maybe she knows who some of these other women are."

Brady's inhalation whistled. "Sounds like a pretty long shot to me, and I don't really get the connection to Rochelle—"

His eyes widened as his words dropped away, and I could almost see the light bulb flare brightly over his head as the tumblers fell into place.

"Her little boy, Joel—"

"Joey," I corrected.

"He's Parker's *son!*"

I avoided his eyes. "I can neither confirm nor deny that."

He threw his head back laughing. "Of course! How did I not see that?"

"Because it isn't something that Rochelle makes a habit of advertising. In fact, she couldn't if she wanted to."

"How so?"

I sighed. "I'm still not entirely comfortable discussing this with you without Rochelle's approval."

"Oh, come *on!* Totally off the record—I swear," he said, placing his hand over his heart. "I'm only trying to be helpful. I don't want to see an innocent woman go to jail for something she didn't do, and let's face it, with Melanie busy taking care of things down south, you could use a sounding board."

"I could always call Mel," I said.

"But you won't because her plate is already too full. Come on. I'm right here. I'll bet by this time tomorrow, I'll have learned who Rochelle's new attorney is and arranged for you to get that in-person visit you wanted, too. Is a little bit of trust too much to ask in return?"

I stared at him and scowled, attempting to weigh options I didn't really have.

"Okay, *fine*," I finally said. "But this is strictly probationary, and the first time I am quoted without prior permission will be the last time I talk to you, capisce?"

He nodded and sat forward in his chair, his eyes glowing like a kid's at Christmas as he eagerly awaited whatever it was I had to say, and I prayed I wasn't making a mistake.

"It would seem that Ghant has a pattern of buying silence from these women by offering them large settlements that are free and clear, provided they sign a non-disclosure agreement," I said.

"What do you mean by 'pattern?' There are others?"

"I've confirmed one, but that's why I'm looking to identify the women in these photos. I suspect there are more."

He sat back in his chair. "The one you've confirmed, what's her name?"

"I'm not at liberty to say. She's entitled to her privacy and isn't interested in violating the NDA, if it even still applies now that Ghant is dead."

"Did she have Ghant's baby, too?"

Brady's inquisitive eyes didn't ever seem to blink, and I was unnerved by the laser-like focus of his rapid-fire questioning and how quickly he was connecting the dots. Still, I wasn't going to lie to him now.

"Yes," I said, and Brady whistled again.

"This sort of thing would *not* play well with some of Ghant's biggest supporters," he said. "So, how did Rochelle come to hire Boggs Investigations? Was she trying to get out of the NDA that she signed?"

"No, quite the opposite," I said, pinching the bridge of my nose. My headache was beginning to worsen. "For whatever reason, she still felt really protective of Ghant and didn't want to upset his family life or career, but she needed his help. Her little boy is really sick."

"Yeah, you mentioned that earlier," said Brady. "How sick is 'really sick?'"

"He's got a form of leukemia that will kill him if he doesn't receive a bone marrow transplant," I said. "In these cases, the best donor matches are usually from other family members. Rochelle was convinced that if only she could talk to Parker, she could make him understand the urgency, and he would be willing to help. The problem was that she couldn't get past the man's team of security goons. She's been trying to hire outside help to get the message delivered, but everyone else has bailed on her. Boggs Investigations has been the only team with enough tenacity to stay on the job."

"More like stupidity," he said, clearly assessing my wrecked face. "This doesn't sound like Doug at all, but it's got your fingerprints all over it. How did you get him to stay on the case?"

I chuckled. "Believe it or not, Loretta is with me on this one. Rochelle's plight managed to prove that the old battleaxe does indeed have a heart." I turned to Anyssa, who stood at the island separating us from the kitchen, blowing the steam from the top of her mug. "I don't suppose I could trouble you for a few more Excedrin?"

"Of course," she said. "Your head's still bothering you? You should really get yourself checked out."

"*Pssh*," I said, waving away her concern. "I just need a good night's rest. I'll be fine."

"If you say so," she said dubiously, bringing me a glass of water and my requested pain relief.

I thanked her and tossed the pills back, swallowing them as one. My eyes wandered back to the search results populating my screen, one of which almost leapt out at me. "Oh, no," I said, clicking the link.

"What is it?" asked Brady, sliding closer to peer at my screen.

"She's dead," I said, impatient for the page to load.

"Who's dead?"

"Doralee Watkins," I said, skimming the scant details divulged by an online ancestry site without signing up for a membership. She had died barely a year after Janet Harper's own entanglement with Parker Ghant. "There's not much to go on here, not even a cause of death."

Brady picked up the printout with Doralee's picture, upon which I had written her name. He added the date of death from the website and stood, pulling his phone from his pocket.

"Let me make a call or two and see if I can get some more information about this," he said, already consulting his contacts as he drifted away into the living room.

Anyssa and I smiled at each other awkwardly across the cooktop. We didn't know each other quite well enough for conversation to come easily, but I genuinely liked Anyssa, despite her questionable choice in men.

"How are things going out on Marble Toe?" I asked, referencing the island where the manor house she owned was located. She was currently in the process of turning it into a premium murder-mystery weekend destination on the Great Lakes. Our trial run over the past Labor Day had gone spectacularly off the rails, indicating a need for more stringent controls in the experience.

"I think we've added the necessary structure to the murder scripts, but winter's been hard on the house," she said. "The last big snowfall came right through the roof in the northwest corner of the attic, and repairs have really put a dent in the margins of my operating budget. I'm optimistic that we'll be ready to give it another go by May. You up for a return engagement?"

She arched an eyebrow at me expectantly, and I laughed. "Thanks, but no thanks. Been there, done that."

She scowled. "Oh, come on. You've got to give it another chance. I mean, what are the odds things could go *that* wrong again?"

"With my luck? A little better than I'd care to admit."

"It wasn't all bad. If it hadn't been for that weekend, I would have never met any of you, and I've grown rather fond of all of you in the time since. I couldn't be happier that you and Melanie have sorted through your differences."

Jasmine's earlier phone call flashed through my aching head, and my smile faltered a bit. "Well, we still have a few things to discuss."

Anyssa's scowl deepened. "Oh, no," she said. "Stop it right there, mister."

I blinked. "Stop what?"

"Typical guy move. You're overthinking things," she said. "Life is too short to worry about all of the ways things can go wrong. Spend your time looking for trouble, and that's all you're ever going to find. You're going to let the best thing that's ever happened to you get away, and what a stupid, senseless mistake that would be. Please tell me you're smarter than that."

I wasn't expecting our conversation to morph into another uninvited counseling session, but I couldn't deny the impact of her impassioned words. Responding, however, was another matter altogether. My mouth worked uselessly for a second before I managed to lamely say, "I'm trying."

She looked less than satisfied with my response, but mercifully, Brady chose that moment to charge back into the room, his excitement evident. "Man, oh man, you're never gonna believe this."

"Well, that was fast," I said.

He smirked. "It pays to have connections in the Pickaway County Coroner's office."

"Yeah?" asked Anyssa. "And what's her name?"

That wiped the smirk right off of Brady's face. "Who said it was a 'her?'"

Anyssa merely cocked her head and stared, folding her arms across her chest. I couldn't keep from laughing.

"Busted, my friend," I said.

"Okay, *fine*, Margie Coldiron is a *former* acquaintance of mine, and I'm leaving it at that," said Brady, as color crept into his cheeks. "We're getting off track here. Doralee Watkins was found dead in her apartment several months after Parker Ghant was sworn into Westerville City Council."

I sat up straighter. "Stabbed?"

"Huh-unh," said Brady, shaking his head. "Suicide. She took an entire bottle of benzos and washed them down with a bottle of vodka. But that ain't all."

He was enjoying his moment of revelation a little too much, his eyes gleaming while he grinned at me expectantly, and I was losing patience with his whole routine. I rolled my eyes and then my hand, encouraging him to get to the point.

"She wasn't alone. It was her screaming toddler that drew the attention of her neighbors," he practically whispered, waiting for my reaction, and finally getting his reward when my mouth fell open. "There were indications that post-partum depression was a contributing factor."

"Anything about the father?" I asked.

Brady shook his head. "Nope, but I've been doing some quick math, and—"

"It might have been Ghant?"

He shrugged. "The timing's approximately right, but—" His phone rang in his hand, startling him to silence. He glanced at the screen and swiped to answer the call. "Talk to me."

The voice on the other end was animated and unintelligible, but my curiosity was piqued as I watched Brady's expression intensify with whatever he was hearing.

"You've got to be kidding me," he said. "Alright, I'll meet you there in fifteen to twenty. We can do breaking news right there in the parking lot if we have to, just bring your camera, and get there as fast you can."

He disconnected the call, already moving toward the front of the house.

"What was that?" I asked as Anyssa and I trailed after him.

"Rochelle Pendleton was attacked by another inmate," he said, tossing me my coat before plucking his own from the rack beside the front door. "She's being transported to Riverside as we speak."

CHAPTER TWENTY-FIVE

I insisted we take my car under the pretext that it was safer in this inclement weather with its all-wheel drive. While this was technically true, it was strictly my survival instinct that prompted the offer. Brady's driving on a good day scared the shit out of me, and I really wanted to see how this story ended.

Brady's source hadn't been able to tell him how bad it was, only that Rochelle had been stabbed by another prisoner named Chardy McMahon—McMurray—McMuffin—*McSomething*. I focused on the road ahead as Brady bounced from call to call on his cell, mobilizing his team in ways I couldn't completely follow, but he was entirely in his element. Traffic was light as I pushed the speed limit on Henderson Road, but the headlights from oncoming traffic reflecting off the damp pavement was exacerbating my headache and making the Italian wrap I had just eaten heavy in my stomach. Of course, it wasn't helped by the acid roiling through my system. The thought of Joey never seeing his mother again was more than I could bear. It was completely inconceivable how quickly things had gone south. It felt more like years than two days since I had spoken to Rochelle over breakfast with her son.

As we traveled south on Olentangy River Road, approaching the sprawling Riverside Methodist campus, I couldn't help but notice the stark contrast between the chaotic OhioHealth campus and the far more sedate

Lymont Memorial, where Sarah was being treated. An air ambulance circled the building waiting for clearance to land while the entrance to Emergency was a sea of police vehicles and ambulances.

"I see my camera guy by the doors," said Brady, as I worked my way closer. "Just let me out here and find someplace to park. I'll catch up with you inside."

He was already halfway out of the car before I had come to a complete stop. "Is there anything I can do?" I asked before he was completely out of earshot.

"Just stay out of the way. Grab a seat in the waiting room and keep your phone handy if you go anywhere. I'll let you know as soon as I find out anything," he called over his shoulder, and then he was gone, sprinting off to meet his colleague.

I sighed, winding my way through haphazardly parked vehicles with their emergency lights pulsing in synchronicity with the throbbing of my head. Riverside's ever-expanding campus was in the middle of another major renovation, adding another nearly 600,000 square feet to its overall footprint. The ongoing construction of what was currently a hulking, skeletal framework of steel girders, along with two ginormous cranes that stood sentinel in the dark, was forcing the closure of some of the most easily accessible parking. This required more people to make use of the parking garages, and I was wondering if I was going to find myself on the roof of the Red Parking Garage when I finally secured a spot on the fourth level. I shivered against the cold as I bypassed the elevator and used the stairs, taking them two at a time to reach the ground floor.

The sidewalks glistened with Safe-T-Salt, and it crunched beneath my shoes as I passed others hurrying to and from the hospital. Most were easily categorized as employee or visitor, based on their attire and the level of distress reflected on their faces. A group of young male Latinos engaged in rapid-fire conversation that I couldn't begin to understand with clouds of smoke billowing around their heads, all while congregating incongruously around a sign that declared this and all OhioHealth campuses smoke-free.

I passed through the sliding doors into the Emergency Room waiting area where chaos had preceded me, but at least it was a little warmer. A middle-aged man with a Julius Caesar hairline was arguing with one of three security guards near the walk-through metal detector about the necessity of the contents of the backpack he carried while the other two kept the short line slowly moving. When it was my turn, I surrendered my laptop bag for pillaging and dropped my keys and loose change into a plastic receptacle, holding my watch over my head as directed as I passed through without incident.

Thankfully, I had remembered to leave my gun locked in my car.

"Take a number, and they'll get you checked in as soon as possible," the stone-faced guard said, reciting a line that was undoubtedly automatic by now.

"I'm just waiting for a friend," I said, collecting my belongings from the plastic tray.

"Oh, I thought—" His gaze lingered on the damage to my face as his voice dropped away, and he waved me on. "You can have a seat over there."

I scanned the packed room and sighed. Most of the seating was occupied, and what wasn't was by choice. No one wanted to sit next to the emaciated woman tweaking and geeking near the water fountain or the three-hundred-pound fella who seemed to be leaking from every visible orifice—and probably a few that weren't. Can a person look like he smells? I'm going to say yes. An admissions nurse called a mother and her young daughter back into the secure triage area as I was passing the loveseat they occupied, and I didn't miss a beat snagging the newly vacated spot before anyone else noticed. I set my laptop bag beside me, not so subtly discouraging anyone from taking its other side. I would grudgingly move it if anyone asked, but I wasn't looking for conversation. I was trying to make sense of everything I had learned in the past few hours, and between the ambient noise filling the waiting room and the steady thud pulsating at my temples, I could barely think at all.

I slipped my phone out of my coat pocket and unlocked it with my thumbprint, pulling up my favorite contacts and tapping the icon with Melanie's face. I could certainly use a friendly voice, and she might just see something I was completely overlooking. It wouldn't be the first time. Her phone rang a handful of times before going to voicemail, and I disconnected without leaving a message. I tapped out a quick text asking her to call me whenever she had a moment before slipping the phone back into my pocket.

I leaned back on the hard plastic cushion and closed my eyes, pinching the bridge of my nose and trying to massage away the pressure that was slowly building behind my brow. I leaned my head back without any consideration whatsoever to who or what else might have leaned against the wall before me. The room felt like it was closing in on me while the bustle and noise receded like the tide being pulled out to sea.

"Dwayne!"

I jerked upright in my seat, my eyes swimming into focus. Brady was uncomfortably close, scrutinizing me with a level of concern that was unfamiliar. I realized my mouth was hanging open, and my tongue felt like sand. I tried to speak but could only cough, elevating Brady's alarm to new heights. He turned to call for help when I grabbed his arm and squeezed.

"I'm fine," I said, my voice like the rusty hinges on an old screen door. I cleared my throat and summoned trace amounts of saliva, but it was like trying to break a drought with a thimbleful of water.

Brady eyed me dubiously. "You don't *look* fine. You're white as a sheet."

"I've probably picked up something from all the disease floating around this room," I said, my voice beginning to sound a little more like my own. I rubbed my eyes before focusing on a clock mounted on the wall across from me.

Ten forty-three.

That couldn't possibly be right. I hadn't really paid much attention to when we arrived but knew I had lost a significant chunk of time. It seemed highly improbable that I had fallen asleep in a crowded hospital waiting room, but apparently, I had. I jerked to my right, certain that my laptop bag would be gone.

It wasn't. It remained undisturbed and exactly where I had laid it. My headache hadn't gone anywhere, either, although it had diminished slightly. I squinted up at Brady.

"Have you heard anything about Rochelle?" I asked.

"She's still in surgery," he said. "We went live with breaking news, and I managed to get a sound bite from one of the officers who escorted her ambulance here, but it didn't amount to much. We've been outside for so long I can barely feel my fingers. I sent my guys down to the cafeteria to get us something warm to drink while we wait for new developments, but this could take a while. You really don't need to stick around—unless you're finally considering getting yourself checked out, which I would highly recommend. You really don't look good, man."

"I'm fine."

"I tried calling you like a million times before I headed in here," he said, moving my laptop bag to the floor and taking the seat beside me.

I pulled my phone from my pocket and looked at its screen. There were eight missed calls, all but one from Brady. The other was from Melanie. She had also left a short text.

Tag. You're It.

317

"I guess I didn't hear it," I said, unable to mask my perplexity.

"I could buy you not hearing it over all the noise in the room, but because you fell *asleep?* Come on. That's not normal."

"I said I'm *fine*," I said irritably. "I'm just tired, that's all."

Brady sighed. "Then you should go home and get some rest."

"How will you get home?" I asked.

"This could be an all-nighter," he said. "I can always get one of my guys to take me home."

"You'll call me if anything changes?"

"I promise," he said. "Now, go. Our meteorologists are reporting another wave of precipitation is moving in within the next hour or so, and it's supposed to bring even more accumulation than before."

I grudgingly got to my feet and put my laptop bag over my shoulder. "Fine."

Brady walked me to the exit. "I'd like you to do me a favor, too."

"What's that?"

"Call or text me when you get home," he said. "I've got too much going on to be worried about you, too."

I nodded as the automatic door swooshed open, admitting a gust of wind that assailed us from all sides. It was decidedly colder than when we had arrived. "Yeah, sure. Whatever."

He grabbed my arm, forcing me to look at him. "Promise?"

I shook my head, fighting back a grin. "Alright, alright! I promise. Now, can I go, please?"

I stepped out into the night, the smile lingering on my face as I headed toward the Red Parking Garage. I would die before admitting it, but it was nice to know that Brady truly cared.

Exiting the parking garage, I drove around the rear of the hospital campus to avoid the service roads that had been closed by the ongoing construction, turning right on Thomas Lane, which essentially turned into a southbound entrance ramp for SR-315 at Olentangy River Road. What should have been an easy drive to I-670 quickly became an exercise in frustration and futility as all three lanes ground to a halt just short of the exit towards Upper Arlington and Lane Avenue. Clearly, there must have been an accident, as an ambulance worked its way past our idling vehicles, using the berm and escorted by a pair of Columbus's finest. I could see more pulsating police lights just beyond a sea of bright red taillights but couldn't quite determine which side of the road the accident was on. I was in the center lane and figured it was as good as any for now. Snow was beginning to fall again, and I just wanted to get home before it got any worse.

With no other choice but to creep along as cars slowly inched forward, I decided to try Melanie once more. Again, I landed in her voicemail, and now I was beginning to worry about *her*. I realized cell service could be spotty at best in some areas around Lymont, but she would've had reception at the hospital or if she'd returned to Sarah's house. Of course, she had mentioned the weather was worse there when we had spoken earlier, and it wasn't difficult to imagine her skidding off any one of the hairpin turns that comprised Brenner Hollow, especially the way Melanie drove. I was working myself toward the edge of panic when it occurred to me that she had said Sarah's parents were watching Jasmine and Jordan, and it was an absolute dead zone for cell service where they lived. I chuckled to myself uneasily as I glommed onto an idea that seemed reasonably probable. Eventually, she'd see my missed text and calls and would call me back. Still, my restless fingers drummed on my steering wheel, my mind finding other worries to entertain.

An image of Joey Pendleton's bright, inquisitive face flashed before me. I could almost hear his exuberant proclamation— *"Dane!"* —and my heart ached. With nothing but time on my hands, my fertile imagination was determined to construct a vivid scenario in which Rochelle hugged and kissed her young son goodbye before departing Lauren's houseboat, reminding him to behave while she was away—it would only be for a short while. Now, she was fighting for her very life in an operating room at Riverside, and the mercifully oblivious child might never see his mother again. Who would take care of the boy if Rochelle didn't pull through? Who would navigate the difficult path of securing a bone marrow donor to give Joey a fighting chance at a normal life? There was simply nobody better suited or more dedicated to the task than the boy's mother, and I found myself getting angrier by the moment at the incredibly unfair hand that had been dealt to Rochelle and her family as well as my own inability to do anything about it.

Vehicles were beginning to gravitate toward the righthand lane, so I activated my turn signal to show my intent and squinted into lights that seemed exceedingly bright in my rearview mirror, waiting for either a good Samaritan or a relatively safe opportunity, whichever came first. I could see the line of patrol cars blocking passage of the southbound corridor and forcing everybody off at Lane Avenue, where we would all have to find alternate routes to our final destinations. My mood only darkened with the realization that major thoroughfares are generally only closed when there are fatalities involved.

I caught a break and worked my way onto the congested exit ramp, trying to decide my best path home, but I wasn't entirely sure that I wanted to go home. Going home felt like giving up, and I wanted more than anything to do something helpful in a situation that seemed exceedingly dire.

Begin at the beginning.

Melanie's words floated into my ears as if whispered from the back seat. "Can you be a little more specific?" I asked aloud. *"Please?"*

I realized the car in front of me had come to an abrupt stop, and I stood on my brake pedal, praying the exit ramp wasn't covered in black ice. My shoulder belt went taut, forcing an involuntary glug from somewhere deep within my throat as it prevented me from braining myself on the steering wheel. My laptop bag toppled forward in the passenger seat, spilling most of its loose contents into the floorboard. Thankfully, I had zipped my laptop into the bag's center compartment, saving it from a similar fate. My eyes landed on the envelope Rochelle had left for me at Lauren's boathouse, and the message contained within returned to taunt me.

I've got some info you should see in the floor safe of the guest cottage. You know the code.

I most certainly did *not* know the code. But I knew where the guest cottage was. How hard could it be to find a floor safe in a building of that size? It seemed that with a knot this tangled, it might be best to focus on pulling at the piece I could get my hands on and worry about the rest in due time. By then, an epiphany might just happen. Admittedly, the odds were akin to hitting the lottery, but you know what they say—you can't win the lottery if you don't take a chance.

When I reached the light at the bottom of the exit ramp, I opted to turn left, crossing under the mess on the freeway overhead before turning left again and rejoining SR-315 in the opposite direction. It was the quickest way to reach the I-270 outer belt and head west to Plain City. It was nearly eleven-thirty, and I hoped the odds of accessing Rochelle's property might be a little more in my favor this time around.

I rolled my window all the way down as I traveled west on US-33 towards Marysville. The inside of my car had gotten a little too warm and comfortable, and I caught my head bobbing just one too many times. This was really unlike me, and after my little incident in the waiting room at Riverside, I was just a bit afraid I'd blink and find myself wrapped around the base of the high masts that illuminated the roadway. The icy cold wind whipped me back to attention, although it didn't do much for the throbbing at my temples.

The precipitation was already morphing from harmless, fluffy snow into something more compact that pinged off my windshield and the roof of my Hyundai, and I adjusted my speed accordingly. Slow and steady wins the race, right? Well, *no*, but it certainly improves your odds on arriving safely at the finish line to congratulate the winner, and as the markings on the highway slowly faded away underneath the steady onslaught, it seemed increasingly prudent.

I was approaching Rochelle's property from a different angle, and while I had been sure of my route when I exited onto US-33, my confidence began to wane when I couldn't quite remember which road I was looking for to reach my destination. The highway was practically deserted at this point, so I took a moment to pull over and idle with my hazard lights on, locating my phone which had fallen into the passenger floorboard along with most of the contents of my laptop bag. I plugged my phone into the SUV's USB port and scooped the rest of the items back into the bag before climbing back behind the wheel and engaging the maps feature available through Android Auto. Rochelle's address was already programmed as a recent destination, so all it took was one tap of the finger to get myself back on track. I eased back onto the highway and took the exit for US-42 into Plain City.

The narrow road leading to Rochelle's property was buried beneath a field of unbroken snow, and my tires crunched audibly as I crept toward my destination. There was no oncoming traffic to blind me on this leg of the journey, but my own headlights reflecting off the snow hurt my eyes, and squinting against the glare was only making my headache worse.

As expected, the entrance to the Pendleton property was deserted. It was also dark and foreboding, and for a fraction of a second, I considered turning back. What if there was a policeman guarding the premises, and his vehicle was parked somewhere I couldn't see? What would I say to explain my presence? Would I be arrested for breaking and entering when I clearly knew how to get through the security gate?

I stared at the obscene collection of offerings that had been left memorializing the late, great Senator Ghant and wondered how these benefactors might feel if they knew half as much about the man as I did. It hardly seemed fair that the man was virtually being canonized while Rochelle was busy touring the seven rings of Hell.

I drove up to the keypad mounted near the entrance and entered the security code. The gate swung inward, and I didn't give myself any more time to question the wisdom of what I was doing. I slipped the gearshift into drive and passed through before I could change my mind. I had barely cleared them before the gates reversed course, and I had the fleeting sensation that I was being trapped inside. I giggled aloud at the ridiculous thought, startling myself with the sound of my own voice.

For shit's sake, get a grip! I thought to myself, shaking my head.

I proceeded, unable to determine where the gravel drive lay beneath the wintry accumulation. The best I could do was inch along, trusting my memory to be my guide while not trusting it enough to drive any faster than five or so miles per hour. Soon enough, the darkened outline of the guest cottage loomed to my left, and from what I could tell, there was nobody standing sentry. Somehow, I thought it should bring some comfort, but it didn't, and now I really had to pee. I pulled close enough to see the yellow crime scene tape that crisscrossed the front entrance and killed my lights and engine, and the resulting silence was deafening, save for the steady ting of icy precipitation falling from the heavens.

I took a deep breath before grabbing my laptop bag from the passenger seat and stepping out into the night. I was almost to the front stoop when I stopped and turned back. I had left my gun locked in the glove compartment.

I was *never* going to get the hang of this shit!

Once I had my weapon stowed safely in its holster, I went back and used the key Rochelle had given me to unlock the front door, pushing it open. I paused, waiting for the beep indicating I would need to disarm the security system, but it never came. For a second, I thought the senator's body was still sprawled out before me on the carpet below, but I blinked and realized it was just the bloody aftermath of where his corpse had been. There were a handful of numbered markers scattered throughout the living room that obviously meant something to officers who had placed them, and although they were meaningless to me, I paid them due deference and cut a wide path to avoid them altogether. There was no need to begin my quest in a room that still reeked with the unmistakably coppery scent of spilled blood. In fact, I hoped to find the safe in another part of the house so I wouldn't have to spend any more time than necessary on my hands and knees in that particular room.

I wandered back to the bedroom I had occupied, noting Dexter's cat carrier sitting beside the makeshift litter box I had left behind in the hallway. I didn't want any of these things back, not even the clothes I had left behind. I could never look at any of it again without thinking of death and how fragile life actually is.

The bedroom was dark, and opening the blinds provided little additional illumination. The moon was obscured behind heavy clouds shedding a wintry mix of precipitation, but I was hesitant to turn on the bedside lamp. It would be a beacon to anyone who might be patrolling the grounds, and I couldn't be certain that nobody was. It seemed like a better idea to use the flashlight on my phone and limit its reach with my hand.

I patted the pockets of my coat.

No phone.

I closed my eyes and sighed. I had left the damned thing hooked to the USB port in my car.

I retraced my steps through the living room, eager to grab my phone and get this search over and done with. I had only opened the front door a crack when I reversed course, slowly easing it closed. I stepped sideways over the blood-stained carpet to peer through the cottage's front window from the shadows. A bright column of light bobbed side to side in the dark, drawing closer.

Somebody was coming.

CHAPTER TWENTY-SIX

I backed into the shadows as the roving beam of light drew closer, already working on what might serve as a plausible excuse for being there. It occurred to me that Detective Burnside might have had the property under observation, and I was probably moments away from being taken into custody and escorted to a cell of my very own—or worse yet, a shared cell with hardened and violent criminals keen to establish dominance over any newcomers such as myself.

My heart raced in my chest with the sudden realization that even the shadows I used for cover were not impervious to the halogen beam scanning the front of the cottage, and I scurried forward, pressing myself flat against the front door where I couldn't be seen. My gun dug into the small of my back, and I briefly considered extracting it from its holster before realizing it was the quickest way to be seen as a lethal threat by the approaching officer. I could almost picture my grotesque tap dance across the living room and into the afterlife as my body was riddled with bullets fired in self-defense.

This wasn't good.

Maybe whoever it is will go away, simply move along after patrolling the area—

Yeah, right.

No amount of wishful thinking was going to make *that* happen. My SUV parked in the drive as well as the crime scene tape I had disturbed upon entry were practically tattling on me. Footsteps crunched in the snow on the stoop, and I held my breath, fearful that the sound of my pounding heart was just as audible on the other side of the door.

I jumped when a series of knocks sounded near my head.

"Dwayne? Are you in there?"

The voice was little more than a whisper, and while it was vaguely familiar, it took a moment to recognize. I peered through the peephole and found Brady shivering on the doorstep. Relief washed over me as I opened the door.

"Brady? What are *you* doing here?" I asked, as he nudged his way past me, stopping on a dime before stepping into the telltale bloodstain on the carpet.

"I could ask you the same," he said, rubbing his gloved hands together to generate a little warmth. "I thought you were going home to get some rest."

I closed the door and sidled over to the window, searching for any other unexpected visitors who might be approaching. The coast was clear.

"I changed my mind," I said, keeping my response vague. "That still doesn't explain why you're here. I thought you were hanging out at Riverside waiting for your next breaking news update."

"It's probably going to be a while," he said. "Rochelle made it through her surgery and is in recovery. She's not out of danger, but it's a step in the right direction. I left my team on site and told them to call me if anything changes. I had a feeling my time would be better spent keeping an eye on you."

"You were *following* me?"

"Not exactly," he said, trying to diffuse my escalating outrage with a cockeyed grin. "At least, not until I checked in with Anyssa. She mentioned that Melanie had called her, looking for you when neither one of us answered our phones. It had to have been when I was on the air, and you were passed out in the hospital waiting room. Melanie's battery was about to die, and she was hoping she might catch you at my place. Anyssa told her what had happened to Rochelle, and Melanie was afraid you were going to do something stupid. Let's face it—stupid is frequently your go-to move. I decided to do a little checking up on your whereabouts." He extracted his phone from his pocket and unlocked it, scrolling through its apps until he found what he was looking for and tapped on its icon.

My teeth were already grinding. "You have *got* to be kidding. You've been tracking me on Mother Knows Best?"

I referenced an app Melanie had secretly installed on my phone after our previous misadventure on Marble Toe Island so she could keep dibs on me. The uninvited invasion of my privacy had been one of the messier points of our breakup, and I had uninstalled the app immediately upon its discovery. The confusion on Brady's face was immediate.

"Mother Knows Best?"

I shook my head. "Never mind. How did you find me?"

His grin morphed into a full-on smirk as he showed me his screen. A Google-like aerial map was displayed of the Pendleton property, a single red light blinking in our approximate location on the grounds. He invaded my personal space without warning and plunged his hand into my right coat pocket, nearly knocking me off balance.

"What in the hell—?" I snarled, attempting to push him away.

He pulled his hand free, clutching something infinitesimal between his thumb and forefinger. Slightly bigger than the pellet from a BB gun, its entire surface was covered in tiny hooks like Velcro. "I slipped this into your pocket when you stopped by for breakfast this morning." His smile was smug and victorious as I stared at him in disbelief.

"You *bugged* me? Son of a *bitch!*"

"Hey, it wasn't my first choice," he said, slipping the device into his own pocket. "I hadn't actually *used* it—well, at least up until now. I was optimistic

328

that you might be willing to actually work with me, and you know what? You've done a lot better with that than I would have ever expected. But you hadn't called or texted to let me know you had gotten home safely, so I couldn't resist taking a peek. It was more out of concern for your well-being than anything else. I told you I was worried."

"What a load of horseshit!"

"As soon as I saw where you were heading, my instincts kicked in, telling me I was following the wrong story, so I borrowed Jimmy's RAV4, and here I am," he said, far more pleased with himself than I was. "So, what are we doing here? Isn't this trespassing? Tampering with a crime scene or some such shit? I can't help but feel that we should get to the point, whatever that point may be. The RAV4 is a whole lot more conspicuous sitting outside the gate than yours is parked all the way up here. How'd you get through the gate, anyway? I only made it on foot because the gate got hung up on some ice and was open just wide enough for me to squeeze through."

"I was staying here before all of this went down," I reminded him. "Rochelle gave me the code, and—*oh!*" A smile slowly spread across my face as Brady stared at me vacantly.

"*Oh?*" he repeated, smiling crookedly through his lack of comprehension. "And would the great Dwayne Morrow care to share his epiphany with the rest of the class?"

I sighed, mulling over my options. We could stand here and bicker all night, or I could take Brady into my confidence, as unnatural as that seemed, and when no viable third option presented itself, I realized we were wasting precious time. I retrieved Rochelle's note from my laptop bag and handed it to Brady.

"I'm looking for a floor safe that's somewhere in this cottage, and I'm pretty sure the gate code will get me into it," I said. "But that's only if I can find it."

"*'I've got some info you should see in the floor safe of the guest cottage,'*" Brady read aloud before looking at me. "What do you think it is?"

"Not a clue, but it's all I've got left to explore, and sitting on my ass feels like a complete waste of time," I said. "Since you're already here, you might as well help me try to locate this safe so we can collect this mysterious information and get the hell out of here before we get caught. I'd suggest keeping your gloves on, so you won't introduce your fingerprints into an already muddled crime scene."

He scoffed, showing me his gloved hands. "Already thought of that. So, any idea where this safe might be?"

I shook my head. "It wasn't part of the official tour when Rochelle was showing me the place, but its footprint is fairly small. There's the living room we're standing in, and over there are the kitchen and dinette. There are two guest rooms down that hall and at the rear of the house, and full bath centered between the two. Halfway down the hall is a linen closet on the right."

"Where would you like to begin?" he asked, and my eyes immediately went to the bloodied carpeting.

"Anywhere but here," I said, leading him toward the hallway and the bedrooms beyond.

• • • • • • ● ◐ ◑ ● • • • • • •

The sight of the bedroom to the right was both daunting and disheartening. Rochelle had mentioned that it was primarily used for storage, so I hadn't given it much consideration during my earlier stay. The bedroom on the left had most recently been occupied by Rochelle before she and Joey had moved back into the main house to care for her father. Its bedclothes had been refreshed, ready for immediate occupancy, so my choice hadn't really been a choice at all.

330

We stood in the other room, surveying a collection of boxes stacked wherever there had once been floor space. I wasn't even sure there was a bed anywhere in the room. Each box was clearly labeled with bold, black lettering that stated the contents of each, and it looked like most of it belonged to Rochelle's late mother. Brady shone the light from his phone on what little of the floor was visible, but we couldn't find anything that looked promising.

The bathroom floor was tile, each square fitting tightly against the next, and it didn't take long before we found ourselves in the room I had occupied during my brief stay. I eyed the clothes I had left behind and still had no desire to take them with me. They were forever tainted, and as far as I was concerned, I didn't want any of the things I had brought with me.

Well—maybe the pet carrier. Those things were freaking *expensive*.

Brady and I crawled around on the floor, me palpating the carpet with my gloved fingertips while he used his phone to light my way in an entirely futile attempt to discover a hidden latch or seam that might reveal the safe's location. We were quickly running out of places to search.

"We should move the bed," I suggested, standing beside the vintage bedframe while Brady groaned.

"This thing's real wood," he whined. "Do you have any idea how heavy it's got to be? Can't you just crawl under it or something?"

I eyed the narrow opening and scowled at him while taking hold of one corner of the headboard. My head continued to throb in time with my heartbeat, and I didn't have the patience for Brady's petulant sarcasm. "Just do it."

He rolled his eyes before grabbing onto the other side of the headboard, and together, we tugged the monstrosity away from the wall.

"Pivot the headboard towards me so we can see the floor below," I barked, my limbs straining as the thick carpeting clung to the bed's clawed feet, adding enough resistance to make the process truly labor intensive.

Once the bed had finally shifted far enough out of position, I came around to the other side and stared at the unbroken and unblemished carpet that was lying beneath.

"Dammit!" I exclaimed, plopping down on the edge of the relocated bed.

"I ain't movin' that back," said Brady, stooping forward with his hands on his knees and laboring to catch his breath. "I'll go to jail first."

"We can't just leave it like this," I said. "Any chance we have to get out of here undetected would be gone the instant someone sees that the bed's been moved."

"Like they're not going to notice the crime scene tape you mangled on the way in?"

"Someone could have done that without ever coming inside," I said. "Stop arguing with me and give me a hand."

He groaned but got into position. "I hate you."

We worked the bed back into position, making sure its feet rested in the divots in the carpet left after years of being in the same position.

Brady moved towards the door. "What's next? The kitchen?"

I shook my head. "It's vinyl flooring and so is the dinette. I think the only place left is—"

"The murder room," he finished for me, and I winced and nodded.

"We'll just have to be extra careful not to disturb anything," I said, standing up only to sit right back down. *"Whoa."*

"Are you alright?"

I nodded carefully as the spinning room settled back into a queasy sort of equilibrium. "Guess I got up too fast," I said, repeating the maneuver successfully, but at a fraction of the speed. "Let's get this over with."

We went into the living room and started in the corner farthest from where the senator had been shot. We worked our way around the room to no avail, saving the bloodstained bit for last. Even from a safe distance, it was apparent there was no break in the carpeting anywhere.

"We're going to have to move more furniture, aren't we?" groaned Brady.

I narrowed my eyes as I scanned the room. "Maybe not. Shine your light over there." I pointed to the far wall, and Brady followed my finger with his phone. "Do you see that?"

"Sure. It's a furnace vent."

"Now shine your light over there, just underneath the picture window," I said, pointing towards the front of the house.

"You know, if anyone's paying attention outside, we're giving them one hell of a light show," he cautioned.

"Would you just *do* it?"

His beam landed on another narrow floor vent centered below the window. Brady was nonplussed when he looked at me. "What am I missing?"

I crossed to the vent below the picture window and knelt. "This is a standard furnace floor vent like you'd find almost anywhere—white to match the carpet, but otherwise nothing fancy, just serviceable." I exercised caution as I stood and crossed to the other vent, followed by Brady and the beam from his phone. I stood above it, pointing. "This one's different."

"*Hmm*," he said, and we dropped to our knees to get a closer look. "It looks older than the other one. It's way bigger, too—almost square. Maybe it's a return instead of a vent."

"Huh-unh," I said, pointing to the hallway where a larger version of the other floor vent was mounted near the top of the wall. "There's your return. It's a different size, but it still clearly comes from the same Home Depot collection, so to speak. This one doesn't have a louver to adjust the direction or amount of air flow, and its grate is—I don't know—*ornate*, sort of like an antique."

333

I slipped my fingers underneath the edges and lifted, revealing the face of what we had been searching for all along.

"A-ha!"

"Nice!" said Brady, feigning a little applause. "And now to test your theory. Try the code for the gate."

I studied the simple keypad staring up at me from its recessed position in the floor. A metal handle pointed downward on its right side, and it wouldn't budge when I tried to turn it. The keypad was laid out like one from an old telephone, complete with an asterisk and pound keys on either side of the '0' in the bottom row.

Could it really be this easy? There was only one way to find out.

I pecked in the numeric sequence Rochelle had given me and held my breath. It worked on the front gate as well as the security alarm for the cottage—and it was the only code she had given me. I was rewarded with a distinct click as the handle turned counterclockwise in my hand. I lifted the face of the safe away and set it aside while Brady leaned in, shining the light from his phone into the safe's recessed compartment. Any thief expecting jewels or other treasures would have been sorely disappointed. Its inner chamber was only wide enough to accommodate letter-sized files, and there was a plethora of them to choose from. I carefully extracted them all, fanning them out on the floor between us. We were practically in each other's laps sharing the narrow beam of light as we each grabbed half of the folders and started perusing.

"Last Will and Testament," said Brady, setting aside the first in his stack.

"Every Pendleton birth certificate from the beginning of time." I added mine to the stack.

"Property deeds," he noted.

"Life insurance policies."

Our pile of discards was growing almost as quickly as my impatience. None of this could be what Rochelle had sent me after. My fingers hesitated as the next folder in my pile was sky blue, a bright beacon buried in a sea of ordinary manila, and it was a thick one. I opened the folder to find a numbered list of names in Rochelle's precise script, and my breath caught as I recognized the first two:

1. Janet Harper
2. Doralee Watkins

"I've got something here," I said, flipping through the pages below and startled to find several of the very same pictures I had collected on my own—but there were so many more. Rochelle had numbered each picture in its upper left corner, and the cover page acted as a legend, putting names to faces for easy reference. Noted on the back of each picture was the year it had been taken, and they acted as a chronological guide to the many notches on Senator Ghant's bedpost.

"Whoa, back up there," said Brady, who was peering over my shoulder. He placed a finger on the bright face of a young woman in the last picture I had viewed. "Isn't that—?"

"Oh, my God, I think it *is*," I said, going back to the list to find the name belonging to Conquest #4. "Cassandra Morgan. It's Ghant's *wife!* I wonder what made her different from all the other women."

Brady snorted. "She's a Morgan, that's what."

It meant absolutely nothing to me, and the look on my face must have conveyed that fact quite clearly.

"L.L. Morgan?" Brady prompted expectantly, sighing as my fog refused to lift. "They only run one of the largest banks in this country, and Perry Morgan has been a regular fixture on Forbes' list of the richest people in the world since about the time we were in diapers. It would be very difficult to buy the silence of someone whose needs are already more than met."

"It's a hell of a foundation to build a relationship on," I said, continuing to peruse through the stack. "It sure didn't stop the man from his future pursuits, though, did it?"

"And I thought *I* had it goin' on," said Brady, whistling at a list that required both the front and back of a piece of lined notebook paper.

"I have to admit, I didn't think it was possible to find anyone more morally bankrupt than you, but I stand corrected," I said.

"Whoa, whoa, *whoa!*" Brady's finger froze on a name near the bottom of that list. "Charlesia McMillan. She's the woman who attacked Rochelle— I'm sure of it."

I sucked my breath in. It was more coincidence than I was willing to buy. "We should take all this and get out of here."

"Agreed," said Brady, shivering. "Being in the same room where the guy was murdered is starting to give me the creeps."

I tucked the contents back into the folder and debated on exactly what I should take. While this particular folder seemed to be what Rochelle had alluded to, there were still quite a few others we hadn't even checked. Odds were better than good that we wouldn't have another opportunity, so I stuffed the entire collection into my laptop bag, testing the limits of its capacity. I lowered the face of the safe back into place and turned the handle, rewarded with the sound of the lock engaging. Brady fitted the false floor vent over the opening, and we stood, prepared to take our findings and run. He switched off the light of his phone, plunging us back into shadowy darkness.

I took a step towards the door and paused, moonlight glinting on something small and shiny embedded in the carpet just beneath the edge of the sofa.

"Hang on," I said. "I think you dropped that goddamned bug you had planted on me."

I stooped to palm it just as Brady gasped and grabbed my arm, pulling me away. I slid it into my pants pocket.

"What the hell, Brady?" I hissed, pulling my arm free as he urgently shushed me.

"I saw a light," he whispered, nodding toward the picture window.

"Are you sure?" I asked, searching the darkness beyond the glass for some sort of visual confirmation. My chest tightened as a bright beam scrolled across the width of the window. "Oh, shit."

"What do we do?" he asked.

"Hide," I said, leading him back through the hallway. I started to turn left before deciding there were more places to take cover in the bedroom used for storage. We slipped through the door, and after we had eased it closed, Brady reactivated the light from his phone.

"What are you *doing?*" I demanded, squelching the beam with both hands.

"Finding a place to hide without knocking everything over in the process," he said pointedly. Realizing the veracity of his point, I moved my hands away from his phone's beacon, and we worked our way through the narrow pathways between boxes, eventually ducking into a large closet in the back corner of the room. He turned the light off, plunging us into complete darkness, the sounds of our labored breathing unnaturally loud in the confined space.

In the distance, the front door of the cottage opened and closed.

"Shit," I repeated as footsteps neared.

First came the sound of the other bedroom door opening, followed only seconds later by the sound of someone entering the room. I nearly gasped as the wall switch was activated, flooding the room with bright light that was clearly visible around the outer edge of the closet door. I held my breath as my heartbeat throbbed at my temples.

"I know you're in here," said a male voice I couldn't quite place. His self-assurance was unsettling. "You may as well show yourselves."

Brady and I stared at each other. *Yourselves?* Clearly, we were busted, but by whom? I couldn't imagine the police taking such obvious pleasure in this game of cat and mouse, and that somehow made me feel a little more confident about the only move I had left. I reached for the gun in the holster at the small of my back, but before I could pull it out, the closet door flew open.

Kevin Moody—aka Mr. Green—blocked our exit, backlit by a blinding halo courtesy of the bedroom's overhead lighting. His ugly sneer was menacing, but not nearly so much as the gun he held in his steady hand.

CHAPTER TWENTY-SEVEN

"**I** could have sworn I told you to steer clear of all this, Morrow, but what do you do? You bring a friend," Moody said, eyeing Brady. "You're even stupider than you look."

"You'll never get away with this, Moody," I said. "I've already reported back to my team at Boggs, and they know you assaulted me earlier. If anything happens to me—"

"Or me," interjected Brady as he used me as his personal shield.

"—or Brady, you'll be the first person they question."

Moody leaned within inches of my face and hissed, "I honestly don't give a *fuck*."

He slammed his forehead into mine, and I dropped like a stone, the world doing its ever-loving best to spin away from me. There was a loud commotion above my head as Moody turned his rage on Brady, but I couldn't really follow what was happening. I was just thankful not to hear any gunfire. The light from the room wasn't nearly so bright anymore, a kaleidoscope of darkness compressing to a pinprick until soon there wasn't any left to see at all.

······•◎◉●·······

I woke with the taste of carpet in my mouth and a chilly wind gusting across my back.

I was lying face-first in the darkened living room with my hands bound behind me, my headache completely off the scale. It was everything I could do not to cry out while my stomach churned with queasiness. I concentrated on my breathing, giving my eyes a chance to adjust. The front door stood open, making the room brighter than before as moonlight peeked through a break in the cloud cover and reflected off the shimmering snow that blanketed the grounds. I struggled against whatever bound me but only strained my shoulder in the process. I could hear Moody tromping around outside, and from the sound of it, he was rifling through my car. Doors opened and closed while I frantically scanned the room for anything that might be useful. My only discovery was Brady's motionless body, his back facing me, and his hands bound by what appeared to be an electric cord. He was eerily still; I couldn't tell if he was breathing.

"Looking for this?" Moody was suddenly in my face, waggling my gun in front of my face before swapping it for his own and pocketing mine. "Mine's bigger. Nice SUV, by the way. Very roomy with the seats down, although I really have to confess, your comfort isn't really much of a concern."

That was more ominous than I cared for. I pushed myself backwards and struggled into an upright position, using Brady's prone form as leverage. I was relieved when he grunted, inadvertently letting me know he was still alive—at least for now. He lay on his side with his hands similarly bound, and I had no idea how we were going to get ourselves out of this. All I could do was stall and hope for the police to patrol as I had been fearing since I let myself into the cottage.

"I don't understand, Moody," I said. "I thought you idolized Parker Ghant. Why would you kill your own hero?"

His expression shifted from rage to surprise in an instant before reverting to its original state. "Why would I—*what?* I didn't kill Senator Grant. I *wouldn't*. But I really have to wonder what *you're* doing here. I'm guessing you're still on that bitch's payroll, planting seeds of doubt about her guilt, but I'm not going to let that happen. Her fingerprints were all over the goddamn murder weapon! She's going to pay for what she's done."

His anger seemed to border on petulance, as if he might just burst into hot, angry tears at any moment.

"That's ridiculous," I said as Brady started to come around, using my back to leverage himself into a seated position. "It doesn't even make sense. The police have already thoroughly documented the scene. Anything added at this point would stand out like a sore thumb, obviously planted after they sealed off the perimeter, which has clearly been breached."

"Then, what in the hell are you doing here? Do *not* bullshit me, I'm warning you," he challenged, and I didn't like the way the veins pulsed at his temples. His knuckles were going white from the iron grip he had on the gun pointed at my face, and it felt like only a matter of time before he pulled the trigger. I jumped as he abruptly shifted it in Brady's direction. "And *you*—who the fuck are you? You look familiar."

"I'm nobody," said Brady, choosing self-preservation over honesty. "Just a friendly neighbor doing the neighborhood watch thing. I noticed Ms. Pendleton's gate was open, and I was just taking a look around. I don't have any idea who this joker is or why he broke into the cottage. I—"

"*Bullshit!*" roared Moody, his fury now manifesting in his tremulous grip on the gun's handle. "Morrow knows your fucking *name!* I warned you—"

His arm moved so quickly I could barely follow as he whipped Brady across the face with the butt of his weapon, knocking him out cold. My heart clenched as he brought the gun up and leveled it at Brady's supine form.

"Stop! Stop!" I shouted. "Put the gun down. I'll tell you what we're doing here, but you probably won't believe me. You seem to have your mind made up, but what's the harm in hearing me out?"

The muscles in his jaw flexed as he ground his teeth together, deliberating his next move. I was happy with anything that bought us a little more time. The tension in his arm lessened, if only a bit, and he shifted his enraged eyes back towards me.

"Go on," he said.

"Rochelle was staying with a friend last Friday night when she got a text from the senator," I said. "He asked her to meet him here to discuss— things." I was flying by the seat of my pants and probably divulging too much, but at this point, I couldn't waste a lot of time filtering my content.

"Things?" He scowled at me. "What sort of things could he possibly have to discuss with *her?"*

"Their son," I said, my words having an unanticipated effect on Moody. His arm holding the gun drooped as he reeled with the information.

"You're lying," he said, but I could see the uncertainty in his eyes.

"I'm not," I said. "That was why Rochelle has been so desperate to hire a private investigator. Her son is very sick. Leukemia, but it's possible for him to get better. She needs to find a bone marrow donor, and a match from family is best. She didn't want to violate the non-disclosure agreement and harm Ghant's career, but she couldn't get close enough to discuss it with him because of the barrier you and your team placed around the man."

"We were doing our job."

"And Rochelle was doing hers," I said. "Don't you get it? She's Joey's *mother.* There isn't a thing she wouldn't do for him. It just doesn't make sense that she would turn around and kill the senator. She *needed* him."

He began to pace the room, struggling to process what I had told him and making me dizzy in the process. Brady hadn't moved an inch.

"Okay," he said. "Let's just say that all of that is true. It still doesn't explain what you're doing here tonight."

"Well, that's pretty much your doing," I said, chuckling mirthlessly at the ironic realization.

He found it decidedly less funny, bringing the gun back around to cover me. "How's that?"

"I really wish you'd get that thing out of my face," I said, feigning a calm I wasn't even close to feeling. "You're going to end up shooting me before I tell you what I know, and if you're telling the truth—that you aren't responsible for killing the senator, then you haven't done anything wrong, at least not yet."

He brought the cool metal of the barrel of his gun to rest against his forehead as he appeared to count to ten, but his patience was clearly running thin. "What could *I* have to do with *your* being here?" he asked through clenched teeth.

"Your little stunt Friday morning with planting a campaign sign on the front lawn of the cottage," I said, pointing through the open front door. "Once I saw how easily you bypassed the security gate, I tried my best to convince Rochelle that she was in danger here, not that she seemed to believe me. I convinced her to take Joey and stay with a friend while I tended to a previous engagement that night. Like I already said, she was there when Ghant allegedly texted her, but apparently, not everything I said was lost on her. She left me a note, just in case things didn't work out the way she was certain they would. She told me to look at some information in a floor safe that's right over there underneath that furnace grate." I nodded my head in the general direction which was only a few feet in front of me.

Moody crossed the room to stand over the grate before kneeling down for a closer look. He lifted the metallic rectangle and set it aside, reaching in to run his fingers over the safe's smooth surface before trying its handle. "It's locked."

"She gave me the code—more or less," I said. "The contents, along with Rochelle's note, are in my laptop bag. You can see for yourself."

He stood, scanning the room. "Where is it? I don't see a fucking bag," he said, before bringing his gun right back into my face again, his hand even shakier than before, and I flinched at his sudden aggression. A sheen of perspiration shone across his mottled brow. "You better not be jerking me around, man."

"I swear, I'm not," I said. "But I can't tell you where the bag is now. I had it on me when we were in the closet where you found us. It's probably still there."

His eyes narrowed suspiciously, and I managed a hiccupy sigh.

"We're not going anywhere, and besides, you've got the gun—both of them, in fact," I said, staring him down. "We're no threat. Maybe the info will mean more to you than it does to me."

I could see that curiosity was nibbling away, and after some lengthy deliberation, he stood, the gun falling to his side once more. "Fine. Just stay put."

He headed back to toward the bedroom, and I wasted no time fumbling with the electric cord that bound my hands behind me. Seeing how Brady was trussed was helpful in knowing how to work at the knots near my own wrists. The plastic shielding of the electric cord prevented it from being pulled as taut as would have been possible with rope or a more flexible restraint, and once I got a thumb hooked into the tangle, it began to loosen fairly quickly—but not quickly enough. I had just managed to extract one hand when Moody reentered the living room, my bag in hand, and he was already sifting through its pockets. I sat on my hand and hoped he was too distracted to notice it was free.

He pulled out the folders and placed them on the floor in front of me, crouching down to examine them. He set one manila folder after another aside, their contents of no obvious interest.

"Can I ask you a question?" He was preoccupied, so I didn't wait for permission. "I've told you why we're here tonight, but how about you? What brought you out on a night like this? Was there a tracker on my car? Have you been following me all this time?"

He had the bright blue folder in his hand when he looked up, his face shrouded in grief. "I was here to pay my respects. Senator Ghant was—" He bit back whatever he was about to say, his mouth clenching into a tight line while his chin trembled. I could swear he was about to cry. "He was the greatest man I've ever known. When I saw a car parked near the entrance with the gate standing open, I needed to see who was trespassing. It felt like—like—*desecration*."

Well, alrighty then. Moody was affording Ghant the reverence of a deity, and it was wholly unnerving. As much as I disliked Moody, I didn't believe he was behind the senator's murder, but I wasn't foolish enough to doubt his capacity to carry out the act.

He flipped the folder open and gave its contents his full attention. I used the opportunity to furtively scan the room, searching for anything I might use to turn the tables, but nothing trumped the gun he still held at his side. Brady hadn't budged since hitting the ground, giving me something else to worry about. Even if I could figure a way to escape, I couldn't just leave him behind.

"What in the hell is *this?*" Moody asked, his finger frozen midway down the handwritten list of names that Rochelle had assembled.

"I believe it's a list of women who worked on Ghant's campaigns and— um, fraternized with him throughout the years," I said, aiming for diplomacy in my choice of words. I didn't want to set Moody off. "Ms. Pendleton had reason to believe that her situation with Senator Ghant was anything but unique, and maybe I'm telling you something you already know. I mean, you were actively trying to enforce the non-disclosure agreements. Surely, you knew what they were about."

The slow shake of his head gained momentum, and his temper was once again on the rise. "There were a lot of non-disclosure agreements, and it wasn't up to us to question their contents. It's how things get done in Washington. There are all sorts of dealings that go on behind the scenes to keep our country safe and strong, things the average voter is too simple to understand. It was our job to protect Senator Ghant's image, not question it. There are thirty-three names here. Are you trying to tell me that Senator Ghant *impregnated* them all?"

"Hey, I'm just trying to get to the bottom of this," I said. "The only thing I can say with any certainty is that he got four of them pregnant—I don't know about the rest. Rochelle Pendleton—obviously, and immediately before her was Lauren DeAngelo. They both signed NDAs and have been raising their sons as single mothers. But it all started with Janet Harper. She never got a chance to raise her child. She was attacked and left for dead in an alley in the Short North. She recovered but lost the baby, as well as her ability to ever have any more children. It literally drove her crazy to see herself replaced by the next name on the list—"

"Doralee Watkins."

There was an undeniable spark of realization on his face as he interrupted me, his voice almost hollow. He held Doralee's picture in his hand as the folder slipped from his fingers, falling to the floor and scattering its contents around the room. He stared at the picture, and the threat of tears suddenly became a reality as his face contorted with his deepest grief yet, his chest hitching as he began to sob. I didn't know how to react.

"You—you couldn't have known her," I said. "She's been gone for longer than you've been alive."

"Not quite," he said, unable to take his eyes from the picture. "She was my mother. I was adopted by the Moodys when I was a baby. I've always known her name, but I've never seen her face before. Oh, my God!" He doubled over as another mournful wail escaped his lips.

My mouth dropped open as I had my own epiphany. "You're telling me that Parker Ghant was your—"

He was already nodding as my words failed me.

"He was my dad. I didn't find out until I was being interviewed for classes at the Academy, and he took me under his wing, said I reminded him so much of himself at my age. What you're implying can't be true," he said, his grief already shifting back to anger. "He would *never* shirk his responsibilities like that. He wasn't that sort of man!"

"And yet he hid the fact that you were his son from the entire world." I was pushing it, but I couldn't seem to help myself. "How does the rest of the family feel about you?"

His gaze fell away as he fumbled with his words. "I—uh, I really couldn't say. We decided it was best to keep this between the two of us. I never wanted to be the cause for any controversy in my father's campaigns."

"Must've been rough," I said. "Standing guard over family dinners instead of taking your rightful place at the table."

"No, no, *no*," he said. "It wasn't like that at all. It was a decision we made *together*. Our relationship was *special*. He wanted to protect it. We didn't want to share it with anyone else."

"How very selfless and considerate of the senator," I said scornfully. "Considering he was the only one with anything to lose."

"*Shut up!*" he roared, his gun back in my face, fury lending an uneasy tremor to his hand. "*You don't have any idea what you're talking about!*"

"I'm sorry," I said, flinching as I narrowed my eyes. I covered my face with hands I was supposed to be hiding.

"What the—? Your *hands*—" His planted his feet at shoulder width, his gun suddenly deathly still.

A thunderous clap of gunfire lit the room like a flashbulb, setting my ears to ringing and the room to spinning, a startled shriek escaping from the upper register of my vocal range. Despite the fact that I felt no more pain than the headache I'd been carrying for days, I frantically inspected my face with my fingers, certain to stumble upon a ruinous point of entry. It was only after Moody dropped to the ground, that I realized it wasn't his gun that had discharged.

Cassandra Ghant stood over me, the exhaust from the barrel of her own gun sending a thin haze of smoke into the chilly evening air.

"Oh, thank God," I said, struggling to my feet. "I really thought I was a goner, there. I—"

"Not so fast," said Cassandra, shifting her gun in my direction. "Stay right where you are and keep your hands where I can see them."

I blinked. "I beg your pardon?"

"You heard me," she said, and there was nothing shaky about her own grip. Her hands were rock steady in designer gloves. "This has gotten a whole lot more complicated than I anticipated. I didn't expect anyone to be here, but it looks like I stumbled into a fucking party. What's going on here?" She stepped over to where Brady lay and used the toe of her insulated boot to roll him over onto his back. "Son of a *bitch!* Is this who I think it is? Brady Garrett? *Shit.*"

Her eyes were drawn to something small that fell from Brady's pocket, and she stooped to pick it up and hold it up in the moonlight.

"What's this?"

My mouth went dry as I recognized the bug that Brady had planted on me. If the bug was in her hand, then what was *I* carrying? I took a chance that she was distracted enough not to notice and hooked a finger into my own pocket to retrieve my earlier find.

348

It was a small emerald earring in the shape of a teardrop. The last time I'd seen it, it was part of a dazzling collection that Cassandra Ghant had worn to Brady's dinner party.

"*Aaah*," she said, delicately plucking it from my palm. "Here's what I've been looking for."

"You did this," I said as the realization dawned. "You killed your own husband."

She regarded me with an ugly sneer as she slipped the earring into the oddly elongated lobe of her left ear. "And I'd do it again in a cold second if I had the chance," she hissed. "Son of a bitch was going to leave me for this—this—*harlot* and their bastard child, and after everything I've put up with throughout all these years tied to that philandering piece of shit."

"Leave you?" I asked, surprised. "Wouldn't that jeopardize his reputation?"

Her laugh was every bit as ugly as her sneer. "What world do you live in, Mr. Morrow? It's exactly the sort of move Parker's followers would applaud, trading in the worn-out model for something younger, prettier, newer. Sure, Parker always had a roving eye, but after a while, I was pretty much grateful that he didn't have any interest in touching me with those filthy hands anymore. I mean, Lord only knew where they'd been. But those were always just flings, and once they were over, he rarely looked back. There have been two exceptions."

She crossed over to where Kevin Moody was bleeding profusely into the off-white carpeting. "He always felt guilty about the suicide of this one's mother and couldn't help but keep an eye out for him, pulling him into our orbit once he felt he was old enough to keep the secret."

"You knew about Moody?"

"Of course, I knew about Kevin. There wasn't much that Parker could keep from me. I tolerated it as long as Kevin was kept completely separate from our own children. They shouldn't have to suffer the shame of their

349

father's constant indiscretions. It's bad enough that we have to deal with the stepchildren from his previous marriage. I wasn't about to publicly acknowledge another heir, and I absolutely forbade Parker to do the same, but *this*." She swept her arm around the room. "This just wasn't going to go away."

"I don't understand."

"It was all this idiot's fault," said Cassandra, angrily kicking Moody's extended leg. "And *yours*." Her gun was directed at me once more, and I have to tell you, I was mighty sick of this perspective.

"Me? What did I do?"

"You wouldn't leave it alone! Kevin was so pleased with himself, convincing the other investigators who were approached by the Pendleton woman to stay clear of the case, but not you. When Parker wondered what made you so persistent, Kevin told him about the boy and his—*condition*." Her face soured like she smelled something foul.

"Joey?"

"Yes, *Joey*," she snapped. "The moment Kevin showed Parker some surveillance pictures he had taken of Pendleton and her little boy, he became fixated. Despite what you think, my husband wasn't a complete monster. He had apparently forgotten how much he enjoyed his time with Ms. Pendleton, and the pictures only served to remind him. He was showering—preparing for his *date* when I saw that he had texted her asking to meet here, the very place where they had conceived that—that—*child*. I knew he was planning to rekindle the affair, and once he did, there would be no turning back. She had replied with the code to the gate and the cottage. She had apparently changed it since his last visit. I got here before he did, waiting in the dark as he came through the door. You should have *seen* the look of surprise when I pulled the trigger."

She paused to savor the memory.

"I left the gun behind, not really thinking too far ahead," she continued. "I couldn't believe my luck when that stupid woman picked the gun up, completely implicating herself. I didn't realize until later that I'd inadvertently left something behind." She touched the emerald earring that somehow managed to sparkle even in the room's scant light. "My luck held when the police overlooked it on the first pass, but I couldn't take the chance that it might still turn up. Besides, it belonged to my grandmother. It's one of a kind and completely irreplaceable. But now, I've got a bigger problem. What to do about all of you."

She scanned the room, deliberating her options.

"I don't suppose you'd believe me if I said I wouldn't tell a soul," I said, my voice not nearly as steady as I'd hoped. It felt like time was running very short.

Her laugh was throaty and unsettling. "I don't suppose I would," she said.

She approached Moody and patted him down, retrieving both his gun and mine. She traded her gun for Moody's and pocketed both mine and hers. "I'm seeing a scenario that should work rather nicely. Kevin confronted you and Brady while you were plundering the cottage, looking for something that might clear your client's good name."

She kept Moody's gun trained on me as she stooped to collect the files and paperwork that had scattered when he fell.

"Of course, you found nothing," she said, straightening the stack as she set it on an end table. "I'll be taking these with me and destroying them. I'm not going to let my children suffer the embarrassment of Parker's legacy, and it isn't like any of you will be alive to say anything different."

"You'll never get away with this," I said, wondering as I said it why people say such ridiculous things at moments like these. Her plan was looking pretty damn serviceable from where I stood.

"Let's see," she said, enjoying her moment. She retrieved my gun from her pocket, thoughtfully examining the weapons in her hand. "Kevin shot Brady, killing him instantly. Then there was a struggle between you and Kevin. You shot Kevin, mortally wounding him, but not before he got one last shot off at you, splattering your brains all over this nice living room. All I have to do is remove your gloves and put the weapons in your hands afterward, tying everything together in a nice tidy package for the police."

"Dwayne?"

It was the last voice I expected to hear, and my breath caught in my throat. Everything slipped into slow motion as Cassandra and I both pivoted to see who was standing in the open doorway. Melanie was framed by moonlight, looking just as confused as I was to find her there. Cassandra's right arm swung around, brandishing Moody's gun in Melanie's direction, and I did something I was always taught I should never, *ever* do.

I punched that bitch in her fucking nose, putting everything I had into the effort.

As Cassandra's head snapped back and her eyes fluttered into unconsciousness, the gun discharged, renewing the painful ringing in my ears as Melanie dropped to the ground. Panic overwhelmed me as I hurried toward the door, fearful of what I might find, but I'd taken no more than two steps before my feet got tangled up in Brady's legs, and I lost my balance, lunging forward.

The last thing I saw was the edge of the end table approaching my forehead at high velocity.

EPILOGUE

I t's almost been four weeks since the events of that terrifying night.

Fortunately for you, I can bring you up to speed fairly quickly—just don't be expecting happy endings all the way around. Life is rarely so accommodating.

Cassandra Ghant was taken into custody and charged with the murder of her husband. Kevin Moody survived the bullet she had pumped into him, and it was his testimony coupled with mine that served as the foundation of a slam-dunk case against the senator's widow. Rochelle Pendleton recovered from her injuries sustained in prison, the victim of another of Parker Ghant's former lovers whose life had degenerated into a series of bad choices once the senator had cast her aside. Charlesia McMillan had given her own child with Ghant up for adoption, turning to a life of liquor, drugs, and prostitution to combat the utter void left behind by Parker's absence. It was pure chance that she and Rochelle were assigned to the same cell block, and Charlesia's belief that Rochelle was guilty of killing the only man she had ever loved prompted an attack borne of pure vengeance. The late senator's inexplicable allure was the gift that kept giving, long after he had departed this mortal plane. As thrilled as Rochelle was to be cleared of the crime and reunited with her son, she couldn't hide her disappointment at being denied another chance at happiness with a man who had done nothing but take her for granted. I just wanted to shake some sense into the woman, but heartbreak is illogical, and nothing I could do would lessen her pain. Hopefully, time will heal that wound.

Speaking of healing, a donor match was found for Joey Pendleton, and I was surprised to learn it was from none other than Kevin Moody. Moody's attitude towards Rochelle and her son changed drastically once he learned that Rochelle wasn't responsible for his father's death. He was adamant in volunteering to be tested, assuming a responsibility he felt certain his father would have expected of him. It will be a while before we know if the transplant is successful, but it's the most encouraging news on that front since Joey's initial diagnosis, and cautious optimism has been contagious. Although our business has officially concluded, Rochelle has promised to keep me posted, and in turn, I have promised to bring Dexter by to visit Joey upon occasion. He really loves that damn cat, and I can't really blame him, now, can I?

While Brady was disappointed to have missed all of the action, he more than made up for it after the fact, breaking the story in a seemingly endless series of updates featuring his first-person narrative of what he almost witnessed. For days on end, you couldn't even turn the television on without being subjected to one earnest account or another, testifying that he had forever been changed by the experience, and for once, he wasn't speaking in metaphors. He carried a scar reminiscent of the lightning bolt on Harry Potter's forehead from where Moody had struck him in the face with his gun, and I'll be *damned* if it didn't somehow magnify his inexplicable appeal with his sizable base of lustful fans. I eventually gave him his fucking exclusive, keeping my end of a bargain I wasn't entirely sure I had actually made, but it was easier than listening to Brady's persistent groveling.

I still haven't approached my dad about The Deep Dark Secret of his first marriage. There really isn't any easy segue into that conversation, especially when he's still being evaluated for his sporadic episodes. Scans have found a tiny "dark spot" on his cerebral cortex, and we're still gathering opinions from specialists while trying not to freak the fuck out. Denial is a surprisingly cozy jacket to slip into.

I think that just about covers everything, doesn't it?

Oh, wait—*Melanie*. You're probably wondering what happened to her. For that, we'll have to go back four weeks to the night in question…

·····•••●◦○●•••·····

The room was bright, and my eyes were having trouble focusing.

I could hear the unmistakable bleep of hospital machinery around me, so no big surprise to find an IV line trailing away from my arm and up to a bag of what I hoped was saline at the head of my bed. Gentle pressure on my hand drew my eyes to an angelic face hovering over me.

Melanie smiled, and I had a powerful sensation of déjà vu, afraid we were back in West Virginia, the birthplace of so many sleepless nights.

"Hey," she said. "Can you hear me?"

I nodded, struggling to speak with a throat like gravel. She handed me a plastic cup of ice chips, and they were the sweetest relief I had ever known.

"Easy there, tiger," she said, pulling the cup away. "You seem more lucid this time, but you still probably shouldn't overdo it."

"This time?" I croaked, and she nodded. "Where are we?"

"You got your very own room at Riverside," she said, adjusting my sheets with one hand while keeping hold of my hand with her other. "I hate to say that we told you so, bu-u-t—congratulations. You are *indeed* suffering from a concussion."

Suddenly, the events from the cottage came racing to mind, and I struggled to sit upright. "You were shot! You were—"

"I was not." Melanie placed her hands gently on my shoulders, keeping me flat on my back. "Fortunately for me, that bitch was a lousy shot. Fortunate for Kevin Moody, too. Word is he'll pull through."

"I don't understand," I said, trying to shake off the agitation brought on by the questions that swirled in my foggy mind. "Why were you even there? You were with Sarah—and where are the kids? How long have I been out?"

"*Shhh*," she said, her fingertips light against the skin of my face. "It's only been a day. The kids are safe and sound with Sarah's parents, and Sarah continues to improve."

I studied her face suspiciously. "That still doesn't explain why you're here. What made you come all this way with freezing rain and snow falling?"

Her smile slowly ebbed as she looked away. "It really wasn't so bad. I borrowed Sarah's Jeep because it handles so much better than my Mazda, and that's why we kept playing phone tag. It doesn't have Bluetooth or a working power outlet for a phone charger, and my phone died halfway here."

"But how did you know where to find me?" I asked.

"When Anyssa told me what happened with Rochelle and I couldn't get hold of either you or Brady, the guest cottage was the only other place I could think of to try. I'm sure glad you mentioned Rochelle's note about the floor safe, and since I am now a member of the Boggs team, I was able to get the Pendletons' address from Loretta." Her smile was reserved, but she was understandably pleased with herself.

"So, what did you want to talk about?"

Her smile turned sheepish. "It can wait," she said. "Really. Let's worry about getting you all better and out of this place, huh?"

I stared at her until she finally returned my gaze. "I'm pretty sure I know what you needed to talk about," I said. "It's about Jordan, right?"

She sighed, dropping her eyes. "Fine. Yes, it's about Jordan. I don't really want to go into this right now, though—*please?*"

I continued to stare as I put my thoughts in order. "How about this— I'll do all of the talking and you just listen, okay? You don't have to say anything if you don't want to."

Her eyes found mine once more. "Alright."

"I think you should pack up your things, Jasmine's things, and Jordan's things," I said. "I think we should rent ourselves a U-Haul and bust our sorry asses getting it all put away where it belongs—in our home."

She stared at me, her mouth dropping open. "Oh—oh no. You must've hit your head harder than they realize. You're not making any sense."

I took her hand in mine and gently squeezed. "I know exactly what I'm saying. I love you, Melanie, and every single thing that comes with you."

She smiled doubtfully. "Jordan is a whole lot more than some 'thing.' You can't know what you're saying. You need to really think about this before saying such things."

I held fast to her hand. "It's all I've been thinking about ever since Jasmine called to read me the riot act," I said.

"Jasmine did *what?*" Melanie was startled.

"She called to let me know in no uncertain terms that she wasn't on board for a bunch of back and forth between us. She explained what should have been obvious—Sarah's not going to be in any condition to care for Jordan for a while, if ever, and it was your intention to bring Jordan back to Columbus."

"I'll kill her," said Melanie, frowning. "I can't believe she went behind my back and—"

"*Shhh.*" It was my turn to do the shushing. I smiled. "She wasn't wrong, and let's face it—she gets this attitude from her mother. But here's the thing—if I've learned anything over this past year, it's that I'm so tired of wasting time. Time is our most precious gift, and we're just squandering it. I realize it might take some time for you to believe me, but I'm done keeping secrets from you, I swear it. Life without you isn't a life I care to live, and I refuse to waste another second."

She continued to stare, the corners of her mouth slowly inching upward. "You're *serious?*"

"I've never been more serious in my entire life," I said. I released her left hand long enough to pluck the oxygen sensor from my fingertip and transfer it to the tip of her fourth finger. "I know it's a sad substitute, but it will have to do until I can replace it with something big and shiny. Melanie McGregor, will you marry me?"

· · · • • • • • ⊝ ⊝ • • • • • · · ·

The parking lot was almost completely empty as I nosed my Hyundai into a spot that wasn't reserved for the resident practitioners working in the two-story, red bricked rectangle. I'm not sure it would have even mattered; they were all empty. The only other vehicle was a white van emblazoned with 'Jason's Janitorial Service' in fading black letters across its broad side. It was almost four o'clock, and the setting sun glistened off the sizable diamond on Melanie's ring finger—I only hoped I'd live long enough to pay that sucker off.

"I don't see the good doctor's fancy Lexus," I noted, killing my engine. "You don't suppose she took the bus?"

She scowled at my gleeful smirk. "Unlikely. Maybe her car's being serviced or something? She was probably dropped off by her husband or a friend. Does it really matter?"

"Not at all," I said, leaning in for a quick kiss. "I just want to get this over with."

"There will be no gloating, do you understand me?"

"I can but try," I said airily, and she playfully pinched the tickly soft flesh on the inside of my arm while I squirmed out of reach.

"You'll do better than try," she said, unfastening her seat belt and opening her door. "I've suffered enough mortification in front of that woman at your hands."

"What? *These* hands?"

She squealed and slid beyond my reach, hopping down to the pavement and closing the door. She blew a raspberry at me through the window.

I grinned at her like a fool. I couldn't have possibly loved her any more.

We held hands like a couple of school kids as we trotted up the few steps to the main entrance, and I held the door for my lady as she entered the lobby with a swish of her cute little backside. She was as happy to be done with these counseling sessions as I was, even if her jubilation was a tad more restrained. The information desk was unmanned at this hour, but that was customary for our late afternoon appointments. At this point, we knew our way around. The building was devoid of activity, save for the sound of an industrial vacuum somewhere above us, and we rocked on our heels as we waited patiently for the elevator car to arrive and carry us to our ultimate destination.

The smell of industrial cleaner was fairly prevalent once we stepped out into the second-floor hallway and turned left, ambling towards Dr. Jillian Whittier's office on blissful autopilot. This was a breakup I would thoroughly enjoy. The sound of the vacuum grew louder as we approached her open doorway, and it soon became apparent it was coming from within the doctor's suite.

"Ladies first," I said, stepping aside so Melanie could take the lead, then nearly ran into her as she froze just inside the door.

"What the—?"

Her voice dropped away as she surveyed the empty outer office. The walls were bare, stripped of every expensive painting that had adorned them, a collection of images carefully calculated to soothe patients while they waited to be called into their private sessions. Divots were visible in the carpet where the receptionist's desk once sat, but not a single piece of furniture remained. The door to the doctor's inner sanctum stood open, and a swarthy, heavyset man kneeled beside a carpet shampooer, using elbow grease to scrub a particularly stubborn section of carpet, affording

359

us an entirely unwarranted view of his butt crack, smiling vertically above his sagging belt line. I leaned out into the hallway to confirm we were in the right place, but the suite number was correct. What I hadn't noticed on our way in was that Dr. Whittier's nameplate was no longer mounted above it.

The carpet cleaner abruptly switched off, and I realized the maintenance man had swiveled, staring at us expectantly.

"Can I help you?" he asked, although the offer seemed a little less than sincere. He made no effort to stand and remained either oblivious or proud of the peep show he was giving us.

I tried to disarm him with a smile. I thought I might stand a chance. The bruises on my face were almost completely faded, and I was scaring fewer children with each passing day. "You must be Jason," I said, and he looked at me like I was from Mars. I pointed in the general direction of the parking lot. "From the van—Jason's Janitorial Services?"

His response was to smirk. "I been working for that company for three years, and I ain't never met no one called Jason," he said. "Let me guess— you must be Dick. You sure look like a Dick to me."

My smile faded. "Dwayne," I said. "And this is Melanie. We're patients of Dr. Whittier's. Did she move offices or something?"

"I got no idea. I don't know the comings and goings of the folks that rent these spaces. We were hired by the building management company to clean out this office. If you want any more information than that, you'll have to ask them. Now, if you don't mind, I'd like to get home at some point this evening."

Melanie and I exchanged an uneasy glance.

"Um, sure," I said, guiding Melanie back out into the hallway. "Sorry to bother you—"

He had already switched the carpet cleaner back on and resumed scrubbing the stubborn stain in front of his knees.

We walked the entire length of the second floor checking each door on both sides of the hallway. There were plenty of other nameplates proclaiming names and specialties, but none belonged to Dr. Jillian Whittier. I flashed upon our prior appointment and the last time I saw the doctor. She had been watching us intently from her window as we argued in the parking lot, fueling my fear of inadvertently sharing anything substantive, especially regarding the fate of my sister. At the time, Melanie had considered my behavior paranoid, but as we returned to my car in silence, it was with the unspoken understanding that we were now on the same page.

My instincts were just fine. Paraphrasing a famous quote from Joseph Heller, just because you're paranoid doesn't mean they aren't out to get you...

THE END

COMING SOON

DELUSION

Dwayne Morrow Mystery #8

ACKNOWLEDGEMENTS

I'm having the hardest time believing this is a wrap on the *seventh* Dwayne Morrow escapade. Actually, it's seven-and-a-half—we can't ignore that bite-sized nugget of comedy gold, *Over Consumption*, co-written with the inimitable V.R. Tapscott and featuring characters from the delightful Jane Bond series. In fact, if you include my *non*-Dwayne Morrow outings, this is my tenth release, and that just feels utterly surreal. I never thought I'd finish writing *one* book, much less ten…

But I'm certainly not doing this alone. Heavens, no.

I am *so* grateful to have my trio of formidable editors back for another go 'round. Teri Lott, Lynne Hobstetter, and Traci Steele—these books are always better for your input, and I can't thank you enough for your time and effort—especially when I've dropped the last two Dwayne books on you just before the holiday season. You are the *best!* Any errors or mistakes that manage to filter through are strictly my doing, including the dramatic license I took with Dwayne and Melanie's counselor. No counselor worth her salt would conduct the session that opened this story as Lynne, a retired psychologist, was quick to point out.

To my ever-expanding network of author friends—Charly Cox, Katie Mettner, Tiffany Ryan, Melissa Nordhoff *aka* lizzie Qnert, Rob Neto, Leslie Noyes, Jethro Wegener, V.R. Tapscott (duh), just to name a few—to have your ear is a privilege I wouldn't trade for anything. Sharing your experiences with this whole publishing thing is a generosity I will never forget.

To all of my Facebook friends, I can't tell you how much your ongoing support means to me. I could start naming names, but these acknowledgements would soon be longer than the book, and I would still manage to omit and offend someone, which would *never* be my intention. Just know that I see you, and I appreciate all of the ratings, reviews, and words of mouth that you have put out there, helping Dwayne (and my other titles) find new readers. They say you should write for yourself, but let's face it—it's writing for you that makes it all worthwhile.

Stay tuned for DMM #8, *Delusion*. It's partially inspired by *Indiana Jones and the Last Crusade*, only in a Midwestern setting—I *swear*, I don't know where these ideas come from…but it's gonna be one hell of a good ride!

Until next time,
Darin Miller
Grove City, Ohio – December 2024

ALSO AVAILABLE

REUNION
Dwayne Morrow Mystery #1

CIRCUMVENTION
Dwayne Morrow Mystery #2

RETRIBUTION
Dwayne Morrow Mystery #3

DIVERSION
Dwayne Morrow Mystery #4

ISOLATION
Dwayne Morrow Mystery #5

ABDUCTION
Dwayne Morrow Mystery #6

DELUSION
Dwayne Morrow Mystery #8

OVER CONSUMPTION
A Dwayne Morrow and Jane Bond
Novella
(Co-written with V.R. Tapscott)

OTHER WORK

BROKEN BITS AND BOBS
A Collection of What Ifs, What Was,
and What Never Should Be

HOUSE OF SECRETS
Every Room Holds a Story
(Contributor, "Redemption")

EQUILIBRIUM

THE LIBRARY CENTENNIAL ANTHOLOGY
Celebrating the Lives and People of the
SPL Community
(Contributor, "Meredith's Bad Day")

DID YOU LIKE ME?

☐ Yes! ☐ No ☐ Maybe?

May I ask a favor?

If you enjoyed reading this book as much as I enjoyed writing it, won't you please consider leaving a rating and/or review on Amazon, Goodreads, Barnes & Noble, BookBub, or anywhere else you might see fit? It only takes a moment to leave a rating and a maybe a couple more for a short review—even a simple 'I would recommend this book!' will do nicely.

Word of mouth is the single most powerful tool in an Indie author's toolkit, and ratings and reviews help more than you may realize in growing our audience. Think of it as a gratuity you might leave a server after an evening of fine dining, but this gratuity doesn't cost a thing—only a few moments of your time.

Thank you for your kind consideration.

Darin

Amazon

Goodreads

Barnes & Noble

BookBub

ABOUT THE AUTHOR

Darin Miller was born in Portsmouth but currently resides in Grove City, both of which are located in Ohio. While he has worked in Information Technology for three decades, he has *not* solved a single, solitary crime to date. He is the BookFest award-winning author of the Ohio-based *Dwayne Morrow Mystery* series, as well as an unrelated short story collection, *Broken Bits and Bobs*, and a standalone psychological horror thriller, *Equilibrium*. With equal parts action, humor, suspense and mystery, the *Dwayne Morrow* series features characters you're sure to love—and in some cases, loathe.

Stay current with updates, short stories, and other special promotions at www.darin-miller.com.

www.ingramcontent.com/pod-product-compliance
Lightning Source LLC
Chambersburg PA
CBHW070621260626
47161CB00007B/2531